The Fae Queen's deadly servants . . .

Gryffid slowly got to his feet. His eyes remained fixed on the faeries and the memory of Oona.

"We hereby advance you to the rank of vigilant," the king said. "For now. You will lead one thousand Wilt-Leaf archers and rangers on Oona's behalf in the coming battle. They shall be completely under your command, just as you shall be under the Fae Queen's. Her victory shall be yours, and ours. Achieve it, and you will become the most favored vigilant who ever lived."

"I will do as my majesties command," Gryffid said.

The king rocked forward on his throne. "For the sake of the hold, for our shared future, Maralen and all who stand with her must die," he said.

. . . and the ravings of a mad giant . . .

Rosheen's scroll was uniquely powerful, as it had been inscribed with all of the oracular giantess's random thoughts and fancies before the Great Aurora came. In it were descriptions of many things that had happened, and more that hadn't happened yet. Rosheen's prophetic magic was as complex as it was potent, and as far as the sapling knew it was impossible to benefit from the scroll without knowledge of the world it described—either through personal experience or from detailed and direct study. The sapling had planned to use the scroll as a touchstone to that world, to increase her understanding of how things were before they became as they are.

Oona's words were loud, piercing. *I am your master. Obey me.*

Maralen did not obey.

. . . threaten the last flickering light of hope in a world of darkness.

Scott McGough and Cory J. Herndon bring the tale of the dual worlds of Lorwyn and Shadowmoor to a stunning conclusion!

MAGIC
The Gathering®

TWO WORLDS,
ONE SERIES

Lorwyn
LORWYN CYCLE
BOOK I
Cory J. Herndon and Scott McGough

Morningtide
LORWYN CYCLE
BOOK II
Cory J. Herndon and Scott McGough

Shadowmoor
SHADOWMOOR CYCLE
ANTHOLOGY
Edited by Philip Athans and Susan J. Morris

Eventide
SHADOWMOOR CYCLE
NOVEL
Scott McGough and Cory J. Herndon

Shadowmoor Cycle • Novel

Scott McGough and Cory J. Herndon

Shadowmoor Cycle Novel
Eventide

©2008 Wizards of the Coast, Inc.

Published by Wizards of the Coast, Inc. MAGIC: THE GATHERING, WIZARDS OF THE COAST, and their respective logos are trademarks of Wizards of the Coast, Inc., in the U.S.A. and other countries.

Printed in the U.S.A.

Cover art by Christopher Moeller
First Printing: June 2008

9 8 7 6 5 4 3 2 1

ISBN: 978-0-7869-4868-0
620-21737740-001-EN

U.S., CANADA,
ASIA, PACIFIC, & LATIN AMERICA
Wizards of the Coast, Inc.
P.O. Box 707
Renton, WA 98057-0707
+1-800-324-6496

EUROPEAN HEADQUARTERS
Hasbro UK Ltd
Caswell Way
Newport, Gwent NP9 0YH
GREAT BRITAIN
Save this address for your records.

Visit our web site at www.wizards.com

Dedication

This book is dedicated to Troy Sandelin,
a good friend who will be missed;
and Casie Leigh Saavedra, the hero of Rose Valley.

Acknowledgements

For inspiration, the authors would like to thank Matt & Trey, Rob Grant & Doug Naylor, Richard Sapir & Warren Murphy, Ricky Gervais & Stephen Merchant, and Garth Ennis & Steve Dillon.

The authors also wish to thank the readers, players, and fans of Magic: the Gathering for all their support and interest.

Scott offers special thanks to Lucy, the Daughter of the Devil, and her dad, along with Becky, the Special Fathers, and the Assassinun.

Cory extends special thanks to S.P. and extra catnip to Bayliss and Remo.

CHAPTER 1

The moon had been hiding for hours behind the distant hills outside Mistmeadow. If the silver orb's truculent mood didn't improve, it would likely continue to sulk alone and out of sight for at least two more. The denizens of this world who thrived under the silver orb's cold, gentle light did the same, for they had learned to stay safely inside during these moonless hours, when starlight too often languished atop thick layers of jealous clouds and smothering fog. Only fools, villains, or determined madmen ventured into Mistmeadow's woods at times like these, for within that absence of light lived the things of true darkness, things that even the moonlight feared.

The ragged bodies of two cinder warriors flickered into view as twin sparks of gold and blue flared in the blackness. The cinders stood revealed for a split second as they labored at the base of the craggy and charred mountainside, and then the inky black sea swallowed them again. They were jagged, gangly, skeletal things dressed in steel mesh breastplates, badly corroded gauntlets, and black ironbark boots. Creatures of flame and stony coal, a cinder's fire perpetually smoldered just shy of ignition.

Unaffected and unconcerned by the return to darkness, the cinders continued their relentless efforts. They conversed with each other sparingly as they worked, speaking in a language more of light and smells than of sound. One of the world's soft and fleshy creatures—a merrow, kithkin, or an accursed elf—would have heard only hollow rasps and growls.

The cinders were restacking a pile of rubble into a wall that, when complete, would block the path that led up the mountainside. The cinder closest to the low wall stooped to slide a piece of flat, cut stone imprecisely between two others. The blackened creature wore a soot-stained golden robe woven from boggart skin and mesh steel which scraped against its brittle torso.

The golden cinder snarled impatiently at his partner, whose sooty robe had a bluish sheen. "She will not wait," the golden cinder said. He waved an impatient hand at the growing light now bleeding into the edge of Shadowmoor's pitch-dark sky. "The wall will never be ready in time."

The smoke of exertion curled up from the eyes of the second cinder as he hauled over another stack of flat stones. The blue cinder hated the golden cinder, but then cinders hated everyone as a rule, including other cinders. In this case the demands of a larger destiny outweighed their everyday maliciousness. They had been thrown together by providence and stayed together through pragmatism, for they shared the same holy purpose. Each also recognized he was far more likely to accomplish that purpose through shared effort.

"The wall will be ready when it is ready," the blue cinder replied. "And she will strike when she strikes." The inherent contempt in the blue cinder's words was clear to the golden cinder, who snorted and took the first shingle from atop the stack.

"I should break you into pieces," he said. "And add your body to the wall."

The blue cinder sneered. "You still wouldn't finish it in time."

The golden cinder lowered his rock. "Sometimes, brother, I doubt your true dedication."

"Then break me, if you can." The blue cinder angrily threw away the stone in his hand. "I'm finished with this. I'm finished with you. I did not come here to build walls."

"No." The golden cinder's face grew calm. "You came here for the same reason we all came: to see the Destroyer first hand. To gaze upon her and know if she is the one we've been waiting for."

Then the ground beneath them began to shake, causing the blue cinder's booted feet to slip. An orange glow appeared, crowning the mountaintop and growing stronger and brighter with each passing second. The gold cinder fell to his knees and clapped his hands together. A small cloud of black dust and grit rose up from his hands. The flesh on his face cracked and split as he smiled. Pale sparks struggled to shine in the depths of his hollow eye sockets.

"She is here," he said. "That is no giant 'rounding the mountainside, no army of migrating treefolk. The Destroyer has come." He raised his head and leveled his eyes at the blue cinder. "And now we shall both see what we came to see."

The blue cinder looked up over the mountain and spoke in a small, half-strangled whisper. "Is it her?" he said. "Are you sure it's really her?"

The golden cinder nodded. "It is, brother."

The blue cinder started. He glanced down at his partner and quickly kneeled beside him. "So there's no more reason to argue," the blue cinder said. "And no more reason to build walls.

"No, brother. In fact I believe we are about to be rewarded for our faithful efforts."

The blue cinder stared into the ever-brightening sky. "She is coming," he said. "She is really coming."

"Yes."

"I want to see her." The blue cinder stood and shook his skeletal fists at the glow, shouting, "I need to see her! I want to feel! I want to burn!"

"You will burn, brother." The golden cinder stood beside the blue and raised his arms in open-handed supplication. "In the darkness, she is the Destroyer, who shall cover the world with fire," the golden cinder intoned. The blue cinder's face remained fixed on the leading edge of the orange glow as it descended the mountain, but his voice joined his partner's and they continued together, "In the sea of flame she becomes the Extinguisher, who shall consume the fire that consumed the world."

Their voices rising, both cinders shouted, "And from the ashes, we are reborn."

The blue cinder screamed, flailing his arms in a paroxysm of ecstatic joy. "I will burn for you!" he said. "I must burn for you!"

"We shall all burn, brother." The golden cinder turned to face the blue. "First for her and then with her. Only after we have helped her set the whole world ablaze will she will turn and call us to join her in that holy fire. And we will go, brother. We will burn."

"Thank you." The blue cinder settled back to his knees, still staring blankly into the sky. "Thank you." He turned to the golden cinder and lunged forward, digging his sharp, brittle fingers into his partner's arm. "She's so beautiful," he hissed.

Then the orange glow enveloped them and the marshy ground below them burst into flame.

* * * * *

A small army of scarecrows moved along the edge of a fogbank just a few miles from the edge of the burning swamp. The shambling, stick-like figures moved not in silence but as a part of the aural landscape, betraying only the rustle of a leaf or the wind blowing through the dense stands of ash. Every so often one of them would turn and attempt to pierce the mists with a spasmodic swing of its spindly arms, only to be thrown backward with a jolt. Powerful spells protected those who lived on the other side of the fog, but the nigh-aimless and mindless scarecrows never seemed to remember.

If they felt frustration over their inability to break through the fog and raid Mistmeadow, the scarecrows kept it to themselves. They also ignored the steadily growing orange glow in the dark cloudless sky, and so none of the shambling monsters saw the pair of tiny, winged figures hovering just a few feet above their heads. The faeries wove back and forth between the crudely formed creatures and the strange blaze at the very edge of the horizon that was currently filling the western sky with a soft golden light.

"Should we warn them, Iliona?" the smaller faerie said.

"Not a chance, Veesa," the larger faerie replied. "I want to see what happens when they burn!"

"Wonderful! Joy!" Veesa squealed and flipped a double-loop in the darkness, but then she froze in midair. "We are talking about the scarecrows, right?"

"Yes," Iliona said. "Though I wouldn't mind seeing some of the treefolk burn, too."

"And the kithkin. But don't we have to warn Her Tallness when we spot fire?"

"No, we have to warn Her Tallness when we spot the big scary fire monster with a horse growing out of its soul. There's a difference."

"I get it. So we'll see the fire long before we see the—what are they calling her now? The Egg-stick—"

"Extinguisher. That's what the cinders call her. Though just about everyone else has settled on the 'Destroyer,' or the 'Fire Monster,' or the 'Please don't burn us *yeeeargh!*' "

Iliona caught herself slipping away into frivolous reverie and forced herself to concentrate. She had been getting lost in thought far too much lately, even if she didn't want to admit it.

Her sister Veesa gave her a sharp kick in the leg. "You know, that fire looks really—"

"Big," Iliona finished for her sister. "And hot."

"I'm not about to get my wings burned off over a few smelly kithkin," Veesa said. "Am I? I'd sooner push an entire kithkin doun off a cliff one-by-one before I'd let myself become a groundling."

"You're missing my point," Iliona said. "Like always. The point is we should get to see lots of stuff burn before we have to go back and report to Lady M."

"Oh!" Veesa exclaimed. "I get it. Say, is that her? The Destroyer?"

"No," Iliona said. "Those are just cinders. Miserable creeps. I wonder why she doesn't just incinerate them all. I mean, look at all that fire! She doesn't need a—a *horde*."

"Does that really qualify as a horde?" Veesa asked. "Really? It looks like a mob to me. Maybe a crowd."

"Or maybe the forward guard," Iliona said. Damnation, the faerie thought, I've gotten pessimistic, too. What a time to get old.

"There goes another treefolk!" Veesa clapped her hands in savage glee. "Boom, scream, crackle-crackle. She must be getting close now."

"Or the fire's just gotten ahead of her. Once she gets started it pretty much goes where it wants."

Veesa shouted again, "And we have our first scarecrow! Burn, you cretin! You'll never swat at another faerie ever again! And another! Ha, ha, stick-man, you should have taken a dip in the Wanderbrine. Might have lasted—"

"Shh," Iliona said. "I think I see something. It's bigger than a cinder, and it's not one of the trees. She's so bright! She's—"

"She's like the sun," Veesa said in awe. "I remember sunlight."

"So do I," said Iliona. The thought of sunlight didn't bring back happier memories of light, beauty, and love. No, sunlight reminded Iliona of the traitor who'd left them to save a tree. *A tree.*

Unsurprisingly echoing Iliona's thoughts, Veesa said, "Endry's going to just die when he learns he missed this."

"Don't say—just don't." The faerie sisters watched silently for a few moments as the scarecrows beneath them incinerated one after the other. The heat pressed against them like a solid, living thing, and Iliona exhaled loudly.

"It's time we were heading back," Iliona said. "Unless you really do want to get your wings burned off."

* * * * *

"Bucket!" Brigid Baeli called from atop her makeshift platform outside the heavily fortified doun of Mistmeadow. The kithkin's wooden perch was reinforced with iron plates and her own shapewater magic, but the flooring still bowed under her as she took a large iron bucket filled with water from the kithkin standing above her. That kithkin in turn leaned down to lift another bucket from a third kithkin standing on a platform similar to Brigid's on the other side of the wall.

The outside platform was also wooden but held together

by shapewater alone so that it could easily be destroyed if the enemy tried to use it to get over the wall. There was another pair of inside/outside platforms about twenty feet east of Brigid, where another pair of kithkin poured water from buckets into a wooden tank the size of a three-story house. Brigid was grateful for the help, as time was short, but everyone knew that Mistmeadow's defenses wouldn't be as formidable without contributions from these two in particular—the doun's new hero, Jack Chierdagh, and its future mayor, Keely (who was also Jack's betrothed).

Brigid dumped her bucketful of water into the moat beneath her feet and handed the empty bucket back to the kithkin atop the wall, and then a moment later took another full one from him. The moat inside the wall had been dug as recently as the two outside. They'd saved this one for last in the hope it wouldn't be needed, but the blaze in the sky in the direction of Mount Kulrath told them they'd be lucky to have the moat half-full by the time the Destroyer and her cinder horde reached the gates.

Brigid called for another bucket, emptied it, and tried not to think of how much the blazing sky reminded her of Lorwyn. She still thought of that place as home, lost and gone though she'd never physically left it. Instead, Lorwyn left her. The Great Aurora happened and Lorwyn became this place they all called Shadowmoor. Brigid, unlike every other kithkin, remembered Lorwyn, that world of endless summer where a golden sun hung in the sky for hours before dipping gracefully toward the horizon and created beautiful vistas of purple, gold, and orange before rolling back up into its apex.

Everything was different now, and everyone. In Lorwyn elves had been a fierce and terrible people, ready to destroy or enslave anything that did not meet their rigid standards of perfection. Now they were the stalwart protectors of beauty and they welcomed Brigid and her companions when she offered to help defend Mistmeadow from the coming fire-storm. In Lorwyn the merrow were friendly merchants and guides who cheerfully offered passage across the Wanderwine. Now they were merciless brigands who extracted a heavy toll in blood and treasure from anyone who dared cross the Wanderbrine. The wise and ancient treefolk who roamed Lorwyn had become rotten with cankerous disease and bit-terness. They'd also grown to tremendous sizes that rivaled the giants, towering into a sky that was no longer blue but an eternal black brightened only by the regular rise and fall of the bright silver moon.

In Lorwyn, kithkin like Brigid shared the bond of thought-weft, a sort of group thinking which made communal decisions with ease and forged a lasting peaceful coexistence with the rest of Lorwyn's tribes. Shadowmoor kithkin closed their gates to their neighbors, drove away strangers, and shared a *mind*weft which to Brigid seemed built on fear and the desperate need for survival in this harsh, dark world.

Shadowmoor kithkin also had eyes as large and white as a dead frog's, and despite having almost a year to get used to them Brigid was still unsettled whenever she gazed into them. She had taken to wearing a cowl and avoiding eye contact entirely, since her own small black orbs would give her away. She was no longer a member of her own tribe, but something the people of Mistmeadow would have attacked en masse as a threat to the doun. Even her own former village of Kinsbaile—Kinscaer— would treat her as a strange and hostile outsider.

The Aurora—the *Great* Aurora, Brigid corrected herself— had created a world of darkness she hardly recognized, and as usual when she dwelled on such things she touched her throat to feel for the pendant known as the Crescent of Morningtide.

The ancient merrow artifact had preserved Brigid's mind and body from the change that altered everything else, though she still did not understand why. The small talisman had belonged to a friend of hers, a merrow named Sygg, but Sygg might be dead now and if he wasn't he wouldn't have remembered Brigid as a friend. If anything she would be an employee to him, and a traitorous one at that.

If Sygg had known what the Crescent was, he hadn't let the secret slip. Brigid learned more from an elemental entity called the Source of the Wanderwine—Wander*brine*—who had informed her of the Crescent's nature. The Source had not told Brigid much more than that, so she was still learning what it could do. It had been less than a year since the Great Aurora, and the Crescent was still with her, so Brigid was still Brigid. Even in the gloomy wasteland that was Shadowmoor, she was thankful for that tiny blessing.

Millions of tiny pinpricks of light called "stars" (Brigid had never heard the word before but had picked it up from Sygg not long after the Aurora) hung in this strange and ominous sky. It had been less than a year, but to ask anyone in Mistmeadow, or the safeholds of Wilt-Leaf, or the underwater redoubts of the merrow brigands, or even the boggarts—assuming they listened—and they would tell you the world had always been this way. The kithkin outsider grappled daily with the fact that the world around her was impossible, a lie, but there was nothing she could do to expose the truth. Brigid knew a small handful of beings who remembered Lorwyn—her current employer was one, the faeries of the Vendilion clique were another (thanks to their connection to Brigid's boss) but these others either couldn't or wouldn't help her bring back Lorwyn and return things to normal.

Not that returning things to normal would stop Ashling the Destroyer, Brigid reckoned. The Great Aurora had given rise to the Destroyer, though Brigid suspected others had been actively involved. The stories had been circulating from one end of Shadowmoor to the other since that day, tales of entire towns and villages burned to the ground. With each telling the monster of living fire and her cinder horde had grown larger, wilder, and more dangerous. Ashling had been an ally in the world that was, her flamekin tribe a proud, intelligent, passionate people. Now the flamekin had become cinders and Ashling the Destroyer threatened to consume the new world that Brigid had been forced to inhabit.

She poured another bucket into the moat and cast an eye over the rest of their defenses. The elves were stationed on the side of the doun most likely to receive the brunt of the horde's onslaught, and among them were kithkin firefighters digging trenches much shallower than the moats, running in lines between the defenders. When the fighting started, the tank that Jack's team had filled would drain slowly into those trenches so the moats protecting Mistmeadow would not boil away. It would not stop or harm the Destroyer, but it would slow her horde's progress. To be honest, Brigid wondered if all the water in the Wanderbrine would be enough to save the doun, much less stop the Destroyer's rampage.

Brigid patted the Crescent again. If her death really was as impending as it seemed, she was glad she was going to die with all of her memories, even if so many of the memories caused her nothing but sadness.

A sound like a small quake shook her back to the present. It took only a few minutes for the entire elven contingent to file in and snap to attention, and the gates slammed shut once the final warrior stepped inside.

She's coming, Brigid thought. And she would be met by a force of arms and magic unlike any she had ever seen before. Elves, kithkin, faeries, and a merrow or two. If she lived to be a hundred years old, Brigid knew she'd never see such a strange alliance again, especially not in this dour and suspicious place. The ground shook again and dreadful orange light flooded the sky.

The kithkin smiled. Good thing I won't live to be a hundred, she thought.

CHAPTER 2

Safewright Gryffid of the Wilt-Leaf elves walked briskly down the line of vinebred warriors. He nodded to each in turn and gave everyone a brief word of encouragement. It was the least he could do, he thought, literally the least he could do. His superior, Vigilant Eidren, had been so busy preparing the defense of Mistmeadow he'd had to give his own second-in-command an insultingly unimportant job. There were trenches to dig, barricades to build, and water to be fetched from the Wanderbrine. Any of these would have been a task more critical than reinspecting the vinebred. There was nothing he could impart to them, nothing for them to say to him beyond what had been said every time he asked. Yes, they were in perfect order. They were confident. They were ready. They could win.

Beneath the ornate growth that gave them their names, the vinebred contingent comprised mostly elves, but Gryffid also nodded to a pair of former kithkin scouts who'd volunteered to be enchanted by the vines to better defend their homes. The safewright had to admit that within the deceptively delicate vines, even a kithkin approached grace.

The vinebred needed no inspection, but Gryffid was determined to do something worthwhile this close to the battle. He was not a great speaker, but the vinebred would not be expecting much. "Warriors," he said as he reached the end of the vinebred line, "You have your orders. The Destroyer is heading this way. Fire brought to us by the forces of nature is a thing of beauty, and as such it keeps the Wilt-Leaf wood strong. This is no natural blaze we face, but a living flame that wants nothing more than to burn us all down to smoldering ash."

Gryffid turned on his heel and marched back down the line the way he had come, giving them a moment to think on what he'd told them. "We are the protectors of all that is good," he said. "And we will die for that which is beautiful and just."

"Well said, Safewright Gryffid." Vigilant Eidren stepped forward and said, "Though I must ask, my friend: what makes you suspect our warriors have forgotten their sacred duty, their very reason for existence?"

"Vigilant," Gryffid said, his voice only just betraying his alarm and embarrassment at having been so introspective he did not hear his superior approaching. "I was—"

"Growing impatient," Eidren said. "I've half a mind to set the forest ablaze myself."

"Sir, that would—"

"Be at ease, Safewright." The vigilant laughed. "Do not let the grace of a modest joke go unnoticed just because you think we're all going to die."

"I—I don't think that at all, sir," Gryffid said. "The kithkin have been industrious, and the shapewater defenses—"

"Will become vapor if exposed to enough heat," Eidren said, still smiling but no longer joking in the slightest. He lowered his voice so as not to be overheard by the vinebred. "And these defenses will burn like paper. But we must succeed here. The Destroyer must be stopped or diverted before she reaches Mistmeadow. For if Mistmeadow falls, the rest of the Wilt-Leaf is open to attack." He grimaced, an expression that looked out of place on his handsome, lean face. "We sacrificed many elves—many friends—luring her this way."

"We will not fail," Gryffid said, "even if I must drag the Destroyer into the river myself."

"I shall hold you to that, Second," Eidren said. "But this is hardly the way for two warriors to speak on the eve of battle." Eidren straightened, and the first hints of returning moonlight flashed against the silvery vinebred armor he wore beneath his golden tunic and shimmering shapewater breastplate. In a loud, clear voice that every elf nearby could hear, Eidren said, "Safewright Gryffid, report on the readiness of your forces."

Gryffid's answer was strong, sure, and immediate. "Vinebred contingents are all at their stations and ready to fight, sir. The kithkin civilians have been led to safety in the deep woods and the kithkin fighters have taken their positions atop the lookout towers and town walls."

"And what of these water wizards, Safewright?"

"The shapewater brigade is maintaining a state of readiness at protected shelters. Shapewater barriers will be available on command."

"Very good." Eidren looked down the main thoroughfare of Mistmeadow. The town had had walls before the Wilt-Leaf elves settled on its strategic importance, but now the doun boasted reinforced barricades built with every scrap of wood, metal, and stone the industrious kithkin had been able to find. Buildings within the tiny doun that could serve the defenders stood reinforced. The kithkin and elves tore down anything else that would have served as fuel for the Destroyer and converted the material into further reinforcement for the town walls. In the moonlight, what rubble remained took on a curious and sad beauty all its own.

A cough from Eidren reminded Gryffid he was still in mid-report. "Shapewater nodes have been attached to key defensive structures, ready for use should the waterline be interrupted."

"Yes, the waterline," the vigilant said. "They must hold out as long as they can. Are you certain this merrow can be trusted?"

"Not at all," Gryffid replied honestly. "And that goes for the kithkin river-brigand too, but the damned—pardon, sir—the mindweft told the dounsfolk to trust them both. They won't hear a single word that runs counter to the opinion of the mindweft. Perhaps it is not too late to evacuate them all—warriors, water wizards, all of them?"

"This will not be our last battle against the Destroyer," said Eidren. "We will need all the allies we can find to protect the safeholds and the Wilt-Leaf. So for now we will respect their mindweft, but if either the merrow or the kithkin brigand does anything to threaten our mission, we must deal with them swiftly and severely. There is simply too much at stake."

"It will be done. As for the waterline, sir, it is fully manned. The merrow is at the river; the brigand is just inside the wall. But should their line be broken—"

"Oh, it will be broken, of that I have no doubt," Eidren said. "The only real question is will they last long enough to make a difference?" He turned and gazed upon the reinforced gate that led to a series of winding paths and the wall of permanent mist that had given the doun its name. The glow in the sky over the tree line grew stronger, illuminating in orange light the black spires of the closest mountain peak. Almost lost in the unnatural brightness was the full moon, now creeping up from the horizon like a stalking cat's eye.

"Their position should keep them safe," Gryffid said.

"And what of your second, our envoy to the stranger?" Eidren asked. The burning sky behind him threw a crown of light around his head pierced by his twin horns, which swept back from his forehead and around the golden helm. "Has Rhys reported to you recently?"

"No," Gryffid said with a scowl and cursed his absent-mindedness. "He accompanied the stranger on her jaunt around the wall. She was meeting with her faerie spies, no doubt."

"I want to know what the stranger's spies told their master. Debrief your second-in-command as soon as you see him," said Eidren. "And I ask you now: Do you believe the stranger's spies can be trusted?"

"I do not. But it doesn't really matter." Gryffid spoke with a bitterness and frustration he never would have risked in a less desperate situation. "They're the only scouts we can risk."

"I suppose so," Eidren replied. "Though I must tell you, Safewright, the stranger worries me. I do not trust that woman, but we had very little choice choice. Better to have her close by, where we can observe her. But for that to help us, she must be observed. Your second—he knows this, and knows to keep a close watch on her?"

"Yes, sir," Gryffid confirmed. "And though I trust second Safewright Rhys, I am curious as to his long absence."

"Then look at the sky," Eidren said with a wave at the ever-growing glow on the horizon. "That is the reason we are here, and the justification for each and every action we take this day. Take a deep breath, my friend. The time is almost upon us. Alert me as soon as Rhys reports to you."

* * * * *

Second Safewright Rhys of the Wilt-Leaf elves had trouble keeping up with his charge. He was overdue to report back to Gryffid, which distracted and slowed him down. Jogging along behind the raven-haired elf maiden he called in a whisper just loud enough to pierce the mist, "Maralen! Slow down, please."

"Taer—*Safewright* Rhys," the stranger said, making the same odd mistake in addressing him she'd already made twice since they stepped outside the town gates, "We can't observe anything in this fog. I'm hurrying because my friends bring news."

"How do you know?" Rhys asked. "If they can tell you at this distance they have news, why don't they just give you the news?"

"They haven't told me," the tall elf woman in black said. Her arched eyebrows accentuated her long face and curiously thick horns. She tapped one ear. "But I can hear them coming."

A moment later, so could Rhys. The faerie sisters bickered furiously and continuously, and though he'd known them only a few days Rhys recognized this as their usual state of affairs. These strange, overly opinionated faeries behaved quite unlike any of the fluttering creatures Rhys had ever met before. They were bolder, more aggressive, and more independent, which resulted in some truly abrasive behavior. He could not make out what the diminutive creatures were saying, but their agitation and the reaction on Maralen's face made it clear that it wasn't good news. It seemed that they were out of time. And then their voices were lost in a sound that started at a high-pitched wail and rapidly descended in tone until it became a dull roar, something like the sound of a single angry giant but coming from a thousand different points within the mist.

"It's my right to tell her, Veesa," Iliona—the larger of the two—was saying, buzzing her wings to get ahead of her smaller, and fast-moving sister.

"It's first-come, first-tell if you ask me," Veesa replied, picking up the pace, but with effort. As they barreled toward them, the sisters took on more distinct shapes until they at last emerged from the mist. Each arrived before the stranger and came to a halt, but the moment one began to speak the other cut her off. The chattering cacophony grew louder and more shrill until the tall elf woman finally clapped her hands together precisely between the Vendilion sisters, silencing them.

"Iliona," Maralen said, "I know what you've seen; you know that. We don't have any secrets, do we? But tell me anyway so my friend Rhys can hear."

"Right, Maralen, your *friend*." Veesa giggled rudely.

"What does that mean?" Rhys asked, but the others ignored him.

"The Destroyer," Iliona said. "She's not far behind us—maybe half a mile."

"You actually saw her," Maralen said with a scowl. "Not a cinder running through the flames, not a burning boggart or a blazing treefolk. You saw Ashling."

"If that's Ashling," Iliona said before her sister could jump in again, "she's changed. Are you sure this isn't just that—you know, the horse-thing, with the fire?"

"The elemental fire is part of her now, yes. And you're dodging my question. Her physical form. You saw it?"

"Yes," Veesa replied, "We both did. Search our minds if you don't believe us."

"That's not necessary," Maralen said. "Now go, get out of range. The two of you won't last a moment against living flames. Get to high ground, preferably someplace already burned, and stay there for a day. If you receive my signal by then, meet me wherever I am."

Though a bystander to this conversation between the strange elf woman and her improbable faerie handmaidens, Rhys couldn't help but notice the faeries didn't move an inch but continued hovering directly before Maralen's face. He felt something tickling the back of his neck and swatted at it, but soon realized it was sweat, not an insect.

It was growing quite warm.

"Maralen," he said with an authority he didn't feel. "We all have to go." The roar was no longer just in front of them; it was coming from the sides. The fires had reached the edge of the mists and were trying to envelop the town like running water over a round stone.

"You heard him," Iliona said.

"And you heard us," Veesa said. "We're not going anywhere."

Rhys said, "We have to get back inside the walls. I'm expected." Already the roaring was giving up other, more distinct sounds, including the terrifyingly guttural tongue of the cinders, creatures that hated all living things and especially those things most beautiful—in other words, everything the elves were sworn to protect.

"Then we should return," Maralen said. To the faeries, she added, "Though I admit, I had not expected such loyalty." With a wry look, Maralen turned on her heel to join Rhys for the short jog back to the doun gate.

"It's not loyalty," Iliona called.

"It's self-preservation," Veesa explained. "What's the kithkin saying? 'Don't kill the rabbit that lays the golden egg'? You're our only rabbit, so we're not going to let you die unless we're here to see it. And then, oh, the eggs we will break."

"You're talking with too much metaphorical whatsit," Iliona said. "Oona won't take us back now. That's the point. We can never go back. It's got nothing to do with eggs."

"Why do you have to be so—"

"All right," Maralen said over her shoulder. "I've already agreed. But if you're incinerated I'm going to be very cross. You're my most valuable agents, ladies."

"Hear that, Veesa? She thinks we're her agents."

"What a laugh," Veesa replied. "*You* might be her agent, but you're both my agents. Rhys, too. My most valuable elf agent, which isn't saying much."

"I'm a what?" Rhys's head was spinning as the air seemed to leave his lungs. The nearing fires were taking the breath out of the very air itself.

"You'll see," the faerie sisters said simultaneously.

Rhys and Maralen arrived at the doun gate. Though not yet visible, the snarling cinders and the intense fires devouring the southern edges of the Wilt-Leaf sounded as if they were right over his shoulder. The smell of burning wood and flesh created an intensely unpleasant cocktail in his nostrils. Maralen helped to support him, and he did the same for her as they pounded on the small, sturdy pass-door built into the much larger gate.

There was no response, and as his air continued to run out Rhys found he could not keep his balance. Leaving the pass-door to Maralen, he turned and pressed his back against the gate itself.

He spotted the vanguard of the Destroyer's horde just as Maralen ordered her faerie attendants to fly over the wall and get one of the kithkin to open the damned door. The attackers were cinders—that much was clear from the way they moved through the advancing mass of fire as if they were part of it. The flames flickered and flared between the oncoming cinders, connecting them each in a web of fire.

"They're sending someone now," Iliona cried from atop the wall. "They said they didn't think the Destroyer would get here so quickly."

"Well, they know now," Maralen snapped and Rhys heard the first clicks of the lock being flung open. "Now get out of range—she'll be here any second!"

Was that another shape among the cinders, Rhys asked himself? It was, and unlike the cinders it did not appear as a half-burned coal in a blazing fiery web. There was nothing skeletal or shambling about this creature; indeed she appeared to be something like what an elf maiden might look like if she were made completely out of flames. This was the Destroyer, he thought dizzily. He grew faint from the lack of fresh air just before the door was flung open and a kithkin emerged to help Maralen guide Rhys back into Mistmeadow.

Once inside the doun gate, Maralen slapped him once, twice, and he stopped her before she could do it a third time. "I'm awake!" he snapped. "And I'm ready. I need to find my superior and—"

With a blast of heat, a billowing cloud of orange fire, and a tremendous boom, the sturdy doun gate of Mistmeadow exploded inward, engulfing Maralen and Rhys in a ton and a half storm of debris and burning wreckage.

* * * * *

Gryffid looked uncertainly at his vigilant superior when the gates imploded. He hoped he and Eidren had not made a tactical error at the very start of the battle that would cost them their necessary victory. If not for the smoke that dimmed her brilliance and the protective magic Gryffid already wore, the wave of heat and the blinding glare of the Destroyer's sudden appearance might have been unbearable.

In fact, with as much rubble and smoke as there was still in the air, Gryffid wasn't certain the brightness was the Destroyer herself or merely the flames preceding her entrance. She had to enter the doun for their plan to have any chance of success, a truly terrifying prospect to the kithkin hiding in the underground passages outside Mistmeadow. The dounsfolk would never have their village back the way they remembered. Gryffid regretted that, and he wished he could pity Mistmeadow, but he had to be pragmatic. The survival of the doun and its inhabitants was of secondary concern to keeping the Destroyer clear of the Wilt-Leaf.

"There, sir!" came the call from a sharp-eyed elf scout, "The cinders!" Gryffid noted with bitter pleasure that the call did not come from one of the vinebred. Despite everything, he did not entirely trust vinebred magic. "Archers, draw," he called softly. "Find your targets, and . . . loose!"

Twin streams of arrows rained on the cinder vanguard from the two strongest fortifications the elves and kithkin had been able to reinforce. One had been the town smithy, the other a distillery, and now each held almost thirty of the finest elf archers in the Wilt-Leaf. Their elevation helped the silver arrows (an expensive precaution, but Eidren hoped the silver might survive the flames) plunge into the raging cinders with enough force to do real damage. The silver projectiles lodged in the heads, shoulders, torsos, and legs of the crumbling cinder brutes, but hope faded as soon as it had sparked when the stricken enemy didn't even flinch. The nearest to Gryffid even now charged toward him, eyes spewing black, oily smoke despite a silver arrow embedded into the top of its head and another transfixing its upper leg. Another arrow's feathered end could be seen waving back and forth behind the cinder like a cat's tail as the raider bounded toward him.

Gryffid ignored the approaching threat and called, "Archers, pick your targets carefully! Aim only for the enemy!" His sword gleamed orange and white in the burning night as he thrust it overhead defiantly. "Vinebred, attack!"

Then Gryffid drew his sword back down and turned to meet the pincushion cinder with a powerful swing. It was not a true chevalblade—only vigilants had the honor of carrying those fearsome magical weapons, though Eidren personally eschewed them—but Gryffid was confident the great sword would do the job against these cinders.

The first strike disappointed him, taking a chip out of the monster's long right arm but not causing it more than a moment's distraction. The cinder responded with a backhanded swat that sent Gryffid flying into a vinebred warrior behind him. The vinebred managed to keep his footing and prevent his superior officer from rolling into harm's way.

Of course, Gryffid told himself, I'm already *in* harm's way. The cinder he'd struck resumed his charge, slavering and intent on finishing the job. Pushing off from the stout-legged vinebred, the safewright regained the initiative and readied his sword. In the moment he had before the cinder reached him, he searched for some weak spot that might actually slow the thing down for more than half a heartbeat. He'd struck it in the arm, and there were arrows deeply embedded in its head, back, and leg. Where could his fine blade cut to make a difference?

Gryffid held the sword steadily, looking at the leg—the knee in particular. It was not at all like an elf's knee, but more like a pair of stones held together by a rope running through a borehole in each. Giant beads on a very short string—to get the beads, one need only cut the thread. There were similar joints at the shoulders, ankles, and neck.

Just as the cinder bore down Gryffid leaped to one side, dragging his sword's edge along the monster's right knee. Wilt-Leaf steel severed something like a thick vine—he could feel it snap when the blade made it all the way through. The cinder's upper leg slipped from its shin and the creature crashed to the ground, rolling into the vinebred's waiting strike, which took off the monster's left arm at the elbow. Completely unbalanced, the cinder struggled in vain to right itself using only a left leg and a right arm.

"Aim for the joints!" Gryffid cried, sweat streaming down his face. His lungs burned as he breathed in an inferno. "Archers! The joints! Take off their limbs at the joints! They'll be helpless!"

For a few shining minutes Gryffid could tell himself they had a chance. Not every blow hit the right spot on the joint, and indeed many did not. Vinebred warriors were tossed and battered, pummeled and smashed, but their resilient armor and powerful magic kept them in the fight.

He ducked a cinder's charred forearm that a precise elven arrow had taken off at the elbow, and then pushed ahead. The archers were safe for now, but if the flame reached the fortifications the shapewater barricades around the base of the makeshift towers might not be enough to keep them from igniting and burning all of his finest hunters. Gryffid did not like such uncertainty when it came to the fate of the elves under his command, but it was another calculated risk he had to take, much as he had in sending Rhys to his doom with orders to meet with the stranger Maralen. He supposed there was a chance those two were alive, but Gryffid had seen no sign of them since the gates came down. Eidren believed the strange elf woman had powerful magic, but with Maralen nowhere to be seen the vigilant would have to work alone.

Eidren's magic, Gryffid knew, was the only thing keeping the wall of flame from flooding the town. From his vantage point on the ground facing the smoking wreckage, the safewright saw his commander atop a third fortified structure, backed by Eidren's own small detachment of vinebred. They had orders to defend the fortification for as long as the vigilant lived.

Eidren was alone, apparently unarmed, and holding both of his palms out toward the shattered entrance. Gryffid felt Eidren meeting the fires with his own vibrant power. A cinder stalked through the barrier Eidren created without difficulty, but the blaze itself could not penetrate. As long as Eidren kept the flames at bay, the Destroyer could not prevail here. She would have to change her course, for she was a creature of flame and surely could not survive without it.

The attacking cinders cared little for their own survival, it seemed. Their assault was as uncoordinated and chaotic as the inferno and they threw themselves in ones and twos at the doun's defenders as the elves continued to find and exploit the thin smoking seams and joints between solid pieces of stony flesh. The safewright took the head off a fresh cinder, a lucky blow meant to cover a feint that instead severed the neck joint, but it was to no avail.

With a roar of frustration and what sounded like physical pain, Eidren abandoned his war against the encroaching flames. The result reminded Gryffid of a natural dam knocked over by a petulant child, except the flood that rolled in over the broken restraint was an ocean of searing orange fire. Most of the defenders had already been driven back far enough from the gates that the immediate blast didn't kill them. The archers also survived the initial blast, but their fate was more uncertain, for fires now lapped at the shapewater barricades and clearly yearned to leap to the top.

Eidren—was he all right? Gryffid didn't dare risk trying to find out, as leaving his warriors on the battlefield would only cause more confusion and hasten what he was still telling himself wasn't completely inevitable. Eidren was the vigilant, and he had plans within plans. Of course he must have anticipated this.

So why, Gryffid asked himself, is the fire running rampant? Had Eidren been mistaken? Was the vigilant's roar actually more serious than mere frustration? He risked a look back at Eidren's tower, and a cold fist squeezed around Gryffid's heart.

The vigilant was gone. There was no sign of Eidren in the ruins of his shelter, nor of his vinebred honor guard. When Gryffid turned back to face his next foe, he saw the Destroyer had at last arrived.

She was a tall, lithesome female shape at the heart of the living blaze. Her features were obscured and distorted by fire and frenzy, but Gryffid saw her clearly in his mind's eye. She was fury personified, a living incarnation of vengeful killing rage.

The kithkin waterline finally finished their preparations, set down their buckets, and scrambled into the last two remaining structures in a transparent attempt to save their own skins. It appeared they left Gryffid and the elves to die, that he was the only thing standing in the way of Mistmeadow's complete and utter annihilation. The Destroyer appeared to hold the fate of the doun—and the entire Wilt-Leaf—in her fiery hands.

But appearances could deceive.

CHAPTER 3

"There's the signal," Jack called to Brigid, who immediately relayed the news to the waterline. This was a crucial moment—if the kithkin outside the walls could not get inside in time, if Gryffid were simply incinerated on the spot, if the Destroyer turned her wrath on the kithkin instead of the elves and simply leveled the last two structures—so much could go wrong.

But then Brigid could hardly believe any of it had gone right, and much of it had so far. As the first of the kithkin scouts clambered down the wall, she directed them to their posts and reminded them to stay there until she gave the orders to attack. Though she couldn't see them, she knew the far ends of each waterline—hers and Jack's—would converge on Wryget and stay there as a last resort to let the hidden civilians reach safety if absolutely everything else, including Eidren, failed.

Inside the former grain silo (now a guard tower filled with desperate defenders), Brigid crouched and waited with some two dozen kithkin under her command. She could not feel a single thought from any of them, and they would see her as a blank spot in the mindweft, but she had prepared for that. As long as she was in charge and acted independently as she gave the orders, they should have the best of both worlds—the quick decision-making of an individual leader and the quicker communication of the mindweft.

Brigid employed a minor scrying spell to look in on the makeshift fort at the opposite end of the wall. She frowned, gazing into the tiny mirror that was magically connected to another mirror inside that fort. The brave vinebred were losing the fight. No matter how many cinders the formidable defenders cut down, more kept coming. The same could not be said about the decidedly finite vinebred warriors—tough as they were, their numbers were already noticeably diminished. With any luck Brigid and her students in both towers would be able to save a few of the elven elite before it was too late. As it was, Gryffid and his squadron were being driven slowly back toward the doun. The safewright retreated slowly and deliberately, he and his warriors a lure to draw in the Destroyer according to Eidren's plan.

All at once the blinding glare of the Destroyer herself forced Brigid to turn her face aside, her eyes instinctively squeezed tight. And a good thing—she realized her hood had slipped off at that moment, and she pulled it back over her eyes before returning to the mirror. Shielding herself from the glare with one hand and looking through her fingers, she nodded. It was Ashling.

Brigid wondered if the flamekin pilgrim (for that was what the Destroyer had been before she became the Destroyer) would remember her, if Ashling recalled a kithkin scout who tried to murder her and dump her in the Wanderwine more than a year ago. Did "the Destroyer" remember anything of Lorwyn? Maralen seemed to think so.

The figure in the center of the living flames was identical in shape and size to the flamekin Brigid had known, but as she watched the flames leap and cavort into the center of Mistmeadow's once-thriving thoroughfare, Brigid realized the

Destroyer was much larger than Ashling's body. The inferno and the horde that came with it were the true Destroyer, and Ashling—who for all Brigid knew wouldn't even recognize her former name—was its heart.

Brigid dismissed such fanciful thoughts—there was a great deal of work to do—and she whispered, "Ready everyone?" The others all responded in the affirmative. "Remember to take your cues from me. Don't try anything too fancy; you're not here to make art. You're here to save your town." She grinned. "To save *our* town. You welcomed me in, a stranger you could not recognize, without judging me harshly. Well, not *too* harshly, Aldo," she added, earning warm laughs from the others and a sheepish smile from the kithkin she'd addressed.

"We're ready," Aldo said. "Just lead the way, Boss."

"She's almost close enough. Is Jack's tower ready? Good."

The Destroyer marched directly toward Gryffid, almost swaggering as she bore down on his zigzagging path. The safe-wright raised his hand again, signaling once more to Brigid.

"Time for the hand-off, kithkin of Mistmeadow," Brigid said. "Now get out there and make Mistmeadow Jack—and all the rest of us—right proud. On my mark. One. Two." Her hand began to drop and she hastily called, "Three . . . *mark!*"

Shapewater magic was a merrow invention as far as Brigid knew, and for some time—both before the Aurora and after—she'd made use of borrowed shapewater magic. She'd used it for simple things like breathing underwater (during a lengthy foray into a merrow redoubt in the old days) or transportation (when she'd been working for Sygg's criminal crew after the world changed).

In the aftermath of the Aurora and its great change, Brigid learned the Crescent of Morningtide allowed her to manipulate water into useful tools as easily as an average merrow could. Mastery of the sort Sygg displayed in both his incarnations had so far eluded her, and even with the Crescent she had trouble keeping a shapewater craft afloat without Wryget's help. The artifact seemed to allow her to tideshape, but deeper magic required more experience or a stronger force of will. And even then, neither of those could grant her merrow stamina.

In the weeks she, Maralen, and the Wilt-Leaf elves had spent preparing for the Destroyer's inevitable attack on Mistmeadow, Brigid had dedicated herself to learning—and teaching other kithkin—how to use the shapewater as a weapon. A very specific weapon for a very specific enemy. Now she would learn whether all of that learning, teaching, and planning was for naught.

The archers in the kithkin shapewater brigade let fly on the enemy; unlike the elves, their target was the Destroyer herself and their missiles were not arrows but cold, icy water Brigid and most of Mistmeadow had been hauling into town for days. Ashling—no, the Destroyer, Brigid corrected herself; she needed no painful memories getting in the way of her decision-making—had walked neatly into their trap. And since baiting that trap had already cost the lives of several vinebred warriors and looked set to destroy several dozen elf archers as well (to say nothing of the village itself), it had better damned well work.

On Brigid's order, water from the huge wooden tank flowed into the trenches. There the river water rose like a dancing line of drunken snakes hypnotized by a kithkin flute-player, a vertical net to prevent the Destroyer from retreating. Brigid had trusted her best shapewater students to hold the net steady. Then, with the help of the others who were not quite as capable with the strange merrow magic, Brigid summoned all the power she could muster and emptied the inner moat, driving all the water it contained toward a single center point—Ashling herself.

The result was phenomenal. Tons of water rose into the air in an untidy ring, and then broke into large transparent globules that flickered with reflected light from the many fires raging within the doun walls. She doubted any of the Mistmeadow kithkin had ever seen such a light, and she was proud they were able to maintain their control of the shapewater even under these circumstances.

Brigid raised an arm and then dropped it like an axe. A moat's worth of icy water slammed into the blindingly bright creature at the heart of the flames with tremendous force. Clouds of steam rose in a fog bank thicker and more searing than Mistmeadow normally endured. The hot, humid smoke erupted from all sides of the Destroyer, obscuring her behind a fluffy wall of orange and sickly white.

Brigid raised a hand and once more summoned all her strength. She felt the magical support from her fellow kithkin, and this time they raised the moat just outside the walls. She dropped her arm and again the borrowed Wanderbrine slammed into the Destroyer from all sides. As the brimstone-stinking cloud spread to nearly all corners of Mistmeadow, Brigid and her shapewater brigade lifted the contents of the third and final moat into the air and hit Ashling with it. Brigid was glad she hadn't needed to teach anything more complicated or strenuous than this, for even she was unable to attack a fourth time. Three was enough; it had to be enough. Surely three moats could put out even the most ferocious blaze, even one at the white-hot heart of an attacking fire.

Brigid felt sick as the wind moved in to disperse the fog. There, unharmed and only slightly dimmer than before, stood Ashling the Destroyer. Though it hurt the kithkin's eyes to stare, she could have sworn she saw an expression of cruel amusement on Ashling's glowing face. Amusement and, as her eyes flashed at Brigid, bitter recognition.

There was nothing for it, Brigid thought, and she called out "Cage!"

Her best students lashed out with the snakes of water, all that remained of the tons and tons Brigid, Jack Chierdagh, Wryget, and dozens of kithkin had carried miles to Mistmeadow. Instead of trying to strike the Destroyer, the tendrils came together in a translucent mesh that closed around the glowing figure until Ashling would have only a foot or two to move in any direction without coming into contact with it.

Brigid watched the bubbles roiling within the watery bars of the cage, and then the cage itself dissolve into steam within a matter of seconds, and she found herself speechless. There was another order to give, and she wanted with every bone in her body not to give it.

"Brigade," Brigid called, her voice strong and clear as she pushed the small doorway to the makeshift fort open and stepped out into the open. She held a silver dirk in one hand and with the other she traced a few symbols in the air. When she was finished, her shapewater armor had sealed around Brigid's body and head, leaving only her face and weapon exposed. "Stand your ground and ready for siege defense."

Two bubbling hisses behind her told her the shapewater barricades of the two fortifications had enveloped the structures in much the same manner, but leaving gaps for arrows and swords to be deployed against an enemy. Which was, Brigid thought sadly, exactly useless against the foe standing before her. Even through the kithkin outcast's magical protection, the heat pumping out from Ashling's body was almost unbearable. It took all of Brigid's courage to take even a step closer to the Destroyer, and then even more to raise her dirk defiantly.

"Destroyer," Brigid said. "In the name of Molla Welk and the citizens of Mistmeadow, I place you under arrest." Brigid staggered and the silver dirk wavered, but she quickly recovered her bluster and added, "Surrender at once."

"Brigid Baeli," the Destroyer said, though Brigid was not sure if being recognized was a good thing. "The hero of Kinsbaile. Fancy meeting you here. You're in my way."

"Yes," Brigid said with an involuntary gulp.

"But because we're such *good* old friends," Ashling continued, "I will allow you, and any you choose to take with you, to flee. You may live in the—" She turned to look over her shoulder at a wall of flames and a nightmare sky from which the stars had been blackened and extinguished by the devastation rising up from below. "You may live on in the new world I'm leaving for you. I regret it is not as bright and optimistic as the one you remember, but you are a survivor. Perhaps when my work is done, we will meet again."

"You're under arrest," Brigid said again. "Though if you leave now I'll let you off with a warning."

* * * * *

Rhys had not seen the monster rampant from such a close vantage point before, but it was clear that the Destroyer was living up to her name. The heat above their heads was unbelievable, but since they were both submerged up to their chins, Rhys and Maralen were able to withstand the Destroyer's entrance into Mistmeadow even if the stinking, brackish moat did not. Most of the solid debris from the hastily constructed gate was piled up on top of the two, but Rhys guessed they could probably push themselves out with little effort once the wreckage stopped burning.

He called Maralen's name and again received no response. She'd been unconscious since the wall collapsed, and Rhys had neither heard nor seen any sign of her faerie attendants. The elf woman was strange in so many ways—whoever heard of the Fae serving elves—that the second safewright had to remind himself that she might not just be unconscious. She might be dead. Reaching out with his one free hand—his legs and left arm were pinned, though nothing felt broken—he was able to tap her on the top of the head. "Maralen. Maralen, wake up."

"What?" came the groggy reply, and in the dim orange light that filtered through the smoldering wreckage he saw her eyes blink open. "Oh. Rhys? Where are—"

"The gate fell on us," Rhys said. "And the Destroyer—she's here, in Mistmeadow. I think she just walked right over us. If not for the water in this moat we'd have been cooked."

"Well, then," Maralen said. "Lucky us." He saw her attempting to move, saw her eyebrows arch in relief. "Nothing broken. We have to get out of here."

"I agree," Rhys said. "I've got to get back to my comrades. Now that you've come around, is there any chance your little friends could help us out of here?"

"If they're still around, I'll be—" She closed her eyes for a moment. "No, they're not. Good. I still need them alive, and they're just too vulnerable. We'll have to get out of here ourselves, and the sooner the better, I'd say. Don't want to miss all the fun." She grunted as she brought a knee up to her chest, and Rhys saw his earlier estimate of the wreckage's remaining mass was correct—it moved easily.

And then all of the water in the moat was pulled unceremoniously out, spinning Maralen around so that she inadvertently kicked Rhys in the face. Fortunately the blow helped him cough up a lungful of the moat water that had, for a second, made him think he was going to drown in perhaps the stupidest fashion possible.

"Sorry," Maralen called. "What just happened?"

"They've sprung the trap," Rhys said. "Come on," he added,

drawing up his knees as Maralen had done before. "No more face-kicking, please. One, two, *push!*"

The pile of smoldering wreckage gave way and scattered with a rattling sound that was lost amid a rush of heat, smoke, and steam that had Rhys coughing again.

It wasn't until the heat hit him that Rhys realized how close they really were to the Destroyer. She stood a mere twenty feet ahead of them, and if she caused this much discomfort at this distance he could only imagine what Brigid Baeli was feeling. The diminutive scout still had her ever-present hood pulled over her eyes, but her shapewater armor had become a shapewater bodysuit that covered her from head to toe. Though he couldn't see her eyes, Rhys registered Brigid's alarm when she spotted him, and the elf officer realized the Destroyer was speaking to Brigid. The faintest movements of her chin to the left and then the right told Rhys the kithkin didn't want his help.

Well, she was going to get it. They had to stop the monster here, and this kithkin water-mage was their best chance—or so Vigilant Eidren said, and Rhys would no more doubt the Vigilant Eidren than he would doubt the existence of the sky.

But what could he do? Rhys had no water magic, was not adept at any of the arcane arts. That was for scholars and princes like Vigilant Eidren. Rhys was but a warrior, and what little magic he did employ came from the soil and what little life force it contained.

Without a choice left, he turned to Maralen. "Stranger," he said, causing her to arch an eyebrow and smirk. "Can you do anything more than talk to Fae?"

"You don't know what I am," Maralen said with an odd grin. Then she added for no reason Rhys could fathom, "That's rather sweet." The grin disappeared and she turned to face him, ignoring the searing heat.

"Just do what you can do," Rhys said, casting an eye toward the burning battlefield where Gryffid was doing his best to gather the wounded together for a counterattack that couldn't possibly succeed.

"Rhys, the power I can use—it's not mine, not exactly." Maralen spoke with that peculiar, protective familiarity Rhys found so disconcerting in someone he'd known for only a short time. "If I use it, the owner of the power will know, and she will use that knowledge to find me. She could be a bigger problem than this, though I know that sounds impossible."

"If we don't stop her here—my home is next," pleaded Rhys, waving toward the Wilt-Leaf. "She won't stop. Even if we can't finish her, we have to send her in the other direction. Delay her. *Some*thing."

Maralen grimaced and her eyes flicked momentarily toward the sky. The grimace turned into a full-blown scowl when Rhys felt something sharp poke him at the base of his skull and then he could feel nothing below his neck. Looking down—no longer able to support his head—he was alarmed to see he was clearing the tops of the tallest fortifications still standing in Mistmeadow.

"There," Iliona said from behind Rhys's ear. "You're saved."

"What are you doing?" An infuriated Maralen hung in the air beside Rhys, her collar held tightly in the claws of Iliona's sister Veesa. Each of the faeries was struggling mightily to gain altitude, and their efforts now had the group almost a hundred feet above and almost two hundred away from Mistmeadow. Below them now the fog appeared, brushing past their feet, refusing to dissipate even though the forest and ground it had once hidden had been devastated by the Destroyer's passage.

"We decided to get you both out of here," Veesa said. "It's hopeless."

"What?" Rhys objected as strongly as he could with his chin rolling back and forth on his chest. "Return me at once. I've a duty—"

"Wasn't your last duty to keep an eye on Miss High and Mighty here?" Iliona asked him, and he knew she meant Maralen.

"It was, but that's irrelevant. My men are being burned alive! I can't flee into the sky paralyzed and carried by *faeries!*"

"We swore to serve this one," Veesa said, tapping Maralen on the head with a giggle that showed she'd wanted to do that for some time, "and that means keeping her alive no matter how foolish she is. You were both going to turn into charcoal if you kept standing there."

"Ladies," Maralen said, her voice as cold as the winds. "You will put us down in Mistmeadow and administer an antidote to whatever was on that little knife of yours, and you'll do it now. Then you'll get to a safe place while I—"

"You can't," Iliona said.

"Yeah!" Veesa said, but she sounded less certain than her sister. "The Great Mother is looking for us. And you stole something that doesn't belong to you, so you keep getting tracked down for it. Because that's how big and enormous and powerful Oona is! You have *no* idea!"

As Veesa continued to rave on about Oona's power, might, peckishness, peevishness, pettiness, prettiness, and odor (among other topics) there was little either Rhys or Maralen could do but try to follow what was happening back in Mistmeadow from a great distance and an increasing height.

"Now all we need is to get flattened by a cloud goat and the humiliation will be complete," Rhys muttered.

* * * * *

Gryffid watched in disbelief and growing fury as Rhys and the stranger floated into the sky and out of the battle. The second safewright hadn't so much as batted at the faeries that had carried him away from Mistmeadow. "This is treasonous," he told the nearest vinebred—an elf who had managed to keep all of his limbs, unlike many of his compatriots. "What is he doing?"

"Sir?" the vinebred asked. The cinders were no longer pouring through the gate—either there were no more, or the Destroyer had sent them on ahead. Gryffid doubted the so-called "tideshapers" had done much good, but for whatever reason the few surviving vinebred and scouts were no longer under direct attack.

The damage was more than done. Gryffid's duty now was to get his scattered warriors back into something like a fighting unit, see to the wounded as best he could, and pursue the enemy. Vigilant Eidren would still be waiting to exercise their weapon of last resort, but the safewright couldn't see the point.

"Gather any wounded who can be saved, help the ones who cannot be saved, and organize here. I've got to stop the vigilant before he wastes his time. Nothing can stop that thing."

"Yes, sir," the vinebred answered before turning to scan the smoke and fog for any sign of additional Wilt-Leaf survivors.

Wilt-Leaf survivors. If they didn't stop the Destroyer here, they could be *all* that survived of the Wilt-Leaf. All because some kind of elemental madwoman decided the world needed to burn.

"On second thought," Gryffid said through clenched teeth, "I will join you, vinebred. We have only one chance now, and it doesn't rely on any of us." He raised a hand and pointed at the tiny figure in green atop the last standing structure in Mistmeadow. The structure was the only physical object between the Destroyer and the Wilt-Leaf; the figure was the only one who could make that matter.

"Sir, he's—"

"Enough. We'd just get in the way. Remember this day," Gryffid added bitterly. "When the greatest of us died to save the least."

* * * * *

Brigid Baeli also watched Rhys and Maralen ascend into the skies on wings of faeries with more than a little disbelief, though hers was tinged with relief and annoyance rather than anger. Relief, because at least Rhys—who had been a friend before the Aurora but remembered none of that now—was going to survive this debacle, even if it meant Maralen, whom Brigid had never trusted no matter how often circumstances threw them together, also escaped unscathed. She watched them go for only a heartbeat, however. She didn't want the thing that had once been Ashling to focus her attention on the two improbably airborne elves.

"I haven't forgotten how you left me to die," the Destroyer seethed. "But petty vengeance of that sort is beyond me now, little kithkin. I can destroy whatever I wish, and I can spare what I wish. You're spared, despite your past crimes against me, to enjoy the fruitful land I have created for you." The heat surrounding Ashling became even hotter, and Brigid felt twinges of burning pain along the seams of her armor as the edges lost cohesion and began to boil.

"You've made your point," the kithkin said. "But I obviously haven't made mine. Turn back, or turn aside; just turn and leave this doun. You can't—I won't *let* you enter the Wilt-Leaf. It's too much to ask as repayment for what a few stupid fools did to you in another lifetime." She hadn't lowered the dirk, but neither could she bring herself to take another step forward to back up the threat.

Ashling replied with a sudden and maddening calm. "You can't do anything to me," she said, "and I'm not interested in killing you." The Destroyer took a step forward, bringing all of Brigid's shapewater armor to a roiling boil that made her want to scream. She bit her lower lip and focused her entire will on the Crescent, pulling through enough river-magic to balance the scales before she cooked, but the effort it took was too great to sustain for long. In seconds, she'd have to at least breathe, and then she'd be done for.

"Oh, very well," Ashling said, and her next step was to one side. Like a dancer made of light, she slipped around the kithkin outcast.

"Don't ignore me," Brigid said, and threw her hands toward the elemental monster. The shapewater armor rolled up her body, down her arms, and flew toward the Destroyer like a net. It enveloped the glowing body but did not yet boil. She closed the seal completely; using every bit of energy the Crescent could bring her to hold it liquid and complete against an unbelievably powerful display of energy within—Ashling did not enjoy confinement. But with the seal achieved, the air within the bubble would run out. No flame, not even living flame, surely, could exist where there was no air.

"Burn out," Brigid muttered, "burn yourself *out* already. Will you just—ow!" She pressed a hand to her temple when a searing pain seemed to slice her skull in half. A tiny beam of impossibly bright light had pierced the skin of the Destroyer's shapewater coffin and struck her in the forehead. Her skull had not, mercifully, actually been sliced in half, but she'd have to get her hood patched.

The pain was more than enough for her full concentration to shatter, and along with it the bubble. Brigid involuntarily backed away—even though Ashling was three times as far from her now as when she'd set her armor boiling, the armor was now gone and little if any water was left in sight. The heat was not something anything made of flesh could withstand for long without running in animal terror, and Brigid was no exception. But to her shock, the Destroyer simply waved like a passerby greeting a neighbor on the path and continued to move around the kithkin outcast.

Unable to keep to her feet any longer, drained of physical and magical energy, Brigid felt herself dizzily returning the wave and stopped herself. The Destroyer—Brigid could no longer think of her as Ashling—was already ignoring her. The kithkin rotated in place watching the elemental thing approach her last obstacle.

"Hello," Eidren said. "Are you through toying with the children? The forest wishes to speak to you."

What happened next Brigid could hardly credit later, but then she'd never seen an entire forest—canker-ridden tree-folk, living trees, elves, birds, rabbits, springjacks, everything that lived and died in the Wilt-Leaf—grant their own power to a single individual elf. Nor had she ever seen a vision of what the elves called "glory," the highest and most divine form of beauty, until she saw Eidren wield that power against a force of complete destruction.

Brigid realized, as a tremendous wave of green energy erupted over Mistmeadow's north wall and washed over Eidren, that the anger, fear, and bloodthirstiness of every living thing in the forest had been a part of that power, and she saw the mistake she'd made. She'd tried to confront the fire directly, but it hadn't been enough. Eidren, on the other hand, was hitting her with a force that could have leveled a mountain whether it was on fire or not. And, Brigid noted grimly, he was letting that force focus itself through his own body.

A column of green lightning slammed into the Destroyer, lifting her off the ground and sending her flying into the sky like a falling star returning home. The analogy became less than perfect when the blazing thing, still pushed along by Eidren's last resort, began to descend back toward the ground. Between the energy forcing her up and her own power pushing down, Ashling was being driven in the direction of Kinscaer, which had so far escaped her wrath. Brigid feared for Kinscaer; she mourned the losses it would undoubtedly suffer, but for now at least part of Mistmeadow had been saved.

The Destroyer's abrupt defeat and departure had left a weird not-quite silence hanging in the air. Spot fires still crackled here and there, and every once in a while a moan or cry from a wounded defender (kithkin or elf, it was not easy to tell since pain was such a universal sound). But it was calm. In only a few seconds, the power of the entire Wilt-Leaf forest had stood up to defend itself, using Eidren, glorious Vigilant Eidren, as its instrument, and no one had yet overcome their shock to react.

The first was Gryffid, who called Eidren's name. He emerged from the smoke on the edge of town and charged up the thoroughfare to the small pile of bone and ashes that was all that remained of his leader and friend.

The next was, to Brigid's surprise, herself. She pushed herself to her feet and staggered after Gryffid, but more to check on the still-enveloped forts where her shapewater brigade now controlled the only water in for miles in any direction. Eidren's death was tragic, though the loss wasn't exactly causing her as much pain as it was causing Gryffid, who even now was shouting his intention to avenge the glorious vigilant who wielded the Wilt-Leaf as a weapon.

The third and fourth were Rhys and Maralen, lowered to the ground by the Vendilion sisters. Rhys was aghast and ashamed, weakly swatting at Iliona as she set him down on the ground; Maralen looked oddly content. Neither was able to remain standing for reasons Brigid had yet to learn, but the kithkin was only able to catch Rhys in time. As Maralen scowled up at Brigid, the one-time scout simply shrugged and said, "Sorry, Boss. He was closest."

"Boss?" Rhys asked as Brigid helped him take a seat.

"Long story," Brigid replied, and then snapped at Iliona, "What did you do to these two? Smells Fae."

"Of course it's Fae," Veesa snapped back as she brandished a tiny blade no bigger than a sewing needle. "We had to make them pliable. Right, Iliona?"

"When this wears off," Maralen said darkly as she struggled to a sitting position, "we're going to have a talk about your priorities."

Brigid turned on the tall elf with the fury of the righteous and more importantly, the right. "Well, we tried to make our stand here," she said. "I did my best." She wasn't defensive; it was a statement of fact.

"The disaster was averted," the elf snapped. "Or at least delayed. That's what's important."

"At the cost of the greatest and finest of the Wilt-Leaf elves," Rhys murmured, the horror of what Eidren had done finally sinking in, it seemed.

"We all knew he was the last resort," Maralen said.

In the distance, Brigid could still hear Gryffid railing against the heavens, and heard Rhys's name among the shouted words. "I'm beginning to think we should leave Mistmeadow," she said. "Now."

"I'm not going anywhere," Rhys said. "If anything, I'm bringing this woman to face justice in the court of—"

"Listen to what your commander is shouting about you," Maralen said. "He thinks you fled the battle."

"I was *taken* out of the battle," Rhys snapped.

"What's done is done," Brigid said. "And unless there are a hundred Eidrens with the power of a hundred Wilt-Leafs, it's not going to do any good. Look." The kithkin outsider pointed in the general direction of Kinscaer, where a column of black smoke atop a bright orange pedestal showed how little Eidren's sacrifice had actually gotten them. The kithkin turned to Maralen. "Elf—Maralen. We have an arrangement."

"One you're really pushing at the moment," said Maralen.

"I'm asking you to trust me. Nothing can stop her except the Source. It's the only way. We've tried the Wilt-Leaf way, and it's at best bought us another day, maybe two, before she reaches the biggest forest in the world and turns it to ash. But I might be able to stop her." Brigid tapped her breast, feeling the comforting shape of the Crescent.

"You?" Maralen asked. "You already tried. She boiled away every attempt to use your merrow magic on her."

"What I have in mind isn't merrow magic. Well, it is," Brigid admitted, "but it's river magic, too. You know what I—how I use the shapewater. I think if I can find Sygg he might be able to do more."

"Isn't Sygg a well known killer?" Rhys asked, his eyes still on Gryffid. "You aren't proposing you share the power with him?"

"I don't know what I intend to propose. He could just try to kill us, and then we're back to me. We'll deal with that when we get there," Brigid said. "But we've got to get there first." She pointed at a gray shadow rising to the northwest, blocking out the black sky but hidden with a few wisps of cloud; the winds were already blowing away most of the smoke the Destroyer had left behind. "Sygg, if he's still hunting his old haunts, is that way, and if we can find him we can convince him to help on our way to the Source."

"We can?" said Maralen.

"I hope," Brigid said. "Otherwise, what's happened there," she gestured in the opposite direction at the path of charred devastation to the southwest, "is going to happen everywhere."

"Another adventure!" Veesa tittered, and swooped low to orbit Rhys's head a few times. "Together again for the first time!"

"No," Maralen told them. "You and your sister, at least, are going to honor your word and *do as I say,* right?"

Iliona gave a heavy, theatrical sigh, but said, "Yes."

"Good," the tall elf said. "I've got a job only the two of you can do."

"Really?" Iliona asked, brightening.

"We're especially good at those!" Veesa exclaimed. "Even better at those than the jobs we can't do!"

"That's what I wanted to hear," Maralen said.

"What's this big important job?" Rhys asked, and Brigid could see he was already looking upon this little band as something he needed to protect. "I don't want them sneaking up on me in the small hours and stabbing me in the neck again." Or not.

"It's time the Vendilion got the clique back together," Maralen said. "Find your brother and don't come back until he's with you. And if you really want to make me happy, you'll bring the sapling with you, too."

"A challenge!" Veesa said.

"Why now?" Iliona asked, skeptical.

"She doesn't think the Source will help us," Brigid said. "She's got another 'last resort' up her sleeve, I'd wager."

As the faeries squabbled with Maralen until at last they agreed to do as they were asked—though they couldn't promise how long it would take—Rhys asked Brigid, "Sapling? What's so important about a sapling?"

"It would really be better to let her explain—the sapling, that is." Brigid shrugged apologetically, and then turned back to Maralen. "The kithkin also have wounded, and they've got—Jack. Where's Jack Chierdagh?"

A clatter and a groan from some twenty feet away revealed a smudged and familiar (to Brigid, anyway) kithkin climbing out from one of the shapewater brigade forts.

"I'm all right!" Jack called. He choked and spat out a throatful of water. "Mostly."

Brigid breathed a sigh of relief. She quickly explained why she had to go, but not where, and then dragged Rhys and the others after her.

* * * * *

"You're just letting them leave, sir?" the vinebred—whose name, Gryffid had learned, was Visk—asked as the odd band of survivors helped each other onto the abandoned waterline platform and over the north wall. "He abandoned his duty."

"Eidren is dead," Gryffid said. "Rhys is secondary."

"Yes, sir," said the vinebred. "But Second Safewright Rhys left in the course of the battle. You wanted to capture him, see him punished. You do remember, sir?"

"Dead," Gryffid replied. Then he stood, hoisting a leather bag that contained the vigilant's mortal remains. "And he must be returned home. That is our priority now. He won us our victory, and we owe it to the greatest of us—"

"Sir, the Destroyer survived. Look, you can see the fires to the south."

"We *owe it to him*," Gryffid growled. "Gather the wounded and leave the dead. We must take Eidren home."

"Very well, sir," the subordinate replied uncertainly.

Gryffid nodded toward Rhys's band. "Take heart, Visk. I

suspect we'll be pulling their corpses from the rubble before all is said and done."

"More failure," the humorless elf growled.

"We have failed," Gryffid said. "And our failure was a costly one. The Wilt-Leaf may never recover from the losses we—from the losses it suffered today." Gryffid raised his frozen hands and said, "But we will endure. There is beauty yet for us to tend, nurture, and protect."

A murmur of assent rose up from the column. The safe-wright moved gingerly down the path toward the live tree, toward the increasing number of live trees that lay beyond. His legs and back screamed in outrage with every step. He stared down at his fingertips, watching them shudder slightly in response to his mental commands to relax.

"But first," Gryffid said, "we must honor Eidren. We must ensure that there are no more Mistmeadows. To die protecting Wilt-Leaf is a great honor. To die protecting anything else is an appalling, damnable waste.

"Those who fell will be remembered. They will be honored. And those who should have fallen but did not—they will know the cost of their good fortune. Their lives were bought and paid for with noble elf blood, and the scales will be balanced."

Gryffid turned his back to them. "On to Cayr Ulios," he said. He shifted his clenched fists in front of him like a bound prisoner. "The king and queen will be told. Accounts will be settled. The Wilt-Leaf Hold will endure."

"To Cayr Ulios," came the reply. Soon the entire column had echoed Gryffid's answer back to him in succession.

CHAPTER 4

Brigid led Maralen and Rhys down the course of the waterline that had temporarily connected Mistmeadow to the Wanderbrine. Without Brigid and Wryget to maintain them, the shapewater buttresses and fortifications back in the doun itself were already starting to degrade and run off. It was only right and proper that their defensive preparations left no lasting impression on Mistmeadow, as the moats and buttresses and fortifications had made no real difference during the battle itself. Jack already had crews filling in the trenches.

The kithkin archer grumbled audibly and tried to cover the sound with a cough. The world had changed around her far too often lately, but so far she had not succumbed to the overwhelming certainty that she was utterly alone and entirely out of her depth. She had not merely managed to survive in these dark and confusing times, but had actually assembled a modest series of minor successes and temporary alliances that enriched and informed her as she learned the new lay of the land. In the Destroyer's wake, however, Brigid's successes seemed laughable and her allies stood as helpless and desperate as she.

Rhys was as noble as ever, every bit the effective hunter, but the solitary elf's face was drawn and his shoulders hunched as he hiked behind Brigid. Some of his fellow Wilt-Leaf had certainly survived the battle, but so far none of Rhys's superiors or subordinates had come looking for him. His face was a grim and stoic cipher, but Brigid saw how keenly he felt the loss of his commanding officer. The battle for Mistmeadow had sent Rhys reeling, but he remained tenacious and resourceful, and these were the qualities Brigid knew they'd need the most in the coming trials.

Maralen was also somber, almost melancholy, but she did not carry herself as one burdened by grief or shock. Without her faerie retainers, Maralen's eyes took on a suspicious aspect that made her seem secretive and shifty—that is, even *more* secretive and shifty. Maralen had looked upon the Destroyer with the same amazement and terror as the rest of them, but the elf maiden also displayed brief flickers of something else, something that competed with her fear and awe. Brigid could not clearly name the complex mixture of emotions she had seen on Maralen's face, but it contained fascination, recognition, and (Brigid shuddered a bit) hunger. Maralen saw the Destroyer as a terrifying destructive force to be confronted and neutralized, but the elf maiden also saw the monster as something to be admired, perhaps even sought after.

These are the allies I have, Brigid reminded herself. These are the circumstances I find myself in. She made a circle out of her thumb and forefinger, spat through the center for luck, and swore to herself, I will make the best of this.

Brigid emerged from a thatch of brambles and beheld the Wanderbrine. Her merrow partner Wryget was floating near the bank, apparently dozing with his arms crossed as his upper torso bobbed on the water. Though the current was swift, Wryget remained where he was as if rooted in place.

Rhys and Maralen stepped up behind Brigid. The Wilt-Leaf safewright's voice floated down to her. "Is that the merrow captain?"

"That's Wryget," Maralen said. "He aided us during the attack."

"Most of the merrow along this part of the river would rob you and use you for bait at the first opportunity."

"Wryget and I go way back," Brigid assured him. She placed her index fingers at the corners of her mouth and blew a shrill whistle. Wryget snorted, sank a bit, and then opened his eyes.

"Landwalkers," the huge merrow brute said amiably. Wryget stretched his arms and yawned, flexing his sharp-clawed fingers. He swam toward Brigid and the others, his bruise-colored skin especially lurid in the light reflecting up from the river's surface.

"All rested up?" Brigid called.

"I'm ready to go," Wryget said. He slowed as he neared the bank so as not to splash those waiting there. "How about you?"

"We're upright," Brigid said. "And we're not standing still."

Wryget stretched again. "Where to?"

"Upriver."

Doubt and concern clouded the merrow's features. "Upriver is bad for me," Wryget said. "Captain Sygg thinks I ought to be dead. I don't want to call his attention to the fact that I ain't."

"You'll be safe," Brigid said, and it wasn't even technically a lie. She had every reason to believe that if Sygg saw Brigid and Wryget at the same time he'd go straight for the kithkin and leave Wryget till later. "But I've got an idea, Wryget, and I think you might be the only one to help me make it happen. I need you to come with us."

"All right," Wryget said, but his assent was slow and hesitant.

Rhys stepped forward and leaned down by Brigid's ear. "What is this all about?" he said. "If the merrow captain has something we need, let's talk to the merrow captain."

"Sygg controls the entire river between Kinscaer and the mountains," Brigid said. "We don't have time to search him out, so I'm taking a different approach. First, Wryget and I know this stretch of the river better than just about anyone else. It's worth a few hours to walk along the riverbanks. If we don't get a sense of Sygg being nearby, there should be an old acquaintance or two we can ask."

"I see," Rhys said dryly. "And if that fails?"

Brigid smiled, her large dark eyes twinkling. "Then we do something loud and messy and disruptive to the river. Merrow cutthroats will come from every direction to sort us out, and word will reach Sygg. That shared history I have with Wryget? We also share something with the good captain. Once he hears our names in connection with this part of the river, he'll want to pull out our vitals and play with them. Personally."

Rhys shook his head angrily. "So you're volunteering to be bait. How will you stop Sygg from killing you when—that is, if he appears?"

"I've got something he wants," Brigid said. "Sygg is a lot of things—murderous brute, ruthless brigand, professional criminal—but business has always been his first concern. It will profit him in the short term to keep me alive, and in the long term to do as I ask." She shrugged.

"Brigid's right about one thing," Maralen said, cutting off Rhys's reply. "It's worth a few hours of our time to check this out."

Rhys said, "How can you sound so sure?"

"Because Brigid knows things I don't," Maralen said smoothly. "About merrow in general and Sygg in particular. It's one of the few ways she's truly useful to have around."

Brigid snorted derisively. "Thanks, Boss."

The elf maiden turned away from Brigid and faced Rhys.

"You saw what we saw back in Mistmeadow. None of us has the power to stop that demon. The entire Wilt-Leaf came up short. Next to your noble vigilant, Sygg wields the strongest power in the region. We need his help."

"And he will give it," Brigid said. "Willingly. Now, then. Wryget? Swim out to the middle of the river and keep pace with us. We'll be marching double-time so you shouldn't get too bored waiting up.

"And what do I do if I see another merrow that works for Sygg and wants to kill me?" Wryget nervously laced and unlaced his fingers. "That would be all of them, by the way."

"If that happens, just shout out my name. I'll be there before you finish the second syllable."

Wryget smiled weakly. "Can I flee downstream while I'm shouting?"

"Absolutely."

"All right, then." The hulking merrow cracked his knuckles. "I'll help if I can. But you have to tell me what to do."

"Happily," Brigid said. "I tell you what, Wryget, letting you and I move on was two of the biggest mistakes Captain Sygg ever made." She turned to Rhys and Maralen. "Let's go."

* * * * *

Hours passed with no sign of any merrow at all. It occurred to Brigid that Sygg must have known about the threat to Mistmeadow—had the good captain pulled his enforcers out of harm's way and temporarily left the river unsupervised?

"There's another," Rhys said. He gestured to a jagged ridge to the northwest where a ragged, misshapen figure was shuffling along the top edge.

They had seen no merrow so far, but they had seen almost a dozen scarecrows. Mistmeadow Jack had described the strange creatures in detail, and according to him scores of them wandered through the hills. To date no one knew where they had come from, or why, or what magical force animated them. They just appeared, and there seemed to be more of them all the time.

Wryget breached at the center of the river and called Brigid's name. The archer tensed for a moment, expecting the worst, but then Wryget surged up from below again, waving furiously. He was not under attack, as far as Brigid could tell. She waved him in.

When Wryget was close enough to be heard without shouting, he said, "How much longer? There were merrow down there not long ago, but it's completely deserted now."

"Well," Brigid said. "Then I guess it's time to get loud and disruptive." She rolled up her left sleeve and said, "Are your shapewater skills up to the challenge? I think between the two of us we should be able to stir the waters enough to draw some attention."

"We could do that," Wryget said. "Or we could just use them." He pointed over Brigid's shoulder toward the ridge beyond.

"Use who?" Brigid said, turning and squinting. "The scarecrow?"

"Sure," Wryget said.

"How do you propose we use the scarecrow?" Maralen said. She wore a smile, but her eyes were steely and fixed on Wryget.

"Yeah," Brigid said. "I saw some during the battle. Seems to me the only thing they're good for is standing still and burning up."

"That's only because someone used fire magic on them," Wryget said. "I've seen them all up and down the river since Sygg cut me loose. They react to whatever spell you use on them—or at least, they react to the person who casts the spell. A fire mage sets them on fire. Poison casters make them poisonous."

Brigid and Maralen exchanged a wicked smile. The archer said, "So if we use water magic to herd them toward the river?"

"They'll take to the river," Maralen said. "And a mob of strange creatures in his river is sure to draw a response from Sygg's minions."

"Wryget, I love you," Brigid said. The huge merrow beamed and fanned out his barbels on each side of his mouth. To Rhys, who was standing by with a mildly disapproving look on his face, Brigid said, "How many of those scarecrows have you counted in the last mile or so?"

"Dozens," Rhys said.

"Do you think you could double back and herd eight or ten of them this way? Wryget and I will prepare the spells if you and Maralen do the leg work."

Rhys suddenly dipped his head down and spoke in a strained, exasperated whisper. "This is becoming a farce," he said. "That flaming demon is over Kinscaer right now, and it will return to Wilt-Leaf territory in a matter of days. And we're moving farther and farther away. I respect your expertise here, kithkin, but—"

"Then trust me to get the job done," Brigid said. "This will work. Sygg made a tactical move, pulling his forces back to avoid their being incinerated, but he's too sharp and too greedy to let someone else move in while he's away."

"And so we draw the merrow captain's attention—what then? What is this mysterious power you think he has? What leverage do you have that will compel him to help us?"

"As I said, old friend, you have to trust me. More words won't convince you I'm right, so let me prove it to you."

"I am as uncomfortable with this plan of yours, 'old friend,' as I am with your presumption of familiarity."

"My apologies, honored, noble Safewright." Brigid avoided Maralen's eyes and fixed Rhys with an earnest and confident stare. "How's that?"

"Better. Though only marginally more respectful."

Maralen stepped forward and placed a soft hand on Rhys's shoulder. "Bear with us a little while longer," she said. "Please."

Rhys grimaced, but Brigid could tell he wasn't ready to abandon them yet.

* * * * *

Luring and herding the scarecrows toward the river was no challenge to an expert ranger like Rhys. In fact, as he effortlessly circled his latest target and guided it toward the Wanderbrine, Rhys began to think this whole endeavor was beneath him.

His temporary companions were earnest and capable, but they were not elves. They would never understand the demands or rewards of duty and discipline as the Wilt-Leaf did. The Destroyer was a far greater threat than Brigid or even Maralen could ever fathom, for the monster wasn't simply devastating villages and killing innocents—she was consuming what little beauty remained in this world. If she were not stopped, there would be nothing left for future generations to cherish.

The women were right about one thing, however: It would require far more powerful allies to stop the Destroyer's rampage. Rhys had learned to respect Brigid's talents, but from what he had seen there was nothing to be gained from locating her elusive merrow quarry. The elemental fires that consumed Eidren were alive, voracious and implacable. What could the merrow offer that could stand against such a monster? What could any tribe?

Before Mistmeadow, Eidren had consulted with the oldest and wisest sages among the elves, kithkin, and treefolk, and none of them had an answer for the Destroyer's wrath. Oracles and augurs saw nothing, and some that looked too hard or too long came away burned, blinded, or broken. It was a creature that did not belong in this world, an elemental force driven by the darkest and most savage mortal emotions.

She is what we made of her, came a soft but sharp feminine voice. *And what she made of herself. No more, no less. All of us—her, you, me, Father. We each bear part of the responsibility for what she has become, and so we each carry part of her salvation.*

Rhys dropped to a crouch and drew his long knife. The voice had come from within, rising from inside his skull, but that did not preclude a physical attack from without.

Do not fear and do not despair, Half-Brother. For I have found you at last, and together we can end this long night as was always intended.

"Show yourself," Rhys said sternly. He brandished his knife. "Face me or withdraw."

I mean you no harm, Half-Brother. I have the answers you seek. I have always had them, but it is only now that I am able to share them with you.

"Who are you?" Rhys said. "Why do you call me brother?"

In another life, the voice said wistfully, *your spiritual father was my literal one. But that is not important now. What is important is that we meet so that I may share with you what I know. We have a great and terrible task to do, one that only we who were chosen by Colfenor can accomplish—and only if we work together.*

"Who are you?" Rhys said again.

I am the last living yew, the voice said. *And the sum total of all my ancestral trees and forests. I am the bearer of a thousand years of lore and knowledge, and many thousands more only half-remembered. I have seen entire races of trees put to the axe and the torch; I have seen armies of treefolk conquer great swaths of this world and rule with benevolent cruelty, aloof and arrogant. I grew from a seed cast by your mentor and master Colfenor the Red, who knew these things and worked his entire life to redeem the treefolk and most especially the yew. I am his last hope and his first success—I am heir to his power. I exist to complete his greatest work.*

Rhys's muscles all stiffened at once. His eyes shot up in their sockets and he felt the knife tumble from his unresponsive fingers. He saw a great and aged yew treefolk wreathed in flames atop a great stone altar. The flames were the Destroyer's, as fierce and as potent as they had been in Mistmeadow, but the treefolk sage was not consumed.

Together, the feminine voice said, *we can stay the monster's wrath. We can save her. And once we have, perhaps we can save much more.*

The rigidity left Rhys's body and he stumbled forward. He did not recognize the presence in his mind, but he did recognize its power. He could not understand her words, but he could not dismiss the truth of them, truth that came to him through his eyes and his ears and the pores of his skin.

"I'm listening, spirit," he said warily. "What shall I call you?"

The voice laughed briefly—a light, breezy sound like Rhys hadn't heard since his childhood. It faded quickly and he longed for its return. *I am no spirit,* the familiar voice said. *But my heart is inextricably bound to yours. You may call me "sapling."*

* * * * *

Brigid assessed the motley assemblage of scarecrows. Rhys and Maralen had done their work well. More than a dozen already were here and more probably on the way, but she decided to proceed now with the test subjects she had.

She and Wryget had erected a simple shapewater fence to keep the dozen-odd scarecrows in one place. It was a foot-thick horizontal ring of water that floated several feet off the ground, flowing around the scarecrows like the outer edge of a whirlpool. Whenever one of the shambling creatures touched the band, they were spun around by the water's velocity and sent stumbling back toward the circle's center.

Wryget rose up beside the riverbank. "What now, Boss?"

"I was just about to ask you the same thing," Brigid said. "You're the one who's seen more of them. How do we rile up this band of misfits enough to catch Sygg's attention?"

Wryget considered this, and as he did Brigid decided she loved the huge, hulking merrow more with each passing moment. His earnest look of intense concentration fell somewhere between that of a serious child and a loyal dog.

"Let's make them walk on water," the former thug said at last. Wryget gestured to the river's flow behind him. "Landwalkers using merrow magic to cross the river. There's no way anyone in Sygg's organization would overlook that. Someone that careless would wind up mounted on the prow of Sygg's ferry as a trophy." The bruise-colored merrow grinned. "Especially if there's a lot of them, and we make it so they're not crossing the river but running up it."

"Another capital idea, Wryget. You'd better be careful or soon I'll be calling you 'boss.' " Brigid moved around the penned scarecrows until she was standing directly opposite Wryget. Another benefit of picking Wryget's brain was that his shapewater skills were no better than hers, so it was impossible for him to suggest a plan that was beyond her abilities. Making the river solid enough to hold up scarecrows was not child's play, but together she and Wryget were at least up to the task.

Brigid started, and Wryget quickly joined in. She felt the strength of the river's flow, the texture of the water streaming by. She called it to her, held it tight, and then examined it. The trick would be to make the surface of the river substantial enough to keep the scarecrows afloat but thin enough so that it didn't get dragged into the current. She turned her attention to their captives, sizing up their collective size, shape, and weight. She was pleased to discover that each scarecrow was uniformly lighter than a same-sized fleshy creature would have been.

The scarecrows responded as soon as Brigid and Wryget began to infuse them with the river's powerful magic. Oddly, the scarecrows did not seem to be directly affected by the spell but by the fact that Brigid and Wryget were casting it near them. Some grew darker, as if doused by a sudden shower, while others swelled and expanded like beans soaking in a pot.

Brigid and Wryget redoubled their efforts. A thin platform of blue liquid formed under the scarecrows' feet and the entire assembly rose several feet into the air.

"I think they're ready, Boss!"

"I agree!" Brigid shouted back. "How about you?"

The big merrow was grinning happily. "Let's send them on their way."

"Done and done," Brigid said. Together, she and Wryget guided the floating platform filled with scarecrows out over the Wanderbrine. They set it down on the river's surface and it flattened the water coursing below it. The still and tranquil platform spread out and began moving upstream. Brigid released her hold on the watery ring that surrounded the scarecrows and it instantly broke apart and splashed down upon the now-floating platform.

"Will you look at that," Brigid said. "It floats all by its—"

Wryget submerged and then surfaced again, spraying Brigid with river water. "That ought to do it, Boss," he said. "What's next?"

"Us waiting," Brigid said. "Once Maralen and Rhys return, we can shadow our floating band as they stumble upriver. We'll think about how to deal with the merrow we meet once we're under way."

An angry splash out on the river caught Brigid's attention. She looked past Wryget to the scarecrows' raft just as a long, lean merrow erupted up through its center. Two of the scarecrows were split into pieces and hurled overboard. The rest staggered and reeled as they fought to keep their balance.

"Or," Brigid said tightly. "We can think about it now."

CHAPTER 5

Led by Gryffid, the surviving Wilt-Leaf elves reached the crossroads just outside the borders of Cayr Ulios, capital of the entire Wilt-Leaf Hold. As Gryffid was about to approach the gates, he heard the voices. Gryffid thought he might be imagining it, but the barely concealed alarm of the pack proved otherwise.

"First Safewright Gryffid," the unseen speaker said. "We've been expecting your triumphant return for some time. We welcome you home and sing your praises to your glory."

Gryffid raised a warning hand to keep his elves from advancing. "Show yourself," he said.

The air above flickered with dusky light as four tiny winged shapes descended from the dark, mossy trees that formed the outer walls of the Wilt-Leaf capital. The city gates were fashioned from two huge trunks that had been trained into the shape of a tall, oblate doorway; the gates themselves were pure hardened silverwood.

"Stay away," Gryffid said. Faeries were not unheard of in Cayr Ulios, but the Fae were never to be trusted or taken at face value in any circumstances. This clique was evenly split between males and females. Their markings were similar enough to pass for a family resemblance, but their colors varied wildly from metallic blue-green to the vivid black and yellow stripes.

The green male drifted ahead of the others. "Ah, but we are where you want to be. Or rather, we are where you are and will be where you're going. We're everywhere, you see. If you don't want to be where we are, how will you get where you're going?"

"I've no interest in your word games." Gryffid glanced back at the other faeries. "I have urgent business with the hold, with the rulers of Wilt-Leaf."

"So you do. We know all about it. Oona herself suggested we come out to greet you."

"I have urgent business with the rulers of Wilt-Leaf," Gryffid said again. "Not your imaginary queen."

The larger of the two females zipped forward, leaving a scintillating trail of purple-white dust. "You're very quick to exclude others," she said. "Still, we'll gladly overlook your insult to the Great Mother as it was she who summoned you here."

"No one summoned me," Gryffid said.

"Not as you would understand it, no." The green male's smile was dazzlingly sharp. "But when a mudslide is flowing down the side of a hill, isn't it silly for one tiny speck of dirt to proclaim it was moving independently of the rest?"

"This conversation is over," Gryffid snarled.

"And not a moment too soon. Your presence is required at another, far more important audience. Oona demands it."

"I am not here for Oona."

"But you are here to see your tribe's most exalted rulers, who are currently receiving ambassadors and envoys from Oona of the Fae."

The pale purple faerie mimicked her brother's smile. "So you see, Mr. Haughty Elf, we're only trying to take you where you want to go. We'd be there by now if you weren't determined to be such a fussbudget about the whole thing."

Gryffid glowered. "The rulers of Cayr Ulios—" he began.

"Are in conference with the ruler of Glen Elendra." The green male bowed and his purple sister curtsied, both in midair. The green said, "That is to say, with her most trusted representatives. And if the urgent business you have is as dire as your expression, do speak."

"It had better be dire," said the purple. "Otherwise there's simply no excuse for his bad manners."

"Then we'd all best be on our way. Just think of us as your temporary heralds."

"I need no heralds. And if I did, they wouldn't be faeries."

"Rude," the purple female said. "Just plain rude." She sniffed, tossed her head, and then zipped back to hover among her siblings.

"So you would prefer that we didn't precede you and announce you as you enter?"

"Prefer? No. And what's more, I will not allow it."

The green male's cheerful, sly expression faded. "May we accompany you as your temporary attendants?"

"No."

"You are indeed a sour-tempered elf, First Safewright Gryffid." The faerie shrugged, nodded back to his siblings, and rose higher into the air. They paralleled his ascent, spreading out until all four were arranged along the top of the gateway. "Welcome home to Cayr Ulios," they all sang together, their pure, clear voices ringing like bells. "The rulers of Shadowmoor await your arrival."

Gryffid sneered up at the clique one last time. He raised his hand and waved the column forward as he himself strode through the gates and entered the Wilt-Leaf capital.

Cayr Ulios was still the most magnificent city in all of Wilt-Leaf, and therefore in the entire world. The elves maintained safeholds all across Shadowmoor to protect places of natural beauty and purity that were truly worth protecting. Cayr Ulios was far grander both in its scale and its purpose, for it was from Cayr Ulios that the king and queen guided the entire Wilt-Leaf tribe's destiny.

The monarchs—the two most powerful male and female lifewards in the Wilt-Leaf Forest—had gathered the hold's other skilled lifewards here to infuse this place with vital magic. There were more live trees in Cayr Ulios than everywhere else in the entire world. More important, the precious dawn-glove flower grew in abundance. The elves' capital represented what the whole world could be if they not only endured but reached out to spread their influence far beyond the borders of the forest. The king had once orated, "Where there is beauty, there is hope," and as long as the capital remained the vibrant, beating heart of the Wilt-Leaf Hold, the elves could believe in a brighter future.

Gryffid led his column down the central tree-lined path, straight from the gates to the great hall and throne room. He noticed hardly any canker on the boughs or trunks he passed, and even these dark, scabby patches were being tended by the lifewards' invigorating magic. A line of flickering green torches cast deceptive shadows back and forth across the path, and Gryffid saw the canker actually retreat from that emerald light.

Gryffid approached the stairs leading up to the great hall and called his column to a halt. Elf sentries stood on each side of the short staircase. Gryffid turned his head to the sentry on his right, but before he could speak the blue-green faerie from the gates fluttered down.

"Please go straight in, Safewright," the faerie said. He bowed as he hovered. "We shall make sure these worthies who follow you are treated well."

Gryffid ignored the faerie and continued to stare at the elf sentry. The warrior straightened, lowered his pike, and nodded to Gryffid. "It will be done," he said.

"Thank you," Gryffid told the sentry. He turned back to face the column and said, "We have arrived. I have business with the monarchs, so take this opportunity to avail yourselves of the food and healing available. If anyone is in need, consult with these noble elves." He indicated the sentries behind him, and then Gryffid drew his sword. "Welcome home," he said loudly. "We muster back here in one hour."

Gryffid saluted the sentries as the rest of the elves who survived Mistmeadow quickly dispersed into Cayr Ulios's sparsely populated paths. The sentries returned Gryffid's salute, and then he strode into the monarchs' great hall. He had been inside just once before, but at that time he had been a subordinate officer at the back of a much larger retinue. Now he was not only alone but expected—though Gryffid still gave the faeries no heed, the elf sentries would never have allowed him to pass so easily unless they had received orders to do so.

The outer chamber was lit by the same eerie green torch-light. It was deserted and empty, a bare room without decoration and without sentries. A strange, musical sound vibrated out from the inner chamber, paused to compose himself, and then he marched into the throne room.

"Hail, First Safewright Gryffid. We welcome you." The king and queen sat gracefully on their huge silverwood thrones. The magical wood glowed softly in the dim light. There were no torches here, but the gleam from the thrones and the shining light from a glowing orb hovering over the doorway allowed Gryffid to see.

The music Gryffid heard also emanated from the orb. He bowed deeply to the king and queen, but as he rose Gryffid tilted his head back to gaze up at the glittering sphere.

The miniature sun was not a single round body, but an array

of four large faeries. Each was a male with hard, metallic skin that shined like polished gold. Soft light emitted from their beating wings and their clasped hands, light that bounced back and forth from their golden bodies and formed a perfectly round nimbus of light.

"Majesties," Gryffid said. He bowed his head, staring furiously into the floor through wide, clear eyes. "I bring an urgent report from Mistmeadow."

"We know all about your tribulations," the king's voice said. From his position, Gryffid could not see the monarch's face, but he knew the king had not moved since Gryffid entered the chamber. "The Destroyer is an enemy to us all, a threat to all tribes everywhere, and she grows more dangerous with each passing day. We are currently reconsidering how to best pool our resources to stop her rampages."

"She has already cost us far too much," the queen added. "Vigilant Eidren will be sorely missed."

"My lieges," Gryffid said. "I wish that I had died in the vigilant's stead. I would rather be rotting in a Mistmeadow gully than standing here now, reporting the full scope of my horrific failure."

"How fitting," The queen's voice was arch and clipped, yet somehow bored. "That would have been our preference as well."

"Majesties," Gryffid said. "My report is done, my duties all discharged. I am at your disposal. I know that nothing I do can truly recoup the loss of Vigilant Eidren, but if my life or my death may yet be of use to the Wilt-Leaf Hold, I hereby offer both. Freely."

"There's no need to be hasty," the king said. "Or so dour. Of course you are still useful to the hold. Oona of the Fae has come to us specifically to discuss that very subject."

"Sire." Gryffid raised his head. "Oona is here? Now?"

"No, First Safewright. These are her envoys." He gestured at the glowing golden quartet above the door. "And they have presented us with a proposition that we find fascinating."

"Majesties," Gryffid said. "Forgive me, but the Fae are notorious tricksters. Even if they do have some sort of grand high queen-mother, can we be certain that these"—he nodded up over the doorway—"speak for her?"

"We are convinced," the queen said. "Nothing more is required."

"We are the voice of Oona," the four golden faeries said in unison. "Welcome, First Safewright Gryffid."

Gryffid paused to glance at the inscrutable faces of the king and queen. "There is much I do not understand, Queen of the Fae. Starting with your purpose here."

"My purpose here is yours," said one of the golden faeries.

"My purpose here is you," said another.

"Once we shared a common enemy," said the third brother.

The fourth faerie added, "And you felt my power through her actions. At the very least, I wish to offer amends."

"I have no idea what you're talking about," Gryffid said. "The only enemies I have are the enemies of the hold."

"And thus our causes overlap. For my enemy travels in the guise of an elf, though she is not. She makes promises as if she speaks on behalf of the Wilt-Leaf Hold, though she does not. She sows strife and discord wherever she goes, seducing the base and the feeble by offering herself up as some sort of savior." The four faeries all turned their faces down and glared at Gryffid. They spoke emphatically, stressing each syllable. "She is not."

Gryffid stole a glance at the monarchs, but the king and queen neither spoke nor stirred. "You speak of Maralen."

The faeries' faces wrinkled at the name. "She is a poison, a disease," the quartet said together. "An accident that should never have happened. But she has happened, and the longer she is allowed to continue, the more devastating her effect on our world."

Gryffid turned once more to the king and queen, but his limbs were thick and slow. Were they talking about the elf Maralen, or the Destroyer? He swooned but caught himself before he stumbled. The monarchs sat silent and still as statues. As the golden light from the faerie quartet intensified around Gryffid, the king and queen faded into the thickening shadows.

"This is a dream," Gryffid said. "Faerie mind-magic."

"A dream indeed," the golden four replied. They spread out, expanding the shining nimbus around them until it almost touched Gryffid's face. While two of the brothers spoke, the others let out a clear, mournful note that grew ever louder and more intense. "But isn't the Wilt-Leaf Hold itself a dream? Your tribe's foundations, its purpose, and its future are all derived from your collective aspirations. You are not content with what is but strive to protect and enrich it while you create something better, truer, and more worthy of your lofty self-image."

"Ours is a dream, Queen of the Fae," Gryffid said. "But it is also a real and tangible thing, a goal worth striving for. You and all that you say, all you may offer—these are not dreams but mere illusion."

The golden faeries' wings buzzed angrily. "Come, little Safewright. I will show you something worth striving for, something real and tangible."

The golden light flared and Gryffid's vision went white. When it cleared, he was no longer indoors in the Cayr Ulios throne room, but standing at the center of an impossibly lush and verdant grove. Flowers, fruit, and faeries were in abundance, but even among the flood of color and noise the majestic figure at the center of the grove commanded Gryffid's attention. He stared agape for a moment, and then Gryffid involuntarily dropped to his knees.

She was taller than a giant, a graceful female head and torso perched atop a mounded thicket of thick, ropy thorn canes. Fat green leaves and stout, sharp spikes covered her lower half. Thousands of colorful flowers carpeted her upper body like a fine gown. Clusters of blood-red berries adorned her wrists, neck, and ears like jewelry. Her face was hidden behind a veil of honeysuckle creepers, but her huge blue-green eyes shone clearly through the curtain. A wreath of sharp-leaved holly and jasmine flowers crowned her head.

"Hear me, Gryffid of the Wilt-Leaf Hold," the divine flower-woman said. "Your entire tribe seeks the good and the beautiful, does it not? That is your driving passion, your collective reason for being. You would all gladly bleed and die for the right to preserve and protect those people, places, and things that you find valuable."

"Yes," Gryffid whispered. The absence of the figure's divine voice was painful to him, and he realized he wanted nothing more than for the creature to continue speaking to him.

"The Wilt-Leaf elves are utterly devoted to beauty, are they not? To its preservation, its protection, its extension across all Shadowmoor. Beauty is your highest ideal, your ultimate goal, and *I am beauty itself.*"

The honeysuckle veil split and separated. Gryffid looked upon the face of Oona and screamed. Weeping tears of profound joy, the elf pitched forward and pressed his head into the rich, fertile soil.

"My enemy is raising an army against me," Oona's voice said. "I would answer with one of my own. Look around you, Safewright. See how my world is. Carve its splendor into your memory, for the whole world will be like this one day, alive and green and vibrant. I swear it. And all I require in return is a small measure of the Wilt-Leaf Hold's power—and its passion."

Gryffid raised his head. He tried to take in the entirety of the magnificent landscape surrounding the great figure, but he could not pry his eyes from the glory of Oona's face.

"Rise, First Safewright Gryffid. The Wilt-Leaf Hold does indeed have a use for you." The king's voice sliced through Gryffid's rapture, ruining it. The safewright felt a nauseous surge rise in his throat and found himself back in the Cayr Ulios throne room, prostate before the quartet of golden faeries overhead.

Gryffid slowly got to his feet. His eyes remained fixed on the faeries and the memory of Oona.

"We hereby advance you to the rank of vigilant," the king said. "For now. You will lead one thousand Wilt-Leaf archers and rangers on Oona's behalf in the coming battle. They shall be completely under your command, just as you shall be under the Fae Queen's. Her victory shall be yours, and ours. Achieve it, and you will become the most favored vigilant who ever lived."

"I will do as my majesties command," Gryffid said.

The king rocked forward on his throne. "For the sake of the hold, for our shared future, Maralen and all who stand with her must die," he said.

The queen tilted forward as well. "For the memory of Eidren."

"I swear it." Gryffid glanced up at the golden quartet. "Maralen will be purged from this world along with all the unworthy elves that stand with her."

Smiling, all four golden faeries began to sing once more. Gryffid's mind dissolved into a paroxysm of joy as Oona's overwhelming beauty filled it to bursting.

CHAPTER 6

Rhys's mind continued to race during his sprint back toward the riverbank. He felt the giddy, buzzing excitement of someone who has just leaped out of a tall tree in total darkness: He could not see where he was heading, but he was headed there quickly and his arrival would be memorable (assuming he arrived intact enough to remember anything).

The sapling, as she called herself, claimed to be descended from Colfenor. In his youth Rhys had studied with Colfenor—one of the only powerful yew sages left in the world—but many of his teachings did not sit well with the sensibilities of the Wilt-Leaf Hold's rulers. When it came time to choose between the ways of a sage and the ways of a warrior, Rhys made his decision without hesitation and with very few regrets, though afterward it became clear that Colfenor would never forgive him. He hadn't seen Colfenor now for almost a decade, and he often wondered what his life might have been had he followed the ways of the yew entirely, as Colfenor intended, instead of adapting the sage's powerful poison magic to an elf warrior's needs. Rhys had not once regretted the decision to part from the old yew's teachings until now, but considering what had become of his life as a Wilt-Leaf elf, perhaps Rhys should have broken with his people and done as the treefolk asked.

Rhys remembered the vision of Colfenor aflame without being consumed. Petty as he was, the old log had been extremely powerful, and it would be foolish to ignore the implications of that particular vision. If this were a trick or a trap of some sort, it was one that had been derived from yew magic, one that had used Colfenor's name and image as the lure. Rhys owed it to his former mentor to investigate.

And more important, the sapling's voice in his mind felt eerily similar to Colfenor's. She was clearly steeped in familiar magic and adept at the specific rituals Rhys and Colfenor used to communicate, and so the sapling herself worth investigating even if her story was pure fiction.

Rhys had only begun to wonder how he would tell Maralen and Brigid about his strange encounter when he recognized the sounds of battle ahead. From the splashes, shouts, and shouted curses he surmised that the merrow had attacked at last.

He cleared a small hill and stopped, allowing his eyes to confirm what his ears concluded. A loud, frothy skirmish had erupted near the bank. Brigid stood at the very edge of the river, and Wryget thrashed in the water nearby. A dozen or more scarecrows were standing in scattered clusters along the surface of the river with some sort of magical blue stepping stones beneath their feet. Random pieces of other scarecrows floated downstream.

There were also merrow in the water, on the banks, and circling the floating scarecrows. They bared their needle-sharp teeth, they slashed at the intruders with metal blades and their own naturally sharp fins, and they sent sheets of water up over their foes and tried to pull them under. Rhys counted eight of the watery brigands visible with many more probably hidden under the surface of the Wanderbrine.

Rhys hesitated, not from fear but from a surfeit of discouraging options. He had no bow, so close-quarters combat was his only option. He had no way of forcing his foes to fight on dry land, and he could not fight effectively in the river against a whole school of merrow. He might dispatch one or two, but the others would surely drown him in short order. He couldn't even support Brigid and Wryget unless they repositioned themselves within arm's reach.

"Rhys!" Maralen came out of the blackened forest at a dead run. She barely glanced at the river, where Brigid had just lopped off a merrow's arm at the elbow and Wryget was wrestling with another who was just as big as he (the two were braided together and seemed hopelessly intertwined), but the elf maiden seemed to have a firm grasp on the situation nonetheless. "What are you waiting for?" she shouted.

Rhys blinked. "An effective strategy," he said.

Maralen stopped in front of Rhys, kicking a small cloud of sticky dust and debris over his hooves. She grabbed his arm urgently and said, "Didn't you hear Wryget?" Maralen pointed to the scarecrows. "They react to spellcasters. 'Poison casters make them poisonous.' That's all the strategy you need."

"What about Brigid?" Rhys's gaze darted between the kithkin in the river and the elf in front of him. "And Wryget?"

"Just do it, Safewright." Maralen cocked her head and smiled cryptically. "The first part of the plan is working. Don't you want to see if the rest pans out?" Without waiting for his answer, Maralen sprinted past Rhys toward the river. "I'll get Brigid and Wryget out," she called back over her shoulder. "Be ready to strike."

Rhys's teeth clenched a bit, but he shouted back, "Agreed." As much as he disliked Maralen's sudden authoritative streak, he disliked the course they were pursuing even more. To his thinking they were pinning far too much hope on Wryget's limited understanding of how the scarecrows would react to magic spells. Also, it had been too long since Rhys had occasion to employ the toxic yew rituals Colfenor taught him, yet here he was preparing to cast them once again, mere moments after discovering that Colfenor himself was not yet through with him.

The battle grew more chaotic and confusing as Maralen joined in. Rhys was not sure exactly what magic the elf maiden was using, but blue-black smoke seemed to follow and precede her every step of the way. When she approached the hostile merrow, they were driven back. When she pointed at them and waved, they were hurled clear out of the water and sent howling downstream.

"Very well," Rhys muttered. He reached into his belt for a small clay bottle, uncorked it, and held it in front of him with both hands. Rhys cleared his mind and closed his eyes. He sent his thoughts back to his days as Colfenor's student. The old log had always been quick to disparage the aggressive ways Rhys applied yew lore but never once acknowledged that many of the ancient spells were clearly intended as weapons. Rhys chose one of the simplest and most effective of these, opened his eyes, and then carefully tilted the bottle over his open palm.

Yew resin dripped slowly out of the bottle. The amber-yellow syrup was thick and sticky and gave off a bitter odor. Rhys watched carefully as the translucent stream descended toward his palm, mentally reciting the incantation that triggered the spell. The moment the resin touched his skin; Rhys flicked his wrist and cast his arm out toward the river, directly at the largest scarecrow.

The huge shambling beast staggered backward, shuddering. It toppled into the water with a wide and promptly sank. Its twig-arms and knotty fingers convulsed as they disappeared below the surface. The battle continued, undiminished and uninterrupted.

"Closer!" Maralen yelled. She was keeping a pair of merrow thugs at bay with the point of her dagger and an open hand. She turned her head slightly and said, "You have to be closer to them!"

Rhys started to reply, to explain how he could not get close enough to the scarecrows without sinking, but Maralen never gave him the chance. "Oh, never mind," she said. Hissing angrily, the elf maiden leaped back from her opponents, turned toward Rhys, and gestured. Rhys felt an invisible force snatch him up, and moments later he was soaring over Brigid and Maralen and Wryget on his way to the largest collection of floating scarecrows.

Instinct took over and Rhys prepared himself to act. He would have time to lay hands on at least two of the scarecrows even if he didn't manage to stay above water once he came down. If that wasn't close enough to get the job done, he was ready to abandon Wryget's half-baked strategy entirely.

Rhys crushed the bottle as he descended, coating his fingers with yew resin. He smeared his hands together until all ten of his fingers were covered with sticky yellow poison and broken clay. The force that propelled him vanished just as he came down upon the head of the tallest scarecrow. Rhys tucked his knees against his torso so that his kneecaps slammed through the scarecrow's upper body. He also spread his arms out wide so that each hand slapped across the faces and shoulders of as many scarecrows as he could touch.

To his surprise, Rhys stopped short when his knees hit the strange blue platform that supported the shambling monsters. There was almost no shock from the sudden impact as the platform and the river cushioned his fall. Rhys jumped back to his feet and stood with his yew-stained hands ready to blight more of the scarecrows.

He quickly saw that no more poison magic was required,

however. The scarecrows he had already touched now shuddered like the first he'd enchanted, but the rest reacted even more strangely. They did not seem to be suffering from the effects of the yew spell so much as becoming part of it. Fascinated despite the dire action around him, Rhys stared as the blue-tinted scarecrows secreted yellowish oil that coated them from top to bottom. The drier parts of their ramshackle bodies—the reeds and twigs and discarded bits of cloth—all darkened and thickened with moisture as if they'd spent years steeping in yew sap.

The phenomenon spread across the river, traveling from the scarecrows nearest Rhys to those farthest away, until each was tinged with the yellow-amber poison. Rhys's fascination broke when he realized he was still alone and unsupported at the center of the river, but once more Maralen acted before Rhys could speak. The same unseen force that had tossed him out onto the river now gathered him up and whisked him back to the bank. He tried to keep his eyes on the scarecrows and the merrow, but Maralen's strange magic did not accommodate him. Seconds later Rhys landed on solid ground beside the elf maiden and Brigid.

Maralen did not even glance at Rhys. "Wryget," she called. "It's now or never." In response, the huge merrow brute shot up out of the water and flopped heavily onto dry land. Once Wryget was clear, Maralen's calm voice said, "Brigid."

"I'm on it, Boss." The kithkin concentrated, squeezing her dark eyes almost shut, and then she waved her hand in a sharp chopping motion. Out on the river, the shattered pieces of the blue magic platform dissolved, dumping all remaining scarecrows into the Wanderbrine.

"There," Maralen said. "That's that."

"That's what?" Rhys demanded. "We don't even know—"

"Yes we do," Maralen said. She turned and smiled her thin smile at Rhys, directing his attention to the river with an elegant wave of her hand.

The river rushed by as always, its surface momentarily free of merrow or scarecrow. Rhys noticed an oily film on the water, a slight discoloration that did not move with the current. Something scaly and blue-gray bobbed to the surface. This new object did move with the current, and as it flowed downstream it rolled, revealing a sharp head-fin, a wide merrow mouth full of sharp teeth, and a pair of dead yellow eyes.

Another merrow corpse appeared beside the first with a makeshift scarecrow arm in its clutches. Rhys and the others continued to watch silently as more bits and pieces of scarecrow appeared, along with a large number of dead fish, a handful of lifeless snakes, and more than a dozen merrow corpses. They watched the ghastly flotilla grow larger for several minutes until the dead had been washed away and the oily film was all but dissolved.

Wryget gasped slightly and shook his head. "Boss," he whispered. "This isn't entirely my fault, is it?"

"Not even close," Brigid said. "And I'll make sure that Sygg knows that. In fact, I'll make sure he never even hears your name in connection with this."

"If you ever see him again," Rhys muttered. He felt sick. For the first time he understood how it must have pained Colfenor to see ancient yew magic used for large-scale slaughter.

"We'll find him for sure now," Brigid said brightly. She turned to Maralen. "That was quick thinking, Boss. I think you saved us all a lot of trouble."

"Congratulate me after we find Sygg," Maralen said, but her face shone with pride that belied her sharp words.

"I will," Brigid said. To Rhys, she added, "Can I congratulate you, Safewright? That was a nice bit of spellwork."

"You may not," Rhys said.

Brigid shrugged. "Suit yourself." She nudged Wryget with her foot. "Back in the water?"

"Only if it's safe," the big merrow replied. He was wheezing, his breathing strained, but he was otherwise relaxed and untroubled.

"It's safe," Brigid said. "All we need to do is put together a shapewater craft of our own and keep heading upriver. The next batch of merrow will approach us with a good deal more caution and respect. If Sygg's not among them, we can give them a message to take to him. A day, two at the most, and we'll be sitting across the table from the terror of the Wanderbrine."

"And then what?" Rhys said sharply. "You still haven't explained how a merrow crime lord is going to help us defeat the Destroyer. Or how you're going to convince him to do so."

"That's my worry," Brigid said, and though she didn't actually wink at Maralen, Rhys felt the gesture was clearly implied.

"And mine," Rhys said, suddenly angry in the face of these two women's smugness. He had endured more than enough of their evasion, their secrets, and their petty conspiracies. "I've been contacted by someone who has offered to help make sense of all this. Someone I deem worth meeting, someone with information worth verifying. I don't feel that's the case with your Captain Sygg."

"Well, you're wrong," Maralen said.

"How do you know?"

"Because I trust Brigid," Maralen said. "And Brigid trusts me."

Rhys shook his head. "That's not good enough anymore."

"What do you propose, then? Return to Wilt-Leaf to rejoin a fighting force that we all know cannot accomplish its mission? Force of arms alone will not stop the Destroyer, Rhys."

"I agree," Rhys said. "That is why I intend to pursue this other option."

"We're a good team," Brigid said, her eyes fixed on Maralen. "It'd be a mistake to break up a good team."

"I wish you luck," Rhys said. He bowed perfunctorily, barely hiding a sneer. "If you really do plan to make a stand against the Destroyer and you do manage to secure some sort of advantage from the merrow, I expect we shall meet again.

"I'm dead certain we will," Brigid said. "If you'll pardon the expression."

"Good-bye, elf guy," Wryget said. "Thanks for helping us."

"I don't want—" Maralen said, but she caught herself and sighed with what sounded like real sorrow and disappointment. "Don't go," she said at last.

"I must," he said. Her forlorn demeanor oddly touched Rhys, but he remained resolute. His voice softened and he said, "The kithkin is right. If we all continue to track the Destroyer, we will meet again. And when we do, it would be better to have as many different assets as we can muster. Go," he said. "Find your merrow. I will do what I can—what I must—on my own."

Maralen's eyes were dry, but her face was sad. "As you wish, Safewright. The Destroyer will strike again sooner or later. I hope that you and I meet sooner, and not only to prevent the attacks to come later."

Rhys held Maralen's eyes. He nodded to the elf maiden and then bowed once more to Brigid and Wryget. Rhys turned and walked away from the river, silently following the memory of the soft voice only he could hear.

* * * * *

The kithkin doun of Kinscaer sat on the western banks of the Wanderbrine, perfectly situated as the nexus of trade and travel between the north and south halves of Shadowmoor. Over the years Kinscaer's leaders had parlayed that location into a lucrative position of prominence, and its current cenn, Donal Alloway, led the doun to new heights of influence and wealth.

Under Cenn Alloway, Kinscaer was easily the largest and best-defended doun in the world, boasting the most formidable warriors and the most powerful spellcasters. Canny and ruthless, Alloway had spent years reaching out to the other kithkin strongholds and bringing them under his protection. His detractors in the kithkin community claimed he was power-mad, that he advanced Kinscaer's cause only to further his own. His ardent supporters, who greatly outnumbered the detractors, said that he had simply made Kinscaer the heart of kithkin society, just as kithkin society was already the heart of Shadowmoor. Cenn Alloway's works benefited all kithkin everywhere far more than they benefited Donal Alloway himself.

The great walled kithkin city was a haven for the weak and a fortress from which the strong could strike at their enemies. Provided the merrow who ran the river were properly compensated, no one had ever successfully mounted an assault on Kinscaer—not boggarts or cinders or even elves. Giants and treefolk rarely visited the doun, but no kithkin who had been to Kinscaer doubted that Alloway's army could easily turn them aside as well.

High above the clouds, invisible to the sleeping kithkin below, the Destroyer looked down upon Kinscaer. Thoughts no other living being could comprehend churned in the terrible cauldron of her mind. Fire raged in the skies around her, flames that were simultaneously solid as rock and fluid as rainwater. She had never seen Kinscaer before, never heard the name

Donal Alloway, but the somehow the merest thought of the doun tore ragged screams of outrage from her throat.

A cacophonous series of impossible sights, sounds, and facts assailed her like bad memories: Kinscaer's leader and the devil tree luring someone here and then sending hired thugs to abduct someone and drag her back when she didn't stay; someone being bound to an altar in the town square while an agonizing ritual was performed; a mind shattered and a life ended as the wicked tree tried to set fire on fire and was itself consumed.

Flames exploded from the Destroyer's body, filling the sky. The clouds below her burned away, bathing distant Kinscaer in the hot orange light of her frenzy. She fell, plummeting toward the doun. With every incremental increase in her speed, the sound of thundering, galloping hooves echoed more loudly within her mind. Kinscaer's existence pained her like an open wound that had been packed with salt. She could not endure it, and she would not.

Screeching her wild fury, the Destroyer blasted through the upper portion of Kinscaer's mighty fortress walls. Jagged bits of flaming rock peppered the entire doun, injuring some, killing others, igniting homes, shops, entire neighborhoods. The living fireball slammed into the town square, razing it to bare rock in places.

Other cries came, sounds of pain and terror that intensified the Destroyer's rage. Fists clenched, she rose several feet into the air and then dropped again, half-burying herself in the stony ground. A rolling shock wave rippled out from the point of impact, and the resulting tremor leveled those buildings that had survived the initial fire blast.

The Destroyer floated up from the crater she had made. Kinscaer's town square was square no longer, but a broad and smoking disk of charred soil and stone. The vengeful monster at its center was the only thing upright for a hundred yards in each direction.

Someone cried out sharply in the distance. The Destroyer watched a volley of arrows arc up from the intact portions of the fortress walls. She laughed and spat at the archers. Their bolts ignited and burned to ashes long before they ever touched her.

The demon paused then as if distracted by some strange sound. Chillingly silent and still at the center of the devastation, the Destroyer stood staring at the nearest intact doorway. Many seconds ticked by, marked only by the sounds of the dying and the crackle of magical fire.

Then the door opened. Slowly but without fear, two kithkin emerged from the building. The male was unusually tall and thin for his tribe, dressed from head to toe in an elegant suit tailored from stiff black animal hide, and he carried a gigantic sword. The woman was squat, aged, and frail, but her wide white eyes were sharp and clear and bright.

The male kithkin stepped forward. "I am Donal Alloway," he declared. "Cenn of Kinscaer. And you should not have come here." He turned to the old woman. "Augur Tarcha?" he said. "Begin."

The old woman opened her hands and began to chant, but the Destroyer paid her no mind. Instead she fixed her fiery gaze on the cenn as the same series of kaleidoscopic images and sensations returned. *Kinscaer's leader luring someone here, sending hired thugs to drag someone back when she didn't stay—an agonizing ritual in the square—a mind shattered. Lives consumed.*

The monster sprang forward, faster than the finest kithkin mage, her hands extended for Alloway's throat. The cenn managed to draw his huge blade and position it between them so that the Destroyer's hands clamped onto it rather than Alloway's neck. The blade bit deep, but she did not bleed.

For a moment the cenn and his fiery assailant stared at each other across the blade's length. Alloway tried to force the sword down or forward while the Destroyer pushed it back. She savored this last moment before Alloway's complete destruction, reveling in the expected sight of his hair and eyebrows crumbling away in the heat. Then Donal Alloway smiled.

"Fool," he said. "Mindless beast. It is not one kithkin you fight today, but all of them. Now, my friends, now!"

Hundreds of kithkin voices rang from inside the building that had concealed Cenn Alloway and Augur Tarcha. At the same moment this song reached the Destroyer's ears, the cenn's sword began to glow. A blue-white envelope of light surrounded the blade, and for the first time in her short, chaotic life, the Destroyer felt her flames cool.

"She's ours!" Alloway shouted. Without breaking eye contact with the Destroyer, he said, "Strike now, Tarcha! Finish this!"

The Destroyer let out a sound that was half-snarl, half-chuckle. She sniffed disdainfully at Alloway, turned her face from his, and spat fire into Tarcha's face.

The old woman wailed and fell back, clutching at her eyes. The sword wavered in Alloway's hands, but the Destroyer did not press the advantage.

"Fool," she hissed, her voice crackling with vicious glee. "It is not one kithkin I seek to kill today, but all of them." Alloway's courage failed. He howled and tried to release the sword, but the Destroyer merely laughed. She sent a brutal surge of fire through the blade that flowed across Alloway's hands, up both his arms, and then enveloped his entire body. Through it all, Donal Alloway screamed.

Still clasping the cenn's sword, the Destroyer forced more killing fire through the blade. A thick column of red-orange heat blasted from Alloway's back and engulfed the doorway behind him. The synchronized chorus of kithkin voices supporting the cenn dissolved into a confused mass of individual wails and shrieks. The bottom floor of the building exploded, belching flames from every window, and then the structure collapsed.

Blackened, both the great sword and its owner crumbled to the ground. The Destroyer flicked melted steel and carbon slag from her hands before turning back to Tarcha.

The old woman's hair was gone and her forehead was hideously burned, but her eyes were intact. In fact, Tarcha's wide orbs were glowing brightly, so brightly they stood out even amid the harsh firelight that surrounded the Destroyer.

Tarcha extended her hands. "Go now," she said softly. A comet of white smoke erupted from her hands and circled her forearms, leaving a corkscrew trail of vapor around the aged kithkin. "Go now. Begone."

The Destroyer prepared to swat this presumptuous, bothersome insect, but something seized her body before she could. Roaring, she reached out a flaming hand to caress Tarcha's throat, but the old woman was now encased within a column of spinning white smoke. When the Destroyer's fingers touched that cocoon, it emitted a flash. The world became silent under a shroud of white, and when it returned, the Destroyer was no longer in Kinscaer, but high atop a lonely mountain peak.

There were no mountains near Kinscaer. Whatever spell Tarcha had cast hadn't hurled the Destroyer away, as Eidren's had, but had transported her instantly to the far edge of the world.

Furious, disoriented, the Destroyer vented her frustration on the peak itself, causing a flood of molten granite to pour down the mountainside. When the initial rush of anger subsided, she turned toward the south, feeling for her quarry as a child feels for its favorite toy in the dark.

Tarcha's magic hadn't spared Kinscaer, only granted it a respite. The monster rose higher into the air and hurtled back to finish her unfinished business. The kithkin hag would regret delaying the Destroyer's vengeance, and not only because the Destroyer herself would make sure Tarcha suffered for it.

Streaking across the sky like a shooting star, the Destroyer let out a laugh that rang in perfect rhythm with the awful sound of thundering hooves.

CHAPTER 7

The Destroyer burned a wide swath of devastation as she quit Mount Kulrath, but there were oases of unscorched land between the furrows of blackened soil. They looked like tiny dying fish floating down an inky river to the third member of the Vendilion clique, who had ascended to a great height to clearly hear what Maralen was telling him.

"You want me to *what?*" Endry asked the empty sky. It wasn't necessary to speak. The words Maralen would hear came through a mental connection, but speaking helped Endry focus. He found it also made others nervous, which he liked. Nervous people were easier to deal with, easier to manipulate. Unfortunately for him, the party to whom he spoke was neither nervous nor easily manipulated.

You heard me, Maralen told him. *Now get to it. You may have gone rogue, little man, but you swore an oath to me. I'm calling in a favor, and you will do what I ask.*

"I swear a lot of oaths." Endry dipped through a puffy white cloud that appeared silver in the moonlight. The inside was anything but—in fact, it was damp and chilly, a feeling exacerbated by the presence of Maralen within his mind. "But I've already broken this one. What makes you think you can just make me do whatever you want?" He slipped from the cloud into a thin band of clear sky above the fog that almost permanently covered this region of Shadowmoor, thinner these days since so much of the landscape had been angrily incinerated, and then veered a little south into as-yet-unburned territory covered with a few sparse, gnarled trees and isolated swamps. "I've got things to *do*."

Nothing is more important than this, Maralen responded. *Rhys is headed your way, wherever you are. He seeks the sapling.*

"So?" Endry said. "I'm seeking a *giant*."

You're what?

"Never mind," the faerie said. "Not relevant."

Endry, there isn't time to impress upon you the importance of this task. The sapling has something very vital to do, and—

"The last time you said that," Endry said, finally spotting what he was looking for, "she almost ended up dead."

And you were right to side against me, Maralen said, somewhat to Endry's surprise—it was not like the fatheaded elf woman to admit a mistake. *But now you have to see why this is important. I hope you're not flying; this may make you a little dizzy.*

"You *know* I'm flying," Endry replied. "It's what I do. I fly like a—*yeeargh!*"

Endry did not even hear himself scream. The vision that flooded his tiny brain didn't leave room for outside sounds to reach his thoughts, for the vision had far too much to tell him. There was fire, more fire than Endry had ever seen, and considering recent events that was a lot of fire. But that was just the start of it. Fire was strong, but there were other things that could snuff it out, for fire had weaknesses—fire needed fuel to burn and air to breathe.

The Great Mother was stronger than fire, for example, and with Oona's stolen power Maralen showed Endry just how much stronger. *I've had a change of heart as far as allies are concerned*, Maralen said. *The sapling and Rhys must reunite, and then you must bring them here.*

Endry realized he was still squeaking hoarsely and ended it with a theatrical cough. "The sapling has other plans," he said proudly, "and I'm helping. I get it, she's important, but she gets it too. And right now she and I have something big to pin down before we do anything."

You're making a joke, aren't you? Maralen said. *You mentioned a giant.*

"That's right," Endry said. "The sapling was hoping to get hold of Rosheen Meanderer's journal, but when I got to her someone else had gotten there first."

I know. The journals are very useful, by the way. Bring the sapling to me, and we can share them.

"I'll tell her," Endry said, and to his own surprise he was completely sincere. "And if she agrees, we'll track you down. But I've really, really got to take care of something else first."

If not Rosheen, what giant are you—?

"In a minute," Endry said. "Now listen, just leave me alone for a bit. I can't hear myself think, and I really need to think if I'm going to pass along your message."

What? What's happening?

With a supreme effort, Endry pushed the oppressive voice into a quiet corner and muttered out of the side of his mouth, "Not *now*. Have to concentrate on not dying."

There was no response.

"That's more like it," Endry said, and then he turned to the nearest of the thirty or so faeries of many cliques hovering in a bowl-shaped formation. He did his best to sound the bold and brave hero he knew himself to be, but his voice suddenly seemed small and nervous. He cleared his throat and tried to lower his voice. "Now what exactly do you faeries want?"

Like Maralen's thoughts, the faeries were silent, but Endry found this silence much more ominous and a thousand times more threatening. He didn't recognize a single one, which meant it was likely these faeries had all been born after the Vendilion clique had left Oona's service—maybe even since the Aurora. They all wore similar expressions of expectancy and arrogance that made Endry want to punch each and every one in the tiny face. Before he could, the first crashing footsteps and babbling rumbles of the giant he'd been seeking shattered the expectant silence.

"Well, I guess I'll be going then," Endry ventured, one eye on the giant and another looking for gaps in the cordon these newcomers had placed around him. The bowl formation was a cruel technique that every faerie knew about but few ever had reason to experience. It was specifically designed to trap a flying enemy without having to cover all directions at once. The trapped flyer couldn't move forward, to the side, or down, and if he fled straight upward—perhaps in the hope he might go "over the wall"—the bowl simply followed him up, never giving the prisoner (who might not even realize he was a prisoner yet) a chance to escape.

"Stay where you are," the nearest faerie answered. "You've been a bad boy, Endry. The Great Mother wants to know when you're coming home."

Endry didn't immediately respond—he was looking for something that shouldn't be too hard to spot, especially since he'd been steadily flying lower and lower while conversing with Maralen.

"Oh, he's too frightened to speak," another faerie said. "He must be getting hard of hearing. Old age does just creep up on you, doesn't it, old-timer?"

The trapped faerie fought his instincts and bit back a witty rejoinder about his age (he was, he had to admit, getting a bit old for a faerie) while he focused on the lumbering, babbling monster below. The other faeries weren't paying the giant any heed, assuming they could flit away from any long swipes of the enormous creature's massive meat hooks. Now Endry just had to figure out how finding the giant Kiel would help him. He couldn't really follow the huge goon with Oona's minions trapping him in place, but as long as he kept the newcomers distracted, Endry's plan might still be successful. He hoped it would be—he'd hate to let down the sapling. Endry had never really had friends before meeting her, and he liked having a friend.

I've sent help, Maralen voice said inside his head. *Do not try to fight her creatures alone. And do not forget who your real friends are.*

"I don't need *their* help," Endry said. "My *real* friends are doing just fine on their own." And with that, he placed two fingers to his tiny lips and released a whistle with a volume that was entirely disproportionate to the faerie's size. The whistle's effect was immediate, and a hundred invisible lines—invisible at this distance, even to Endry, but woven by silverback spiders and tough enough to pin even something as strong as Kiel—dropped from the treetops above the giant's head. Strong as they were, the lines would have fluttered away on the wind were the ends of each not weighed down by a tiny wingless faerie called a groundling. The groundlings held the spider-silk as they plummeted like tiny knives, shouting cries of tiny, squealing defiance. Their shouts told Endry they hadn't lost their nerve no matter how confusing they found their task.

No matter how many times Endry told his groundling subjects—no, that wasn't the word. *Minions.* Beloved minions. No matter how many times Endry told his beloved groundling minions how the world used to be brighter than now, which wasn't bright at all; no matter how often he reminded them of how he'd heroically spared their homes from destruction before forming them into a finely honed squad of tiny wingless killers despite their deformities; no matter how much Endry wanted Nora—the fiery little groundling who'd been their leader before Endry came along—now matter how much he wanted Nora to remember the way she'd smiled at him when they brought down the big rock monster thing with the smashy fists and—

A sound less like the tremendous crash he'd expected and much more like a big, wet splat broke Endry's train of thought, and he cursed himself for daydreaming. He'd been doing it more often of late, letting his thoughts wander onto whatever fancy—another splat, just in time.

The faerie looked down through the cluster of fresh new-borns trying—and failing—to make faces frightening enough to intimidate him. The giant Kiel had fallen to his knees into the mud, and then the groundlings at the shoulder-lines hauled with all their considerable might and brought the giant down onto his forearms. Kiel's babbling became angrier, but it had not yet occurred to him to attack the two hundred groundlings standing around him, if he even saw Nora and her army of wingless Fae.

Endry looked up at the nearest loudmouth Oona-lover and reached behind his back to draw a silver blade. With his other hand he pulled an object somewhat like a reddish acorn from a pouch on his belt.

"You are going to fight us, elder?" asked the faerie, a female who seemed to have a permanent sneer.

"No, but if you try to keep me from doing what I want to do, new-growth, I'm going to throw this acorn at you. Isn't it pretty? Have you seen one before? I especially like the red. It's a bit obvious, I suppose, since—"

"Since *what?*" shrieked Oona's spokesfaerie.

"Since the particular *kind* of yew poison it's got in it, which I'm completely protected from, by the way, thanks to a friend of mind who's—well, never you mind." He cackled. "It'll make blood shoot out of your eyes, all right? And that's just the beginning. Your skin will dissolve, and so will your wings, but I think there'll still be enough of you when you hit the ground to feel it." Endry smiled.

Oh my, Maralen interrupted, to the faerie's annoyance. *Yes, the sapling is going to be very important to all of us.*

For once Endry forced himself not to speak his response aloud—he was still smiling wickedly and brandishing an acorn, after all. *Just leave me alone and I'll talk to her about it. I'm busy.*

Fair enough, Maralen told him. *Tell your sisters to bring your reply to me. I'll be disappointed if you don't come with them as well. Good luck.*

The entire exchange took less than a second, and by the time the word "luck" finished echoing in Endry's head he saw the sneering faerie had begun sneering some more sneers in his direction.

"So you can see we have nothing to worry about. Oona protects us."

"Oona protects you," Endry repeated, hoping he was catching up to the right conversation. He decided to try another threat in the hopes the loudmouth would repeat herself. "But even she can't withstand yew magic!" He waved the acorn at a cluster of smaller, freshly budded faeries who leaped back with a satisfying jolt.

"That's—that's not proven," the faerie stammered, but quickly recovered her composure. "Besides, you wouldn't be throwing it at Oona—you'd be throwing it at us!"

"Er—Anjie? How's that a good thing?" the second faerie asked. "Yew magic would be able to hurt us, wouldn't it?"

"Shut it, Drimlo," the spokesfaerie Anjie snapped at her companion, and the Vendilion brother couldn't resist the opportunity to press his point.

"I think Drimlo is right, Anjie," he said, still smiling confidently. "I think you all should think about Oona's lack of concern for the lives of her own children." He hovered in midair, still watching the groundlings struggle to keep the giant pinned. He could hear their tiny voices crying with exertion, but typical of their arrogance the other faeries didn't appear to pay them any heed at all. Endry could hardly believe he'd once been that way. "My sisters and I, we don't have to do Oona's dirty work any more. And we don't have to die in needless servility."

"You'd kill your own kind!" Anjie said. "And there is no such thing as 'dirty work' where Oona is concerned. She is the Mother of us all. You're ill, Endry. You and your sisters have been infected. You're to come with us. You can even—" She swallowed hard, and Endry though he detected actual fear in her voice. He couldn't be sure; actual fear wasn't often something he sought. "You can keep your—your acorn," she finished.

He laughed a bold, heroic laugh and casually tossed the acorn into the air, catching it in one hand. The entire bowl of faeries moved back as he caught the reddish nut. "I told you, I don't do Oona's bidding. I have a new—that is, I'm my own master, and I work for whomever I like, and I don't like Oona anymore. Neither should any of you, but if you choose Oona over your own kind, well, you'll die. It's really that simple." He tossed the nut again. A second time they all moved a little bit back.

"We'll tell the Great Mother!" the male called Drimlo cried, and received a cuff alongside the head from Anjie. "Just put that acorn down!"

"For the love of—Drimlo, we outnumber him. A lot."

"I don't care, Anjie, he could kill us all with one nut! A *nut!* He's right! It's crazy that she—that the—"

"That had better not be seditious talk," Anjie warned. But the warning was driven more by frustration, Endry guessed, than any real concern about sedition in the ranks. He had her, and she knew it. "Endry, we will leave you to your pursuits. But you cannot flee the Great Mother forever. We will be watching.

"Good." He tossed the acorn in the air a third time, beginning to enjoy himself. "I'll be watching you too, Sweet Wings." Unfortunately, as the acorn reached its zenith, Endry took a moment to wink at Anjie, and that lapse in concentration was all it took for the acorn to completely miss Endry's upturned palm and plummet toward the part of the "bowl" that was thickest—the bottom. Endry covered his ears at the terrified screams as every faerie below him moved hurriedly out of the way of the falling object. Every one of them froze in midair, watching in horror as the acorn dropped, dropped, landed with a bounce on Kiel's upper back, and disappeared from even the faerie's sharp eyes.

"Great mother!" Endry said after more awkward silence than he could stand. "My lunch!" Without another word, he tucked his wings and dropped like a stone through the gap in the bottom of the faerie bowl formation.

Endry didn't look back, but raised his tiny sword—envenomed with a sleep-inducing, nonlethal mixture that was nevertheless strong enough to put down a giant for a short time—as he dropped. With slight adjustments to his wings, he was able to guide his freefall until he was aiming exactly where he wanted—the base of Kiel's hairy, smelly neck.

The impact drove the faerie blade into the giant's hide and the velocity of the fall drove Endry in after it up to his waist. Unable to breathe, he released the blade and wriggled his body mightily, but to no avail. He was already feeling groggy; if he remained embedded in Kiel's flesh he'd never be found after he suffocated. *I just wanted to administer the poison,* he thought. *I didn't want to be an arrow.*

I told you I sent help, Maralen replied. *They should be there—*

He felt a small hand clamp onto each of his ankles and begin to pull. The pressure on his wings was painful, but he'd had worse.

Right about now, Maralen finished.

Kiel slowly settled onto the ground with his face turned to the side, tremendous, tusklike teeth protruding in three directions, and fell into a slumber just as Endry slipped from the wound that had knocked him out. He found himself standing atop the giant's neck, the center of faerie attention—surrounded by two hundred groundlings, watched by around thirty of Oona's faeries in the sky, and flanked by two others whose presence surprised him but probably shouldn't have. After all, what other help would Maralen have sent?

"Who in the name of the sapling and all that's holy are they?" asked Nora, the leader of the groundlings (not counting Endry, who wasn't so much for the day-to-day aspects of leadership, preferring instead to focus on big ideas like capturing a giant for his friend the sapling).

"The ones up there?" Endry asked, pointing at the buzzing Oona loyalists. "Or do you mean—"

"We're his sisters," Iliona said, "and we came to help."

"Yeah," Veesa said, "And what's so holy about the sapling? She's just a stupid tree, you know."

"Ladies," Endry said, pointing up. "Let's discuss all this later. I smell trouble. See?"

* * * * *

Rhys entered this unfamiliar section of the Wilt-Leaf. Even though he'd never been here before, it already looked familiar.

You're getting closer, the sapling said to him. *It won't be far now.*

I think I'm lost, he shot back angrily. He was beginning to feel the familiar sensation of being manipulated, a feeling that had led to him once leaving Colfenor's apprenticeship. *Where are you?* he asked for the thousandth time.

You are about to encounter your first landmark, the sapling told him. *Look for the giant. I am nearby.*

"The giant?" Rhys spoke aloud, and then he thought, *The giant? What giant?*

He possesses knowledge, knowledge he does not know. I need him. But not as much as I need you to help me become what I am meant to be.

I'll look for a giant, Rhys thought, and pushed through another section of densely wooded forest. Like most of the Wilt-Leaf, the greenery here was not from the trees—many of them were dead from the canker—but from vines, ferns, moss, and dense, hard grasses that grew tall and jagged. Even Rhys, who was as adept at moving through these woods as any safewright, found it hard going. His practiced eyes sought the natural gaps in the tangled tendrils and barbed undergrowth and he pushed through them, widening gaps big enough for a thin, nimble elf to slip through without too much trouble. At least that was the theory, he mused when his left hoof became ensnared in a coiling, rough-edged vine that tripped him up just before he fell flat on his face.

Rhys rolled onto his back and raised himself to a sitting position, eyeing the vine that held his ankle in its painful grip. The tendril had coiled around itself a number of times and had somehow wrapped all the way around his leg below the knee. He decided that if he couldn't risk a sword blade on the potentially metal-eating vine sap, he could afford to risk a dagger. He leaned forward and pulled the long, double-bladed knife from the sheath he wore strapped to one leg. Rhys slipped the silver blade beneath the vines and carefully pulled it back toward him, making sure the pressure from the cutting, upward-facing edge was firm but even. The vine refused to be cut, even when a gentle sawing motion was applied, and Rhys grew concerned.

When the vine began to constrict around his leg and crawl up past his knee, the safewright's concern multiplied tenfold. When it pressed the edge of the dagger into his leg and the blade sliced into the flesh of his calf, he shouted in pain and alarm.

Her reach is long, the sapling whispered. *But she cannot take you from me.*

Who? Rhys replied. *Who is reaching—Ow, this really hurts.*

"She cannot take you from me!" the sapling repeated, and it took a moment for Rhys to realize he'd heard the words reach his ears before he heard them in his head. Then he felt a wave of familiar, deadly energy wash overhead, just missing him—and he felt the vine around his leg crumble to dust. He winced and sat up abruptly, pressing a hand against the knife cut—it wasn't deep—and twisting to see where the voice had come from.

It did not take Rhys long to spot the sapling. Though he was certain he had never seen her before, she was unmistakable— the only yew in the entire Wilt-Leaf, as far as he could tell. She stood some twelve to fifteen feet tall; a young tree, but certainly her name was not quite accurate—this tree had not been a sapling for some time. Her boughs were lush green and glittering red, the bark covering her strong limbs a rich, healthy ochre untouched by canker or disease. Her face was almost like the face of an elf carved into the bark, long and narrow beneath a crown of reddish needles and a wooden mouth cut in an almost permanent half-smile. The sapling was in fact more vibrant than any tree he'd ever seen in his home forest, even those lining the moonlit paths of Cayr Ulios, and Rhys felt an instinctive need to ensure her absolute safety.

"Student of my sire," the sapling said, "Brother. Colfenor chose well when he chose you, Rhys of the Gilt-Leaf."

"Gilt-Leaf?" Rhys asked, puzzled.

"Wilt-Leaf, then," the sapling said wryly. "You remember Colfenor, yes?"

"Of course," said Rhys. "He was my mentor in certain arts my colleagues wanted to discourage." The safewright pushed himself to his feet and tested his weight on the wounded leg. No trouble there—the cut was superficial, no matter how painful it had seemed at the time. He eyed the yew skeptically. "I left his tutelage a long time ago, and he never mentioned any offspring."

"Not to you, Rhys of the Wilt-Leaf," the sapling said. "To Rhys of the Gilt-Leaf."

"You're not making any more sense now than you were before," the elf objected. "What was that? Not what you did— I'm familiar with that—but what was the vine? It was—it was in my head, making my thoughts—"

"It is all right now," the sapling said. "I had hoped my friend Endry would bring you to me, but he's fallen a bit behind schedule thanks to your friend—the one who calls herself by another's name."

"What are you talking about?" Rhys asked.

"Your friend Maralen. I will explain on the way to Kiel," the sapling said. "We will have to walk to Kinscaer, I'm afraid. Captain Sygg cannot help us this time."

"Sygg the merrow criminal?"

"No, Sygg the merrow ferryman. Do not worry; even if I told you a thousand times I doubt you would remember. It is difficult, some days, even for me. And you had no protection against the Aurora." The sapling let out a remarkably kithkin-like sigh. "I do wonder what's going to happen to Brigid Baeli."

Rhys started to back away from the sapling. This was a mistake; it had to be. This was treefolk treachery, trying to use the memory of a beloved mentor to trick him into believing a load of nonsense—or maybe just to trap him and wrench the secrets of the magic barriers protecting Cayr Ulios from his mind.

If I wanted to wrench any barriers from your mind, the sapling's voice said from inside Rhys's mind, *I already would have done it. Come, Rhys. Let us speak with an oracle, and let his knowledge of the past help us light our way.*

Oracle? Rhys thought, and then added aloud, "Oracle? I thought we were going to see a giant."

"They are one and the same," the sapling said. "Now, let us—"

"Wait." Through the moonlit trees, Rhys eyed the destruction that marked the Destroyer's progress through this remote stretch of the wood. He was alone and far from home, but now he had the chance to help—and protect—true beauty.

"Time is not short yet, but it is not in great supply. Please, student of—please, Rhys," the sapling said, "we must retrieve Kiel and the others."

Rhys nodded. "Lead the way."

CHAPTER 8

Brigid had gotten used to seeing drastic changes in the world around her, but this was the first time she'd seen such devastating change strike the Shadowmoor she'd known for only a short time. Brigid wondered what it was like for the ones who couldn't remember what the lush hillsides lining this stretch of the Wanderbrine had looked like in the full bloom of sun-drenched noon. To them, the world had been this way forever and those lush hillsides and idyllic meadowlands never existed.

The skeletal trees were now piles of ash amid smoldering dirt and charred rocks. The wrecked, smoldering mountaintop in the distance had once shone silver in the moonlight but now bore jagged craters at its summit like glowing wounds, illuminating the endless night. The marshes were parched and cracked, the tributaries dry and sandy, the meadowlands scorched and barren, and all of it meant the end of the world to the blissfully ignorant folk who, unlike her, hadn't carelessly lifted a ludicrously powerful trinket from a friend at exactly the wrong moment.

At first Brigid hadn't thought of it that way—a *wrong* moment. Only of late had it truly begun to sink in that she might well have been much better off without the Crescent of Morningtide, which by all rights should have been Sygg's.

She could befriend however many of this world's kithkin as she liked, she could try to do all the good she could, but the Crescent of Morningtide wasn't going to bring Lorwyn back to her, nor her to Lorwyn. At least not at Brigid's behest. It wasn't going to put Kinsbaile back in place of Kinscaer, it wouldn't turn Sygg back into a gruff but loveable river guide with a penchant for long stories of dubious veracity, and it wouldn't make Brigid fit in, ever.

She wasn't about to tell the others, but Brigid wasn't just hoping to learn how to stop the Destroyer. The kithkin intended to find out *why* the world changed, even if she couldn't change it back. What seemed a lifetime ago, but was to Brigid just over a year, she'd raced up these banks with Sygg's help, and songbirds had taken wing as they approached. Now a gang of wild bats erupted from a grasping snag standing improbably amid the smoldering devastation, one of the islands of withered, dying life left behind by Ashling's rampage. Now it was Brigid (and, admittedly, the Crescent) moving them upriver, and the kithkin hoped she could avoid running into the Crescent's rightful owner altogether, though she suspected it might eventually prove necessary.

"We're wasting time," Maralen called above the sounds of splashing merrow fins, whistling wind, and fast-moving whitewater. "We should go directly to Sygg."

"Are you reading my mind, elf?" Brigid snapped.

"Don't be ridiculous," Maralen snapped right back. "I've got plenty on my own mind. But I'm not surprised we're thinking of the same thing. You're never going to convince the—convince the *river* it should help us." She scowled at the kithkin, who had lifted her hood to better allow her to see what she was doing as they sped upriver on a small shapewater skiff. Wryget was doing most of the work of moving the translucent craft, but Brigid and the Crescent were what held it together.

Fortunately, it wasn't difficult, especially compared to what they'd gone through at Mistmeadow and after. The whitewater, though worrisome to Maralen, was nothing a simple skiff like this one couldn't handle. The shapewater was as much shape as water, as old Captain Sygg had told Brigid a long time ago when the sun still shined. This simple fact of shapewater physics meant that when the skiff hit the whitewater rapids it would absorb the roughest of the impact by taking the whitewater into the shape of the craft, and that simple fact put Brigid a bit too much at ease. Naturally, her second traveling companion couldn't let it last.

"Brigid," Wryget called with the same amiable air he might use to describe a change in the weather or a new joke he'd heard in Mistmeadow, "that whitewater isn't natural. I didn't notice until just now, the landscape's changed a bit since I came through here last."

"What isn't natural?" she asked. "Quickly, they're getting closer. If we're going to need to turn—"

"Be right back," Wryget said before he ducked back under the water and shot upriver much faster than the shapewater skiff could move, at least as long as she was the one maintaining it. The merrow wasn't gone long but returned to the surface closer to the stern where Brigid gave a mild start that made the skiff shimmer.

"What did you see?"

"The rapids aren't running over rocks," Wryget said. "That's why I said they weren't natural. They were running over—"

"What did you see?" asked Brigid.

"Here, I brought one back. Careful now, I'm going to toss it up onto the skiff." Wryget let out a good-natured snort and then heaved his cargo onto the translucent deck. It wasn't complete, but the badly decomposed body of a cinder was easy to recognize once you accounted for the peculiar gray-green coloring.

Brigid guessed the green was algae and other slimy things that grew on rocks, but the light, almost spongy complexion of the stone was nothing like what she expected.

"Didn't weigh much," Wryget said. "I'd say she's been in the water for a long time, maybe eight, nine months. There's plenty more where that came from. The whole of these new rapids are made up of—of *those*."

Brigid turned to Maralen to ask her opinion and saw the elf's eyes were closed—communing with her faerie minions, no doubt. Well, what she wasn't paying any attention to wouldn't hurt her, the kithkin hoped. Not that she bore Maralen a great deal of affection, but Brigid had sworn to serve the elf woman in exchange for a large favor, and Brigid Baeli upheld her oaths. Besides, at least Maralen was someone else who remembered, and such folk were rare.

"Wryget," said Brigid, "let's bring her to a stop for a moment." There was a slight lurch as their already slowing forward momentum came to a halt. "Thanks. Now, how do you know how long the body was in the water?"

"Oh, easy," Wryget said. "I've seen it before. Captain Sygg, you know, he used to have to deal with 'em encroaching on our territory. They blamed the river for all their problems, and sometimes they'd come out and try to divert the water away from their mountain. Foolish, you know."

"The mountain is where the Source is," Brigid agreed. "You'd never be able to divert it completely."

"Right," Wryget said. "Ironic, that. Or maybe coincidental. I can never keep those straight."

"Wryget—"

"Right. So then a funny thing happened. When the cinders started showing up and causing trouble, Sygg had us catch a couple—painful, that—and dip 'em into the old Wanderbrine as an example to the others."

"Dead examples?" Brigid asked.

"Well," said Wryget, suddenly embarrassed, "Sygg always said those were the best kind. Didn't talk your earfins off with threats of revenge and the like."

"That's not very funny," the kithkin said.

"Oh, that's not the funny bit," Wryget said, eager to move on. "The funny bit is, once the cinders saw the examples we made, they started wailing and snarling. They tore those bodies to pieces, until they weren't anything but charcoal. From what we could make out of what they were saying—the captain had us watching, of course, to see how they'd take the loss of their pals—they were *jealous* of the dead ones. Seemed their religion, or what have you, prevents 'em from voluntarily jumping into water, else more of the sad bastards would be snuffing themselves out every other day."

"You know a lot about this, Wryget," Brigid said. "I'm impressed."

Wryget's gillfins fluttered against his face, a gesture Brigid knew was a sign of further embarrassment. "I'm not trying to boast," he said sheepishly. "The captain, he's the one who figured out most of it. I was just along as muscle."

"You still haven't gotten to how you know exactly how long that corpse had been in the water," Brigid said.

"Oh, right!" said Wryget. "Sorry, I get—"

"Distracted," Brigid finished. "Now go on. The cinders were destroying their own dead in a mass fit of jealous pique. You watched."

"That part's mostly over. Now it was a few weeks later we started seeing a dead cinder in the water once, maybe twice a week. You think they sink like rocks when they drop into the water, and they do, but the stuff that makes 'em heavy, and alive, I assume, doesn't last long. After about a week in the water, a dead cinder is light enough to be moved by the current. But it gets hung up on things, rivergrass, freshwater kelp, slime, frogs, and things like that. Eventually they'd get caught in the fishing nets, *all* the fishing nets." At this, Brigid nodded, realizing Wryget was speaking not only of the nets that kept most merrow in the Wanderbrine fed, but also the larger nets meant to snare bigger prey—including unsuspecting merrow not of Sygg's Razorfin school. "The captain would send us down to clear them out. Got to be a pretty good judge of their age."

"Eight or nine months," Brigid said. "Could these bodies be from Rosheen? Did she kill a cinder village? Please tell me she killed a cinder village. Or three."

"Rosheen?" Wryget asked, puzzled. "I don't—oh, that giant. No, I doubt it. They'd be flatter, I'd think."

"And they couldn't be stragglers from her recent passage," Brigid said, eyeing the blackened, charred riverbanks. They were holding their position in the current between two wide swatches of destruction that had left a thin strip of green between them, mostly grasses and some vines that would probably consume all the life in the soil before the entire patch died, a brown island in a sea of carbonized soil. "They'd be much fresher."

"I can't say for sure they're all quite that old, by the way," Wryget said. "Just the one we brought up. Tricky to judge underwater, especially with the moon sinking."

"But they're all old?"

"Yes."

"They're from the period after the Aurora," Maralen interrupted. "Ashling—the Destroyer, she must have gone after the Source first. She had cinder followers by then, and they must have jumped into the fray with gusto."

Brigid, annoyed, asked, "How long have you been awake?"

"The whole time," Maralen said. "And before you ask, yes, I was also listening." She cocked her head to one side like a bird, considering, then added, "It would explain why it's taken her this long to do this much damage. She wasted time and resources on the Source." She raised an eyebrow. "You may be right after all, Brigid. The sooner we see whether the Source will help us, the better."

Brigid nodded. "Wryget, it sounds like these are the relics of a battle that's been over for months. I think we can safely go over them."

"Oh, I'm sure you can," he said. "Me, I'm going to have to do some leaping around, but I reckon I've still got it in me."

The ride over the rapids was relatively painless, but far more disturbing to Brigid than she'd expected. The blank, dead stone faces of the fallen cinders all seemed to stare at her accusingly through the smooth deck of the skiff. Most were in pieces, and those few that looked intact might well crumble into silt with a good swift kick.

The landscape changed little beyond the rapids, though the current against which Brigid strove increased with every inch of incline as they neared the foothills around the mountain cinders called Mount Kulrath.

"It's been a few months since she's been through here, I'd guess," said the merrow over one shoulder, pointing at the new growth lining the fast-moving river. Long grasses cradled a few scattered flowers clinging to the charred banks, hardy vines were already clutching the soil jealously to keep the river from eroding any more away than had already been lost, and tall cattails twice Brigid's height stood strong against the eddies of current.

All at once a thud against the bottom of the skiff jolted Brigid into instant readiness.

"Something in the water," Brigid gasped. "Not water. In—in

the water." The object passed with a few bouncing thuds beneath them before disappearing down the rushing Wanderbrine.

"That was a—" Maralen began.

"Dead merrow," Brigid said. "And it was fresh."

"Ladies," Wryget said, surfacing a few yards ahead. "I think we should stop again for a moment."

"Why?" asked Brigid, already fearing the answer.

"I've found Sygg," Wryget said. "I think he's dying."

Another thud, and this time Brigid's craft came to a halt without her permission against another shapewater form, this one a sphere that surfaced between Wryget and the skiff. The sphere's occupant pushed himself upright against the translucent substance and blinked large, lantern-like eyes as he frowned at the kithkin.

"A skiff, eh?" Sygg spat. "Lazy. Should've killed you years ago."

"You can criticize me later," Brigid said. "First tell us—"

Three more spheres surfaced, and now the skiff was surrounded. Brigid recognized the injured form of Kasella, Sygg's former wife and reejerey—a sort of merrow queen back in Lorwyn—slumped inside one of them. The other two were in similar shape, though Brigid knew neither the sleek, green eel-like merrow to port, nor the huge blue bruiser to starboard.

"Oh, I'll tell you," Sygg said. "Then you'll give me back that little bit of jewelry you stole. Traitor."

* * * * *

Endry was proud of his groundling troops on that day they came to call the Battle of Mount Kiel. Well, they'd come to call it that if Endry had anything to say about it, and if any of the groundling troops standing astride the toppled mountain of a creature actually survived the battle. So far all were more or less intact, but there was no denying that even two hundred wingless faeries would be hard-pressed to defeat more than thirty of the flying variety. True, the groundlings had Endry, and Endry *appeared* to have his sisters Iliona and Veesa. He wasn't entirely positive since they hadn't stopped bickering since pulling him out of Kiel's neck. Even as Endry called the groundlings to nail down their lines and take defensive positions astride Kiel, even as he sent the Groundling Wing Guard (a name Endry had come up with himself and of which he was perhaps inordinately proud) to their magpies, Iliona and Veesa would not stop pecking at each other.

"We should just take him back," Veesa was saying. "We don't want to fight them."

"We don't?" Iliona replied. "*I* do. *Endry* does. Those little ground-bound cretins do."

"We're not cretins!" Nora cried from over Endry's shoulder. "Who are they, Endry? Tell them we're not cretins."

"They're my sisters," Endry said. "Ignore them and focus on the others. Good luck." He placed a hand on the groundling's shoulder and smiled as bravely as he could. "You're very brave, Nora."

"Chief, I can't go if you don't let go of my shoulder."

"Right," Endry said, suddenly awash in an embarrassing tide of memories from a world that was gone. "Fight well, Wing Leader."

"Yes, sir!" Nora answered with a rough salute. She hopped astride a black bird fitted with a small saddle and harness. With a kick of her heels she took to the sky at the head of a flock of three.

"Oh, look," Iliona said. "He's sad."

"Aw," Veesa chimed in. "Poor little guy. Bet he wishes he hadn't abandoned us for his cretins."

Endry finally noticed the sisters were speaking of him, and clenched his teeth. He sprang from atop Kiel's head and hovered before them.

"My cretins—my *groundlings*—are fighting back against *her*. The mother." Endry pointed at them in turn. "What have you done? The least you had to, and now you're standing there bickering like new growth while the Groundling Wing Guard goes heroically into battle. The sapling wants this giant, and she's going to get this giant. And we're going to keep those slaves in the sky from taking him instead. If you want to help, help, if not, you'll have to excuse me."

"This isn't about fighting the—about fighting *her*," Veesa said. "It's about freedom from her. Who said we had to fight her?"

"What did you think was going to happen?" Endry was surprised to hear Iliona asking the question he was about to ask himself. Subtly, Iliona took a step to the side—closer to him.

"Oh, no," Veesa said. "You two are *not* teaming up against me. Think about this. There are thirty of them here, but you both know how many of them—of us—there are! We can't. They're us."

"We can," Endry said, "and I will. They're not us. They haven't seen what we've seen and they don't remember what we all remember, and I don't think they're going to wait for us to explain it to them."

With that, he sped into the air after Nora's magpie, scanning the sky for the nearest target. He'd given up trying to think tactically; he just wanted to punch something, from embarrassment, desperation, or anger he wasn't sure—probably all three.

He spotted the perfect target after a few seconds. He pulled ahead of Nora, who signaled she'd found her own target: a pair of females who had uncoiled a silver line between them—a razor sharp line Endry knew was woven by a unique spider that lived in burrows at the heart of Glen Elendra. When Nora kicked her mount in the side before he could shout a warning, he decided to leave the mean-looking male he'd been intending to hit and join the groundling wing leader.

"The line!" Endry called after Nora, his wings beating furiously against the smoky air to catch up with the swift black bird. "Don't touch it!"

Nora nodded her understanding, but Endry saw with horror his warning had come too late. The twin faeries dived toward her before Nora could rein up the magpie. With a flash of silver and an explosion of blood that shone black in the moonlight, they drew the line through the magpie's neck.

"Nora!" Endry called as the screaming groundling bird rider felt her mount turn to dead weight beneath her knees. Then she was dropping from the sky, and the murderous faerie twins were circling for another pass. Endry folded his wings against his back and dived after the plummeting bird.

It was fortunate, he supposed, that the wicked twins had only taken the bird's head—the magpie's dead, splayed wings provided some wind resistance and slowed Nora's drop, but also caught enough of the warm air to carry her forward, away from the aerial battleground the sky above the fallen giant had suddenly become. Endry let his own wings slide outward but did not flex them, instead using them to guide himself along the same path the dead bird followed.

Nora twisted around in the saddle, covered with blood but still as fearless as ever. "What do I do?" she called. "We're going to hit the ground too fast!"

"Get out of the saddle!" Endry said. "Now!"

Just as he reached the same altitude as the dead magpie, Endry flexed his wings at last and shot forward, hoping Nora finished unbuckling herself from the saddle before he reached her. She managed it just in time, and he scooped the groundling up under the arms moments before the bird's corpse smashed into a rock still hot from the simmering fires burning in the loamy soil below. It sizzled grotesquely.

"Take me back to the fight," Nora said angrily. "I'm going to make them pay for that."

"But you don't have your bird," Endry said, finding himself a bit tongue-tied at this proximity to the groundling. She doesn't remember me, he thought, but that doesn't mean she wouldn't be open to the idea of—

"Endry!" Nora exclaimed, and he swerved to the right just in time to avoid the clutching branches of another improbably whole tree.

"Sorry about that," he said sheepishly.

"I don't have my bird," Nora said, "but I've got you. Can you manage the extra weight?"

"If you keep them off our backs, I'll keep them off our fronts," Endry said, and he hoped he did so heroically.

"You've got it," Nora said, drawing a tiny sling into which she placed a five-pronged bramble, one of many she'd dipped in widow venom before the battle. Originally she'd intended to use the poison on the giant to paralyze Kiel's legs if Endry failed to put him to sleep. They'd both hoped it wouldn't be necessary, and it hadn't been.

"One of those has enough venom to kill a faerie," Endry observed uncertainly.

"Yes," Nora said. "The sapling will understand."

Endry grimaced. "I hope so. Can you aim?"

"Just hold me steady," the groundling replied, and Endry heard the sling began to whir in the air as Nora spun it in place, choosing which of the twins she would hit first. She barked an objection when a sudden gust of air sent Endry bobbing sideways for a moment. Iliona's wings beat like mad, forcing her brother to shift the tilt of his wings to compensate, and he called an apology to his passenger.

"You're not going to stop me," he told Iliona. "Where's Veesa?"

"She's standing by," said Iliona with a roll of her eyes. "In protest."

"What?" Endry said. "We need flyers! Why isn't she going to help?"

"She can't make up her mind," Iliona said irritably. "Says she wants to see who wins, and she'll go with them. Maralen's not going to like that. She's breaking our oath."

"Wonderful," Nora snapped. "Now will you two shut up?"

"Groundworm—"

"Iliona," Endry said.

"Ground*ling*, you are taking the one on the left?"

"Yes," Nora said.

"Well, you can have it. I shall have the one on the right. And groundling? Don't miss."

CHAPTER 9

"What is that sound, sapling?" Rhys asked. "I've never heard the like."

"The Fae are killing each other," the sapling said. "Or rather, a number of faeries are doing their best to kill a few faeries who wish to part from their Great Mother. It saddens me that so few seeds fall very far from that particular tree."

"The Great Mother of the Fae is a tree? Like you?"

"No," the sapling said. "Oona wears the living things of this world like a kithkin wears a cloak—or more accurately, like the elves of the forest wear the vines. The real Oona is within Glen Elendra, a place no one has ever seen. Certainly not me."

"Why do they fight each other?" asked the elf. He found it easy to ask questions of this yew, so much like the Colfenor he'd known, but with less of the old tree's arrogance and presumption. "Doesn't the Destroyer threaten Oona as much as the rest of us? Last I checked, that monster wasn't being particular about whom or what she burned, and faeries don't strike me as particularly fireproof."

"Before this ends, more will fight their own kind," the sapling said, her voice very much reminding Rhys of Colfenor's at that moment. "Especially the Fae. They will choose whom to serve and will go to war with those who serve the wrong mistress."

"Which one is the wrong mistress?"

"I do not have that answer," the sapling said. "I can only tell you what I think. Oona's reign must end."

"Oona's reign?" Rhys said. "She is only the queen of the Fae, and most of the world thinks she's a legend. She does not control the elves, or the treefolk, or the boggarts. She doesn't control the kithkin, and nobody controls the merrow."

"My student," the sapling said. "Rhys. Your presence has all but opened Colfenor's legacy to me. I can feel him in my mind, waiting to tell me all he knows, but for now he tantalizes. If I am to know more, if we are to achieve the destiny the Red Yew put before us both long ago, we must ignore the fighting for a time. The Fae must battle, and we must shut out everything else. We must join our minds, and you must help me unlock the bonds holding Colfenor's memories back."

"How do you know I can help?" Rhys said. "I don't even know you. I'm taking you at your word that you even knew Colfenor." He stopped, realizing he'd been strolling alongside the sapling for almost a mile now with no real idea of their destination.

"Let me show you," the sapling said. She held out her wide, branching hands and held them palms upward. "Place your hands in mine and we will find Colfenor together."

Rhys had done it before he even really had a chance to consider the implications—and the dangers—of trusting this strange creature. Colfenor was long gone, but old habits died hard. He'd trusted Colfenor a great deal despite their frequent arguments, and he found it difficult to resist the sapling's suggestion. He placed his hands in her woody appendages and didn't make a sound as tiny tendrils snaked from the ends of her fingers and coiled around his. Nor did he object when even tinier needles sprang from the coils to pierce the skin on the back of his hands in a thousand places. And then Rhys didn't see the coils or feel the needles, because he was in a world of light.

That was all Rhys could see at first, the light. It was blinding, unbelievably bright, as if the entire Wilt-Leaf had been put to the torch in an instant and then burned for eternity. Then his eyes adjusted and he saw the brightness filled not only the sky but bounced off anything and everything it touched in an explosion of color and life unlike anything that had ever existed in the world.

"What—what is it?" he asked the sapling. "What did you do?"

"I have merely shown you what was," the sapling's voice said, but it wasn't just her voice anymore. It was also Colfenor's, she was Colfenor, and Rhys realized in that moment there wasn't really any difference. Then the moment passed, and Colfenor was gone, and Rhys was walking through this strange landscape of light and color—light without burning, color without death—at the sapling's side.

"Colfenor is here somewhere," Rhys said, irritated that he seemed to be full of nothing but questions and determined to make a statement for once. "We're looking for him. Why do you need me?"

"Another question." The sapling laughed. "And yet I can tell you are trying not to ask them. Why?"

"Because you're not particularly forthcoming with answers. Why have you brought me here?"

The sapling laughed again, and this time Rhys detected Colfenor's tone again, at once welcome and frustrating. "Still you don't understand, and it is my fault, brother. You were always meant to be the one who helped me achieve my potential—who helped me bring Colfenor forward into this world, where he does not belong. That is the only reason he is here with us now. Much of this you will not understand, because you cannot, but know that your old mentor has told me we are on the right path. I know where we must go and what we must do."

"You will help us stop the Destroyer," Rhys said. "Surely if you have Colfenor's power, you can—"

"I have his knowledge and his soul, for lack of a better word. The power I have—what I have—is my own. He could not send *that* forward into the new world."

"New world?" Rhys said. "What are you talking about?"

The sapling ignored his question. "Your very presence here is what was needed. What he needed. Now we must go away to the place I thought we were to go back then. The timing was wrong then, you see. Too soon." The sapling stopped, and the bright light began to shimmer like the illusion it always had been. The golden light turned to silver, the blue sky faded to grays and blacks, and the colors slipped into monochrome. "Shadowmoor is your world now. You are the Rhys I need, not the Rhys that was."

"You made a lot more sense before," Rhys said, "and even then you sounded crazy."

"Forgive me," the sapling replied. "We have, I see, gone as far as we can at the moment. But I must make you understand what we will fight for, when the time comes. We will travel to the kithkin doun known as Kinscaer, and there we will stop the Destroyer, for she too will be needed."

"The Destroyer can't be needed and stopped at the same time."

"It all depends on how we stop her," the sapling said. "But I can hear the fight raging on out there, and now we must return to our friends."

"Our friends?"

"The faerie called Endry, and the others. It would not have done for me to come to their rescue. They must be able to stand and fight on their own if Oona's grip is to be broken."

In a rush of cold air and moonlight like a bucket of water to the face of a sleeping man, Rhys felt himself returning to the real world, uncertain now whether it was quite so real. The sounds of the battling Fae returned, certainly no more than a hundred yards away.

"But now," said Rhys, "we can help them."

"Oh, yes," the sapling said, uncoiling the tendrils of her fingers from his hands. She hummed softly, and her branches seemed to grow even darker in the moonlight, her hands disappearing in black inky clouds of yew magic.

Without a word, Rhys felt himself drawing upon the same power, and it was easier than it had ever been. There had always been something holding him back—perhaps deep down he'd simply been waiting for Colfenor's permission. He raised a fist hidden within the deadly energy. "One last question, then: Shall we?"

* * * * *

"Nora, behind us!" Endry called.

"Easy," the groundling replied, and Endry could hear the sling whirring in the air. "I don't have many more of these, and I don't want to waste my shot."

Despite Nora's instructions, Endry found he had to duck and maneuver just to keep from being pelted by the thorns, needles, and tiny bolts of energy from the Oona loyalists. "Why are they after me, specifically?" he muttered. "What did I do to them?"

"I think you're a marked man," Nora replied. "You're the only one with a passenger. One of only two with actual wings, for that matter."

"Ah, yes," Endry agreed. "You've gotten so skilled with the birds, I'd almost forgotten."

"Charming," Nora said. "Now hold still for another few seconds. There." The whirring sound ceased abruptly as the groundling released the toxic bramble, and a few seconds later Endry heard, but didn't see, a faerie scream in pain as the shot scored.

"How many is that now?" Endry said.

"Better question is how many are left," Iliona said, rising to meet them with a half-mad grin on her face and a bloody Fae needle-sword clutched in one hand. In the other she held a single faerie wing with mercifully unfamiliar markings. "They'll have to turn back soon."

"No," Endry said, "I don't think so. Not while they can always just retreat and attack again from above." He grimaced. "Besides, if they turn back they'll just report everything to the Great Mother. Everything the Great Mother doesn't already know, that is."

I know a great deal, Little Endry. I know exactly where you are. I know what you are trying to do and what you think you serve. You are wrong, but I forgive you. I love you, Little Endry, and will always welcome you home.

"What?" Endry said, but found he was unable to say anything more. Nora didn't seem to notice; Endry heard another shot whirring in her sling and decided to let her be. The voice was compelling and immediately familiar. *Oona,* his heart cried, *Mother of Us All.* This was nothing like the crude, blunt telepathy Maralen used to order "her" faeries around, a yoke he'd already thrown off on his own. This was the mind of the being that had created him, focused directly upon his own. And though Endry was certainly strong-willed for a faerie, he was no match for the Great Mother.

Continue your fight; it is of no consequence. I will tell you how you can finish it, and then I will allow you to speak again. You will not betray me.

Endry didn't have to respond, because he knew it was true.

It took some convincing, especially where Iliona was concerned—Endry, at Oona's suggestion, sent Iliona to lead a wing of bird-riders to flank the loyalists—but a few minutes later Nora was relaying the order to the groundling warriors below. Their numbers were dwindling, cut down by teams of loyalists wielding razor wire and needle-swords, so perhaps that was why they seemed cheered by this new tactic. Surely it was better than picking off the loyalists one at a time. Besides, Endry thought, what happened when Oona sent reinforcements?

Surely Oona was right. The best way to defeat Oona was to do as Oona asked.

"On my mark, cut him loose!" Endry called to the groundling warriors stationed at the lines. "Mark!"

Thank you, Little Endry, Oona told the renegade faerie. *Now you must do your part.*

Standing astride the still sleeping giant, Endry drove his blade into the giant's neck—a point with much thinner hide, Oona said—and allowed the antidote to his sleep poison to enter Kiel's blood stream. He left the sword lodged in the giant's neck and leaped clear as the rumbling began.

Very good. It was good of you to break free of the imposter's sway, because I have missed you and your sisters. But do not come home, my child; do not come home to Glen Elendra. Stay with your sapling and your vermin. Guide them to Kinscaer. They believe they will defeat the Destroyer there, and so must you believe it. Even though they will fail and the imposter will die.

Endry believed it with all his heart.

I will leave you again for now, Little Endry. I will not burden you with memories. You may best serve me where you are, when I choose, so continue your journey. You had a brilliant inspiration, and you freed the giant to fight your enemies, who even now are retreating. You have saved the vermin, the tree, and freed the giant to fight the Destroyer. Endry looked to the sky and saw that it was true—the loyalists were retreating even though the groundlings were on the verge of defeat. Then the sky disappeared behind fifty-odd feet of stinking, leathery, hairy and growling giant.

The faerie stopped short and hovered in midair as Kiel railed at the sky. When the giant paused to catch his breath, Endry heard a welcome and familiar voice rising up from the boughs of a red yew who stood tall for her age. The voice, however, was not happy.

"Endry!" the sapling cried. "What have you done?"

"I saved us all, didn't I?" Endry said. "And now we have a way to fight the Destroyer, too! Isn't that why you wanted him?" He spotted the elf at the sapling's side as he dipped below her upper boughs and Endry exclaimed, "Rhys! Sapling, you found Rhys!"

"Have we met?" Rhys asked. "Why does everyone know me?"

"Fire! Smoke! Catastrophe!" bellowed Kiel, shaking his fist at the fleeing loyalists who were already well out of his reach. "Kinsbaile!" Groundlings scattered as he took a single step toward them, and he added, "Fire in the night!"

"He possesses the blood of Rosheen," the sapling said, her voice leveling off from the full Colfenor to a slightly deeper timbre Endry found equally unsettling. "He has knowledge I need to—" she broke off, eyeing the faerie oddly. "Endry? Why did you free the giant?"

"To fight!"

"You have to admit," Rhys said, "he would be a big help."

"I cannot simply seize control of a giant," the sapling said. "Not without help."

"So don't seize control," Iliona said, returning to the

group—from where, Endry did not see. Her groundling contingent had detached to help those on the ground avoid getting squashed. "Convince him."

"He is—" The sapling winced. "He has knowledge I need. True, I had hoped he would also fight on our side in the—against the Destroyer. But I intended to coax him into doing that while he was fast asleep and I could speak directly to his fractured mind."

Kiel took another step, still disoriented. His stream of babble had not begun again, and he swayed like a drunken kithkin: in no real danger of falling over but giving the appearance of extreme unsteadiness.

"There's only one person who has any influence over Kiel," Endry said, feeling a sudden inspiration from out of nowhere—the place he got all of his best ideas. "That's Rosheen, right?"

"Right," Iliona said, and then she added, "That is, I think so. Was a time he wouldn't shut up about her. Rosheen this. Rosheen that. Tell me a story. Remember?"

"So we just need to convince him that one of us is Rosheen."

"Not me," Nora and Iliona said almost simultaneously. Endry turned to the sapling. "You are pretty tall, Yewling," the faerie said. "You've grown up so fast."

"I don't like this," the sapling said.

"Just keep your mouth shut unless I wave at you behind my back. And then just release a stream of babble like Kiel here does. But not for too long."

"But I look nothing like a giant!" the sapling said, reminding Endry for the first time in a great while of the raw, untested tree he'd befriended more than a year ago.

"You were enchanted by Oona!" Endry said. "Enchanted into a tree."

"Mention goats, too," Iliona said. "Goats are key."

"And the Destroyer," Rhys said. "Or am I the only one who remembers what and who we're trying to stop?"

Endry was pleased to find Kiel didn't need the wild story in the end. He may have been a rambling giant, but he seemed to fixate on Rhys almost immediately. Though it clearly made the elf uncomfortable, Endry couldn't say he minded. Anything to keep his friend the sapling out of danger.

Danger is everywhere, little Endry.

Endry shivered but wasn't sure why.

* * * * *

Brigid took Sygg's clawed hand in her own, mustering enough courage not to shiver as she shook it. The merrow crime lord floated in a column of shapewater, part of a larger craft he'd easily called forth once his wounds were seen to. "Sygg," she said, intentionally omitting his title. "It's been a while. Didn't expect you to shake my hand so readily."

"Consider that a sign of how desperate I am," the merrow replied. "You tried to kill me, traitor. More than once. Lots of things, lots of people try to kill me. Time was I could deal with them easily. The river was always on my side, her currents serving my ends and her eddies confusing my enemies. But the river doesn't listen to her children anymore. The lanes are quiet and cold, and the Destroyer has tainted the Source."

Maralen stood, uneasily grasping at a rail Brigid called up for her. "Why does this matter to us?" she said with forced nonchalance. "Are you certain it's the Destroyer and not just a change in the weather?" The last was directed at the kithkin, and Brigid thought it remarkably unsubtle of the woman to whom she'd sworn her loyalty. The long trip on the Wanderbrine seemed to be getting to the elf like little else the kithkin outsider had seen. It wasn't nausea, exactly—to Brigid it looked more like exhaustion and hunger, which didn't make much sense when one considered Maralen was getting as much rest and food as the rest of them.

"Because the lanes are quiet, but the Source," Sygg said as he flashed a smile filled with needlelike teeth, "The Source has spoken to me. She spoke to me after we sought her out, but not before she killed many of us." The smile disappeared, and the bulbous lantern-eyes became slits. "There is a reason the lanes are cold, and it's more than the Destroyer. She can only do so much harm. The water never dies."

Brigid's hand went instinctively to her neck, and Sygg nodded. "She said you have something that belongs to the merrow, and insinuated it specifically belongs to me. The Source of the Wanderbrine said you took something from me. Funny thing, but I don't remember that at all."

"Why would the Source lie to you?" Brigid asked, raising a hand to keep Maralen from snapping off a retort. Sygg had agreed to join them, and he'd also said he'd explain what happened along the way while his surviving merrow subordinates rested and healed. There was no reason to antagonize him, even if Sygg was baiting them.

"I don't think she did," Sygg said, "which you know perfectly well, I think."

"All right," Brigid said. "Let's say I'm wearing—that I possess something of yours. Why did I take it? Why don't *you* take it? I'm right here."

"Aside from the fact that I'm not quite up to snuff, which I freely admit," Sygg said, "You're protected. No merrow can do you harm. Surely you've noticed." Brigid fought back a grin when she saw Maralen was for once truly surprised by something. The kithkin was surprised too, but she probably should have guessed—she *had* been inordinately lucky on occasion over the last year or so, and she'd spent an awful lot of that time on the river and in the company of merrow who would normally as soon cut a landwalker's throat as work with her. Yet she'd done just that for many months after Lorwyn became Shadowmoor.

"Then I don't see any reason to give it back," Brigid said.

"Oh, there's a very good reason," Sygg said. "You'll want to hear me out. But first, let me introduce you to my crew, or what's left of 'em."

"Brigid?" Wryget asked from his position at the bow of the enlarged shapewater skiff. "Is everything—"

"Everything's fine," Brigid called.

"You should have killed him," Sygg snorted. "I'll be happy to take care of that for you, free of charge," he added, fingering one of the knives he wore across his chest.

"Wryget's not the subject, Sygg," Brigid said darkly. "Consider him *my* crew."

"Suit yourself," the merrow said, and he gestured to one of the three other columns of shapewater. "You remember Kasella."

"More than you know," Brigid muttered, and then she said more loudly, "Your 'personal assassin,' wasn't it? How goes the murder business, Kass?"

"I am more than an assassin, landwalker," the female merrow said coldly. "I look forward to showing you just how much more when you return what you stole. You are an abomination, and you will not see me before you feel my blade at your throat."

"Always a pleasure to be threatened by your crazy Inkfathom concubine, Sygg," said Brigid. "But who are the other two?"

"The green fellow is Scathak," Sygg said. "I found him working for a competitor in one of the northern tributaries, but he always refused my offers of employment. The Destroyer took care of my competitor, so now he works for me."

The green merrow simply nodded to Brigid, which sent a chill down her spine. He was wearing three times as many knives as Sygg, and seemed to give off waves of ice.

"I'd ask what he does, but I think I can guess."

"Oh, all three are accomplished killers. The big one, Artio," Sygg said. "He's not particularly talkative either, but he's strong as a storm current. He can squeeze the life out of anything he can fit between his claws and squeeze the life out of anything else with shapewater."

"And yet you're all just the survivors of the last meeting you had with the Source," Maralen interjected. "Brigid, we don't need them. *You* have the Crescent. Given time—"

"But the Source will not cooperate for a landwalker," Sygg said, "no matter what she wears around her neck. The Source will stop your Destroyer, but only if I, Sygg, use the Crescent to make it so."

"I'm not giving the Crescent up until the Destroyer is finished," Brigid said, before the implications sunk in. Even when they did, she felt almost relieved—soon she'd know one way or the other if she'd forget her past. "That's the deal. It's the only one you're going to get."

"Of course," the merrow replied. "That is why you will also be a part of this. You cannot stop the Destroyer without us, but we cannot stop her without you. And we all want her stopped, do we not?"

"We do," Maralen said. She might have been about to say something more, but then her attention—and the attention of everyone aboard the shapewater skiff—was distracted by the unexpected sound of an argument coming from overhead, and getting closer.

"You shouldn't have done that, Iliona! It was wrong!"

"You can't keep going on about this. What's done is done."

"They were Fae!"

"They were going to kill us!"

"They were going to kill *Endry*. I don't trust him anymore."

"What news from the second front, ladies?" Maralen asked.

"Lots," Veesa said. "Iliona killed—"

"That's not important," the larger faerie interrupted. "They're going to Kinscaer."

"The yewling said the Destroyer was headed there," Veesa said.

"Who?" Brigid asked. "Who said that?"

Iliona looked around at the merrow, all of whom were watching the new arrivals with intense curiosity—merrow and faeries rarely mixed. "I'm not sure I should say in front of—"

"Who?" Maralen demanded. "There are no secrets here." Brigid had to stifle a bitter laugh when she heard that.

"Rhys, the sapling, the giant, and Endry," Iliona said. "Endry and his vermin, I should say. They're going to make a stand there. Maybe they're going to have the giant step on her?"

"I doubt it," Maralen said. "I think I may have underestimated that fluff-headed yew. She already knew we'd be coming, and that we'd be bringing the power to stop the Destroyer. I'd say she's counting on it, and I have to agree." She turned to Brigid. "Kinscaer. That's where we'll make our stand."

"It's as good a place as any," Sygg said to break the silence. "River's close. If the Source cooperates, of course."

"She'll have to, won't she?" Brigid said, patting the Crescent of Morningtide. "Now, Captain," she added, deliberately nodding with respect to the merrow criminal who had been a friend and an enemy to her in two different lives, "why don't you start going over the specifics of this magic that can stop the Destroyer? It sounds like I'll be up to my neck in it."

CHAPTER 10

High above Kinscaer, the Destroyer's rage seared the sky with fire. Huge plumes of flame jetted from her body, arcing high into the midnight clouds above, where they cooled, hardened, and fell again as smoking boulders of red-hot rock. Swirling rings of eerie orange fire ignited above and behind her until the sky itself seemed armored in flaming mail.

The roaring demon pointed both hands down at Kinscaer. The fiery array above her collapsed and merged into a single swirling vortex. A flaming funnel dropped from the ring and plunged toward the doun below. The cyclone's tail slammed into Kinscaer, which vanished under a ball of blinding light and waves of blistering heat, but the Destroyer's magical fury never reached the doun. When the terrible glare faded, the great walled kithkin village stood exactly as it had been. Virtually all of the countryside around the doun stood ablaze with unchecked wildfires spreading to the north, west, and south, but Kinscaer itself remained as it was, unchanged since the Destroyer had breached its outer walls and leveled its town square.

The monster howled in frustration. Her power grew ever hotter and more intense, but the kithkin had gone to ground like the miserable little beetles they were, huddling in a wretched ball with their hard backs facing outward. She ought to be able to cook them in their holes with an angry glare, to crack their shells and bake their innards with a thought. But it was clear now that as long as the witch Tarcha remained alive, Kinscaer was beyond the Destroyer's reach. Here, as there had been at Mistmeadow, was magic strong enough to counter hers and a caster skilled enough to employ it.

The flames surrounding the Destroyer contracted. The energies within her demanded release and she longed to indulge them, but her fury would not allow her to turn away from Kinscaer. The cenn was dead, but the doun itself endured, and so her vengeance remained maddeningly incomplete. Stretched between these two undeniable urges, the Destroyer could not move toward either. She was a creature of impulse and action but now, perhaps for the first time since her endless rampage began, the Destroyer was forced to pause.

Her vague and ragged thoughts flickered like candlelight, their frantic dance slowly cooling as the gallop of hooves in her ears settled into a calm, even canter. It was her nature to move forward, to settle on a target, raze it to the ground, and then settle on a new target. Before Mistmeadow, nothing she attacked had ever survived beyond a few traumatized witnesses, whom she spared to tell the world of her terrible glory.

Intuition and inspiration collided, striking sparks that cascaded through the Destroyer's mind. These scintillating bits of thought aligned themselves into rows, and then the rows braided themselves together and came to a needle-sharp point that stabbed upward from deep inside her skull. For one glorious, majestic moment, she understood her place in the world, her role in it, and her impact on it. Vivid jags of crimson lightning flashed from her hands, and thunder shook Kinscaer below to its foundations. The Destroyer threw back her head and howled her mad joy up into the sky.

If it was her nature to act, it was also the world's nature to react. Though its vital force was dim and muted, Shadowmoor was still a living place, populated by living creatures that employed living magic. The longer the Destroyer's campaign went on, the more time places like Mistmeadow and Kinscaer had to prepare for her arrival. As the wake of destruction grew wider and more terrifying behind her, the communities in the path ahead would fight all the harder and more desperately to keep from becoming part of it.

The Destroyer laughed again. It seemed so simple now, so obvious. Her quarry was adapting to her tactics, and so she must adapt to theirs. She snarled down at Kinscaer one last time. Her body stiffened and hung rigid in the sky. Slowly, the Destroyer turned her head back and rotated forward until she was looking down on the complex series of marinas and docks that dotted the banks of the nearby Wanderbrine.

With malevolent flames dancing in her eyes and searing yellow sparks streaming from her hair, the Destroyer plummeted face-first toward the river.

* * * * *

Augur Tarcha kneeled at the center of the burned-out Kinscaer town square. Hundreds of her fellow villagers stood around her, chanting softly in quiet vigil, their blank white eyes wide and unblinking.

The kithkin augur pressed her hands together as she struggled to maintain her focus without raising her voice above the crowd. Her spells and charms were potent, but they required perfect harmony from the communal mass-mind and she couldn't afford to stand out. The mindweft that connected them all was already fractured and discordant without Cenn Alloway's commanding presence. Tarcha feared it would weaken further if the assembly started focusing on her as its new leader instead of on maintaining the protective spell.

Warree Tarcha was no leader, no cenn, and she could no more plan the doun's next move than she could drive the Destroyer away for good. Even if Tarcha could spare the concentration to start planning ahead, she did not have the force of personality to organize them for action.

So the doun itself would have to decide and then act as a single entity—and their mindweft was already gravely wounded, even crippled. The formerly robust Kinscaer collective was missing almost a third of its voices. Beyond that, Tarcha reckoned that between the scores of kithkin who died during the Destroyer's first attack and those who were now simply too scared to think, the doun had little more than half its usual muster. She was grateful the mindweft kept growing incrementally stronger as survivors overcame their panic. As each realized Tarcha's efforts were the only thing keeping Kinscaer alive, they each then joined in to help fuel the ritual.

The citizens of Kinscaer drew courage and hope from the fact that despite her best efforts, the Destroyer had failed. That renewed the barrier's strength, but Tarcha herself was another matter. Everyone knew Augur Tarcha was old, and no one knew it better than Tarcha herself. She had lived a long life and stood now as a respected mother, grandmother, and great-grandmother to successive generations of kithkin. Though her spells were stronger than ever, maintaining this one in this fashion had already taken a terrible toll on her. She didn't know how much longer she could last,

"Hail to you, brave kithkin." The rich, soothing voices seemed to float down from the empty air above Tarcha. "We are the voice of Oona, Queen of the Fae, and we have come to offer her assistance."

The kithkin chanting continued unabated. Tarcha spared a single thought for the newcomers, but she was the only one. Everyone knew the Fae were not to be trusted, that they delighted in distracting others at crucial moments.

Four large male faeries floated down from above, their gleaming golden bodies arranged in a tight diamond formation. Glittering golden dust fell from their wings, and they spoke in unison. "Well met, defenders of Kinscaer. Help has arrived at last, and with it a guarantee of your doun's survival. Will you take it?"

Tarcha was not able to acknowledge them, so she simply stared.

The lowest faerie in the array bowed. "Rejoice, O wise and noble Warree Tarcha. Your enemy has withdrawn. And though we would never wish to distract you from the defense of your doun, we do crave an audience. Relent, as the Destroyer has, and speak with us. Oona would mourn the loss of this rare opportunity to stand with Kinscaer."

Tarcha did not respond, but she felt concern and distrust spreading through the mindweft. These faeries were not of Kinscaer. They weren't even kithkin. It would not be easy for the dounsfolk to hear the faeries' offer, much less accept it.

Careful not to alter the volume or pitch of her chanting, the old woman glanced up through the translucent barrier that shielded the doun and on into the empty sky above.

"You see?" said the lowest faerie. "The Destroyer's hunger has driven her to seek easier targets. We have time to discuss certain unpleasant realities and their remedies, but only if we begin quickly."

Tarcha stood up straight, using her gnarled wooden cane to maintain her balance. The mindweft wavered, but she coaxed it back to full strength with a warm and encouraging push. She stopped chanting, looked up at the glittering quartet, and then Tarcha bowed. "Children of the Fae. What do you want here?"

"To stop that mindless, destructive thing," all four faeries said together. "We would see her removed entirely from this world. She should not be here. She should not *be* at all. The power she wields cannot be permitted to run wild, and less so the malicious will that guides it. This Destroyer is unnatural and an abomination."

An indignant ripple swept across the mindweft. "She is terrible to behold," Tarcha admitted. "But she is fueled by elemental fire. Such creatures are the embodiment of deep, wild magic. Here in Kinscaer, we hold those fierce spirits sacred. They cannot be unnatural, cannot be abominations."

"And yet your whole life has been devoted to magically neutralizing their power."

"You are much mistaken," Tarcha said stiffly. "I am an augur. I have learned to focus the flow of elemental magic in order to understand its character and direction."

"And in doing so, you have also learned to redirect that flow, to shunt it aside from those it might harm. Do not be fooled, Tarcha of Kinscaer: the Destroyer is no sacred elemental, but something darker and far more loathsome. She is no divine spirit, but a damned demon of bloody-minded vengeance."

The faeries spread, maintaining their diamond shape across a much larger area. "Was the destruction of your town square a sacred act? Was the murder of Donal Alloway and all who stood with him? The Destroyer is indeed fueled by elemental fire, so it is not surprising someone as sensitive as you mistook her for a true elemental spirit.

"She is not. She is a corruption of that sacred power, a twisted and defiled incarnation of something ancient and profound. On behalf of our Queen Mother, we seek your help to stop the Destroyer here, to end her wretched life and cage the raw power she commands."

Tarcha shook her head. "What you ask is impossible," she said. "Kinscaer's strength is fading. We can barely defend ourselves."

"But you are no longer alone. Together, Kinscaer and the Fae can do more than forestall the Destroyer's frenzy. We can stop her completely. We can unmake her and negate the threat she poses."

A ghastly orange glow suddenly illuminated the skies to the east, and a rumble rolled in from the Wanderbrine River. Tarcha smelled fresh smoke and saw clouds of soot and steam rising.

The topmost faerie broke formation and descended to Tarcha's eye. "She will not stay at the river for long," the golden male said. "She will return here and renew her assault on your doun. Are you strong enough to stop her?"

"I am," Tarcha said sternly.

"Then do so. That is all Oona asks of Kinscaer. Fend off the Destroyer's attacks while the Fae engage her directly. We will confront her, defeat her, and in so doing save your homes and neighbors."

Tarcha's own thoughts mirrored those of the larger mind-weft. No one trusted the faeries, but no one really believed the doun could hold out much longer on its own.

"You hesitate," the lead faerie said. "But Oona is not offended. Rather, she is flattered that your close-knit community would even entertain such an offer from an outsider. Now, having entertained it, Kinscaer must decide." The sparkling winged figure zipped up and rejoined his brothers in formation.

"Here," they said. "Allow us to demonstrate Oona's good faith. The healers and herbalists of Kinscaer know much about the restorative power of certain plants. Oona knows more, far more. In aid of achieving our shared goals, the Queen of the Fae offers Kinscaer this."

The faeries flew along the edges of their diamond formation, stopping only when there was a golden brother at each corner. The continued to switch places, rotating in and out of these fixed positions so quickly that they never seemed to move, yet left solid trails of golden light in their wake. A small greenish sphere formed in the center of their array. Tarcha heard the soft puff of imploding air before a shower of seeds clattered to the stony ground.

The seeds immediately split open to release green shoots that crawled across the blackened surface of the town square. As Tarcha watched, a thick cluster of vines grew waist-high beside her, with blue sharp-pointed leaves sheltering clusters of purple-black berries.

"What is that?" the kithkin sage asked.

"Sustenance." The faeries' eyes glittered. "When the time is right and your collective strength is failing, the slightest touch of these vines will enrich and restore you. Even if you do not accept Oona's offer, accept this as a gift, a token of her hopes for Kinscaer's future."

Tarcha stared at the faeries for a moment and then she looked down on the increasingly large tangle of vines. She waited for the mindweft to provide the doun's verdict, or at least for some indication of how Kinscaer wanted to proceed, but the collective was too weary to decide, too confused and frightened. The longer Tarcha looked for an answer, the deeper into the mindweft she sank, and the more certain she became that the final decision had to be hers alone.

Kinscaer, its citizens, and its mindweft were all accustomed to relying on a strong leader. They had accepted the subordinate role in the *lanamnas* between governor and governed, and so while everyone knew Warree Tarcha was no cenn (and certainly no Donal Alloway), everyone expected her to stand up and take charge all the same.

"We accept," Tarcha said. "Though we have nothing to offer your queen in return for her aid."

"Oona requires no offering," the faeries said. "Acting in concert against the Destroyer is reward enough." The topmost faerie came forward and down, adding, "You have chosen well, Kinscaer. The entire world will benefit from your wisdom and bravery." An explosion boomed and a cloud of fire and smoke rose over the Wanderbrine. The lone faerie quickly darted back up to his brothers and all four bowed to Tarcha before rising gracefully into the sky.

"Stand fast, Kinscaer," they called. "Resist the Destroyer with all your might and do not despair. Help is here. We shall be ready to strike when her attention is fully fixed on you. Until then, draw upon the strength of Oona's gift and bask in the endless warmth of her love."

The Fae envoys disappeared from view. Tarcha carefully lowered herself back to a sitting position, pointedly turning her back on the vine thicket. No one liked owing faeries favors, but with a little bit of extra luck, they might survive this night without the Fae Queen's help.

Tarcha cleared her mind, lifted her voice, and stepped back into the mindweft.

* * * * *

The Destroyer circled over the center of the river outside Kinscaer, expanding outward in ever-increasing spirals. Below her sat the remains of the Kinscaer docks, now little more than a crude heap of broken boards and shattered beams. Decades of kithkin labor had been reduced to a single gigantic bonfire, a smoldering mound large enough to choke the river and force the Wanderbrine to fork around it on each side.

She reached the apex of her ascent and howled down at

the obscene wreck she had made. Kinscaer was now mortally wounded. Without access to the Wanderbrine for irrigation, drinking water, and the rare kithkin trade convoys who led springjacks along the river valley, the doun would wither in a matter of days. Even if the Destroyer moved on and left Kinscaer intact under its protective bubble, the doun would never rebuild in time, never recover from the injury she'd inflicted. Its citizens would become refugees, forced to seek out safety and shelter they would never find. She would see to that.

But of course the Destroyer had no intention of moving on. She reveled in anticipation of the ordeal she had already begun to visit on Kinscaer. No matter how well stocked they were now, the kithkin huddled inside the doun would soon fall to thirst and exhaustion. As they did, the magic spells protecting them would also weaken. Kinscaer's strength would diminish bit by agonizing bit until the Destroyer could punch through their protective barrier, or until they became so desperate that they came out to fight. No matter which course they pursued or how long they lasted, in the end the Destroyer would take them all, doun and residents alike.

She followed the billowing column of smoke down to its source. Her manic glee subsided somewhat—the bonfire looked far smaller and less impressive from this height. The river itself did not extinguish the magically created flames that licked up from the ragged pile, but they were definitely dimmer, muted. She tilted her head and glanced upriver, a new and even grander scheme forming behind her eyes.

Her original aim had been simply to sever Kinscaer from the river, now but she saw a way to increase both the scale and the impact of her efforts. As it was, the bonfire made sure that the river no longer flowed properly past Kinscaer, but it did still flow. Why had she settled for one doun when she could ruin every riverside community touching the Wanderbrine?

New purpose flooded the Destroyer's mind, and with it a dizzying surge of raw power. Intense heat distorted her view of the world as the flames in her hair and eyes went white-hot. She spread her arms and soared higher, smoothly rolling and banking like a bird of prey about to swoop. Her eyes settled on the Wanderwine's eastern banks several hundred yards upriver from the bonfire. The sound of hooves filled her ears, and for the first time she didn't simply revel in the ominous sound but called out to it and demanded more. The air itself ignited around her and she fell, screaming in wild abandon.

The Destroyer plowed into the rocky ground and vanished. A geyser of mud and water shot high into the air, followed by a thick cloud of dust and greasy smoke that obscured the surface of the river from one bank to the other. The soil around the smoking hole she'd made shuddered and heaved like a living thing.

The ground cracked and split, riven by wide sheets of bright yellow fire. A wide section of riverbank broke away and collapsed, and countless tons of soil, rocks, and dead trees slid into the water. The Wanderbrine had only a second or two to adjust to its suddenly narrowed passageway, and then the Destroyer exploded from beneath the spreading landslide in a great blast of fire and heat. She flashed across the river like a comet and buried herself in the banks along the Kinscaer side. Once more the ground shook, and then the Destroyer erupted back into the sky. Behind her, the western banks of the river collapsed and fell in beside the remains of their eastern counterparts.

Hovering just above the shifting, spreading mass, the Destroyer howled anew. The Wanderbrine's flow hadn't been stopped, but it had been choked to a mere trickle. The Destroyer's bonfire flared brighter, sending towers of flame into the sky. She brayed mad laughter that echoed off the frothy mix of mud, stone, and river water. The Wanderbrine, the life's blood of Shadowmoor, no longer flowed freely past Kinscaer, nor did it run on to replenish the lands downstream.

The crashing waves and shifting soil made it seem as if the river itself were bellowing in outrage. The Destroyer smiled savagely, but something troubling nagged at her. A tingling sensation started in the back of her skull, and she registered the unwelcome presence of someone, some *thing* else.

You are a fascinating monster. But you are wrong. The strange voice that came to the Destroyer's ears was strong and musical, somehow commanding and soothing at the same time. The fiery demon snarled, her eyes darting and her head jerking as she sought out the speaker.

You will never take Kinscaer or anyone in it. Your strength is unparalleled, but the kithkin have the perfect antidote to your madness, and its name is Warree Tarcha.

"That ancient kithkin witch?" the Destroyer hissed. "Old trees will topple in a strong wind," she said. "And then they burn like all the rest."

This old tree's roots run deep. Even without additional support, you would never have the force to topple Tarcha.

"Additional support," the Destroyer said. "Meaning you?"

Have a care, abominable thing, the voice said. *I am Oona, Queen of the Fae. I am your enemy. I stand with Tarcha and with Kinscaer.*

"Then you will die with them."

Foolish little matchstick. How brightly you burn! But do you really believe you can outshine the light that has caressed and protected the world for countless generations? Shadowmoor is as I wish it to be. No more, no less. It always has and shall ever be.

"Then it is your world that will burn at my command, Oona of the Fae," the Destroyer said. "Starting with Kinscaer. Your wishes are nothing to me. *You* are nothing to me."

Then come, Oona whispered. *Come to Kinscaer. The doun mocks you with its continued existence. Tarcha's magic mocks you. I mock you. Together, we say, "Do your worst."*

The Destroyer roared. Tendrils of fire swept out from her body, curling and grasping like blind snakes. The tingling presence withdrew, flowing toward Kinscaer like a stiff breeze. The Destroyer gathered her strength and prepared to follow, but movement on the riverbanks below distracted her.

Dozens of grim, shadowy shapes had emerged from the scrub forest along the road leading north. Some were as tall as elves, others short and stocky, but each of the dark silhouettes was irregular or incomplete. The taller figures smelled and felt familiar, though the Destroyer had not yet recognized them as members of one tribe or another. Still furious from her exchange with Oona, the Destroyer was nonetheless intrigued enough to descend and inspect these new arrivals.

The Destroyer's stiff, mask-like features crinkled in disgust as her feet touched down. She stood amid a large collection of miscreants from two of the most miserable and degraded tribes in the entire world: cinders and boggarts. Well over a hundred were already in view, with more shuffling out of the woods. In the darkness, they all seemed to be coated with a scabby veneer of crumbling black, with only the odd glowing eye or gleaming tooth standing out against the gloom.

The Destroyer sneered. The assembly stopped short. Was this what her horde looked like up close? She had known that clusters of the mad and the malevolent had taken to following in her wake, but she had never spared them more than a thought or two. Until now they had never mattered enough to warrant her full attention.

Two cinders at the front of the mob came forward, walking in lock step. The one on the left reflected her fire light as a ghostly blue shine that danced across its blackened torso, and the other glinted soft gold. Without a word, both cinders fell to their knees and pressed their foreheads into the soil.

"We serve the Extinguisher," they said together, the words barely discernable amid the harsh, cracking rasps of their breathing. "We are yours."

"The Extinguisher?" The flaming monster spat on the ground in front of the two kneeling figures. "I extinguish nothing, fools. I seek to build an inferno that will engulf the entire world."

"Fire is life," the gold-tinged cinder intoned.

The blue cinder replied, "And it shall consume all that is."

"When there is nothing left to burn, the fire will die."

"But from its ashes new life springs."

"We pledge our lives to the fire," they said together. "To she who is and commands the fire. Burn us up, Master. Burn us out. Extinguish us, that we may be reignited in the world to come."

The Destroyer's eyes narrowed. The rest of the tall figures in the growing mob all fell to their knees in silent supplication. Even the boggarts stood silent and still, seemingly paralyzed in their reverent awe.

A sharp smile curled at the corners of the Destroyer's stony face. "Perhaps I can put you to good use after all," she said.

CHAPTER 11

As his strange party approached Kinscaer, Rhys prepared himself for the devastation he knew they'd find. Despite the sapling's strangely confident, oft-repeated opinion that the doun would be still be standing when they arrived, Rhys was not encouraged. He had seen far too many safeholds and kithkin douns after the Destroyer was through with them, strolled through too many smoking ruins and counted too many charred bodies to be hopeful, especially after Mistmeadow.

The memory of Eidren's final effort pained Rhys, but it also hardened his resolve. The vigilant's sacrifice proved the Destroyer could be stopped by the right people with the right magic. The sapling was heir to Colfenor's wisdom, so she could indeed have the right magic. Rhys vowed to be the right person: if it cost him his life, he would make sure the sapling got the chance to use her inherited knowledge. The Destroyer must be stopped. Shadowmoor's beauty must be preserved.

They had one more hill to clear before they'd have a clear line of sight to the doun, but what they could see was disheartening. The sky directly over the kithkin stronghold was thick with smoke tinged by the dreadfully familiar orange glow.

Rhys held up his hand to stop the procession. The sapling drifted to a halt beside him—he didn't think he'd ever get used to the way she seemed to glide along the soil without actually moving her lower extremities—and peered intently over the hill in front of them. Endry hovered just behind the sapling, followed on the ground by a phalanx of his wingless faerie infantry and in the sky by a squadron of groundlings mounted on magpies. Kiel followed at a distance, treading lightly and taking incremental strides so as not to trample his cohorts or shake the ground below their feet.

Rhys's sharp ears heard the sounds of battle: screams of valor and terror, arrows whistling through the air, blades cleaving through flesh and bone. He carefully mounted the top of the hill, but there was too much smoke and haze between them and the doun. He could barely see the Wanderbrine itself from where he stood. Rhys gestured for the sapling to join him, and as she approached he called out to Kiel in the distance, "Can you see? Is the doun still standing?"

Kiel rose up on his toes so that his long beard barely scraped the ground. "Still there," he rumbled.

"Then we're luckier than we deserve," Rhys said.

"Not luck," the sapling said vacantly. She was staring not at the smoke and fire that enveloped Kinscaer, but straight out over it, into the empty sky above. "Something has baffled her for the moment."

The sounds of fighting continued, and Rhys shook his head. "It doesn't sound like anything's baffled down there." To Kiel he said, "Do you see the Destroyer?"

Kiel grunted in the negative. Endry floated forward to Rhys and said, "Sapling's right. There's more than fire and swords at play here. Something familiar. I don't like it."

"A barrier," the sapling said. "The Kinscaer mindweft has erected a barrier against her power. The Destroyer is unable to get through, so the kithkin are safe for now."

"I don't know about barriers," Endry said, truculently folding his arms. "But I know when I'm being watched. Somebody is lurking down there and they don't want to be seen."

"The Destroyer doesn't hide," Rhys said.

Endry huffed angrily and turned away. He zipped down to ground level and chided his platoon for not standing at complete attention.

Rhys said to the sapling, "Then again, it's never taken her more than a few hours to burn down a village before, either. How sure are you about this barrier?"

"Quite sure," the sapling said. "I can hear them singing, hundreds of them. They're singing to one of their own, and she is turning their song into a protective shield." She turned to Rhys, her eyes clear and bright. "It's beautiful."

"Can we get through the barrier?"

"Oh, yes. That is, I believe so. It blocks elemental magic, and we don't have any."

Rhys nodded. "Then all we need to do is reach the gates? Once we're inside, it will protect us, too?"

"I don't see why not."

"All right," Rhys said. "Kiel, Endry, listen closely. We are going straight for the main gate. There will be boggarts and cinders and who knows what else between here and there, but we aren't looking for a fight with them. Defend yourselves as necessary, but don't stop."

"We'll go first!" Endry said. "Me and my groundlings!"

"Kiel goes first," Rhys said. "The rest of us are riding." He looked up into the giant's small, beady eyes. "All right with you?"

Kiel nodded. "All right, Boss."

"That's no fun at all," Endry said.

"It's not supposed to be."

Endry grumbled, but instead of arguing the point he lighted atop a small stump near his groundling infantry. "Climb the giant!" he ordered. "Spread out and hang on." He waved at the squadron of magpie-riders. "You too! Pick a level spot on one of his shoulders and dig in!"

As the column of wingless faeries marched up Kiel's boot and the magpies arranged themselves on his shoulders, Rhys spoke to the sapling. "Once we reach Kinscaer," he said. "What are you planning to do?"

The sapling blinked. "I think our first step should be to consult the cenn."

"Don't be clever with me," Rhys said. "I'm not Endry. What do you intend to do?"

"I don't mean to be clever," The sapling's expression was open and innocent. "I just don't understand."

"You keep talking about 'Colfenor's wisdom' and 'Colfenor's purpose,' but you haven't ever explained what that means. When the Destroyer comes, what are you going to do?"

"You and I are going to stop her once and for all. She must not be allowed to continue."

"So you mean to kill her?"

"I sincerely hope not. She and I already have too many sins balanced against one another."

Rhys brushed that sentiment aside with a wave of his hand. "What, then? Do you have magic that can counter hers?"

"I do. Though it will not be easy to work that magic while she is enraged and at the peak of her strength. Once we are inside Kinscaer, we must find a way to subdue her."

"And so we're back where we started," Rhys said. "How do we accomplish any of this?"

"Once we are inside Kinscaer," the sapling said again. "And I have examined this barrier more closely."

Rhys clenched his jaw. "All right," he said. "But once we are inside and safe, you will tell me everything you know."

The sapling smiled. "That would take several lifetimes," she said. She extended a branch and clasped his shoulder. "Do not fear, Half-Brother. I can do this. We can do this. And we will not need to sacrifice me, or you, or any of us."

"I'm not worried about that," Rhys said brusquely.

"Excellent," the sapling said. "Then there's nothing more to discuss."

Rhys fumed for a moment. He waved to Kiel, who asked, "Ready, Boss?" Rhys nodded and the giant reached out two long arms to scoop up Rhys in one hand and the sapling in the other. He cradled these last two passengers against his torso in the crook of his elbow and lumbered up to the top of the hill.

"Whenever you're ready," Rhys said. "Go."

The giant started slowly, lurching down the hill in a sort of controlled topple that made Rhys feel as if he were trapped in the first few seconds of a long fall. Endry and the groundlings let out a rousing cheer and Kiel picked up speed, his short legs pumping, his broad flat feet driving into the ground.

When the reached the bottom of the hill, Rhys caught his first clear glimpse of Kinscaer and the carnage taking place outside the doun's walls. The walls themselves had been breached—so much for the doun's protective barrier—and a jagged hole zigzagged from the top of the walls down to its center. Broken stones and debris from that hole had mounded directly below it, and the mound was all but covered with Kinscaer's defenders as well as its invaders.

Rhys counted dozens of kithkin archers and spearmen on the ramparts astride the hole and scores more on the pile of debris. The battle was too broad and too complicated for him to safely gauge which side was winning, but during his brief assessment he didn't see a single kithkin arrow miss its target. He had heard of the doun's militia, and from what he saw now their formidable reputation was well deserved.

Their enemy was nowhere near as disciplined or as organized, but they were every bit as effective. As it had been at

Mistmeadow, the ravening horde that followed the Destroyer was composed mostly of black, brittle-seeming cinders and a small army of boggarts. The boggarts favored mass attacks, swarming over the stony debris and hurling themselves in waves against the walls of Kinscaer and the doun's defenders, all the while gibbering like rabid beasts. The cinders were silent and less numerous, but no less terrible—though none of the skeletal figures was fully aflame, thick smoke drifted up from their joints and sparks flew from their corroded black blades. They towered over their boggart cohorts, swiftly moving from place to place, pausing only to skewer or decapitate those kithkin warriors who had become mired in the wriggling bodies of feral boggarts.

In single combat, the kithkin were more than a match for the boggarts, and the little fiends' bodies littered the blood-slick ground beyond the walls, each with a single kithkin arrow protruding from some vital spot. The kithkin warriors even proved a match for the much larger cinders, whose speed and ferocity did not seem to matter against kithkin skill and training. Kinscaer's archers had already learned the hard lesson of Mistmeadow and were targeting the cinder's joints, and so every one of the ragged skeletal figures that got close to the walls lost at least one limb. Once more Rhys could not help but admire Kinscaer's militia. Though outnumbered, the kithkin did not allow any of the enemy through the crack in their walls.

Rhys's military experience told him Kinscaer was in a hopeless situation, however. Despite their bravery and their mettle, the kithkin could not prevail. The invaders were focused exclusively on overrunning the gap in the doun's defenses, and more of them materialized out of the haze with each passing second. It was all the defenders could do to keep the Destroyer's horde out. What sort of chance did they have once the Destroyer herself re-entered the battle?

"Kiel," Rhys shouted. "Change of plans! Run to that hole in the outer wall!"

Kiel obligingly changed course without losing momentum. He trampled a cluster of boggarts with a sickening sound, and Rhys heard all of the groundlings on the giant's back cry out in disgust.

"Shut it!" Endry yelled at his army. "This is war! You have to expect squishy!"

Kiel plowed on without slowing, scattering the invaders as he thundered toward the wall.

"What are you doing?" the sapling said.

"All that I can," Rhys replied. "Kiel! Keep going! Straight up that pile of rocks!"

Kiel grunted. As his foot touched the base of the mound, the giant leaped forward, bounding halfway up. Stone shattered under him and boulder-sized chunks of masonry rolled down the pile. Boggarts and kithkin screamed as the mound began to collapse. Rhys found himself momentarily at eye-level with a band of hissing, spitting cinders before Kiel's next step sent them all flying.

The kithkin on the walls recognized this strange new development as a potential boon as well as a potential hazard, and so Kinscaer's defenders weathered Kiel's charge far better than the invaders. The giant's wake was littered with crushed and broken bodies, and as the mound of jagged stone broke apart, everyone but Kiel abandoned it. The giant paused to maintain his balance on the shifting heap of stone. As he slid back toward the ground he said, "What next, Boss?"

"All the way to the top," Rhys said. "And then—jump!"

Kiel bounded forward. His disproportionably small legs were a blur and his free hand clawed through the rocks as he scrabbled up. When he hit the top of the pile, Kiel let out a single, bellowed "Ha!" though Rhys could not tell if it was from amusement or exertion. Kiel's feet kicked down hard and he drove himself off the topmost stone just as it fell out from under him. Once aloft, Kiel twisted his wide body sideways so that he barely cleared the jagged edges of the broken wall on each side as he soared through. The giant's muscles tightened around Rhys, but Kiel was careful not to crush his passengers.

"We're flying!" the groundlings cheered. "Hooray!"

"Quiet in the ranks!" Endry barked.

Rhys was more concerned with their landing. There was no way to slow or alter their course, but fortunately they were heading right for the wide, flat expanse of Kinscaer's town square. Something had blasted the area flat, and while there were a large number of kithkin gathered at the far side, there was plenty of room for a giant to come crashing down without flattening anything or anyone.

At least not directly. Kiel's landing shook the entire doun, and some of the half-destroyed buildings that bordered the square simply gave up and crumbled. No one moved or spoke for a moment or two after Kiel's arrival. The battle continued outside the walls, but the sounds of bloodshed were now dim and distant.

"We are here," the sapling said. "Where it began and must end." She stretched her face up over Kiel's thumb and said to Rhys, "Once she realizes I have returned, she will come for me."

Rhys didn't like the sound of that at all, but before he could object, a peal of thunder split the sky overhead. A pinwheel of fire formed, swirling and expanding outward until it filled the sky over Kinscaer—and then it exploded, sending streamers of flame far and wide in all directions. For a moment the Destroyer's howl of rage drowned out the sound of the kithkins' monotonous chant. Rhys briefly wondered how these citizens

149

of Kinscaer were able to ignore a giant dropping out of the sky onto their town square.

"She has come," the sapling said, staring up at the fire in the sky. There was neither dread nor delight in her voice.

"Hoy. You up there. On the giant."

Rhys cast his eyes down to a small kithkin delegation that had gathered at Kiel's feet. The male at the front of the group had a sword in his hand and a bloody bandage across his forehead. He looked grim but his tone was decidedly irritated as he shouted, "Who are you? What have you done?" His hand tightened on the hilt of his sword. "Why have you come here?"

"Defenders of Kinscaer," the sapling said, her voice louder and more forceful than Rhys had ever heard it before. "We are your natural allies. We fought our way through to reach you." The sapling bowed her face forward. "And we have come to help you stand against the Destroyer."

Rhys half-expected a hail of arrows in response, but the kithkin warrior simply stared. He seemed to be thinking, but Rhys knew he was listening to the collective thoughts of the entire assembly.

"Come down and come forward," the kithkin said at last. "Wise yew, noble elf. Acting Cenn Warree Tarcha would speak with you both."

* * * * *

The sapling cast her eyes back and forth across the broken wall and the devastated center of Kinscaer. Except for the crowd of kithkin at the far edge, nothing remained upright in the broad circle of flattened ash before her. No living thing was visible outside the blast zone besides a tangle of healing vines that crept low along the outer edges of the square.

Tarcha, the old kithkin augur, was a marvel, though the sapling did not believe anyone else could tell just how marvelous. Though its acting cenn was uniquely qualified to defend the doun against the Destroyer, the Kinscaer community was losing hope, and with it strength. The dark-berried vines seemed to restore and sustain their bodies, but their mindweft required more than physical vigor. Fear and frustration were eating away at the doun's protective barrier as the Destroyer's fire flashed across the sky and her horde worked its way closer, step by bloody step. The dounfolk were lucky to have such powerful magic to protect their homes and invigorate their bodies, but even creatures as superstitious as these could not depend on luck forever. Kinscaer needed to mount more than a strong defense, and quickly, else the wounds it had already suffered might prove fatal.

It was no mystery to the sapling why the Destroyer had come back here, to the place where Colfenor ignited the fires of her wrath. It was in Kinscaer that the great yew sage brought them together and bound them to one another: Rhys to the sapling, the sapling to Ashling, Ashling to the elemental fire. Colfenor was guided by the accumulated knowledge of his ancestors and prompted by the noblest of intentions, but he was no less stubborn or vain than he had ever been in the execution of his lofty goals, and certainly no more forthcoming. The sage had not even considered approaching those he had chosen to be his instruments before he pressed them into his service, and he never fully considered the effect his actions would have on them in the aftermath. Worst of all, he had never imagined that the actions of others would send his own efforts so horribly awry.

The sapling cleared her mind and then refocused her thoughts and her eyes on the strange conversation between Rhys and Tarcha. The kithkin were characteristically suspicious of the newcomers, but it was also clear that they were ready to accept outside assistance. It took very little time for Rhys to present his offer and less for Tarcha to accept it. The sapling smiled briefly. As Endry might say, all sorts of strange things happen when one is besieged by a mad primal entity.

Rhys and Tarcha nodded to each other, stepped back, and then bowed. The kithkin rejoined the rest of the dounsfolk, already spreading the details of Kinscaer's arrangement with the elf through the mindweft. Rhys himself turned and marched back toward the sapling and Kiel, who still carried Endry and the groundling faeries as a great bear carried fleas.

As always, Rhys's approach conjured from the sapling a wealth of both competing and complimentary emotions. She respected his discipline and his lifetime of experience; she admired his bravery and natural leadership. The sapling loved his selflessness and dedication to his ideals, but at the same time she was mystified by his violent pragmatism and frustrated by his shortsighted devotion to his own tribe above all others. His stubbornness and vanity mirrored Colfenor's.

"Welcome to the Kinscaer militia," Rhys said. He stopped beside the sapling and cast an eye toward Kiel. "Unofficially, of course, and extremely temporarily. Tarcha agreed to let us do whatever we like outside the barrier. She thanks us and wishes us luck, but she cannot contribute to our efforts beyond the kithkin warriors already on the walls. She and the others are wholly dedicated to maintaining their defensive spell." He crossed his arms and clenched his jaw. "So I wouldn't say they trust us, but they are willing to let us get ourselves killed on their behalf."

"They don't need to trust us," the sapling said. "They just need to defend themselves so we can confront the Destroyer."

"Then we're all agreed," Rhys said. "Now. You haven't told

me what your role is, but you did say that the Destroyer needs to be weakened before you act."

"That is the case."

"It took Eidren's life to divert her from Mistmeadow," Rhys said. "As well as an army of elves and kithkin."

"But this time you've got a better army." Endry appeared from among the saplings boughs, grinning confidently, his eyes bright. "Mine." A hundred tiny cheers wafted over the tops of Kiel's shoulders from the groundlings clinging to his broad back.

Rhys moved his eyes toward Endry without turning his head, and then shifted them back to the sapling. "We also have a giant, which we didn't have at Mistmeadow. And Tarcha's barrier spell."

Endry buzzed in front of Rhys's face. "The only thing we don't have is the Destroyer."

"She's here," Rhys said. "We just haven't seen her in person yet. She hasn't ever removed herself from the action before, and until now she's always led the attack. Tarcha's barrier has stymied her, confused her, and maybe even frightened her. We can use that."

The male Vendilion flew around Rhys's head, encasing the safewright's horns in a crown of blue-white smoke and dust. "You have a battle plan, General?"

"I do. And you might be surprised to hear that you and your army play a key role in it."

"I might be surprised, but I'm not." Endry zipped away from Rhys and hovered between the elf and the sapling. "Because really, who else can you turn to? We're all you've got."

Rhys nodded, but he said, "That's not true." He looked up. "Kiel?" he called.

"Mmm?" the giant rumbled.

"The Destroyer is out there," Rhys said.

Kiel nodded. "Ashling," he said. "All burned up, but she keeps on burning."

"Er—yes. But right now she's sitting back and letting her followers do her work for her." Rhys indicated himself and the sapling. "We want to confront Ashling in person, so we need to clear the field. We need to make her come out and fight for herself."

Kiel carelessly wound his long beard around his fist. His jaw worked back and forth as he considered Rhys's words.

"I'll handle this," Endry said sharply. He floated up so that he was halfway between Rhys and Kiel, cupped his hands around his mouth, and shouted, "Hey! Giant! Remember all those boggarts and cinders we trampled on the way in?"

Kiel's beard-wrapped fist touched his chin. He rested his face on his knuckles for a moment, and then started unwinding his beard. "Yes."

"Well, the boss here wants us to go back out and trample the rest." Endry's eyes crackled, spitting out tiny jags of blue lightning. "All of them."

Kiel released the end of his beard so that it fell and trailed in the ashes and dust. He leaned to one side so that he was looking past Endry to Rhys.

"All of them," Rhys said.

The giant's dull eyes grew sharp and a broad smile slowly spread across his face. He pressed his clenched fist into his open palm, squeezed, and then all of his knuckles cracked with a series of ragged pops so loud they drew concerned looks from several of the kithkin in the square. "Now, Boss?"

Rhys looked at the sapling, and she felt the same complicated surge of hope and concern. She nodded.

Rhys nodded back. "Now," he said to the giant.

CHAPTER 12

Kiel carried the sapling as far as the break in Kinscaer's outer walls. She insisted on coming that far and would have stood by them in the skirmish to come, but Rhys was not willing to risk her safety—certainly not until he understood what she meant to do.

Once the sapling was safely deposited atop the wall, however, Rhys's course was perfectly clear—the kithkin militia was keeping the horde at bay for now, but the mound of dead invaders was nearly as large as the broken pile of stone had been before Kiel flattened it. If more boggarts and cinders kept streaming in to replace those that had fallen, the new arrivals would have the makings of a new and far more grisly ramp at their disposal, one that would soon be large enough to clear even the unbroken sections of Kinscaer's defensive walls.

The Destroyer's horde was slowly overwhelming the doun's defenses. Numbering in the hundreds, the host of cinders and boggarts were not so much organized as driven by the same relentless, murderous impulse. The vicious mob was chaotic and inefficient by elf standards, but it was also every bit as dangerous as a crack squadron of the Wilt-Leaf's finest warriors. An ugly victory was still a victory, one that Kinscaer would not survive.

"Endry?" Rhys said.

"Ready."

"Kiel?"

"Mmm."

Rhys tightened his grip on a lock of Kiel's hair and dug his hooves into the back of the giant's neck. He could hear and feel the groundlings moving all around him, but they were invisible in the dark. "Kiel," he said again. "Go."

The giant grabbed the crumbling tops of the wall on each side of the jagged gap. Kiel used his extra-long arms to hurl himself up through the crack and out over the battlefield. He was aloft for a second or two before he descended, and as he did Rhys scanned the ground below. Kiel would flatten everything when he came down, but once he did the horde would have him surrounded. Rhys was certain the horde would close in on Kiel quickly, just as he was certain the thick-skinned giant would easily weather their counterattack.

Rhys himself planned to be elsewhere when the horde received Kiel. While the giant and Endry whittled down the horde's superior numbers, Rhys would observe the enemy's tactics, single out its leaders, and remove them from the field. If no leaders emerged from this festering rabble, he would single out its most accomplished fighters.

Rhys spotted a clearing in the chaos that would allow him to land and recover without being overrun. He tensed his long legs and sprang up over Kiel's bald head just as the giant's thick boots slammed into the blood-soaked mud. Scores of invaders vanished beneath a cloud of soil and filthy water, and dozens more were driven to their knees by the resultant tremor. Behind them, the cracks in Kinscaer's walls lengthened and huge ragged chunks of meticulously laid stone fell, along with a handful of kithkin defenders.

Rhys himself sailed on, arcing away from Kiel as his momentum carried him over the boggarts and cinders who had kept to their feet and advanced toward the giant. Rhys landed on a dry patch of hard, blackened dirt, tumbled forward, and then rolled to his feet. He drew his sword as he turned back to face Kinscaer, but not a single one of the assembled hundreds attacking the doun had attention to spare.

Kiel stood embedded up to his knees in the ground, though he seemed more annoyed than concerned about his lack of mobility. Chunks of stuff like broken clay clung to his legs—the surface of the marsh, baked by the Destroyer's passage but already sinking into the murky sludge and stinking bogwater. He planted one hand on the ground in an effort to work himself free, but by then the first howling members of the horde had reached him. Black cinder blades shattered against his forearm, leaving dark scratches that seethed and smoked like hot charcoal, while a dozen boggarts swarmed up Kiel's leg and scrabbled for purchase on his heavily muscled torso.

Grunting, Kiel swung his arm parallel to the ground like a scythe. The cinders that had cut him shattered, smeared against his forearm like greasy black chalk. Kiel continued this smooth motion, rotated his elbow, and then slapped his hand flat against his chest. Most of the boggarts climbing him were lucky enough to be killed instantly under that blow, but many were sundered into pieces, some large enough to sustain life for many agonizing minutes.

A crimson-black smear slid down Kiel's chest and a shower of ghastly red droplets stained his beard. The giant dug his fingers into the ground, the overdeveloped muscles in his upper arms bulged, and then Kiel dragged himself free. A squadron of boggarts charged him, chattering and howling. Kiel wind-milled his long arms as he waded into their midst, and soon he had become the center of a chaotic storm of gnashing teeth, crude weapons, and flying boggart bodies.

Rhys still held his sword ready, but as far as he could tell the horde hadn't even noticed him yet. Every cinder and boggart in the vicinity was howling or snarling or spitting foam at Kiel. As Rhys had expected, the invaders all oriented on the giant, allowing the elf plenty of time to pick his targets.

His task became infinitely simpler as two flickering figures appeared on the road leading to the river. Simpler, but far more dire. Unlike the rest of the cinders who merely smoked and smoldered without ever fully igniting, these two had actual flames dancing in their eye sockets and small rows of fire running along the tops of their mask-like faces. Their flames were small and dim, no brighter than a candle's, but they still outshone everything else on the battlefield and lit the surrounding area. One glowed soft blue and the other muted gold, and the light from their inner fire cast twisted shadows across the battlefield.

The two burning cinders came straight at Rhys, clearly having chosen him as their target as quickly and as surely as he chose them. He went forward to meet them with his sword drawn. Whatever had ignited them, these two were different from the other cinders. Their movements were sharper and more precise, their reactions quicker, their expressions more savage and cunning. He considered himself more than a match for any pair of cinders alive, no matter how fiery they seemed, but there was too much at stake to trust in his sword skills alone. As he closed the gap between himself and the hot cinders, Rhys pulled a vial of yew resin from his belt and smeared a few drops along the edge of his blade. He was ten paces from his foes when a familiar voice shouted joyfully in his ear.

"Well, look at that!" Endry shouted. "Cinders on fire. And colorful, too! Stand back, Mr. Big Elf. Endry's army will handle this."

"No," Rhys started, but Endry let out a sharp, piercing whistle. The sound was still echoing through the air when a dozen magpie-riders took wing from Kiel's shoulders and a swarm of groundling faeries poured down the giant's arms. Endry swept past Rhys, leading the charge as he and his two-pronged groundling force drove headlong at the softly glowing cinders.

An identical look of feral glee crossed the faces of the two ignited cinders. They stopped short and, without so much as a shared glance, each extended one hand toward Endry and the approaching groundlings. Though tiny and too numerous to count, Endry's army moved quickly and without hesitation. They crashed headfirst into the sheets of pale blue flame the first cinder released from his charred, bony fingers.

The magpies reached the enemy first, and so they were the first to die screaming. Endry himself managed to swerve up and out of harm's way, but most of the bird-riders could not avoid plunging into the thin wall of flames.

Getting into the fire was one thing; getting through it was another matter. The magpies burned to a crisp as soon as they touched the blue fire, and dropped to the ground without advancing another inch. The groundling riders burst through the wall, screaming and covered with flames. The stink of burning meat and feathers wafted over Rhys, and he shouted for Endry to withdraw.

If Endry replied, neither Rhys nor the groundlings heard. The miniature infantry let out a collective battle cry and pressed on. The golden cinder stepped out ahead of his blue companion. He drew his arm back as if preparing to throw a spear, and a blinding ball of golden fire ignited in his cupped hand. He hurled the fireball straight into the front of the advancing groundling formation, where it exploded.

Rhys felt the heat and the pressure from where he stood, so he could imagine how intense the explosion was at the point of impact. He heard wails of agony and saw tiny charred bodies hurtling through the air. The groundlings who survived the initial blast sent up a new chorus of horrified screams as the magical flame spread, racing from body to body, eventually igniting each one. The groundling platoon broke apart and scattered, but the golden fire continued to burn until it consumed them all.

Endry voice was choked, anguished. "No fair," he said, and then twin columns of blue and gold fire stabbed up from the cinders' hands and enveloped him.

Rhys roared. Too late to save Endry, he charged on and buried his sword in the gold cinder's naked ribcage. The blade slid all the way through the cinder's body and severed the monster's spine. The wound was mortal but the cinder did not drop until the yew poison took effect. For a second Rhys's eyes were inches away from the twin golden flames flickering in the cinder's eye sockets. Rhys stared into those glowing sockets until the light within dimmed. The gold cinder's jaw dropped open and he let out a long, wheeze. Rhys ducked under a blow thrown by the blue cinder behind him, yanked his sword free, and then decapitated the golden cinder with a sweeping circular swing of his blade that struck directly between the exposed bones in its neck.

Rhys turned to face the surviving hot cinder. The villain's blue color had grown darker, more malevolent, and his body radiated withering heat. The cinder drew his own blackened, crumbling blade and circled the elf, forcing Rhys to turn his back on Kinscaer and the larger battle behind him.

"Hey," came a familiar voice. "I'm alive. Hooray for me!"

Rhys kept his eyes fixed on the blue cinder. "Endry?" he called.

"Right here," Endry said. "But don't ask me how."

Rhys circled with his opponent until he saw Kiel in his peripheral vision. The giant was still engaged against scores of boggarts, and as Rhys watched Kiel somersaulted forward, crushing his enemies. Once the giant was gone Rhys caught sight of the sapling. She had descended from the top of the wall and moved through the melee entirely unnoticed.

"What are you doing here?" he shouted. The blue cinder took advantage of his distraction and slashed at Rhys, but the elf nimbly leaped aside. To the sapling he called, "Get back inside the walls!"

"The time has come for me to do my part," she said. "And so I am doing it." One of her branches was extended high over Rhys's head and it stretched past his line of sight to where Endry had almost been immolated. "For General Endry is my friend, and Tarcha is not the only one who knows how to baffle fire."

The treefolk's words sent a visible shock through the blue cinder, as though the sound itself pained and appalled him. The fire in his eyes flared out to form a cloud that lingered over his head. His arms dropped to his sides and his sword clattered to the ground. Shuddering, he tilted his head back until his face was pointed at the sky.

Rhys did not understand his reaction, but he was not about to let such an opportunity pass. He sprang forward with his sword ready, but a painful stinging stopped him in his tracks as surely as if he had run into a wall of rock.

Blue sparks danced in every one of the hot cinder's joints. Rhys saw a bolus of azure flame form in the cinder's skeletal chest. The small cloud swelled to fill the brigand's hollow torso, and then it erupted from his open mouth. The gout of flame hung in the air and grew larger still. Without that flame, the formerly hot blue cinder groaned, toppled backward, and clattered to the ground.

The blue ball of fire brightened to pale orange and contracted. Its shape changed as its color shifted again from orange to yellow. It stretched from a sphere to an oval. Crude limbs sprouted from its underbelly. A thick, strong neck grew from its anterior end, and from that emerged a long, rectangular face. The half-formed creature stamped its forelimb in the air.

The furious sounds of battle vanished as each member of the Destroyer's horde turned to stare at the equine shape. Kiel continued to squash boggarts, but the fight had gone out of them. They barely moved or tried to protect themselves from the giant's sweeping blows. Eventually even Kiel stopped fighting and stared at the flaming horse-figure hovering over the battlefield.

The rough, featureless shape reared. Fire flared from its mane and hooves. It sprang forward and then banked left, tracing a flaming ring over the fallen blue cinder below as the galloping sound of its hooves grew loud enough to shake rocks from Kinscaer's walls. With a final toss of his head, the horse-thing pivoted in mid-circle and streaked toward the Wanderbrine, leaving a trail of smoke and fire in its wake. The remaining cinders and boggarts retreated into the darkness and shadows, each silent as they glared at Kinscaer's defenders.

When the enemy was gone and the battlefield silent, the sapling said, "Well done, Safewright." She had drawn in her long branch, and as she came toward Rhys she cradled Endry in a funnel of gently curving wood.

"Hardly," Rhys said. "Kiel! Take Endry and the sapling back inside. Now."

Confusion and disappointment crawled over the sapling's broad features. "But why? We've achieved the first goal we set out to—"

"We set out to confront the Destroyer and weaken her," Rhys said. "But all we've done is bloody her minions and infuriate her. You saw how that cinder reacted to you. It's not safe yet. Go back inside."

"But she is coming—"

"I know. That's why you have to go back inside."

"At least let me stay," Endry said. "I've got to marshal what are left of my troops."

"You've done for today, General," Rhys said dryly. "You and your groundlings were supposed to stick with the giant." He turned. "Kiel! Take them inside, now!"

The giant lumbered forward, and as he approached he spread his long arms wide on each side of the sapling. She and Endry fixed their silent, somber eyes on Rhys as Kiel's fingers closed around them.

An arrow-thin stream of fire lanced out of the darkness into Kiel's left shoulder. The bolt slammed into the giant's meaty body and pierced straight through, emerging out of Kiel's back and continuing on to char the broken walls of Kinscaer. The force of the blow straightened Kiel's back and spun him halfway around, his arms flailing wildly. The giant staggered a half step toward Kinscaer, teetered drunkenly, and then collapsed.

The sapling's eyes went wide with shock. Staring fixedly at the sky behind Rhys, she said, "Forgive me, Brother. You were right." She uncoiled her protective grip on Endry and the faerie went directly to Kiel. Endry lit on the giant's shoulder as Kiel struggled to get back to his feet. His left arm hung limp and his right hand was pressed tight against the smoking wound in his shoulder.

Rhys spun in place as quickly as he could, but his movements seemed slow and dreamlike. There was fire in the skies overhead, a bright, glowing ball of yellow-orange flame with a familiar and dreadful figure at its center. The Destroyer's approach and attack had been silent, but now she let out a mad, grating shriek. Her face twisted into a terrifying rictus of fury and hatred, her burning eyes fixed on the sapling.

"Yew devil." Though she addressed the sapling, the Destroyer's voice ripped through Rhys's mind like a saw blade. "You who were the author of my misery shall now be fuel for my fire." Colorful flames billowed around her. She extended her arms out straight and the fire rushed to her hands, surrounding them in twin balls of light and heat and smoke.

Without thinking, Rhys hurled his envenomed blade up at the Destroyer. The fine elf sword tumbled end over end toward his target's torso, but as it came within arm's reach it burst into flame and exploded. Hot metal slag rained down and a hissing cloud of amber smoke formed in front of the Destroyer.

The elf did not hesitate. He focused his mind on the amber cloud, whispering the ancient and all-but-forgotten incantations that had been drilled into him as Colfenor's student. The cloud of yew vapor was toxic all on its own, but under Rhys's spell it sought out victims like a living thing. The amber wisps rushed past the corona of fire that surrounded the Destroyer and flowed directly into her face, filling her eyes, nose, and mouth. She winced, she choked, she shuddered and staggered, but she still swung both arms forward and unleashed a wide gout of red flames directly at the sapling.

Rhys's attack was not enough to cripple or kill the Destroyer, but it was enough to throw off her aim and blunt the strength of her strike. The sapling screamed as the flames rolled over her upper branches. She was not quick enough to avoid them entirely, but by hurling herself to one side she spared herself from complete immolation. As it was, two of her boughs instantly withered to ash and a third ignited. The sapling hit the ground and rolled toward Kinscaer to extinguish the flames.

The light and heat from the Destroyer intensified, burning away the sting of yew magic. She floated backward and up, away from her enemies, and now her terrifying gaze was locked on Rhys. He saw many things flickering in those flaming sockets—pain, rage, frenzy, and madness. His own death. The death of everyone he knew, and a Shadowmoor burned clean of life, cold and dark. A chill ran down his spine but Rhys defiantly returned the glare, determined to find a way to prevent what burned in the Destroyer's eyes.

"Kiel," Rhys shouted, not taking his eyes off the Destroyer. "Take the others and go. Go now." He didn't know if the giant could hear him, or if Kiel was able to act on his commands, but Rhys knew he was the only thing standing between the Destroyer and the sapling. He still believed the sapling had the best chance of defeating the Destroyer once and for all, and so she had to survive. The elf drew the last vial of yew poison from his belt and prepared to make his stand.

Rhys popped the cork from the vial with his thumb and drew his arm back. He felt something light and sharp touch his shoulder and then Endry whispered, "Hang on." Icy blue dust surrounded Rhys and he felt light, weightless. A cool breeze blew in from the river, and Rhys's feet left the ground. He had to abandon the vial as he tumbled through the air on the magical updraft, or risk scattering yew poison everywhere. The world rolled past his vision in cycles: Kiel, then Kinscaer, then the sky, then the Destroyer, then the ground, then Kiel again. The bottom of his hooves thumped against something solid and Rhys fell against the giant's thick, knotty skull.

"Go, giant, go!" shouted Endry. Still dizzy, Rhys looked down and saw the half-burned sapling cradled once more in the crook of Kiel's elbow. The giant kicked a broken chunk of stone toward the Destroyer, turned, and then charged toward the crack in Kinscaer's walls.

Rhys dug his fingers into Kiel's flesh and held on. As the giant clumsily climbed up and forced himself through Kinscaer's walls, the Destroyer's howls of rage echoed off the broken stone. Kiel had to turn himself sideways to fit through the crack, and so Rhys had one final glimpse of the Destroyer hurtling toward them just before the giant dropped safely inside the doun's walls. The Destroyer's renewed screams of rage and frustration confirmed that Tarcha's magic still protected the doun.

Rhys breathed and tried to gather his thoughts. "That was it. My best effort," he muttered. "And she shrugged it off like everything else." All the most powerful elf, kithkin, and treefolk spells at their disposal, and now they were no better off. They were still bottled up by the Destroyer's horde, still wounded and weakening as the siege continued, and still unable to strike back in any meaningful way. He had been a fool to abandon his fellow Wilt-Leaf warriors—had he stayed with his command, at least he could have died among his tribal peers.

Ah, said a silky, seductive voice. *But you don't have to die at all, noble Safewright. Not if you choose your allies a bit more carefully from now on.*

Rhys was instantly alert. "Who's there?"

I am the only one who can help you achieve your goals. And I feel I ought to, especially after you've returned my prodigal boy to me.

"Who are you?"

A soft but magnificently rich chorus of voices rose behind the unseen speaker's dulcet words. *I am Oona, Queen of the Fae,* she said. *And you will find me with Tarcha in the doun square.*

CHAPTER 13

Brigid Baeli was restless. Their little group had reached a stretch of the Wanderbrine where the destruction of Ashling's passage gave way to hardy mountain shrubs, wildflowers, and brambles. There were even a few short green stalks to mark the inevitable return of alpine trees who might someday become treefolk.

They were miles from the Source, working their way through a series of short but steep rapids that would require Brigid's full concentration if the skiff were to reach their destination safely. For now the shapewater magic was stable enough to sustain itself, more or less, and she was free to stalk the rear half of the skiff, deep in thought, with one hand batting the other away every time it crept up toward the Crescent.

"I'm sorry you have to give that up," Maralen said. She sat on a softly swaying deck chair Wryget had formed at her request, bonding it to the kithkin's skiff with magic that wouldn't interfere with Brigid's own.

"Give what up?" Brigid snapped, feeling foolish and fighting the urge to grab for the Crescent. She wasn't certain whether she'd remain herself if she lost it, but she didn't want to find out anytime soon.

"Sygg and his remaining crew—a useful bunch, from the looks of them—are at best a quarter mile away and won't be back for hours," said Maralen. "Your pet merrow went with them."

"Wryget's a friend."

"What is it that makes you always try to kill your friends?"

"That was business," Brigid replied. "Wryget understood, and I made amends."

"Like you always do," said Maralen. "You carry an awful lot of guilt, little kithkin. But don't worry. The Crescent isn't going anywhere just yet. And you don't know you'll change if you give it up."

"I don't know I won't," the kithkin replied.

"You worry your eyes are going to go white and you won't be the same," Maralen said. "I understand that. Believe me, I understand that." She turned her palms upward in a curiously kithkin gesture. "What can I do? Sygg won't do anything on my say-so. You can't use the river to stop her unless Sygg makes it happen. The last time you tried to talk to the Source, it didn't go well."

"How do you know when I last talked—tried to talk—"

"My dear, before you agreed to enter my service, I had a few others in my employ."

"You had the faeries. That's two."

"There's Endry."

"Endry quit. Went native. Which one watched me?"

"They both did. It wasn't long after the Aurora and I wanted to do a quick survey of those I knew and—I appreciated."

"And you appreciated me?" The kithkin laughed. "No, it's the other one, isn't it?"

"I especially wanted to find you," Maralen said, not joining in with Brigid's attempt to lighten the mood. "Because Oona already had. She wanted you for her own, but I proved too much of a distraction."

"You're joking," said Brigid. Suddenly the rocking of the skiff was making her woozy, and she stopped pacing and took a seat on a second deck chair of her own make and size. "How long did you have me watched?"

"Off and on until you entered my service," Maralen said. "You're forgetting the point. The Source told you to give the Crescent back. It called you vermin. Told you, 'A landwalking creature of your limited intellect and pitiable scope merits not the Crescent.' You think the Source is going to take it back, that it'll overwhelm you."

"Sygg thinks he can change her mind."

"Sygg thinks he's going to get the Crescent when the Destroyer is stopped."

"He is," Brigid said. She rose to her feet and found the wooziness hadn't left. She clutched at a translucent handhold that rose from the deck as she stumbled dangerously close to the edge of the skiff. "Damn it," she swore. "Don't know what's wrong with me."

"You're nervous," said Maralen. "You shouldn't be. You don't have to follow through on a promise to someone like him, do you?"

Brigid whirled on the elf and jabbed a finger at her face. "You would have me betray my word."

"Your *word?* Are you out of your mind? You have knowledge possessed by fewer beings than you can count on your fingers. Don't you want to preserve it if you can? Keep it? I can help you."

"How can you do that?" Brigid asked, grudgingly curious.

"Sygg doesn't have to survive his heroic effort to help us stop the Destroyer," Maralen explained. "He could instead perform a noble sacrifice, as Eidren did."

"Sygg wouldn't like to hear you say that," Brigid said. "And neither do I."

"Let's not quarrel about things that might happen. You're still of great use to me, and I don't intend to release you from your obligation until you aren't," said Maralen with finality, and she sat back in her chair. She closed her eyes and crossed her arms across her chest. "You gave me your word, remember?"

"But according to you, I don't have to honor my word."

"Only to your friends. And those to whom you owe favors. Not to Sygg."

"Are you suggesting we're friends?" Brigid said.

"Not as such. But I did do you a favor. I saved Jack from his foolish hero's errand, and ever since he has certainly been a boon for you." Maralen said without opening her eyes. "A truly supportive fellow. Let's ask him what he thinks—oh, bother, he's back with his kithkin sweetheart in his foggy little doun that you couldn't save from the Destroyer on your own."

"This isn't about his having a sweetheart."

"Odd you'd focus on that. Did I strike a nerve?"

"What you did—what I asked you to do—was to help save Mistmeadow."

"You asked me to save Jack Chierdagh," the elf said. "Not Mistmeadow."

"True," Brigid said. "But saving him saved Mistmeadow. That was why I agreed to work for you, Maralen, so that at least one kithkin doun would survive that giant's rampage."

"Now the giant's off who knows where," said Maralen sleepily. "And the Destroyer hit Mistmeadow anyway. Are you trying to talk your way out of our agreement?" Maralen's eyes opened, and to Brigid's surprise they scintillated with faint sparks of magic. "I have ways of enforcing your compliance."

Another wave of nausea struck Brigid, and she slumped to the deck. If she hadn't maintained her grip on the handhold, she might have rolled off into the water rushing past the skiff.

"Stop it," Brigid coughed, glad she hadn't eaten in almost two days. "You don't have to—just stop."

The nausea subsided. Throughout it all, Maralen never moved except her eyes, which flashed with tiny jags of power.

"Let's just get to the Source and see what Sygg can do. You can share the Crescent, if you really think it possible. Just don't hand it over until I tell you to."

"I won't betray—"

"You'll have to betray somebody. You can't serve two masters, and this one hasn't released you yet."

Brigid was glad the nausea had retreated but started to feel sick in a different way—sick of having masters.

The Source of the Wanderbrine was near the summit of Shadowmoor's Mount Kulrath (which in Lorwyn had been Mount Tanufel), overlooking the Wilt-Leaf and parts beyond. It didn't look much like the mountain Brigid had known most of her life—the Destroyer had sheared off much of the crest and left a charred, blackened stump in its place.

Brigid couldn't say for certain whether the Source had the power to stop the Destroyer, or Oona, if that was Maralen's ultimate intention. The kithkin had only just met that Source when the Aurora changed everything except the Source. Or so she'd thought.

As it happened the Source did change, slowly, like melting ice, except to Brigid it seemed the incarnation of the river had grown colder instead of warm. The Source she'd last met was cruel, practical, and logical; now it seemed jealous, destructive, and fickle.

Knowing that Maralen had been watching her was unsettling, but also embarrassing. Odd that it troubled her even more than the servitude, which merely chafed at her pride—and she hadn't much of that left. Brigid had returned to the Source that last time intending to learn as much as she could about the Crescent, and to find out if removing the trinket would also cause her to become like the Shadowmoor kithkin. She'd never gotten her answer, but the Source had taken the time to belittle Brigid before it attempted to take back the Crescent by force. Only her feet, raw panic, and a great deal of terror-driven tideshaping had gotten the kithkin clear of the Source's reach, though she now had to wonder if she'd had any unseen faerie assistance. She didn't understand how the Crescent allowed her to utilize shapewater, or why the Source hadn't tried—or been able—to cut her off from the trinket.

"Do you see fins?" Maralen asked. Brigid snapped out of her introspection and scanned the river ahead.

"I see one . . . two . . . five." The kithkin exhaled a breath she hadn't known she'd held. "They're all safe."

"All that's left of them," Maralen corrected. "Let's see what our dear captain has to say for himself."

"Don't antagonize him," Brigid said. "He's barely willing to help us as it is."

"Wouldn't think of it," Maralen said.

Wryget reached them first and waved for Brigid to meet him at the bow of the skiff. The news was not good, but Brigid couldn't think of much that could have been.

"The others will be here soon," he reported, gills flapping quickly as he kept himself elevated in the water without coming aboard. "Sygg didn't want me to tell you how bad it really was, but there's no point in lying about it. It's bad."

"How bad?" Brigid asked quietly, aware Sygg and the others could return any second.

"The Source wouldn't even talk to him," Wryget said.

"Don't know why he expected it would," Maralen offered. "After what just happened."

"It wasn't a refusal to speak, exactly," the merrow continued.

"The falls are lined with barricades, and the approach is filled with corpses. She's been busy."

"What he means is we couldn't get close enough to even try," Sygg said, surfacing not far from Wryget. Brigid had forgotten the captain's hearing was so sharp. "The Source has been hunting boggarts, from the look of it. There are hundreds of them, all around her lake. A land approach was foolhardy before; now I'd classify it as impossible."

"Why did you try this alone?" Brigid said irritably. "We should go together. You and your crew barely survived the last attempt. We can't afford to lose any of you."

Sygg scowled at her. She'd forgotten his sharp hearing, but there was no way Brigid could forget how she'd left the captain's employ, and clearly he hadn't forgotten either. "So now you're concerned about my survival," he said. "I'm touched."

"You could have gotten yourself killed," Brigid snapped.

"Hardly," said another merrow, the female called Kasella. Brigid hadn't even seen her surface, but then that was Kasella's specialty. The merrow concubine was Sygg's personal assassin, and she'd always given Brigid the willies.

"You're telling me you think you can kill the Source, Kasella?" Brigid asked. "You're good, I'm sure, but you're not that good."

"This one giving you trouble, Kass?" asked the bruiser named Artio. He was even bigger than Wryget, who'd worked the same line for Sygg before going independent. Artio, however, was much more accomplished when it came to shaping the river's waters.

"No trouble at all," Kasella said with a fishy sneer. She slipped a clawed hand from the water and with a flick of her wrist produced a long, thin shapewater blade. She threw the weapon like a knife, and it tumbled toward Brigid in a flash. The kithkin had to move quickly to stop the blade in midair, and her meager skills would never have stopped the weapon without the Crescent's power backing her. As it was, Brigid's attempt to turn the blade back on Kasella failed spectacularly when the shapewater weapon exploded into steam and vapor.

"Guess I overdid that," Brigid muttered to herself. "Or maybe the closer I get to the Source—could it be that simple?"

"Speak up," Maralen said.

"I think I have an idea," she said more loudly. "Sygg, I'm going to need your help."

"I figured as much," the merrow growled. "Why not just give me the trinket, and I can solve this entire problem?" From the simmering hate that never quite left his bulbous black eyes, Brigid felt certain Sygg wasn't just talking about the problem of the Destroyer.

"That's not going to happen," Brigid and Maralen said almost simultaneously. "Not yet," Brigid added. "But I learned at Mistmeadow that I can share the power with others who are attuned to it." A kind way of describing her shapewater brigade, the kithkin reckoned, but more or less true. "We have to try this sometime. Might as well be now. Sygg, Kasella, Artio, Wryget, if you're willing to join with me, I think we can—"

"Don't leave me out," a sinuous voice came from the stern of the skiff. Scathak had emerged without a sound, almost as stealthy as Kasella, but Brigid had learned the merrow was far more skilled at ranged fighting, transforming the waters of the Wanderbrine into razor-sharp projectiles that made Kasella's single targeted blade something of an afterthought.

"So, what are we going to do?" Maralen asked. "They can't even get to the Source, which has killed a lot of merrow already. And you just said there are boggarts." Brigid could see Maralen was distracted—probably communicating with the faeries. One of these days she was going to figure out how the elf managed to steal away even three of Oona's children.

"That's the truth," Sygg muttered, his face a mask of bitterness. "We can't get to her. I say there's only one thing to do, and that's—well, I say we retreat. I don't like saying it, but there it is. We just have to wait for the Destroyer to burn herself out."

"Well said, Boss," Artio growled. "Besides—"

"Besides, we can just hide out in the river? It's the landwalkers' problem?" Wryget interrupted, to Brigid's surprise. "Look around you, bruiser; there's a whole world dying and we've got to live in it. What'll the merrow do when there's no one to shake down for thread? When there's no fish to eat because they all got cooked? When the Destroyer decides to just dry up the river because she's got nothing left to burn?"

"It's all right, Wryget," Brigid began. "I can fight my own—"

"With respect, Brigid, don't interrupt me," Wryget said. His eyes bored into Sygg, who started to look distinctly uncomfortable. The other merrow were all looking away from their boss, actual shame showing on their piscine faces.

"By all means," Brigid said, taking a step back.

"Thanks," Wryget said without looking back. "When she burns everything that'll burn, she'll come for us. You've seen what she can do. The water won't protect us forever. Now, I don't know how we can get the Source to do what we want it to do, but I do know who can: Brigid. She could have left me for dead a long time ago, but she found me and made sure I was all right."

"After she almost got you killed," Sygg said.

"Not how I remember it, Captain," Wryget said. "And you're not listening. We do this now, or we go and hide and wait to die. I'm not going to do that. I'm going to listen to Brigid's idea—"

"Really, Wryget," Brigid said, more nervously than before. "You don't have to—"

"I'm going to listen to Brigid's idea, and then I'm going to see if I can help her pull it off. And if none of you are going to do the same, well, I guess we'll just have to do it all ourselves. But if you try to come to us afterward and take anything from my kithkin friend," Wryget said, his voice growing menacing, "you're going to have to come through the meanest, maddest, most exhausted merrow you've ever met. Me, that is. Because we're going to tame the Source, and we're going to stop the Destroyer, and you're all going to be a bunch of has-been losers!"

The only sound was a distant chirping bird and the gentle lapping of water against the skiff.

"I see," Sygg said, and the others began to whisper to each other, taking positions closer to their captain. "Quiet, all of you," he commanded, holding up a webbed hand. "All right, Wryget, we'll wait and hear of you friend's newfound genius. You've shamed me." The look on the merrow crime lord's face was anything but chastened, Brigid thought, but she wasn't truly paying attention to his features. She had to think of something, fast. Wryget's faith in her was welcome and even endearing, but it had put her in something of a spot, to say the least. "Well?" Sygg asked Brigid. "Let's hear it."

They couldn't get to the Source, and if they couldn't secure the Source's cooperation Brigid didn't know of a power that could stop Ashling the Destroyer. She found herself staring at the water rushing down the mountain slope, the current rushing through the shapewater skiff as if trying to escape the darkness up the mountainside. Brigid wondered how the Source could keep it all flowing when the banks narrowed more and more as they went up the mountain.

Maralen coughed uncomfortably. Brigid scowled at the elf.

"If we're going to beat the Destroyer," Brigid spoke with as much confidence as she could muster, "we'll need to be able to call on the Source. And if the Source won't let us come up for a visit, we'll just have to bring the Source to us."

"How are we going to do that?" Artio rumbled.

"First," the kithkin said, the idea taking on sharper form in her mind, "we have to get her attention."

* * * * *

"Report, Baeli!" Veesa barked as she snapped her body ramrod straight. The faerie hovered before Brigid's face at a safe distance; a lot of raw power emanated from the Crescent, which seemed to unsettle both Vendilion sisters. Maralen called them back to serve as messengers for this effort, but the kithkin outsider suspected the faeries had been due to return regardless. The elf woman had been spending a lot of time distracted lately, communing with the tiny creatures.

That did not mean Brigid had to tolerate abrasiveness from an arrogant little thing no bigger than a sparrow. "Hush, you. I'm concentrating here," she said. "And anyway, we're all set on this side."

"I know *they're* all set," Veesa said. "*They* reported when I asked them to report."

"So did I."

"Yes, but they weren't as casual about it. They all snapped at me, threatened me, and generally gave me reasons to take petty revenge at a later date. It was so much fun! You, on the other hand, are unbearably dull. 'I'm concentrating.' 'We're all set.' What a yawn-inducer you are."

"You want me to fight you?" Brigid said. "Why?"

"Oh, you just don't understand fun, kithkin," Veesa said. "I remember a time you were selfish and traitorous. Remember that time you killed—"

The rest of Veesa's reminiscence was swallowed up inside a sudden shapewater bubble along with Veesa herself. Indignant, the faerie railed soundlessly inside the bubble and tried without success to find a way through the shapewater skin of her tiny prison.

"She'll suffocate," Maralen said. "Please don't."

"She said she wanted fun," Brigid said. "And why in hell won't you people leave me alone? This isn't easy. Sygg already wants the damned Crescent; if I can't do this then I might as well give it to him now."

The faerie's wing beats began to slow. Brigid flicked a finger and a small hole appeared in Veesa's spherical cage. Brigid moved the finger again and the bubble dropped into Maralen's extended palm and popped. Veesa was lying on her back, gasping but unharmed.

Maralen's head cocked to one side. "Iliona tells me the second team is ready. I admit I'm a little concerned about your friend Wryget."

"He's as skilled a tideshaper as I've met," Brigid said. After a moment she added, "All right, he's better than average. And I trust him. We need someone on the other team we can be sure we trust."

"So that you and I are free to keep an eye on Sygg and his concubine? Really, this plan of yours just gets better and better. Good thing you're not making it up as you go."

"Perish the thought," Brigid said, and for the first time she took her eyes off the soft glowing energy between her hands, looking up at Maralen and the faerie. "You two should go. Just to the bank." She waved her hand and a narrow but steady bridge of shapewater lifted from the current and joined the skiff to the shore. "Hurry, please, I'm borrowing power to make that bridge, power I'm really going to need in a minute."

Maralen turned her attention to the creature in her palm. "Stop being melodramatic, Veesa." Without turning back to the kithkin she stalked across the bridge and onto the bank of the Wanderbrine. Once her mistress set foot on shore, the faerie took back to the air, buzzed out over the water toward Brigid with a battle cry, but stopped at a barked command from Maralen and returned to the elf's side.

"At last," Brigid said, "I can move on from the merely unpleasant to the truly wicked." More loudly, she called, "Sygg! You ready?"

"Of course." The captain's gruff voice floated out the mist concealing his position. "Kasella?" he called down the line into the mist.

The female merrow purred from the far side of the river, "Ready." Though Brigid couldn't quite make him out, Sygg was in about the center of the current. "And so far quite unimpressed, landwalker."

"That's because you're not touching the Crescent yet," Brigid said, the power at her command making her a bit cocky. "Just wait for it. Just a few more." The magic that created shapewater wanted cohesion, form, solidity. She'd needed to focus to draw so much in without using it, but now she had to do something she'd never tried before—she had to distribute it, slowly, and give most of it away. Sygg had been the one to suggest it, and Brigid wondered what else the Crescent could do that she didn't know about.

Finally she could contain the surge no more. She slowly she drew her hands apart at the center of her skiff, effortlessly fighting the current. Blue beams of eldritch light lanced out into the mist, searching for their new home, for familiar contact, slipping free of the cage that was Brigid Baeli and embracing two of the Source's own children.

The kithkin hadn't known what to expect, but she certainly

hadn't expected the contact to feel like someone had smacked her in the jaw.

"Keep yourself together, landwalker," Kasella called. "Or I'll kill you."

Brigid made a mental note to thank the merrow later; the threat was just what the kithkin outsider needed to bring herself back from the brink of fainting. "I'm together," she said, then repeated it more loudly. "I'm together!" She felt the powerful connection between herself and the two merrow stabilize, and the effect was like wearing three Crescents at the same time.

"Now or never," Brigid shouted. Threats wouldn't bring the Source to them or allow them to get to the Source. So Brigid had hit upon another idea. She and the others were going to cut the Source off from the rest of the river. "On three. One, two . . . *three!*"

The kithkin could never have explained exactly how she did what she did next—she had never been formally trained with shapewater by any means; she simply focused on the effect she wanted, and the connection the Crescent offered turned those thoughts into tideshaping magic. Even so, she had always suspected she was barely dipping her toes in the current, and now that she felt the difference between a lone kithkin and a lone kithkin backed by two expert tideshapers, she was certain she'd been right.

The first part of their effort blocked off the current from the rest of the river by forming a solid dam of shapewater. Brigid could feel the skiff dropping slowly as the water ran away downriver, but she kept her eyes on the glasslike wall ahead that separated her from the steadily rising river on the other side.

The mist had blown away, revealing two merrow holding themselves up in the mud on their small fin-legs. Like Brigid, their arms were splayed and their focus was on the shape-water dam.

"Now," Brigid barked, "lift and reverse!"

Certain the wall was sturdy, they shifted their attention to the water behind it. By curving the shape of the wall just so, they caused the current to push back upon itself, and by adding a touch of magic to gravity they forced the water to flow back upriver, against the current. Before long, the Source would begin flooding itself.

This was, Brigid now realized, the truly hard part. They had to maintain the spell, forcing the mightiest river in the world to reverse its course until the Source sat up and paid attention. Would it work? She had been sure it would, the merrow had agreed it was their best shot, and even Maralen believed the plan was sound, but as Brigid continued to channel shapewater magic through the artifact on her chest, the strain started to take its toll on her.

She risked a sideways glance to see Sygg balancing easily in the muck below, betraying no signs of pressure, and Brigid resolved not to give him the satisfaction of seeing her tire. She set her jaw and focused on the task at hand, imagining the gallons and gallons of water flowing upriver as a fist, and that she was punching this entire ridiculous midnight world in the face.

The mental image was enough to keep her going another fifteen minutes or so when pure physical exhaustion set in. Brigid could see Kasella and Sygg both wavering as well. "The Source," she gasped, "had better arrive soon."

As if in response, the upturned wave of water split down the middle as if flowing around a stone. Through the split emerged a translucent blue shape, vaguely female and almost ten feet tall. The only solid parts of her were twin blue jewels where a creature of flesh and blood's eyes would be. The jewels flashed in furious anger, blue sparks crowning the Source's shapewater head.

"What is this foolishness?" the Source asked in a voice like a crashing waterfall—thunderous and cold. Yet despite her question, Brigid couldn't help but notice the Source hadn't crossed their dam or stopped the backward flow of the river.

"Source of the Wanderbrine," said Brigid, "we need your help. The Destroyer is steadily devastating all the lands and peoples of—of this world, and only you, great and magnificent and wondrous, er, majesty, can stop her." Easy, Brigid, she thought. Babbling is for brooks.

"And why should I care about such things?" the Source boomed. "I am the river. I am eternal."

"Right." Brigid said. "Well, you might be eternal, but I remember a time when you weren't such a—"

"Source of the Wanderbrine," Sygg interrupted. "The landwalker bears the Crescent of Morningtide, which is linked to the very source stones you left your children throughout the lanes. She received the object as an honor bestowed by the Razorfin school. She is—" Brigid could see the merrow was struggling to keep from clenching his sharp teeth. "She is a hero of the river's children, and speaks for the Razorfin. As do I."

"And I," Kasella added.

"You, I am not surprised," the Source said, her great translucent head turning to focus on Sygg's concubine. "But you, Sygg of the Razorfin, were not meant to bow and scrape before a landwalker."

"I know, Source of the Wanderbrine," Sygg said obsequiously.

"Yes, he knows," Brigid interrupted. "But that is not the point. The point is—" She nodded to Maralen, who cocked her head for a split second and nodded in reply.

"What is 'the point,' landwalker?" the Source asked.

"The point is," Brigid continued, her confidence returning, "our second team has just cut you off from the actual *source* of the Wanderbrine. You may be the river's soul, but as of right now you're not part of the river at all. Go on. Flow upstream or whatever it is you do. See if you can get back to your isolated lake with your towering cliffs and your accidental boggart guards.

The Source disappeared for a few minutes but soon returned, eyes burning even brighter and her blue form shimmering in anger.

"You will regret this, landwalker," the Source said. "Insect. I am the Source. I am not to be toyed with or manipulated."

"Good to know," Brigid said. "Now are you going to help us?"

Almost half a minute of silence followed the question, and Brigid began to grow nervous. They couldn't keep this up much longer, and only surprise on the Source's part had allowed it in the first place. To use the full power of the river they needed the Source's help. Would the soul of the Wanderbrine realize she actually held all the cards? It was an enormous and dangerous bluff.

The kithkin was about to repeat her question when the Source answered at last.

"I will help you fight the beast of flames. When you need the power, call on me and it will be yours."

"I'm just supposed to trust you?" Brigid asked.

"Yes," Sygg said, for once not elaborating. He almost sounded afraid, in fact. Brigid took that as a sign she should listen.

"We have a deal," Brigid said. "We will release you, and then we will make haste to the port town of Kinscaer. That is where we will make our stand."

"I will be ready," the Source said. "And when your destroyer is extinguished, there will be a reckoning."

"Let's worry about the extinguishing first," Brigid said. "One reckoning at a time."

CHAPTER 14

Rhys approached the doun center carefully, straining his keen eyes and ears with each wary step. The sapling kept pace just behind him, and behind her was Kiel, still wounded but bearing the surviving members of Endry's army on his back. The air was filled with the sounds of battle from outside the walls, and with the Destroyer's endless howls of rage, but Rhys pushed the sustained clamor to the back of his mind and focused on the streets of Kinscaer around him.

Though he and the others had been moving much faster the last time they walked these cobblestone lanes, he spotted even fewer signs of life this time. The roads were eerily empty and silent. A nameless chill made Rhys shudder. This was a dead place, he realized. The doun wasn't empty because it had been abandoned or evacuated, or because the kithkin were all communing over the same shared spell, but because there was almost no life left in it. The stillness here was one of finality, the lingering voices of a dead mindweft that was slowly coming apart.

His companions shared his unease. Kiel was even terser and more withdrawn than usual as he nursed his wounded shoulder. Even Endry and the groundlings were somber and quiet, all but unseen and unheard on the giant's back. The sapling was physically untroubled by the boughs she had lost in the battle, but her face was creased with concern, eyes blank and distracted. She had been distant and preoccupied ever since they reentered the doun—or more accurately, ever since Oona addressed them.

No one with any common sense would take a disembodied Fae voice at its word, but the voice they heard spoke with confidence and conviction that even the strongest glamer could not convey. If Oona's presence behind that voice turned out to be some sort of magical ruse or illusory lie, it was an extremely well constructed and convincing lie, one that both Rhys and the sapling believed. Neither knew what to expect in the doun square, but each was certain the legendary Queen of the Fae was waiting there.

The sapling slowed just before the square came into view, and Rhys stopped. He peered into the milky white fog ahead and then turned back to the sapling with a questioning expression.

"I'm afraid," the sapling said. "Our enemy is too close, too powerful, and there's still so much to do—so much to make you understand. And I don't have all the answers for you yet."

"Some answers may lie straight ahead," Rhys said. He gestured toward the softly glowing cloud that covered the doun square. "As long as Tarcha's magic holds, we can seek those answers in relative safety.

The sapling stopped moving. "I'm sorry, Half-Brother," she said. She folded two long boughs around her middle and declared, "I am staying here. I prefer not to engage the Queen of the Fae."

"That is only wise," Rhys said. "But—"

"You should not, either. Something is terribly wrong here."

"And has been since before we arrived," Rhys said. "Kinscaer is besieged, sapling, and us along with it. At the moment we are in no shape to confront the Destroyer again, but I am quite ready—eager, in fact—to confront this 'Oona' who awaits us in the square."

"It will be dangerous," the sapling said. "Especially so for you and me."

"Then by all means, wait here," Rhys said. "If anything untoward happens to me, you will survive to carry on. You may even learn something valuable from my mistake. But in any case, I am going."

The sapling sighed, half-weary and half-exasperated. "I cannot let you go alone."

"I am going," Rhys repeated.

"Then I must accompany you," the sapling said. "But I will not speak. If Oona addresses me, you must answer."

"Of course." Rhys shrugged.

"Me, too." Endry's voice was muffled as it floated down from Kiel's shoulder. The faerie himself was nowhere to be seen. "Oona's kind of mad at me these days, so I'll just keep my head down and let you do all the talking."

"Fine," Rhys said. "Kiel can keep quiet, too, if that's what he wants. Let's just go." Rhys marched toward the square. Though the others kept pace as they had before, completing each step now seemed far more of a struggle.

Both the mist and the unsettling aura grew heavier and more oppressive as they entered the doun square. Rhys strode in proudly with his back straight and his head held high, preparing to formally greet the great and powerful Oona. He squinted through the haze, barely able to discern the host of small, upright kithkin figures at the very center of the square. He opened his mouth wide to declare himself and issue an appropriately ceremonial greeting, but his breath failed him as the crowd before him became more distinct.

Tarcha, the aged kithkin augur, stood between Rhys and

the assembled population of Kinscaer. She was facing the elf but oblivious to his presence, her blank eyes wide and unseeing. Her head was tilted all the way back and her face held a vacant, blissful expression. Her arms were spread wide, her palms were open and upturned, and her feet hovered several feet off the ground. Where she had been wearing a simple kithkin peasant's costume of tanned hides and rough-textured fabric, now Tarcha was clad in a long, elegant gown that had been woven from colorful flowers and rich green leaves.

The sapling gasped softly behind him. Rhys felt her urgent caress upon his shoulder, urging him to look past Tarcha. He tore his eyes from the mesmerizing figure and focused on the hundreds of kithkin huddled beyond.

The last time he had seen this crowd they had not moved much, but now the indistinct figures in the mist did not move at all. Their mouths no longer formed silent words, their throats no longer swelled with their internal song, and their chests did not rise or fall. The kithkins' eyes remained open, but their clasped hands did not tighten and loosen as the assembly strengthened and supported one another.

Four golden torches ignited in a diamond pattern over Tarcha's head. The additional illumination cast harsh angular shadows across the ground as it revealed more of the assembled throng. The sapling's grip on Rhys's shoulder tightened, but he shrugged her off and stepped forward, numbly trying to convince himself that what he saw was only an illusion, some trick or glamer set up by mischievous faeries.

But the ghoulish scene was all too real. Except for Tarcha, each and every kithkin in the square had a thick, sturdy vine wrapped tightly around his or her throat. There were scores of dead kithkin standing behind the augur, perhaps even hundreds, and beyond them a throng of upright corpses that stretched off into the mist past the limits of Rhys vision. They all stood frozen, each a lifeless marionette tethered in place by a cruel puppet-master's single string. Rhys forced himself to breathe evenly as his eyes followed the vine-nooses from their victims down to the thick patch of blue-flowered canes that snarled the outer edges of the doun square like an ill-tended hedgerow.

Rhys turned his head, dragging his eyes over the dead, silent mob. Had some of Kinscaer's citizens escaped before the Destroyer arrived, before Tarcha's barrier sealed them in for their own protection? He hoped so. If bringing him here had been some sort of Fae trick, then Oona and her ilk had played a far worse one on the dounfolk.

As soon as Rhys thought the Fae Queen's name, the four golden torches let loose with a burst of singing. The lights drifted down and separated, and Rhys saw that they were four large golden faeries. From the rapturous tone of their song, he guessed it was a hymn of praise to their queen and mother.

"Oona," Rhys said. His throat was tight and his teeth ground together as he spoke. "What happened here?"

From her position overhead, Tarcha started. The kithkin augur blinked and then stretched as if her muscles had atrophied and she was reacquainting herself with their proper use. She flexed her arms, legs, and fingers repeatedly until a satisfied smile crossed her features, and only then did she look down at Rhys.

"Oona?" Tarcha said. "No, no, noble Safewright. I am Warree Tarcha, and despite what you have been told, I am no cenn. I am, however, the current protector and guardian of Kinscaer. My magic kept the Destroyer at bay, and soon it will do far more than that." Tarcha's flower-gown rustled as she stepped forward and dropped lightly to the ground. "Kinscaer currently has no hero, and I must say it would amuse me to be thought of as such." Though her voice was unchanged from when Rhys last heard it, everything Tarcha said sounded like a lie, misdirection.

"I shall call you Tarcha, then," Rhys said. "If you insist on using that stolen name. Your friends and neighbors are all dead behind you, Tarcha. It would seem those 'healing vines' do not live up to their name."

Tarcha's bright expression did not change when she craned her head back for a glance at the throng, or when she turned again to face Rhys. "A terrible tragedy," she said. The chorus of faerie voices grew somber as the hymn momentarily became a dirge. "They will be mourned and honored appropriately, I assure you. But theirs was a necessary sacrifice."

"Necessary for whom?"

"For everyone who truly matters." The mournful chorus recovered its jauntier tone. "Things are not yet as they should be, but with this seemingly minor success, they will be soon."

"Oona," Rhys said sharply. "You called me here with talk of aid and alliances. What did—"

"Tarcha, my dear boy." The kithkin augur's face remained frozen as she curtsied. "I am Tarcha of Kinscaer."

"You are not. You stand attended by golden faeries," Rhys said. "You are clad in the living raiment of a magical queen. You smile and banter before the bodies of your murdered friends and neighbors. Your voice and your body may be kithkin, milady, but your mind is pure Fae."

"Oh, dear." Tarcha's voice grew wistful and her happy expression slightly more pensive. The faerie song that accompanied her softened, dropping so low as to be almost inaudible. "I had hoped to make a better first impression than this, noble elf. If only I had allowed more time; if only your powers of observation were not so keen."

Tarcha tossed her head and smiled anew. "Still," she said. "I have managed things far better this time. You can scarcely imagine the trouble I caused for myself when I tried something similar and didn't give it my full attention. A momentary lapse in concentration, a poorly chosen time and place. You think the lives of these kithkin were wasted? What about a whole host of elves cut down by yew spells flaring out of control? That would never have happened if I had not made her, if I had not created her to get close to you. I erred, Safewright, I can admit it now. But I have also learned from my mistakes. Surely you can see that."

"If I do, Fae Queen, I still do not understand it."

"Oh? That is surprising. I thought you of all people would have special insight into this matter. You were Colfenor's menial, after all." Tarcha looked past Rhys to the sapling, and her eyes narrowed. The corners of her mouth curled up, giving her face an amused, almost hungry aspect. "And you were Colfenor himself. By rights we should be enemies, little sapling, but my victory is at hand and it amuses me to see your sad folly play itself out."

Rhys stepped between Tarcha and the sapling. "What do you want from us?"

Tarcha laughed merrily, her mirth echoed by the quartet of golden faeries. "Nothing. I have already come to an arrangement with the Wilt-Leaf king and queen, and Kinscaer has already given me what I came for."

"Then why did you call out to us? To me?"

"You don't believe me about your own king and queen, do you? I would be impressed by your sharp thinking if it weren't so wasted. Do not fool yourself, Safewright. These suspicions and denials aren't due to your superior instincts, but to your increasingly deep isolation from your own tribe. If you were a true and loyal elf, you would already know your duty.

"But I will answer your question, if only to preserve the hope that you will come to your senses. I called out to you because you still have a choice to make." Tarcha strode forward and her frivolous, jovial demeanor evaporated. The kithkin augur's eyes blazed and a second voice rose behind her words—a terrible, glorious voice. "The Destroyer will fall. I have seen to that. Her elemental fire will be taken from her, and then you must choose. Which path will you follow? Will you pursue your sworn duty to the Wilt-Leaf Hold? Or will you throw in with the selfish ambitions of a doomed abomination that was never what she appeared or claimed to be? Or, perhaps you'll simply continue to accept the frothy ravings of that delusional yew."

"Deceiver," the sapling hissed. "Dream-spinner, glamer-weaver." Rhys saw branches rustling and moving in his peripheral vision but he kept his eyes on Tarcha. "Lorwyn-Shadowmoor is no longer your playground, and its people are no longer your toys. My sire gave his life to ensure that I could end your lies and break your unnatural grip on the heart and soul of this world."

"Unnatural?" Tarcha sneered, briefly baring her teeth. "That is highly amusing, coming from you, who should not even exist. I should have studied your example more closely before I adapted Colfenor's methods. Your numerous and painfully evident shortcomings would have provided me with perfect examples of what to avoid."

Rhys turned to remind the sapling that she had chosen to remain silent, but as he did a whip-like yew branch slashed through the air beside his cheek. He instinctively dropped to his knees, and then he heard a wet impact as the tip of the branch plunged in to a live body. Rhys snapped his head toward Tarcha and found the kithkin augur hovering above the ground once more, only now she hung from the smooth yew branch that had impaled her through the chest.

Tarcha's head lolled but her expression remained sly and sharply amused. Amber-yellow resin spread outward from the wound, quickly covering the surface of Tarcha's flowered gown. Beneath this veneer of yew poison, the lush vibrant petals and leaves grew wan and brittle.

"Well struck," Tarcha said. The kithkin's voice was now weaker, subordinate to the glorious, ringing tones that also emanated from her throat. As she continued to speak, Tarcha's voice faded away entirely, leaving only Oona. "But ultimately meaningless. In fact, you've done me a bit of a favor. This construct body was already doomed, you see. I would have killed it and reabsorbed it in any case, as I shall not allow another of my little diversions to rebel." Tarcha's eyes suddenly gleamed with golden light. "I spoke truly before when I said that I have learned from past mistakes." Tarcha's hands reached out and her fingers wrapped themselves around the yew branch that had skewered her. The kithkin squeezed, and the sapling let out a pained shriek. She pulled herself away from Tarcha and staggered back.

Free once more, Tarcha's limp body floated up with the quartet of golden faeries circling around her head. The yew poison continued to spread over her body, with bits of dead vegetation and rotting flesh falling from her in a steady flow, but she ignored it all. With her head resting awkwardly on her shoulder, Tarcha extended her hands high and then brought them both down together.

"The barrier has been removed," Oona's voice said. "The Destroyer is coming. Stand back and watch closely, Safewright. Like Tarcha, the Destroyer's power will be mine. And when it is—when her horde has been broken and there is no one left to attack or defend Kinscaer—I will ask you to choose." Under the continued assault of yew poison, the dead kithkin augur's flesh took on a sickly gray pallor and her extremities blackened.

"And you will serve me as your king and queen demand, or I shall take you along with your sapling and your giant."

Screams from the far wall reached Rhys's ears. Oona turned Tarcha's body toward the oven-hot blast of wind that blew in from the river. Brilliant orange fire lit the sky, illuminating the doun square below. Oona turned Tarcha's face up to the light, smiled confidently, and then waited as the Destroyer raged over the walls and descended upon them all.

* * * * *

Outside the walls of Kinscaer, the Destroyer felt the kithkin's protective barrier waver. Her first elated impulse was to charge forward and seize the opportunity while it lasted, but she hesitated, and far below her the horde of cinders and boggarts did the same.

The flames around her grew white-hot and she focused her thoughts. So far her fire had no effect on the barrier, yet it was buckling all the same. Either her strategy of using the horde to wear down Kinscaer's strength was working, or her enemies wanted the Destroyer to believe it was.

Her enemies. Thoughts of their betrayals stoked the fires within. She saw the hated sapling, wracked with pain but still wide-eyed and naïve in the mawkish pursuit of her sire's approval; the elf with stern eyes, whose stubborn pride prevented him from accepting any leader as worth following, or any followers as worth leading; the smug, disembodied voice that defied her to storm Kinscaer and do her worst; and Kinscaer itself, where she had been brutalized and violated by the doun's leaders and the passive complicity of its citizens. Perhaps she should briefly forestall her vengeance: the longer she stayed at Kinscaer, the more reasons she had to raze it to the ground, and the more satisfying its destruction would be.

The Destroyer felt the same strange tingling in her head before Oona's silky voice said, *Well, demon? Kinscaer still stands and those within await your return.*

The Destroyer said nothing, but fresh rage glowed red in her eyes.

Don't tell me you've grown lazy. There was a time when I would watch you galloping endlessly across the skies from one end of the horizon to the other. You were the Wanderwine's mirror image, a fiery river in the sky to match the watery one in the ground. You have fallen far indeed since you were shackled to that pitiful mortal shell. What a waste.

Tell me, spirit: Are you so degraded now that you cannot even act according to your own nature? Here, Oona said. *I shall extend an unmistakably clear invitation.*

Then the barrier protecting Kinscaer disappeared, and as it fell, the Destroyer's skull throbbed with the renewed urge to act. The horde below her broke free of its paralysis and surged forward.

Come to me now, Oona said. *It is your nature to tear down what others have made. This world that you rage against and ruin one piece at a time—this is my world. You are the Destroyer; I am the maker. We cannot coexist.* The silky voice dropped to a whisper that was far louder than anything the Destroyer had heard it say so far. *Kill me, or die. Anything less is unworthy of us both.*

The Destroyer's composure broke, and she roared in fury. Curling red streamers of flame erupted from her hands, feet, and eyes. The fiery orange-red tendrils spread out, bathing Kinscaer in a lurid glow. The entire horde charged toward the doun, straight through a withering hail of arrows from the defenders atop the walls. Boggarts and cinders fell by the score, only to be trampled by those that came after. In the momentary pause while the kithkin reloaded their bows, the horde's second wave reached the wall. By the time Kinscaer's defenders loosed their second volley of arrows, the invaders had scaled halfway up the wall toward the ragged hole the Destroyer had made.

Still roaring, the Destroyer did not wait for her horde—they were followers, so let them follow. She shot high into the air and then plunged down, leaving a fiery wake as she soared over the walls and straight toward the devastated doun square.

The first thing she noticed was the throng of dead kithkin, which emboldened her. Here was the true reason behind the barrier's failure—Oona's insults had been mere bluster to conceal how vulnerable she truly was. The Destroyer spotted the rest of her enemies as she descended, each standing in a cluster at the far end of the square—Tarcha, the elf, the sapling, and the long-armed giant. She could feel the powerful, oddly familiar magic they had gathered here, and she snorted contemptuously. The forces aligned against her were considerable, but they were not superior to her own. And those who wielded those forces were far from invulnerable.

She landed near the center of the square and immediately unleashed a torrent of fire at Tarcha. The stream exploded once it hit the augur's slack body, and the kithkin vanished in the maelstrom. The explosion sent the elf diving for cover as the giant scooped up the sapling with his uninjured arm and turned away, protecting the yew from the blast with his thick skin and considerable bulk.

The Destroyer rejoiced. The kithkin hag would raise no more protective barriers. The first and most troublesome of her targets was now a thing of charred flesh, blackened bones, and sputtering suet. The others would soon follow.

The Destroyer's exultance faded as Tarcha emerged from the lingering fireball. The kithkin augur was indeed burned black, but the ruined, smoking body seemed unconcerned by its sorry state, perhaps even unaware of it. The scorched figure floated up, accompanied by four golden faerie lights, and Tarcha's blistered features twisted into a cruel smile.

Everyone's being so helpful today, Oona's voice said, though it came through Tarcha's body. *Poisoning my construct for me once it has served its purpose, cremating the body—and all this from my sworn enemies! The mind boggles at the useful services you could all perform if you served me willingly. No matter: The end result will be the same.*

"Ashling." The sapling's voice echoed across the empty square. The Destroyer turned her head just long enough to send a withering beam of red light lancing toward the yew and the giant who carried her. Kiel bounced away from the beam, and it tore through the building behind him.

"I can help you," the sapling called, unperturbed by the casual attempt on her life. "Rhys and I can help you. But you must go no farther. Withdraw, and call off your horde."

"I shall kill you all," the Destroyer said, her eyes fixed on Tarcha's blackened body. "Starting with the kithkin witch."

"That is not Tarcha," the sapling said.

"I know who she is," the Destroyer growled.

No. You truly don't. Oona's voice came no longer from Tarcha, but from everywhere, pressing in on the Destroyer from all sides. *But I shall teach you.*

The Destroyer channeled her mounting rage into a fresh blast of fire. Arcane power, wild and frenzied, built up inside her, but when she tried to release it, nothing happened. Doubt blossomed in her chest, a cold and unfamiliar sensation. She snapped both hands out straight, mentally hurling a blistering ball of heat at Tarcha, but no flames came.

Wonderful! Tarcha's body clapped its hands merrily, breaking off several charred fingers. *And as I suspected. The kithkin's protective magic is remarkable, but she never plumbed the depths of its power. It is a far more versatile tool in my hands. Tarcha could barely keep your elemental fire out of Kinscaer, and it took the entire doun's support to do that. Whereas I have easily contained that same fire within the very body that houses it, and I have done so without assistance.*

The tiny marble of doubt in the Destroyer's chest expanded, restricting her breathing. She glanced down at her hands and saw that she was covered with a skin-tight layer of white mist, so pale as to be nearly invisible. The fire and smoke that normally rose from her joints were gone, fully contained by the magical veneer. The Destroyer turned back toward the sapling and the giant, but the killing stream of fire she conjured never emerged from her eyes.

Your rampage ends here, little matchstick. Tarcha's rapidly disintegrating body floated forward and the faeries above her began to sing. *Farewell.*

The Destroyer threw her head back and screamed in frustration. She did not wait for Tarcha to come to her, but rushed forward to meet her enemy head on. Her magic lent speed and force to her stride—Tarcha's barrier prevented the elemental fire from doing direct harm, but it could not stop the Destroyer from focusing it on herself. The stones exploded under her feet, hurling her headlong at Tarcha, and as the Destroyer slammed into the kithkin's midsection a truly rewarding look of astonishment crossed that ruined face.

The impact of the flying tackle sundered Tarcha's fragile body to pieces—her limbs separated from the torso and dropped, the torso split in two at the waist, and the head shot off into the crowd of dead kithkin. The Destroyer sailed clear through and then tumbled clumsily to the ground.

She bounced back to her feet with a vicious grin plastered across her flaming features, and then whirled to face Tarcha's remains. Though the pieces of the kithkin's body were still and lifeless, the Destroyer was still cocooned, her power still contained within the skin-tight blister.

A great boom from across the square shook the ground. The Destroyer ignored it and continued to stare at Tarcha's body, ready to charge forward and stomp the scattered pieces into gritty paste. She heard the sapling and the elf calling out to her, shouting the name "Ashling" over and over, and pleading with her to relent. The name meant little—she was the Destroyer, and the Destroyer ignored them. She had been right to choose Tarcha as her initial target, and now that she had the advantage she would not relent until the kithkin hag was well and truly dead.

And so she did not notice the giant descending upon her until it was far too late. Kiel had taken a prodigious leap straight up and over the center of Kinscaer, and by the time the Destroyer tore her gaze from Tarcha and looked up, all she could see were the soles of the giant's boots.

Kiel's landing cracked the foundations of buildings all across Kinscaer. It also sent up a cloud of dust, dirt, and broken rock that entirely obscured the area around himself, the Destroyer, and Tarcha's remains.

Below him, painfully crushed between the giant's feet and the bedrock that supported Kinscaer, the Destroyer's angry glow reasserted itself. She was dazed and pinned where she lay, but her body was far harder and more durable than stone. Her entire being was suffused with wild magic, and her physical form had been tempered by elemental fire. It would take more than a giant's weight to damage her, even if it were dropped from the top of a mountain.

Getting out from under the stump-legged brute was another matter. The Destroyer did not have the strength or the leverage to simply toss Kiel off—not at the moment. Since she could not channel her magic outward as withering fire, she channeled it inward. The giant grew steadily lighter as the power seeped into her muscles. She shifted and strained with all her might, and the giant perched atop her began to give.

Kiel must have sensed the Destroyer was about to burst free, for the crushing weight above her suddenly vanished. The Destroyer tried to hang on to the giant's feet as they withdrew, but she lost her grip as the broken rocks below her shifted. For a moment she lay prone and motionless, staring up into the hazy night sky.

The giant's face appeared at the edge of the hole and he fixed his small, piggish eyes upon her with an expression of startling tenderness and regret. "Pilgrim," Kiel said, and then he lunged in and slammed his fist down on the Destroyer's body. The blow drove her even deeper into the ragged hole, and once it landed the giant held his awkward position, with all of his weight balanced on knuckles that were still pressing down on the Destroyer.

Dazed but still uninjured, the Destroyer concentrated on the giant's fist. She was still surrounded by Tarcha's protective barrier but she was also more determined than ever to burn through it. She focused her fury on a single spot directly before her eyes, fiercely willing her heat to penetrate the shield and consume Kiel's hand.

Sadly, the time has come to end this. Oona's voice sounded inside the Destroyer's head. *Kinscaer is about to become much more crowded, and I'm a firm believer in finishing one task before starting another. In that we are alike, my little matchstick.*

But do not despair, Oona continued. *You were destined to serve my purposes in the end. Everyone is. As I told you before, the world and everyone in it is how I want them to be. No more and no less. Even you, Destroyer. Especially you. It was a simple matter to contain the elemental fire that drives you. Now I shall relieve you of it once and for all.*

The Destroyer's stomach rolled, and her vision blurred. She felt a nauseous internal wrench as something vital and essential pulled away from her. She heard the panicked thunder of galloping hooves. For the first time the noise started out strong and urgent, and then grew softer and more distant.

The Destroyer screamed then, and the wail that poured from her body was as much a horse's neigh as a demon's cry. In her mind's eye she saw herself bound to an altar as an ancient yew treefolk presided over her. All that she valued was being taken from her once more, her magic, her purpose, and her very identity. Once more she was utterly helpless to stop it.

No, she told herself. I will not be contained. The Destroyer forced herself upward. The bones in the giant's hand cracked. Kiel's knuckles split, and the giant yanked his fist away. Overbalanced, Kiel toppled to the ground, his awkward body stretched around the curving edge of the pit that contained the Destroyer.

The Destroyer did not hesitate this time, but sprang straight up into the empty air above the doun square. Blood and fire pounded in her veins, in her temples, and she heard nothing and saw no one as she rocketed up and over the walls of Kinscaer. Her body grew hotter and her spirit rose as she moved away from the doun square toward the river. She was dimly aware of concern and consternation behind her.

She ignored that and pressed on toward the Wanderbrine. Her horde would buy her the time she needed to shed the magical barrier that prevented the full expression of her fury, and then she would return. The doun's defenders had baffled her again, but she would never relent until Kinscaer was nothing more than dust and ashes. As Oona said, in that they were alike.

When she was halfway between Kinscaer and the river, the Destroyer noticed the riverbed was empty. The crude dam she had gouged into the soil was only enough to choke the Wanderbrine, not stop it completely. Her mind raced as her eyes raked the battlefield below—there was her horde, there was the bonfire she had made of Kinscaer's docks, but where was the water?

The Destroyer's gaze was drawn to a single slender figure near the riverbank. It was an elf maiden, and though she was too distant to be seen clearly, the Destroyer recognized her as one of the elves from Mistmeadow. The elf's elegant horns tilted as the maiden craned her head up toward the Destroyer. Her posture was intent as she raised her hand and crisply brought it down in some sort of signal.

The furious sounds of whitewater rapids came down on the Destroyer from above. With Kiel's sneak attack fresh in her mind, the Destroyer turned sharply and darted away in the hopes of getting out from under whatever was about to fall on her head.

As she streaked along the riverbanks mere feet above the ground, the Destroyer rolled over and looked up to see a gigantic tunnel of water hurtling down at her. The leading edge of the column was wide enough to cover half the riverbed and half the distance to Kinscaer. Her sudden burst of speed had been for naught; there was no way to dodge the full force of the Wanderbrine River as it slammed into her from above.

CHAPTER 15

Maralen steeled herself as the Destroyer erupted from Kinscaer and hurtled toward the river. She herself had stood as a kind of midwife at the Destroyer's emergence, and had since seen the rampant monster vent its fury firsthand, but Maralen was no less awestruck by her fierce and terrible beauty and no less resolved to stop the demon's bloody campaign.

The elf maiden did not allow herself to ponder why Kinscaer was still standing or why the Destroyer seemed to be fleeing the doun rather than assaulting it. Instead, Maralen emptied her mind of all conscious thought. Within its own calm, blank tranquility, her mind stretched out to those of her companions.

Iliona and Veesa were waiting nearby, sheltered from Sygg's magic but ready to follow up once the blow had been struck. Wryget was positioned back at the Source to guarantee that the flow of magic and water did not waver. Sygg's team was ready and in position, while Sygg himself was waiting around the first sharp bend upriver, floating high on a shapewater tower. The merrow had been crafting their most important spell even before the group arrived in Kinscaer, and though there were only five actual merrow involved, together they were shaping magic powerful enough to drown mountains.

Alongside Sygg on his floating tower was Brigid, and between them the Crescent of Morningtide. Brigid acknowledged

Maralen's presence, and then the archer's thoughts confirmed what Maralen already knew: If not for Brigid's firm grip and the Crescent's strong silver chain, Sygg would already be swimming rapidly upstream alone with the artifact between his teeth.

Maralen didn't need to be told they were ready, but she was reassured to find them so. They didn't need to be told when to strike, but as Maralen's thoughts brushed up against theirs, they all acted as one in tight, coordinated sequence. The spell was cast. The blow would soon fall, its descent guided by Brigid and the merrow.

The Destroyer blasted closer to the Wanderbrine. As she approached Maralen's position, her fiery eyes found the elf maiden's. Maralen did not flinch but stared back, her admiration for the Destroyer's primal beauty tinged with regret. It seemed wrong to stifle such a joyful, unrestrained spirit even if it was vicious and misguided. This regret quickly evaporated in the glare of Maralen's fierce and pragmatic survival instinct, however. No matter how much she valued the Destroyer's joyous lack of restraint, she valued the collective weight of everything else in the world even more.

The Destroyer continued to watch Maralen, and so she did not see the Wanderbrine rising behind her like some frothy blue-green serpent poised to strike. The fire-demon could not have seen the river's approach had she been staring straight at it—Kasella's Inkfathom magic had seen to that—so she was perhaps the only living thing to see the full majesty of what Sygg and his team had accomplished.

The Wanderbrine was airborne—miles and miles of furious rushing water cut loose from its riverbed and diverted into the skies over Kinscaer. The great unbroken rope of water was hundreds of feet wide, and it stretched back into the darkness and disappeared behind the horizon.

Under Sygg's expert guidance, the river's forward edge swung down to intersect the Destroyer's path. The Destroyer suddenly accelerated; weaving as she went. Her expression told Maralen that the monster finally recognized an ambush was in progress. The flaming figure rolled over in mid-flight to check the sky above her, and so caught the full force of the entire Wanderbrine squarely in the face.

Maralen was well clear of the deluge's initial impact, but she was all but submerged in the aftermath. Everything between Kinscaer and the riverbed vanished under a surge of foaming mud and stinging spray. Maralen was swept off her feet and she covered her mouth and nose, not to keep air in but to keep the driving water out.

The river continued to smash down upon the Destroyer—a steady, uninterrupted flood focused on a single point. The torrential blowback continued to batter Maralen as she found solid ground below her and struggled to stand. Wave after knee-high wave of silt and muddy water threatened to tear her loose from her temporary mooring and hurl her into the riverbed. Though Maralen was not the spell's main target and had seen the river coming, Sygg's attack had almost killed her and still might. She could scarcely imagine what it had been like for Ashling.

Maralen coughed and sputtered. The airborne stream of Wanderbrine became too thin to maintain an unbroken line between here and the horizon, so Sygg was forced to relent at last. The roar of the sky rapids dwindled, leaving behind a deceptively gentle lapping sound. Soft, slow waves toyed with the walls of Kinscaer as the vast, shimmering pools of flood water slowly drained back into the riverbed.

Maralen shook her head and wiped her face clean. She scanned the flooded field for the Destroyer and, not surprisingly, found Ashling where the river had first caught her. The

Destroyer was down on her hands and knees in a muddy bog, submerged almost up to her hips and shoulders. The tip of her nose barely touched the surface of the mud and her hot, ragged breaths churned the slurry directly below her lips. Steam bubbled up from her submerged arms and legs. The Destroyer's fire still burned, but it sputtered and flickered.

Maralen spotted something huge and blue skimming under the surface of the shallow water around Ashling—Sygg's man Artio, coming to further incapacitate the Destroyer. According to Sygg, once Artio had Ashling in his grip, Kasella would reveal herself and attempt to strike a final blow. If the assassin missed or the Destroyer broke free, Scathak would step in with his throwing knives while Artio and Kasella regrouped and struck again.

Maralen smiled slightly. That was according to Sygg, and so far everything had gone precisely as Sygg intended. Sygg's plan only went so far, however, and Maralen intended to take it in a far more constructive direction once the Destroyer was truly subdued. She carefully reached into her belt and drew a small, tightly folded scroll. Her nose wrinkled from the stench wafting up from the scroll, but Maralen smiled nonetheless.

Artio had no trouble getting close to his target, as the Destroyer still recovering from their opening gambit. The huge blue merrow surfaced and Maralen wondered once more how such a large creature managed to disappear in less than a foot of water. As the merrow bruiser folded himself over and around Ashling's kneeling body, Maralen saw Artio was half-covered in a shapewater breastplate, and that both his arms were enveloped in a thick sheaf of magically contained water.

The big merrow curled his long, flexible body around Ashling, engulfing her. The shapewater on his arms and chest abandoned his body and flowed over Artio and his captive alike. Artio cinched his grip and drew more water from the pools around him. In a matter of moments Ashling had disappeared under a thick layer of merrow bone and muscle that was in turn covered by a thick layer of shapewater. The strange mound shimmered and shook in the dim light, but none of the Destroyer's fire emerged from its center. Maralen was uncertain if Ashling was even trying to break loose and concerned for Artio once she did.

Maralen inhaled and held her breath as she carefully unfolded the scroll. Obtaining this document had been a costly and complicated business, but if it functioned as Maralen intended it would be well worth both the trouble and the stench.

Rusty ocher light flashed once from within the mound of shapewater. Maralen watched the outer edge of the construct bulge outward, but Artio and his magic held on. The Destroyer was fighting back at last, and what's worse, she seemed to be recovering her strength. If Kasella didn't strike soon, Maralen would have to act without her.

That will be sufficient, thank you very much.

Maralen almost dropped the scroll when she heard the familiar voice. Fear bolted through her stomach and on up her spine, but hatred quickly overwhelmed rising panic. Oona was here. The Fae Queen was not visible and probably not even corporeal at the moment, but now that she had spoken Maralen felt her presence in the air like a cloying, flowery scent.

Maralen was bound to Oona in ways neither of them dared admit, ways even they didn't yet understand, and so it was not surprising they had seemingly overlooked each other at such close range. Disquieting, to be sure, but not surprising. Each of them had put so much effort into hiding their thoughts from the other it would have been more of a shock if they had noticed each other.

So far Oona had not acknowledged Maralen's presence here, and the elf maiden was determined to keep it that way as long as she could. She had never before been able to observe Oona unaware and she was eager to see what she could learn from the unguarded Fae Queen. Gripping the scroll, Maralen quietly stepped back and crouched to watch.

Artio was a consummate professional. He did not relax his grip on Ashling when Oona spoke, or even turn his head to see who or what had addressed him. This was of course an unforgivable slight to a patrician like the Fae Queen, who wasted no time with her rebuke.

You there, the disembodied voice said. *Merrow oaf. Stand aside for your betters.* Artio did not reply but instead tightened his hold on the Destroyer.

Oona's voice dripped contempt. *So be it.* Four golden lights rose over Kinscaer, and then four golden faeries flew toward the river in a perfect diamond shape. They held strands of something between them. The quartet swooped low, and as they passed over Artio in his mound they dropped the strands.

Maralen watched these strange lengths of blue-flowered vine tumble down. She only recognized them as they splashed into Artio's outer layer of shapewater, and with that recognition came a dark, almost solemn feeling of numbness. The vines wriggled down through the shapewater until they found Artio's thick hide. They settled onto his body, twisting and grasping until they had arranged themselves into one single unbroken length. The line of vines let out a terrifying screech that stung Maralen's ears even through the shapewater shroud. One end of the vine rose and plunged into Artio's flesh while the other slithered up and wrapped itself tightly around his throat.

The big merrow winced and shuddered while the vines burrowed in. The surface of the shapewater churned and shook like a rain-swollen river. Below that, Artio's meaty arms shifted and separated, releasing a thin line of gleaming firelight. Maralen raised the scroll. The grappler's grip had been broken, and the entire affair was now in jeopardy.

Sensing things had gone wrong, Kasella materialized in the shadows behind Artio with a gleaming blue dagger in her fist. "Hold her," the Inkfathom assassin shouted. "Just a few seconds more." She raised the dagger and lunged forward, but Artio could not endure.

The shapewater dome erupted with a sickening sound. Artio thrashed and flopped away from the Destroyer, clawing at the vine around his throat and tearing at the section that had burrowed into his skin. Kasella ignored him and continued the lunge she had already begun, driving the point of the vibrant blue dagger toward the Destroyer's exposed back.

The strike never landed, for Ashling was no longer half-drowning in a puddle of filth but kneeling on a concave bed of hard-baked mud. Without Artio and his shapewater magic to douse her flames, the Destroyer's killing fire had returned and quickly gathered strength. Kasella's weapon very nearly touched Ashling's body, but the merrow arm holding it withered in the intense heat. Kasella's scorched fingers fell open and the assassin's dagger slipped from her grasp. The merrow screamed and threw herself backward toward the Wanderbrine, cradling her crippled arm as she fell.

We'll have no more of that, either. Maralen saw a thin white mist descend around Ashling and cling to the Destroyer like a second skin. The water closest to the monster stopped boiling; the waves of heat distortion rippling from her body vanished. Maralen felt the intensity of Ashling's flame diminish, and once again she was afraid. Oona had discovered magic powerful enough to dampen the Destroyer, and she didn't require five merrow and a river to get the job done. Where had she found it? And why didn't Maralen know about it before now?

The Destroyer rose on unsteady legs. She stared down at the misty coating on her hands and arms for a moment, and then she clenched her fists. Bending at the knee, Ashling sprang out of the bowl she had baked into the ground and landed once more on the muddy fields of Kinscaer. She was visibly weakened, her fires had cooled, but she was unbroken and unbowed.

Maralen dismissed her own fears, replacing them once more with anger and determination. Oona had surprised her with this unfamiliar magic, so it was only fair that Maralen should return the favor. Careful not to betray her presence there, the elf maiden reached out to Brigid with her mind. With her hands, she finished unfolding the pungent scroll.

* * * * *

Brigid heard Maralen's thoughts and silently acknowledged the elf maiden's request. Behind her, the Wanderbrine was starting to resume its normal ground-bound course. Water trickled into the riverbed below them as Brigid, still floating beside Sygg atop the merrow's column of water, lowered the Crescent so that she and Sygg were face-to-face.

"It's over," she said. "We failed."

"What? What do you mean? How do you know?"

"I know. We've got to bring the Crescent to Maralen."

"What for?" Sygg managed to sound exasperated, infuriated, and plaintive at the same time. "What can she do with it that I can't?"

"Get the job done," Brigid said. "And our deal was always clear: You don't get the Crescent until the job is done."

Sygg squeezed the curved pendant hard between his fingers. "Give it to me now, Brigid," he said. "You owe me everything, and you don't owe her anything. It's not yours, and you know it. You know it was never meant to be yours, but mine. The Source set it aside for me."

"But I'm the one who has it," Brigid said. "And you're in real danger of breaking our deal, Captain. Is that the news you want spreading up and down the river? That Sygg can't be trusted to hold up his end of a bargain?"

The merrow's eyes glittered. "You'd have to be alive to spread such slanderous talk."

"And you can probably kill me before I do. But can you kill Maralen before she tells this ugly little story? Can you stop her faeries from whispering it in every ear between here and the mountains?" She did not pull the Crescent toward her and she did not tighten her grip but instead stared calmly into the merrow's wide, inscrutable face. "We had a deal and we will see it through. I will take this to Maralen, and she will put it to good use. After that—no matter which way it goes—your treasure will be returned to you."

The merrow's gills flexed angrily and the barbels on his face stood out straight. "It's not treasure, you stumpy little landwalker; it's my destiny. Do you really imagine I would put up with you and that elf over a mere bit of wealth?" Sygg spat noisily over his shoulder. "I could buy and sell ten Kinscaers with the loot from any one of my secret caches. This was never about treasure, kithkin. It's about who I am, what I can do, and who I'm meant to be."

"It must be nice to know your place," Brigid said. "Most of us—me, for example—don't have the luxury of being sure about who we're meant to be." She shrugged. "So, back to the issue at hand: Do we both trust each other and honor the deal we made, or are you going to act like the unprincipled scum everyone says you are?"

Sygg squeezed the Crescent one last time and tried half-heartedly to pull it out of Brigid's grip. "Damn you and your elf boss, anyway," Sygg said. He released the Crescent and waved his hand parallel to the surface of the tower that supported them, which obligingly softened and sank back into the riverbed.

CHAPTER 16

The sapling stood beside Rhys on the walls of Kinscaer as the Destroyer endured the river. Sygg and his accomplices put on an amazing display, their spells driven by a primal force every bit as potent as the one driving Ashling. It may not have defeated the Destroyer, but rerouting the Wanderbrine onto the battlefield had swept away her horde. It would take hours, if not days, for them to regroup, and during the interval the survivors of Kinscaer would be safe.

No sooner had the river's sudden rush receded when a huge merrow engulfed the downed Destroyer and attempt to complete the job of smothering her flames. The sapling's heart went out to the brave blue warrior and she fervently wished him well, for it was clear to her that even after such a devastating attack, the Destroyer was far from beaten.

The sapling also spotted Maralen on the field, who was watching the struggle intently. Maralen's presence meant Iliona, Veesa, and Brigid were also close by. The sapling turned and glanced back into Kinscaer, where Kiel was being treated for his wounds and Endry was organizing the remains of his groundlings into rows and columns. She wondered if Endry was ready for a Vendilion reunion. More important, she wondered if she was ready to face Maralen.

The dark-eyed elf woman remained as much of a mystery

to the sapling as she was to everyone else. Maralen was unique, beyond even Colfenor's understanding, and so the sapling had to rely on her experience to form her own opinion. So far, she was not yet confident in her ability to evaluate. She wanted to like Maralen, to take the elf at face value and rely on her without reservation. She even sympathized with Maralen, or rather she sympathized with what she little she understood and believed about Maralen. They were both seeking a place for themselves in a world that was not kind to outsiders. They were both striving to achieve a specific measure of freedom for themselves and others. They were both heading for a confrontation with the same ancient, subtle, and implacable foe.

The sapling stole a guilty sideways glance at Rhys. Unlike her, he had the ability to assess and then act without second-guessing himself. She longed to be that self-assured, and if not that she at least wanted to agree with Rhys's acceptance of the dark-haired elf maiden—but she wasn't and didn't.

The sapling had seen Maralen do things that could not easily be put into words, terrible things that required grim, unshakable resolve despite their obviously dire consequences. Ashling had suffered terribly from the elf maiden's machinations, as had the sapling herself. She wondered what Rhys would think if he knew the truth about Maralen's actions on the night the Great Aurora came, if he knew what the sapling knew about the Destroyer's true origins. She hadn't told him yet because in the end, the sapling didn't believe Maralen was malicious. The elf maiden was aloof, callous, and very selfish, but she was not malicious. Sadly, the sapling had learned that in this dark world, there was very little practical difference.

"We should do something." Rhys's throat was tight, and he muttered his words through clenched teeth. "But I've no idea what."

The sapling shared Rhys's anxiety, and in fact felt it as keenly as her own. They had both come to batter the Destroyer into submission and then rescue Ashling from the elemental fire—and to rescue it from Ashling in the bargain. They had tried, and they had failed. Now Kinscaer was largely unprotected, Maralen and her cohorts had done most of the battering, and Oona was determined to absorb the Destroyer's power as she had Tarcha's. Once the Fae Queen had done that, the sapling was sure that she'd also discard Ashling's remains as casually as she had Tarcha's.

"We must go to her," the sapling said. She leaned forward and allowed herself to slowly topple over the edge of the wall, catching the edge of the rampart with one of her branches. She steadied herself against the wall with another and smoothly descended.

"Wait!" Rhys's concerned face peered down as he called out to her. "To whom must we go, Ashling or Maralen?"

"Brigid is here as well," said the sapling, "and the Vendilion sisters."

"Let's start with the two I actually asked about."

"Forgive me. I was initially speaking of Ashling. She is under attack by powerful beings who do not understand how dangerous she is."

"But we've all seen what she can do," Rhys said. "There isn't a tribe in all Shadowmoor that doesn't respect her as a threat."

"You misunderstand. Ashling is dangerous because of the power she wields and the vengeful fury within her, but she's all the more dangerous because she can't control either. Right now she is little more than an engine of destruction with an effectively limitless fuel supply. Such an engine must be dismantled carefully and delicately or the results will be even more devastating than allowing her to maraud unchecked."

She stopped lowering herself and turned to face Rhys above. "Please, Half-Brother. I cannot succeed without you."

Rhys's face creased. "All right," he said. He nimbly hopped up on the top edge of the wall and stepped out onto the branch supporting the sapling's weight. Rhys bent his knees and slid down the smooth bough until he reached the sapling's trunk, and then he bounded lightly to the ground below.

She joined him at the base of the wall just as the Destroyer broke free from the big merrow's embrace. Rhys instinctively stepped in front of the sapling when the Destroyer's fire flared, an endearing but totally unnecessary act. The renewed flames revealed another merrow, who struck at Ashling but was easily rebuffed. This smaller merrow fell back into puddles that were no longer deep enough to conceal her, and she splashed and struggled to get clear of the Destroyer.

We'll have no more of that, either. Oona's voice hit the sapling like a slap across the face. She reflexively searched the battlefield but saw no evidence that the Fae Queen was physically present. All the same, a white mist that was eerily similar to the barrier Tarcha erected around Kinscaer settled over Ashling's body, and then the Destroyer's fire all but vanished. Ashling convulsed and staggered, her eyes wide and her mouth open, though the envelope of mist around her canceled any sounds she made.

"What's happening?" Rhys asked. The sapling could not answer, for the events as she perceived them were almost beyond her ability to comprehend, much less articulate.

Oona had the Destroyer's body completely under her power—Tarcha's power, the sapling reminded herself. If the sapling viewed the world as patterns of magical force, she saw Oona as a vast and endless sea of blue-green flowers and the Destroyer as an ingot of pure, solid fire. The fiery spike floated on this leafy sea, surrounded by it, held fast by it, yet entirely separate from it. As the sapling watched, the ingot sank out of sight and the leafy sea converged around it, squeezing it tight. For a moment the sapling saw nothing but the flowers and heard nothing but a pulsating force, and then a single devastating crack echoed across her mind.

Oona's swell of triumph was like an ear-splitting shriek, though in fact it made no sound. The sapling realized the Fae Queen had found a seam between Ashling and her rampant elemental spirit, the boundary line that marked where the two had been fused into one. Using Tarcha's power, Oona exerted unimaginable pressure on that seam until it cracked. She recreated the separation between the two that had been one, and her power quickly wormed its way inside the divide, widening it.

Rhys shouted in surprise as the sapling swept him up in her boughs and rushed forward. "Hey!" he said. "Where are we going?"

In truth, the sapling didn't know what she intended to do, so she did not answer. She knew what Oona was attempting even if she couldn't explain it to her half-brother, and she also knew they could not allow it. Of all the terrible potential outcomes they faced, Oona becoming greater and stronger was by far the worst. It was the antithesis of what Colfenor wanted them to achieve, the exact opposite of what he had given his life to make possible. Oona's grip on the world would not be weakened but strengthened, and future generations would continue to suffer her hidden tyranny.

In Ashling's hands, the Destroyer's power was a nigh-unstoppable force. She was crazed and violent, but her moves could be anticipated and, with the right preparations, countered. The Queen of the Fae was another matter. Oona was far too old and crafty to trust with such devastating strength. She would use this newfound might quietly and according to her own grand designs over hundreds of years, as she had done on Lorwyn and Shadowmoor for centuries. No one alive understood that particular danger better than the sapling. Whole generations of mortal beings would live and die before anyone realized how profoundly the Fae Queen wielding elemental fire had affected the world, and by then it would be far too late.

As she drew close to the Destroyer, the sapling smoothly deposited Rhys on the ground without slowing. He was the only one who could carry on Colfenor's work if the sapling fell, but he was completely unprepared to stand against Oona. The sapling herself was only slightly better off on that score, but she carried knowledge and lore that was at least as old as the Fae Queen. She hoped that it was also as potent and that she would divine how to employ that knowledge before Oona became so mighty they'd never be able to stand against her.

When the sapling was but a stone's throw away from Ashling, the Destroyer's convulsions stopped. Ashling floated freely above the ground, rotating slowly, but the sapling did not stop her forward charge until Oona addressed her directly.

That's far enough, you toxic little weed. A pressure wave slammed into the sapling's face and halted her progress. *It's only fitting that Colfenor's clipping should be here to witness his failure firsthand, but you must mind your manners. How many times has the elemental fire consumed you, sapling? I would not expect you to be so eager to try it again. But be patient. Soon I will control the Destroyer's power, and then I shall be happy to bathe you in it until you've had your fill.*

The sapling reached deep within to call forth the magic Colfenor spent his last decades preparing. The time was wrong, the place was wrong, and the circumstances were wrong, but if she didn't use them now she might never get the chance. Curious or perhaps simply amused, Oona watched silently as the sapling simultaneously drew raw magical energy from the land itself and called upon Rhys to help her shape it.

I'm ready. Rhys's thoughts were as steady and strong as his voice. *What must I do?*

Yes, little yew weed. Tell us, tell us all. What must he do?

The sapling ignored Oona's taunts and prepared to share all she knew with her half-brother. She stopped when Brigid and Sygg sailed into view atop a short column of water. The Wanderbrine had recovered only a few inches of its usual depth, but those few inches carried the strange pair as quickly as if the river was swollen to flood levels.

"Sapling?" Rhys called.

A moment, Half-Brother. There was something strange in Brigid's hand—physically, it was small and insubstantial, but it radiated waves of the same staggering power that had raised the Wanderbrine into the sky. The silver pendant was a conduit for vast elemental power that seemed familiar to Colfenor's memories. The sapling could only guess why Brigid had brought it here or what effect it would have on their desperate situation.

Maralen stepped forward from the riverbed. The sapling noted that Oona had not noticed the elf maiden's presence, and she quietly exulted. If Maralen could slip past Oona's notice, the Fae Queen's defenses were far from perfect.

"Queen of the Fae," the sapling called. "Show yourself. Face me or I will know you fear me." If she could keep Oona talking, Oona wouldn't be able to do any more harm to Ashling or notice Maralen, and the sapling would have time to observe Brigid and learn what the kithkin was up to.

I have many faces, silly child.

Brigid and Sygg floated up to the river's edge. The kithkin smoothly leaped from the tower to solid ground and sprinted to Maralen's side.

But you are not worthy of my true presence, so you will have to make do with my absence and the slight regard I have for you. It is all you deserve.

Brigid held the pendant out to Maralen, but she did not remove it from her neck. The elf nodded and gingerly took hold of the crescent-shaped necklace between her fingers. With the other hand, she held a long, coarsely made scroll up to her face.

"What will you do with the elemental fire, O Queen?" The sapling spoke with force and confidence she did not feel. "The world has already collapsed under the crippling weight of your glamer. This world and everyone in it are submerged in your lies. You rule Shadowmoor, yet no one even knows you exist. How can you possibly crave more power, greater control? What could you possibly do with it?"

I will do as I have always done, as I please. With whatever and whomever I please. You—

Nearby, Maralen began to read. The first syllables had barely passed her lips when Oona's voice twisted into an inarticulate hiss of outrage. Ashling's body bobbed like a cork in the water, still contained within its second skin of white mist. Oona recovered her voice and her control over Ashling, but she had lost much of her composure.

You, she snarled. Ashling's body rotated until it was facing Maralen. The elf continued to read from the scroll in her outstretched hand. She also extended her other hand so that Brigid had to step forward to keep the chain from digging into her neck.

You will regret coming here, Oona said. *You're too late, by the way, and now you have no chance of—what are you doing, vile beast?*

The sapling also wondered, but as Maralen continued to read, the sapling understood. The scroll belonged to Rosheen

Meanderer, and it was the very same one the sapling sent Endry to retrieve. Endry had said other faeries beat him to it, but he never mentioned those faeries were his own sisters—who had no doubt delivered it to Maralen.

Stop this at once, Oona said. *Or I shall erase the very memory of you. To dream of you will be punishable by death.*

Maralen did not stop. Her voice echoed and boomed like thunder as she pronounced the words on the scroll. The crescent pendant shined brighter than the full moon.

Rosheen's scroll was uniquely powerful, as it had been inscribed with all of the oracular giantess's random thoughts and fancies before the Great Aurora came. In it were descriptions of many things that had happened, and more that hadn't happened yet. Rosheen's prophetic magic was as complex as it was potent, and as far as the sapling knew it was impossible to benefit from the scroll without knowledge of the world it described—either through personal experience or from detailed and direct study. The sapling had planned to use the scroll as a touchstone to that world, to increase her understanding of how things were before they became as they are.

Oona's words were loud, piercing. *I am your master. Obey me.*

Maralen did not obey. She was employing the scroll differently than the sapling intended. In the elf's hands, the scroll's totemic magic combined with the force being channeled through the crescent pendant. Earlier, by altering her perceptions, the sapling had seen Ashling as a flaming ingot against the endless tide of Oona's magic. Through those same perceptions, she now saw the power of the scroll mingle with that of the crescent like two streams merging into large river—though these particular streams never truly blended. Instead, they remained distinct, two irregular halves that formed an elegant, symmetrical whole.

In her previous vision, Ashling stood as a physical representation of the Destroyer's fire. The crescent filled that same role in the actual world, a living, active piece of elemental magic that existed to counterbalance the Destroyer's own. Someone connected to that power through the crescent—as Maralen was—would be on equal terms with the Destroyer for as long as her magic and her willpower held out.

The braided coils of arcane energy swam across the gap between Maralen and the Destroyer. They washed over her, surrounded her. The white mist around Ashling reflected the crescent's blue glow and the scroll's pale yellow shine until the Destroyer was shrouded in a swirling kaleidoscope of scintillating colors.

Four golden faeries appeared above Ashling. They streaked toward Maralen and Brigid, but only two managed to get close. The other pair stopped short in midair as if running into an invisible wall—or another pair of faeries.

"Gotcha!" Veesa howled. She yanked her pin-sized blade out of the male faerie's torso and hurled his body to the ground.

"Vendilion rule the skies!" Iliona added. She wiped blood from her weapon on the second dead faerie's shining robe before letting him fall. "You golden boys sing nice, but you're nothing compared to real fighting Fae!"

The remaining pair of Oona's faeries continued on toward Maralen, ignoring the deaths of their brothers. They flew inside her arm's reach, but before they could strike each was swept aside and hurled backward by a powerful unseen wind.

How dare you? Oona sounded petulant, a child deprived of her favorite treat, a bully robbed of her favorite victim.

Maralen did not reply. Instead, she raised her voice and shouted the incomprehensible words on Rosheen's scroll. She raised the crescent as high as the chain and Brigid's height allowed.

Stop! You will stop!

The form-fitting shape around Ashling let out a long, sibilant sound like a lover's sigh, a sound that did not have the awful sudden finality of the one that accompanied Oona's attempt to pry Ashling away from the Destroyer's fire. It was the rich, encouraging sound of a seed coat cracking open, or that of a fresh green shoot pushing up through frozen soil.

A vertical line appeared on Ashling's forehead and raced down the center of her face. Oona roared, and her rage was every bit as loud and terrifying as the Destroyer's. A thunderous tremor shook the ground, followed by another, and another. The overwhelming drumbeat of pounding hooves grew louder and more rapid until it seemed to be one single, sustained sound that had no beginning and no end.

The chrysalis of magic around the Destroyer shattered, bringing simultaneous screams from Ashling, Maralen, and Brigid. A gout of flame exploded up from Ashling's body, and as it rose into the sky it swelled and expanded until it was larger than Kinscaer itself. Below, Ashling crumpled to the ground with eyes closed and limbs slack. Her skin had taken on a hard, burnished texture—jet black but for a series of graceful bone white shapes and swirls. The only vestiges of flame visible on her body now were those on her scalp, and these danced and flickered atop her skull like the wind-blown tresses of a storybook princess.

The great mass of fire hung in the air for a moment. The sapling felt her uppermost needles and branches crinkling in the heat, but she did not look away. So it was that she saw the fireball coalesce and contract into a four-legged equine shape. The horse-thing reared and stomped the air with each leg in succession. It stamped and snorted until its fearsome body was whole.

Now complete, the white horse's gigantic muscles rippled

across its flanks. Its flaming mane ran halfway down the length of its broad back, and its gleaming black hooves struck sparks from the air that continued to burn long after they drifted to the soggy ground below. The air itself bent around the heat from its dazzling white coat.

The sapling tried, but she could not tear her eyes from the glorious creature. If yew tears flowed more freely, she would have openly wept from the sheer majesty of the elemental spirit.

Maralen was not so awestruck. She and Brigid both faltered when the horse broke free, but now the kithkin had regained her balance and the elf held her arms out straight and steady. Maralen brandished both scroll and crescent. She read from the text and her voice echoed like whispers in a madman's dream.

The sapling's paralysis broke. She dropped her gaze from the fiery horse to Ashling below, searching for the power Maralen had braided together and sent at the Destroyer. She found it halfway between the horse and the ground, a flowing helix of translucent force snaking its way upward. It seemed pale and sickly under the horse's fiery light, and it was not moving quickly enough to catch its vibrant and robust quarry.

The horse sensed the approach of Maralen's spell, and it twisted its muscular neck to spot the oncoming braid over its own shoulder. The flames in its eyes and along its mane contracted but grew infinitely brighter. It peered intently at the spell effect, gauging it as a potential threat or nuisance. The great horse suddenly wheeled and reared high and slashed the air with its forelegs.

Maralen shouted her final words and then snapped her jaws shut with a click. She lowered the scroll first, and then the crescent, to Brigid's visible relief. The braided spell sank away from the horse immediately, drifting down as slowly and as steadily as it had climbed. The dark-eyed elf smiled sharply and looked up at the fiery elemental horse. She cocked her head to one side, crossed her arms over her chest, and waited.

The horse snorted. It tossed its head, snorted again, and then it followed the spell column's descent. Its flames grew longer and paler, flickering through a rainbow of vivid colors. The braided magic retreated past Ashling's unmoving form and approached Maralen, who still stood staring quizzically up at the great wild spirit.

The elemental let out a nervous whinny, pawed the air once, and then dived at Maralen. The sapling instinctively fell back and crouched with her branches folded in front of her face. Even Brigid dived for cover, but Maralen simply stood and stared.

The braided spell and the fiery horse struck Maralen's body at the same time. The horse's nose collapsed down to the size of a heavy spear and disappeared into Maralen's face. The rest of its body followed the same impossible path, pouring into the elf's body through a funnel of spectral light and howling winds. The last bit of the final hoof vanished into Maralen, and then finally the elf's body moved. Maralen's neck straightened and her arms and legs snapped out rigid. Her eyes rolled back and her head thrashed from left to right. An invisible wave of force radiated from her body in a perfect circle, boiling away all the water and baking the ground dry below her. Maralen dropped, staggered forward, and then pitched face-first onto the ground.

Brigid quickly stepped forward and crouched beside her comrade. She glanced over at the sapling and called, "She's alive." She rocked back on her seat and crossed her legs. "I'm just going to wait until she wakes up, if it's all the same to you."

"What has she done?" The sapling wasn't entirely if she should rejoice or bemoan the fact that Maralen had survived, and the archer's half-hearted shrug did nothing to help resolve her feelings.

She has made me very angry, Oona's voice said. *And she has sealed your doom ten times over. Each and every one of you.*

"Is that supposed to be a scary threat?" Iliona rose up from the riverbed and buzzed over to circle Maralen. "You're the one who sounds scared, Great Mother."

Iliona. You were always my least favorite.

"And don't think I haven't done all I can to be worthy of that high opinion," Iliona said. "First born, least loved. I'm ashamed, Mother. How dare you be so petty with your own children?"

See to your false mother, turncoat, Oona said. *Or better still, go and collect your sister and your wastrel brother. I would have words with the Vendilion clique.*

Iliona sneered. She streaked back toward Maralen and the sapling lost sight of her.

Now, then. little weed. Attend me.

The sapling concentrated to keep the Fae Queen from digging any deeper into her mind. "We are enemies, O Queen. What do we have to discuss?"

We need not be enemies, Oona said. *But let me speak of more urgent matters. Iliona is wrong, as usual. She is shortsighted, vainglorious, and stubborn, as are all my children. She brings an especially irksome brand of caprice to the family.*

But I digress. Iliona is wrong in that I do not threaten or bluster when I say you are doomed. My part in your nasty little lives is over. The abomination you call Maralen will bring about your deaths more surely and swiftly than even I could. She is the one who truly threatens you. I possess the balm that soothes all elemental fire. The power she stole from the Destroyer is useless against me. You are not only doomed but damned and fools if you believe I was the only one "Maralen the Destroyer" would see burned.

The sapling considered Oona's words carefully. "Why tell me this?"

Because I have lost this battle. But the war goes on, and I shall win that in short order. Maralen cannot defeat me, never ever, and though I could best her by simply withdrawing for a hundred years or so until she died, I prefer to remove her sooner. It's pride, I'm afraid. I cannot stand to be reminded of my own folly. Would that she never existed. But as she does, I can never truly rest until I ensure she does not.

"Your meaning eludes me, Queen of the Fae."

Oona continued as if she were alone and musing to herself. *Tarcha—now there was a passing fancy of which I can be proud. When I made my Tarcha, she had none of the flaws or shortcomings my Maralen had. She was loyal, she served me well, and then she died. Quite like one of my actual children. Speaking of . . . welcome, Veesa, Iliona, Endry. It's time to come home. Now.*

Iliona buzzed her wings angrily and hovered precisely where she was. "Get stuffed, Great Mother."

I see. Very well. You shall be missed, and you shall be mourned. You shall be killed first, of course, but it's all the same in the end. And your siblings?

Veesa swept into view with Endry close behind. The male faerie's face was downcast and he dipped and hitched as he flew, as if he were dragging his feet.

The pretender is unconscious, Oona said. *And so we all can stop pretending. End your ridiculous rebellion. The Vendilion clique is no more; the Vendilion twins may yet be salvaged. Stand by me once more. All will be forgiven.*

Neither Veesa nor Endry moved. Iliona shouted, "Tell her to get stuffed! I did!"

Silence, Oona said. Iliona yelped and fell to the ground, where she thrashed and swore. *Veesa. You are the sharpest of the three, and perhaps the most pragmatic. I remember the day you stepped from your pod. I knew your name instantly. You were always Veesa. Do you remember that, my child?*

Veesa muttered, "Yes, Great Mother."

Stand by me once more, Oona said again. *All will be forgiven.* The ground just outside the blasted circle surrounding Maralen erupted in a string of white mushroom caps. The gleaming toadstools formed a perfect ring in the muddy soil, and the sapling thought she heard a distant hum of ethereal voices.

Veesa glanced sideways at her brother Endry, and then across the stretch of blasted ground to Maralen's prone form, where Iliona was still struggling to become airborne. Veesa looked down into the center of the faerie ring.

"Yes, Great Mother." To the surprise of all but Oona herself, Veesa sadly drifted forward over the ring of mushrooms. Veesa's body flickered and shimmered at first, and then it disappeared completely. The ring of mushrooms wilted and folded back to the soil, only to be replaced by a fresh new ring that gleamed in the darkness.

Endry?

The male faerie lifted his head. "No, Great Mother. We talked about this, remember? The sapling needs me. I choose her. Not you and not the elf."

Curious. I am disappointed.

"I know, Great Mother."

But I would see what becomes of you. Do fare well, Endry. And keep in touch. We wouldn't want Veesa to waste away worrying about you.

Oona's presence gradually slipped away, but even after she was gone it was a very long time before anyone spoke.

CHAPTER 17

Brigid opened her eyes and stared at the sky. It took her a moment to remember where she was and what she had been doing, and when she did she sat bolt upright.

At least she was among friends. Maralen lay next to her and Rhys stood nearby, along with the sapling and Ashling. The flamekin was a flamekin again: not a doun-killing destroyer or a blackened, skeletal cinder, but an actual burning flamekin from before the Great Aurora.

Iliona fluttered down, facing Brigid sternly with her arms crossed. "Wake up, you lazy sack." She kicked the tip of the kithkin archer's nose with her sharp-toed foot.

"Hey!" Brigid waved her back and stood up. "I'm awake."

"Your eyes are open, chunky, but your brain is still asleep," Iliona said. "I recognize that gormless, pie-eyed expression." She smirked. "I know what goes on in that irregular-shaped melon of yours because I've been inside your dreams, remember?"

"I'm the only one who does remember," Brigid said. "And if you call me 'chunky' again I'm going to snap you in half like a stale crust of bread."

Maralen stirred. Brigid and Iliona abandoned their argument and both approached Maralen as the elf maiden quickly rose to her feet.

"It worked." Maralen's face showed none of the foggy confusion that still plagued Brigid. The elf's dark eyes glittered. She raised her hand and a small cone of flame ignited over her open palm. "The fire is mine." She started, and then focused her eyes on Iliona through the flame. "Where are your siblings?"

Iliona petulantly tossed her head and turned her back on Maralen. "Veesa went back to the Great Mother," she said. "And Endry is still following the sapling around with that mawkish expression of his."

Maralen considered this. "And Oona has withdrawn?"

"She has," Iliona said. "Though I don't know why she didn't kill you before she left. You were a pretty easy target while you were napping."

"I'm sure you saw it that way," Maralen said. She shook her hand, and the cone of fire flickered out. "But it's far more complicated than that. Oona wouldn't take the risk of my surprising her, especially not after I stole the elemental fire out from under her nose.

"Your Great Mother is a patient thing, but only because time is usually on her side. I'm sure she's holed up somewhere right now, plotting her schemes and gathering her resources. She'll return to hunt me down eventually."

Brigid stepped forward. "I think you mean 'hunt *us* down,' Boss. You weren't awake for this, but Oona more or less drew a line and told everybody to pick a side: hers or yours. And she was keeping close track of who chose whom."

"Oh, I was awake," Maralen said. "I chose not to participate. And rest easy, my friend. I won't forget who chose to stand with me anymore than Oona will."

"Glad to hear it," Brigid said. "So, what's our next move? Do we regroup, consider our options, and—"

"We find Oona and kill her," Maralen said.

"Oh," Brigid said. "Who's 'we' in your view?"

"That remains to be seen," the elf said, and Brigid did not like the reckless gleam in Maralen's eye when she said it. "I need to sort a few things out here before we move on, but we're leaving straight after that."

"Where? Where are we going?"

Maralen turned to Iliona. "Cayr Ulios?" The faerie nodded. "Cayr Ulios."

"The elf capital? Why? How do you know—"?

"Just because Veesa and I are no longer speaking doesn't mean I don't know where she is," Iliona said. "She's still my sister. I always know where she is just like I know my hands are at the end of my arms."

"Then Veesa knows where you are," Brigid said. "And she'll know you're coming. She'll tell Oona." The archer turned to Maralen. "It's a trap, Boss."

Maralen nodded. "A very obvious one."

Brigid waited a moment, and then said, "You're going to walk into it anyway, aren't you?"

"We are indeed."

"Oh, are 'we'? You know, that isn't the kind of command decision that inspires confidence in one's leader."

"Oona is afraid," Maralen said. "She gave me a small portion of her power, which I kept even though she tried to take it back. I have the elemental fire, which I stole from her. I have Rosheen's scroll, which I stole from her. I have the Crescent of Morningtide—"

"Which belongs to Sygg," Brigid said. "And we have to give it back. That was the deal."

"But not now," Maralen said. "Listen. I have obtained nearly every major advantage Oona has sought. Now she's not sure just how powerful I am and she's not willing to let me take anything else. She's not seeking a direct confrontation, and so that's what we're going to give her."

Brigid nodded. "I see a flaw in that plan, Boss. If you're not actually strong enough to beat Oona—"

"Oh, I'm not," Maralen said.

Brigid paused. "All right, then. Since you're not actually strong enough to beat Oona—"

"We won't win or lose based on raw strength, Brigid," Maralen said. "A kithkin can kill a giant if she knows where to stab."

"And you know where to stab Oona."

"In a manner of speaking."

"I wish you luck in that endeavor, ladies." Sygg rose up from the diminished Wanderbrine. "But our business is hereby concluded." His serpentine body followed his sleek, scaled head as he slithered up onto the riverbank. He drew his tail up behind him, curled it tight, and then shoved himself forward on his tough, stubby fins. "We had a deal. My team did the job. I'm here for payment."

"You'll get it," Brigid said. "The boss and I were just talking about that."

"You were talking about it," Sygg said. He stopped short of Brigid and the others and fanned his gills. "She was changing the subject. And as I'm sure you remember, Brigid, I get nervous when people who owe me dance around the topic of making good."

"Captain," Maralen said. "Brigid is right: You will get what we promised you."

"But," Sygg said, sarcastically drawing out the word and rolling his eyes. "Go ahead, I know you're about to say it."

Maralen smiled. "But," she said, matching Sygg's acerbic pronunciation exactly. "I'd like to propose a short delay. You'll be paid in full, just—"

"Just not now," Sygg said. He fixed his huge yellow eyes on Brigid and sneered. "We had a deal."

"We still do," Maralen said.

"No," Sygg said. "We have a problem." He shot up on his coiled tail so that he towered over Maralen and Brigid. Sygg's throat rippled and he let out a strange, hollow keening that vibrated in Brigid's skull. Scathak surged up from the river and slithered up on the banks. He had one lanky arm wrapped tightly around Artio's shoulder, and he gently deposited the blue bruiser on the sodden ground. He looked to Sygg, who nodded, and then Scathak threw his arms out wide. Muddy water sprayed from his scales, but the liquid froze in place rather than falling to the ground. Scathak drew his hands in to his chest, collecting the sharp, thin sticks of water until his palms were filled with needlelike darts.

"We bled for you," Sygg said angrily. "Artio here might not survive and you ask us to wait like servants, like docile pets?"

"I don't see Kasella," Brigid whispered. "That means she's already here."

"I know." Maralen stared hard at Sygg, her face all but expressionless.

"We aren't waiting," Sygg said. "We're taking the Crescent and leaving. If either of you interfere, I'll have you chopped into tiny pieces and baited on hooks."

"Then our business really is concluded." Maralen's voice was grim and even. "Thank you for your contributions, Captain. We couldn't have done it without you."

Sygg continued to stare, clearly not trusting Maralen's sudden capitulation. "Scathak," he said. "I'm going to take the Crescent off Brigid now. If any of them move—the elf, the faerie, any of them—kill Brigid first."

"Thanks, old friend," Brigid said. She didn't believe for a moment that she was Sygg's first concern if things turned violent. The fact that Sygg hadn't even mentioned Maralen meant the elf was Kasella's target, and that the stealthy Inkfathom assassin was poised to strike.

Maralen spoke quietly. "Stand still, Brigid. This will be over soon."

"That's what I'm afraid of."

Maralen inhaled deeply. "Iliona?"

"The fish-woman is right behind you to the left," the Vendilion faerie said. "Lurking in your blind spot."

"Thank you." Maralen did not move, did not so much as blink, but her eyes became like two black gemstones in their sockets. A swirling stream of purple smoke whipped up behind Maralen and curled into a tall vortex. Brigid saw Kasella through the smoke and dust, one arm withered and pressed tightly to her side, the other bearing a vicious blue-bladed dagger.

The Inkfathom assassin coughed and sputtered. She struck at the smoke with her knife but the ephemeral stuff simply swirled around the blade. With her eyes on Sygg, Maralen cocked her head to one side. Behind her, Kasella shouted in shock and surprise as the cyclone shot into the air. The Inkfathom assassin's cries dwindled as she hurtled high into the sky and disappeared.

Scathak threw a handful of watery needles toward Maralen and Brigid. The elf maiden waved her arm, and a second plume of black smoke followed her moving hand. The needles struck the smoky trail and stopped dead. Maralen pirouetted like a dancer, spinning entirely around and drawing a looping line of smoke as she went. The shapewater needles splashed to the ground behind her, and when she was once more facing Sygg, Maralen slapped her arm out straight and let out a short, savage cry.

Smoke puffed into existence below Sygg, Scathak, and Artio. Scathak hissed and keened and sluggish Artio groaned as all three were dragged up into the night sky, but Captain Sygg made no sound. He simply stared straight into Brigid's eyes, his pupils tightening to sharp vertical slits. His wide blue lips pulled back to reveal sharp, white teeth.

"Baited on hooks," Sygg growled. "I swear it." And then Sygg was gone, hurtling up and out of sight amid a cloud of Maralen's stolen magic.

For a moment the riverbed was silent, and then Iliona said, "Good riddance. I hate the smell of fish."

Brigid still watched the sky, staring at the last place she had seen Sygg. "That was a mistake, Boss."

"Perhaps," Maralen said. "If it was, at least we'll live to regret it."

"You should have killed him if you were going to break the deal," Brigid said. "He'll come after us. In force."

"And we'll worry about that when it happens," Maralen said. "Now. You two check in with Rhys and the others. Find out what they intend to do. Encourage them to join us in Cayr Ulios. Oona has already made an alliance with the elves there. I want all the help we can get."

"Will do," Brigid said. "But what will you do, Boss?"

Maralen smiled. "I'm going to give the cinder horde its new orders."

* * * * *

Rhys stared at the jet-black porcelain-skinned creature sleeping in front of him. Ashling was no longer the Destroyer, but she was also nothing else he recognized. As a vengeful demon, she had appeared to be a skeletal figure surrounded by a body of solid flames. Now her body was flesh again—stony flesh, to be sure, but flesh all the same. Instead of surrounding her, flames now merely licked out from her shoulders, elbows, and knees. A brilliant mane of fiery tresses crowned her head and when her eyelids fluttered they revealed flames crackling deep within her skull.

Was this what cinders were supposed to be—living furnaces who barely contained their inner fire? Or had fusing with the elemental spirit made Ashling into some sort of freak who burned brighter and hotter than the rest of her tribe?

"Is she alive?" Brigid Baeli stood beside the sapling with a look of genuine concern. Iliona hovered over the kithkin archer's shoulder. Rhys shifted so he could see and hear the new arrivals without leaving Ashling's side.

"She is alive," the sapling said. She slid between Brigid and Ashling, facing the archer to keep her from passing. "Your master has done a terrible thing here today. What are your intentions?"

"I'm just trying to keep up," Brigid said. "Oona and Maralen are headed for a showdown. It's time to pick a side."

"That is no choice at all. Neither of them can be trusted, they've proven that. And with the power they have—"

"Trust is hard to come by these days," Brigid said. "Shadowmoor is a cold, dark place. You need to stop thinking about this in moral terms, as if there's a good choice to make. There isn't. Start thinking about it practically.

"This isn't about the right thing," Brigid continued. "It's about the smart thing. Good and bad don't really apply here; it's all a matter of decisions and consequences. For me the choice is easy. Oona wants me dead, so I can't side with her." Brigid glanced over to Rhys and Ashling, and continued. "Maralen wants Oona dead, and I swore an oath to Maralen. So here I am." She shrugged. "She wants to know where you stand. I can't tell you what to do—or force you to agree with me—but you've got to decide now, and you have to be smart about it."

"Brigid." Rhys stood up. He had heard enough, and now his

clear voice rang across the field. "I'm going to ask you questions and you're going to answer. Plainly. We can't decide anything until you do. What did Maralen do to Ashling?"

Brigid turned. She waved half-heartedly at Rhys. He stared at her, his eyes fierce and cold until she said, "She took the Destroyer's power."

"Why?"

"To use against Oona."

"How?"

"That I do not know."

Rhys nodded. "You're honest, at least. What will Maralen do next?"

"She—" Brigid began, but the sapling let out a pained wail and staggered forward before the kithkin could continue.

"The fire, the fire," the sapling moaned. "It must not be used this way."

"What way?" Rhys stepped around Ashling. "What do you see?"

Overhead, two tear-shaped sheets of fire ignited and began to spread across the sky. The wide ends expanded and stretched, growing ever longer and taller until they were two vast fiery wings. The thin ends came almost to a point, but they were separated by a small, lithe figure that hung suspended between them. Like some great flaming angel, Maralen spread her burning wings and called down to the world below.

"Cinders of Shadowmoor," she intoned, and her echoing voice shook dust from the broken walls of Kinscaer. "Behold your savior. Those of you who came seeking the Extinguisher, yearning to join her righteous cause and burn yourselves out in her name: *Rejoice*. The Destroyer gathered you here, as was always intended, and then yielded her power to me.

"I am that Extinguisher, she who will lead you from this dismal, dead world. I shall rekindle the ultimate flame, the final inferno that cleanses away all misery, all confusion. I shall build a pyre from your entire tribe, and the light and heat from that great fire will blaze us a path to the next world, a world of splendor and glory that even now awaits you all.

"Join me," Maralen thundered. "Follow me. Burn for me."

Rhys heard a chilling chorus of hisses and groans all along the dark edges of the battlefield. Maralen flexed her wings, stretching them to cover the sky, and then she folded them back in. The fiery sheaths retreated into her body, dwindling as she descended.

"What was that?" he snapped at Brigid.

"Don't ask me." The archer defensively held up her hands. "Everything she says and does lately surprises me."

"The sapling isn't surprised," Rhys said. The slender yew was nearly doubled over, still clutching the sides of her face with her thickest branches. "She's traumatized. I'm not surprised, either; I'm horrified."

Brigid shook her head. "I can't answer for Maralen."

"But I can." Maralen floated down and landed between Rhys and Brigid. Rhys noticed the last vestiges of fire withering into nothingness along Maralen's shoulder blades. "I'm glad to find you here, all of you. We've been through a great deal together, but the end is finally in sight. Oona has gone to ground in Cayr Ulios. If we confront her there, she will fall. If she falls, all our troubles will be over."

"That's completely ridiculous," Rhys said.

"Not completely," said the sapling. Now that Maralen had doused her wings of flame, the sapling recovered her composure. She slid forward across the dirt toward Rhys and Maralen. "Oona must be defeated. That is what Colfenor wanted, what I was created for." She looked sharply at Rhys. "What you were trained for."

"Trained? I learned yew magic from Colfenor—poison and meditation—how does that prepare me to fight Oona?"

"You still have a part to play."

"So you're saying we should go with Maralen?"

"No," the sapling said firmly. "Never. I am saying we must choose neither side in the struggle between Oona and her rebellious creation. To do what we were born and bred to do, we must look elsewhere."

"She's wrong," Maralen said. "You belong with me, Rhys. We are connected and have been since before we met."

"Connected—like you're connected to the cinders?" Rhys shook his head. "You just used stolen magic to trick an entire tribe into seeing you as some sort of messiah. How can I believe anything you tell me?"

Maralen laughed lightly. "That was impressive, wasn't it? A sharp bit of improvisation, if you don't mind my saying so. I think I was very convincing."

Rhys felt his eyes widen with pure astonishment. He stared at Maralen, amazed. "What are you?" he said softly.

Maralen's smile hardened. "You know what I am. You heard Oona."

"I heard what Oona said," Rhys admitted. "But I'm asking you. Are you Maralen the elf? Or did Oona's vines make another Maralen like they made another Tarcha?"

The elf maiden's eyes filmed over and her voice sounded very far away. "I was born just over a year ago, on the border between Mornsong and the Gilt-Leaf. There was a procession, a wedding. We were meant to embody a newly forged link between your great tribe and our lesser one. But the procession was attacked. *I* was attacked. I heard Oona's voice, and then I—Maralen of Mornsong—died.

"The next thing I remember was yearning for you, Safewright. You were a hunter then, a pack leader. You could have been a taercenn. I found myself wandering in the sun-soaked woods with no idea of who I was or how I had gotten there. But I knew you, Rhys. I could feel you working yew magic nearby. I longed only to be with you, to be near you. I reached out for you—and everything went wrong.

"Your friends were killed. Your horns were shattered. And Oona's voice was no longer the only one I heard. I was made to stand by you, Rhys, and once I could I refused to consider doing otherwise. Not then and not now."

"I don't understand this. Any of it." Rhys's hands went instinctively to his forehead, to his fully intact horns. "And if I did I'm not sure I believe it."

"You are my opposite number, Maralen," the sapling said gravely.

The elf woman cast her cold, dark eyes on the sapling, but she did not speak.

The sapling said, "I was created by Colfenor to be his agent against Oona in the new world, this Shadowmoor. Oona learned of his intentions, of course—there is no secret the Fae cannot uncover—and so she created you to prevent me from rising. She sent you to insinuate yourself with Rhys, to attach yourself to the prized student Colfenor had selected to plant and tend his seedcone, from which I grew. You were meant to stop my emergence, or at least to learn my purpose for being so Oona could have it stopped. In a very real sense, Maralen, we were born to oppose each other. How can you ask me to join you now?"

"Because I have become far more than what my creator intended," Maralen said. "I thought you had, as well. That you have not causes me great sadness." She turned to Rhys and for a moment her gaze was so intense he felt dizzy. "I have done terrible things," Maralen said. "And I have much more to accomplish before I can allow myself to rest. I have lied to you, all of you. I have used you to keep Oona from reclaiming me, from asserting her will over me. I exploited Colfenor's grand plan for my own benefit, and thus I am partially responsible for turning a kind and noble pilgrim into a vengeful monster. These are my sins, all of them, and I would not shrink from doing them all again without hesitation. Oona must fall. The sapling herself agrees—"

"I agree with nothing that comes out of your mouth, Oona's shadow."

"The sapling agrees that Oona's influence must be broken. And since Oona and I cannot exist in the same world, we all share a common enemy and a common cause. You do not have to forgive me for the past or trust me in the future, but you have to accept that our purposes converge. We want the same things, Rhys. Work with me to achieve them."

Rhys turned toward the sapling, who still regarded Maralen with a defiant eye. He glanced at Brigid, who seemed truly dismal, and Iliona, who seemed truly disinterested. He looked down upon Ashling's sleeping form, and for the first time in months he saw the true beauty of her fire.

"No," he said, and the pain his words brought to Maralen's face was entirely genuine. "I do not hate you, Maralen, but I cannot stand with you. It is not down to me to forgive you, and I cannot speak to the grand designs of Colfenor, or Oona, or yourself. But I've learned how this woman"—he gestured at Ashling—"has suffered because of them. I cannot undo what has been done, but I can make sure that it leads to something worthwhile. Colfenor was wise and powerful. If I do not complete the work he started, all of her suffering, all of everyone's suffering, has been for nothing."

"So," Maralen said bitterly. "You will abandon the Wilt-Leaf Hold, your own tribe, to serve a treefolk's whim. Again."

"I will do what I must," Rhys said. "To preserve what little beauty and value this world has left. You and Oona would both destroy that in your zeal to destroy each other."

"I was made to seek you out," Maralen said. "To stand by you. And now I see that is impossible." She bowed deeply, her hands reverently clasped in front of her. As she straightened, Maralen said, "Stay alive, Safewright. When I have bested Oona, I will find you. Maybe then you will reconsider."

"I wish you well, Maralen."

The dark-eyed maiden nodded. She jerked her head toward Iliona and Brigid and made a soft clicking sound in her cheek.

A hot wind blew in from above and swirled around Maralen, Iliona, and Brigid.

"Good-bye," Brigid called. "I'm sorry."

"Die screaming, Endry," Iliona shouted. "I'll give Veesa your regards, you stinking coward."

Rhys lost sight of the three figures in the driving, gritty haze just before the smoky cloud shot into the sky and vanished.

"Well," Endry said. He peeked out from the sapling's upper branches. "That could have gone better." He swiveled his head left and right, and then floated out into the air over Ashling. "What do we do now?"

Rhys turned to the sapling. "You're the one who has Colfenor's knowledge," he said. "Did the old log's wisdom extend this far?"

"It did," the sapling said. "Though the situation is far from what he envisioned."

Rhys scowled. "Does that mean we have no plan?"

"Not at all." The sapling straightened out, stretching to her full height. "It means that Colfenor's original scheme needs to be altered, adapted, and improved." She stretched out a long branch to Rhys, beckoning him to take it. "And I know how."

Rhys took the sapling's branch in his hand. "I'm with you," he said.

"Hooray!" Endry shouted. "But no one has answered my question: What are we going to do now?"

"Oona's magic is crushing the world under its accumulated weight," the sapling said. "That is why we endure the cycles of perpetual light and perpetual darkness. If her hold is broken, a more natural balance will be restored. We will all be free."

"All right," Endry said. "How do we break her hold?"

"We travel to her place of power," the sapling said. "We find the soil that sustains her, and then we act."

Rhys realized what the sapling meant, and he nodded coldly. "I see."

"I don't," Endry whined.

"It's very simple," the sapling said. "Once we reach the place that tethers Oona to this world . . ."

"We uproot her," Rhys concluded.

Endry glanced between them, grinned sharply, and then clapped his hands together. "Sounds like fun."

"It won't be," Rhys said, and from the sapling's solemn expression of concern he knew he was right.

CHAPTER 18

Brigid missed Wryget. She hoped the big merrow found his way to some safe place on his own. For her part, Brigid doubted she'd remember that she even knew a merrow named Wryget for much longer. As the time came to give up the Crescent, she'd grown more and more certain that its loss would erase whom she'd been—whom she still was. It was only a matter of time before Maralen seized the pendant for herself.

Wryget would have had something to say as they soared on unseen currents of air over the Wilt-Leaf Forest—perhaps he would have observed how much of the woodland remained after the Destroyer's rampages, which Brigid chalked up in no small part to the efforts of herself and a small band of friends who seemed to spend far more time as enemies. Or maybe Wryget just would have spent most of his time screaming—the nearest water was a long way down.

The cinders were also a long way down, which was a blessing in Brigid's estimation. They moved as a smoldering mass, running to keep up with their new mistress but unable to wreak the same devastation as before—their power was diminished under Maralen's tighter control, and there was simply less left to burn.

And here was Maralen, leading them into the last great stretch of relatively untouched forest in the world where, perhaps, they'd be able to ignite natural fires that wouldn't be stopped by rivers or willpower. Though she had sworn to herself she was going to keep quiet and ride this through to the end no matter what happened, the kithkin's second thoughts were rapidly moving to the front of the line. She waited until Maralen drifted within earshot, and said, "So this was your plan?"

"You make it sound so sinister, Brigid," Maralen said.

"It was a plan, wasn't it?" the kithkin persisted. "You wanted the elemental the whole time. Now you're the Destroyer, and you're going to—what, destroy the world to spite your mother?"

"Oh, dear," the elf said. She rolled lazily in the air and moved closer to the kithkin. She stopped rolling when she was a foot or so away from Brigid, and her expression became intent and a little bloodthirsty. "That's ridiculous. I'm going to use this power, of course, but only get rid of her once and for all. Haven't you listened to a thing I said? This"—she waved at the night sky—"isn't how it's supposed to be. There's supposed to be a sun in the sky, and a moon in the sky, and they're supposed to rise and fall on a scale of hours, not centuries. And the night is not supposed to be so long and cruel, nor the day so pure and bright. She caused it. She ruined it. She broke it."

"Why didn't anyone try to fix it before?" Brigid asked.

"She's never allowed something like me to happen before. She finally grew too confident, too careless. She thinks the world can't exist without her, but she's all wrong—it's her that can't exist without it. She's a bit like me in that regard: a vibrant distillation of something much larger and less cohesive, one that developed its own point of view. But she's nothing more than a problem to be solved at this point. Shadowmoor doesn't need her, and neither does Lorwyn."

"I wonder," Brigid said thoughtfully, "if she suspected this might happen. What you are, what you did. Maybe she wants you to try this, and fail. Or even—what if you destroy her, but you can't change it back?"

"That—well. I suppose it's possible. If that happens, I will fill the void as best I can."

"And a new Oona is born."

"What are you getting at?" Maralen snapped.

"This could be how she has lived so long—if what you said is true. Maybe she fully intended to create you. Make you hate her, hunt her, destroy her, and take her place. You *are* her in more ways than that sapling is old Colfenor."

Maralen frowned, which gave Brigid a momentary feeling of bitter satisfaction. Let the new Destroyer doubt herself a little.

"You should get some rest," the elf said suddenly, her smile returning but insincere. "We'll be there soon."

"Not likely," Brigid muttered. The verbal jousting portion of the flight was over, she guessed.

"Have we been spotted, Iliona?" Maralen asked the faerie. Someone who hadn't spent so much time around this elf—this simulacrum of an elf, she corrected herself—probably wouldn't have noticed the fiery edge in her voice, but anyone would have detected the curious rasping echo that followed every word.

"Something stuck in your throat?" Iliona asked. "Chicken bone, maybe? That can be rough." Brigid stifled a chuckle and continued to watch the pair; anything was better than looking down for any length of time, though sleep had been a ludicrous suggestion. The kithkin had expected the elf—well, why not, Brigid told herself, it was as good a word as any for what Maralen was—to reply to the faerie's ribbing with a sharp retort or a barked order. Maralen had certainly rebuked the Vendilion enough. But she didn't. Maralen only smiled at the little creature, and Brigid could tell it was one of the only times she'd ever seen a true expression on the elf woman's face. Maralen really did appreciate Iliona choosing to side with her, and Iliona's ribbing was a form of Fae affection, if such a thing existed.

That was when Brigid noticed the buzzing. It was distant, far below them, which meant she'd have to look down. The kithkin truly despised being so reliant on someone else's abilities to keep her aloft and moving, especially after so long on the river, in control—mostly—of the transportation. But there was nothing for it; she had to look.

"We've been spotted," Iliona finally confirmed. "I count at least twenty cliques." Her face wrinkled, and she added, "Correction—twenty cliques' *worth*. They're a jumble down there."

"Time to get ready, my loyal friend," Maralen said. "You're to be my envoy to the Fae. Whether or not we are able to overcome your—our—oppressive mother, you must be strong and confident." Brigid stifled a derisive snort. "You are Vendilion," the elf continued, "and this gives you strength. But you are also free, Iliona. You joined me by your choice, and others will want to do the same."

D*oo* the*he* same*ame*, Brigid repeated to herself, mimicking Maralen's unsettling echo. She risked a stomach-churning look down to face the sources of the buzzing. Even though she knew what she'd see, she wasn't at all prepared for how beautiful they looked. For once Brigid forgot the effect the height had on her nerves.

Twenty cliques' worth at three to four faeries per clique. That meant at least eighty faeries approached from the direction of Glen Elendra, the distant home of Oona. Each one glowed in the moonlight, silvery wings like swimming stars against the darkened ground so far below.

Brigid forced her eyes back onto Maralen and Iliona, a warning on her lips. It stayed there for the time being as her panicked brain remembered Maralen's words. Clearly the boss had seen them, otherwise why prepare Iliona to be an envoy?

In moments the eldest of the Vendilion clique had been transformed into quite an envoy indeed. Her spiky hair had become luminous gold. Her golden carapace was now adorned with jade armor that glittered beneath Shadowmoor's full moon, and her silver wings had taken on a crystalline sheen sharp enough to cut bone. She clutched in her tiny hands a long silver spear with a complicated and ornate barbed tip that looked simultaneously regal and deadly without being ostentatious.

Maralen ignored the kithkin's justifiable awe for the moment and turned to the faerie. "Tell them they are welcome, my herald," she said. So much for not being ostentatious, Brigid mused. "They have heard the call, and they are but the first."

"Wait, those faeries down there—they're on our side?" Brigid blurted. "And how did you turn Iliona into whatever you've turned her into?"

"Brigid," Maralen said, the elemental rasp in her voice rising to the surface for a moment, "I have become something other than the Queen of the Fae. I was of her, but now with the elemental—I can feel everything. The entire world. I can create the things she can create, and I will do more. The long night is going to end."

"You're not really telling me anything," Brigid said, taking up the argument once more, unable to help herself. "Dire, vague predictions don't tell me what you're really going to do."

So suspicious, Maralen's voice rang in Brigid's head.

"Stop it," Brigid said.

As you wish.

"That's not stopping it."

"Iliona," Maralen said with a smirk Brigid knew was directed at her, "Go now, and tell them what I have told you. You may also improvise, within reason. But remember, no matter what they may have done before, they want their freedom now, so they are siding with us. No name-calling."

"Aw," Iliona said "But I'm really *good* at name-calling, you big, fat elf."

"No, you are really not," Maralen said. "And don't do that again. Now go." Again, the sincere smile. Iliona beamed for a moment in the glow of her mistress's love, and then she disappeared in a cloud of sparkling light as she dived to meet the new arrivals.

"Brigid, Brigid, Brigid," the elf said, the smile still on her face. "What shall we do with you?" She waved her hand vaguely in the air, and Brigid suddenly felt a familiar weight in her hand. Surprised, she almost dropped the wingbow that appeared in her grip from out of nowhere.

"How—"

"A sliver of your old weapon lodged in your glove," Maralen said. "I coaxed it into a more pleasing shape. Do you approve? After all, I may become distracted soon, and you may need to take to the air on your own."

"All right," Brigid said. She wanted to test the wingbow, but at this height—

"I know what you're thinking," Maralen said. "I really do. You want to test the wingbow, but you worry that no kithkin archer has ever flown a wingbow this high. Unfurling those wings could spell your doom. But what if you could also manipulate the air, the way I'm doing to keep us aloft?"

"Well, you've got wings," Brigid pointed out.

"An affectation," Maralen shrugged. "I don't need them." With a flash the wings disappeared—in fact, Brigid thought, Maralen appeared to absorb them. "With the Crescent, you can manipulate the waters of the Wanderbrine, correct?"

"Yes," Brigid said. "Though I'm not as good as Sygg. Or even Artio."

"Poor Artio," Maralen said. "A tragic loss. But best not to dwell on what we cannot change. My point is you think the Crescent lets you manipulate the river, but that's because it's all you've tried to do. There is water everywhere. There are tiny drops of water in that cloud, in the fog that fills that valley, even floating unseen in the air we're passing through as we speak. Can you feel it?"

Brigid closed her eyes and tried to picture the tiny drops of water in the air, on the ground, and in the skies above. It helped to visualize wind currents, so much like the currents of the river but bound by neither bed nor bank. The Crescent was cool against her breast and growing colder.

The currents shimmered into view, air that moved with invisible fluidity, and within the air, millions—billions—of tiny drops of water. Every one of them responded to her mind's touch, and she pulled them gently to her as much by instinct as anything else.

Soon there was a soft cushion of fog beneath her, moving along at the same speed through the warm winds Maralen continued to call to them.

"Good," Maralen said. "Very good. You may still use your wingbow to stay aloft, manipulating the air beneath you, even at this height. Here, I'll show you."

Brigid's eyes flickered open and she saw what the wind in her face told her was true. Maralen had just dropped her.

She had perhaps ten seconds before she collided with the canopy of trees below. The fog beneath her was gone—it had been intermingled with the waves of heat Maralen used to stay aloft. She couldn't do this on her own.

Eight seconds. "No kithkin in the world has ever had the kind of power you have, and that's but a sliver of what you've been wasting," Maralen called.

Five seconds. Then Brigid's eyes closed and the Crescent

went cold as ice. The winds slowed, stopped, and a cool, soft blanket enveloped her.

Two seconds. Eyes open.

Brigid hovered some hundred or so feet off the ground, suspended by a small cloud of thick vapor. On all sides spiky, broken, splintered trees thrust into the sky, reaching almost twenty feet above her current elevation. The kithkin had stopped her own fall—and without using the wingbow she still clutched uselessly in one hand.

You almost made it, Maralen's voice echoed in her head. *I nudged the trees out of your way, of course. Well done.*

Brigid looked up through the cloud of faeries at the tiny figure leading them into the heart of the Wilt-Leaf on translucent silver wings. "I'll show you 'well done,'" she muttered. Forcing herself to keep her eyes open, the kithkin extended her forearms and rode a column of water vapor straight into the sky. A cloud of faeries squealed in equal parts delight and panic when she blasted through them, and Brigid didn't bring herself to a stop until she'd risen alongside the boss.

"You've learned a simple thing, Brigid, but a useful one," Maralen said. "Don't let it go to your head."

That last had an unsettlingly bitter ring to it. No, not bitterness. Jealousy. It brought Brigid's hand involuntarily to the Crescent beneath her tunic.

If I wanted it, I would take it, Maralen's voice said in her mind. *It is of more use to me—you are of more use to me, as you said—if you can operate independently. When this is over, perhaps I shall take it. You do not know. But do not defy me, my kithkin friend. Instead, I recommend you think of ways to help me defeat our enemy.*

"You're certain she's in Cayr Ulios? Why?"

"The elves," Maralen said. "They'll protect her, and now that she's seeing defections on this scale, she doesn't trust all of her children to do the job. By barricading herself in there, she forces them to defend her in order to defend themselves—and the fools will believe it's their idea." The elf's face took on an almost plausible cast of concern. "Are you all right? You're sweating."

The kithkin grunted. "No problem," she said, though the chill of the Crescent against her breast was beginning to cause her entire chest to ache. The exhilaration of her rapid ascent was giving way to the exhaustion of constantly focusing her mind on the pendant.

"Allow me," Maralen said. "You should conserve your strength." From anyone else it might have sounded like a kindness, but Brigid didn't kid herself. The elf was being eminently pragmatic.

Brigid slung the wingbow onto her back, where it rested like a familiar old friend, and let the warm cushion of air beneath her lift her up. She allowed the cooler cloud of moist air to dissipate, but still felt all that water above and below at the edges of her awareness, waiting for her call.

"Barricaded is right." Brigid observed, gesturing toward the capital of the Wilt-Leaf many thousands of feet below. "Looks as if they're still defending themselves against the first Destroyer. I guess they hoped they could survive an attack by letting everything burn away except their city."

"I agree," Maralen said. "Fortunately I intend to be more than just a destroyer, as you know." She snapped her fingers, and the blazing wings she'd dismissed moments earlier returned, burning bright and golden in the darkened sky.

* * * * *

"I wish Kiel were here," Endry said for at least the twelfth time in ten minutes.

"Kiel is here, Endry," Rhys said. "We're on his shoulders. Look down."

"Ah!" the faerie exclaimed. "Right. Sorry, I've been so very busy playing lookout. I, General Endry of the Such and Such, reduced to scout duty."

"It's not getting any funnier," Rhys muttered. "And you're not doing much scouting, are you?"

"Your problem is, you don't know how to make long trips enjoyable," Endry replied. "You should work on that. You used to be different. Anyway, we're going to have to leave the big fellow behind before we get there, won't we?"

"I wish it weren't so," Rhys said, pointedly ignoring the reference to some other him he was getting tired of hearing about, "but we're sneaking in and giants don't sneak. He'll have to stay behind, at least at first."

"And upon his return, his presence will help keep Kinscaer safe," added the sapling, "In time he may help them rebuild."

"If the kithkin don't eat him," Endry said.

"You have a really peculiar view of the kithkin, Endry," Rhys said.

"You know the old saying," Endry said. "Nothing lower than a low-down, bright-eyed, creepy kithkin." Endry fluttered back to his lookout position several feet above and a few feet ahead of the main group. "I really wish Kiel were here."

The trail they'd followed from the devastated kithkin doun hadn't been much of a trail at all until the sapling coaxed it into existence. By crafting the trail as they went, the sapling also guided the giant, who cheerfully followed whichever path lay open before him. The rest of the little band rode upon Kiel's broad back—Endry, the sapling, Rhys, a dozen or so of the remaining groundlings (twice as many had remained in Kinscaer to help with rebuilding, a fact of which Endry was justifiably proud), and of course the silent erstwhile Destroyer herself.

"Destroyer" wasn't really a fair description of the flamekin woman who clung to the giant's back at Rhys's side, however. Not anymore. Ashling hadn't spoken a word since they'd set out, but her fiery eyes appeared to see something new and remarkable with every glance. The only time he saw anything but surprise, wonder, or curiosity in Ashling's eyes was when they lit upon one of the many patches of scorched dirt the Destroyer had left in her wake. Those times, to Rhys's unexpected relief, Ashling's head drooped in shame.

She did not speak, but her presence was oddly comforting to Rhys in a way he couldn't explain. Something familiar in this bizarre creature—not a cinder, not a destroyer, neither wretch nor wrecker. Though all of them (except perhaps the giant) had been concerned about the flaming passenger igniting the forest of fur that covered Kiel's broad shoulders, there had been no problems so far. The flamekin, it seemed, could manipulate her fire to burn as cool to the touch as a glass of lukewarm water.

A flamekin was what Ashling had been before—before something. The elf still hadn't worked it all out. There was a world before, the sapling said, with a different name and a different history. But there had been a Rhys and an Ashling, as well as a Brigid and a Sygg.

Or so the sapling had said. She wasn't the only one who knew of this other world, either. The kithkin outcast Brigid Baeli knew. Ashling might know. Kiel? Probably. Rhys didn't know if it were true, but considering the things he'd seen of late it made as much sense as anything else.

He found it easier to dwell on the Destroyer's fate than his own. The sapling had insisted they bring Ashling, lest the survivors of Kinscaer tear her apart—not that Rhys would have blamed them. Rhys could still hardly believe the sapling's plan, let alone that it had been Colfenor's, or that the extinguished Destroyer had a part in it. He had to admit the idea was sound, but the safewright just wished he were not the one who had to help the sapling make it real.

"Endry," he called. "What can you see of the Wilt-Leaf?"

"Same I could see a few minutes ago, Chief," the faerie said with casual but not mean-spirited insolence. "Lots of lights in the sky, faerie lights. A little smoke far, far away. No explosions, just lights."

"Well, what are the lights doing?" Rhys snapped.

"Hey!" Endry said, insolence quickly giving way to indignation. "I'm a free faerie. Freer than either of my sisters is ever going to be. You do not get to push me around." He fluttered down to hover before Rhys and stab a finger at the elf's left eye, "Clatterfoot."

Rhys struggled to keep his composure. He couldn't remember when last he'd slept, and even the frayed edges of his nerves were frayed. In the end, composure won. "The lights, Endry."

"Oh right, the lights!" Endry snapped, making Rhys wonder when faeries slept if they ever did. "The lights are fighting! They're fighting lights, lighting up the night! Right?"

"So the faeries are fighting each other?"

"That'd be my best guess," Endry said. "That means—Great Mother." Endry's face grew deadly serious. "They're choosing sides. They're really choosing sides between the Great Mother and *her*."

"Endry," Rhys said, "I need to know you're with us, here. Tell me now: Are you planning to return to Oona?"

Endry snorted. "I should think not, hoofy. Both of them rejected my groundling brothers and sisters, so I reject both of them. Let 'em destroy each other." Rhys noticed the faerie turned away when he said the word "sisters," and he knew the Vendilion wasn't speaking merely of the greater Fae family.

"If this works," Rhys said, "we'll stop them from destroying each other."

"Really?" Endry's face was a mixture of relief and disappointment, though over which aspects of Rhys's statement the elf couldn't tell.

"Most of them," Rhys offered. "Some of them," he amended. "A few of them. Maybe."

Endry brightened. "All right then. Though I admit I don't like the idea of—you know."

"Do not worry, my friend," the sapling said, momentarily startling Rhys. He'd almost forgotten the tree was there—needless to say, she blended into the tree line along the magically carved path. "Your kind will not die out. I will not allow it."

"No offense, Yewling," Endry said, "But you—well, you were injured. You yourself could die out. There, I said it. I'm sorry, but I just had to tell you. It's got me worried, what we're doing here, and I'm not the only one. Nora's not the type to bother you with this sort of thing, but the groundlings are worried, too."

"I see," the sapling said. "Then allow me to show you something." The sapling brought two boughs together before her, muttered a few soft incantations and rustled her needles. When she pulled the boughs apart, an image of another oddly familiar sight greeted Rhys. It was called the Weeping Bosk, a secluded refuge where Colfenor had given Rhys most of his non-elf training. Amid the towering trees were rows and rows of vines growing on small green stalks—symbiotic stalks that together created the miraculous buds which, when ripe, burst open with living, breathing faeries. Every time Rhys had ever heard of these buds they were attached to Oona, or at least to Glen Elendra, never growing independently.

"Your kind will survive," the sapling said.

"And all those waiting to burst forth?"

"Their fate is less certain," the sapling said, "though every effort will be made to spare them. Oona sought to destroy me by having the Bosk leveled and burned before I was born. It is only fitting that it be the seed bed from which all future Fae spring."

Endry seemed to consider this, and he finally nodded. "Good enough. All right, then, it's time I tell you what you *don't* know about Glen Elendra."

Rhys stopped. "What we don't know?"

"That's right," Endry said. "For one thing, you'll die the moment you set foot inside."

"Really," Rhys said.

"At a time like this, all of the mother's defenses will be up, except those sparklers to the north. And that's why you need me. I'll get you in and you can poison whatever you need to poison, do whatever you need to do. Just try not to kill too many of the family, eh, hard-toes? We're not bad folk—we just have an overbearing mother."

"Well, that is the plan," Rhys said.

Endry buzzed up to take another look at the flashing horizon. He called back to report nothing major seemed to have changed in the lights—still flying at each other, looping back, flying at each other again, and when the twin clouds of Fae collided there were sparks, bolts, and explosions of every color imaginable and several that weren't.

After another few minutes he called down, "I wish Kiel were here."

"You know this means war," Iliona said.

"You've said that already," Brigid replied.

"Yes, but then we'd just been joined by what, two hundred pieces of catapult fodder? Now we've got almost a thousand. And they're all working for me!"

"I wouldn't be so sure of that," Brigid muttered, eyeing Maralen high above. The glittering wings she'd displayed before had been replaced with a striking pair of bladelike projections that formed a **V**-shape behind her back. They were made of fire, but seemed hung on a skeletal frame of flexing vines.

You look ridiculous, she thought as hard as she could at the elf and received no mental response. Good, she was leaving Brigid be for the time being and the kithkin could complete her thought. "I doubt Maralen is that concerned with the Fae surviving any of this. She's pretty intent on destroying Oona to the exclusion of anything else. Are you certain? A lot of faeries are going to die here, Iliona. Are they ready? Are you?"

"They'd better be," Iliona replied. "Or I'll have to whip them into fighting perfection in about an hour."

"That soon?" Brigid asked.

"That's what I hear."

"Doesn't it bother you? Killing your own kind?"

The faerie looked uncharacteristically introspective for a

moment, stroking her chin, and after a few seconds offered, "No. Not anymore. They made their choices; I made mine."

"Don't you wonder why?" Brigid asked, still troubled by the thought she'd had earlier—that perhaps Oona was manufacturing this entire Fae against Fae conflict for her own purposes. The Destroyer—Ashling, at least—had been incidental to it all, or a means to an end for Oona at best. Or was it for Maralen? Was there really a difference?

"Why it doesn't bother me?" Iliona sneered. "Now you're being ridiculous, kithkin. It doesn't bother me because they deserve it! They deserve every snapped limb and severed wing they get."

"You aim to injure, then?" Brigid asked.

"I aim to fight," Iliona said with surprising sharpness. "Out with the old. In with the new."

"You don't need more than that?" Brigid asked.

"No," Iliona said. "It's only natural." Without further explanation, she threw the kithkin a salute and buzzed off to shout at the lead formation of her flying Fae army. They were arrayed beneath Maralen, who was gliding along like a winged comet, and the swarm outnumbered the stars and outshone the moon's brilliance with their dazzling multicolored lights. From Brigid's lower perspective, they looked as if they would enshroud the entire world. The kithkin summoned enough of the vapor stream to lift herself to a better vantage point—her current elevation was a result of her insistence on resuming flight under her own power after relying on Maralen to carry her while she caught a few hours of much-needed sleep. It was a testament to the life Brigid had led in the last few years that taking a nap several thousand feet on a cushion of air was not the strangest thing that had ever happened to her.

Don't wander off, my friend, Maralen called to her. *Our quarry is in sight.*

Brigid automatically scanned the horizon for a glimpse of Cayr Ulios, the capital safehold of the Wilt-Leaf elves and home to their king and queen. She spotted it immediately, or rather spotted what parts of it emerged from the fog and mist that enshrouded it. It seemed to be much the same stuff Oona had used at Kinscaer to smother Ashling and help wrest the elemental from her body, and that was when Brigid saw it all before her as if it had been written onto a Kinsbaile broadsheet and nailed to the door of the town pub.

Oona wanted this war. She wanted to unleash a power like the Destroyer—perhaps even wanted the Source roused into action, causing more upheaval in the world. She wanted that power for herself, and had created Maralen to help her get it. Now here was Maralen bringing it to her, and she didn't even seem to realize she was part of a— a *scheme* to help Oona grow even more powerful, more perfect, more utterly and completely in control of everything.

Lost in thought, Brigid didn't notice Maralen swooping down to confront her until it was too late, and she feared the expression on her face told the woman everything she'd been thinking about. As Maralen's grin grew wide and wicked, Brigid realized with a start that her expression had done no such thing.

No, little fool, Maralen said. *You did. And it's not as if I didn't warn you I would be poking around in that tiny little hovel you call a mind.*

Brigid felt the old familiar nausea return, but this time it was accompanied by paralysis and the sudden sensation of plummeting. Maralen must have caught her on a cushion of air, because the sensation ended as soon as it began.

The kithkin tried to squirm as the elf woman approached her; the blazing wings remarkably cool—like a flamekin's fire—and her face equally devoid of warmth or mercy. "You think too much, Brigid Baeli," Maralen said. "I was going to allow you to go on serving me. Even though you've unlocked the true potential of this little trinket now, even though it could do so much more in my hands, I was going to let you keep it. I enjoyed having you around, you know. As a reminder of simpler times. Before I truly knew what I was. Why I was." The elf woman pulled the pendant from beneath Brigid's tunic and laughed when the kithkin's eyed bulged wide.

"Maralen," Brigid gasped. It took a remarkable effort to speak, let alone breathe, and she could already feel herself growing faint. "They'll stop you."

"Who?" Maralen asked. "The sapling? Rhys? They ran away home. They'll be part of my world soon enough, and there's nothing they can do to prevent it. But you, on the other hand? I'm afraid your time is done. I'll just be needing this." With a sharp jerk the elf pulled the Crescent of Morningtide from around Brigid's neck. There was a moment of shock, then confusion, and then the pain of impact as the kithkin's body collided with the upper boughs of a towering Wilt-Leaf maple.

For Brigid Baeli, the world disappeared under a shroud of black.

* * * * *

Iliona could hardly believe her eyes. She debated for a moment whether to try to catch the plummeting kithkin, but by the time she made up her mind she saw the tree branches break Brigid's fall. Maralen didn't appear too concerned and was holding something shiny in her hand.

Though it broke every protocol she'd just made up over the last few hours, she left the lead wing of the Glorious Sky-Army of Freedom (Iliona had been allowed to name the force herself) in command of her lieutenant and sped through the dazzling sky to Maralen's side.

"What happened?" she said. "Why did she fall?" The faerie had a thought that made her smile. "Should I fly down there and stab her?"

"No," Maralen said, her eyes glued to the Crescent hanging from its chain. "She's no longer of any importance." The elf let the trinket rest against her chest and then arched her back as if she'd just been shot with an arrow. She took in a hiss of air, and Iliona realized it was the result of physical contact with the pendant.

As Maralen writhed in midair, soaking in more and more power, Iliona looked at the forest below for some sign of the fallen kithkin. She saw none.

"This doesn't—this isn't right," Iliona said. "You're not going to stop her; you're going to become her. And why did you do that to Brigid, who—"

"She would never have survived this," Maralen said. "I did her a favor. With the Crescent, there's a chance. One elemental alone wasn't enough to stop Oona."

"Then why drag Brigid all the way out here?"

"I was sentimental," Maralen said. "I should not have allowed her to keep the Crescent once the fiery horse was tamed. I should have taken it then and saved us the trouble."

"You didn't have to do it at all," Iliona said more quietly.

Maralen erupted in a blazing fit of rage. "Did you think we would all live blissfully for the rest of our days in a mansion atop a hill in the sunny countryside?" the elf said. "No, I'm afraid not." The pendant on her breast flashed with energy, summoning a roiling bank of thunderclouds that blotted out the moon and cast the forest in darkness. More light now came from within the fog—the lights of the elves' most sacred safehold—than from the sky, though Oona's rogue creation did her best to compensate with her blazing **V**-shaped wings.

Iliona couldn't think of anything else to say. She'd made her choice, and the hundreds of faeries in the skies below were counting on her to lead them to victory. Maralen was depending on her. She could almost hear Maralen's voice in her head, telling her so.

Of course the kithkin had to fall. Better to fall here than in a battle where she didn't belong. This war was Fae business, and all the others were just onlookers. Even, Iliona thought, if they believed they were taking part.

* * * * *

"Will you stay here, Kiel?" the sapling asked the giant as he squatted on his uneven legs and held out an arm for the others to scramble down. Rhys had been planning to ask the same question, but the young yew had beaten him to it. The sapling was the last one down, and Rhys helped her with her step.

"Sure," the giant rumbled. "I'll stay here."

"Kiel, this is important. We might need you. Will you keep one ear open?" Rhys asked.

"Sure," the giant said. "I could sit for a while. Tired. With one ear open."

"Wait," Rhys said, finding his voice as the giant shifted his stance. "Kiel, don't—just sit over there. *There*. Thanks." The giant dropped onto his massive buttocks, and soon afterward he was rumbling and snoring contentedly.

"Endry," Rhys called. "It's time."

The faerie buzzed down to confer with his groundling troops—specifically the one called Nora, who didn't like what she was hearing.

"I'm going with you, Endry."

"You've got to stay here," the male Vendilion protested. "You're the only one who can bring the giant if we need him."

"I can facilitate mental contact between you, Nora," the sapling said. "Rest assured we will be in touch if we are in trouble."

The sapling's words seemed to assuage the stubborn little groundling, who kissed Endry on the cheek—to his delight and apparent surprise, judging from the loops he flew in the air afterward—and took a position with her groundling troops around the slumbering giant's feet. She was armed with a long thorn the sapling had given her which would rouse Kiel quickly if he were needed.

"So we're just going to walk into Glen Elendra," Rhys said.

"Yes," the sapling said. "And we must do so together, Rhys. You and I have the power to do what must be done here. The others may not."

Rhys followed the sapling's gesturing hand to see Ashling still sitting—awake but unresponsive. "What about her?"

"I had hoped she would come with us," the sapling said sadly. "But perhaps we will have to go in without Ashling of Tanufel. It is too bad. Such an ally would have been useful."

Their impromptu camp was perhaps half a mile from Glen Elendra, and Rhys found it hard to believe they'd not yet been noticed. When they approached, he saw the reason why. A thousand, perhaps tens of thousands of Fae were rising into the sky and headed north—directly toward Cayr Ulios. The battle was joined, and no one was looking for a walking tree, a disgraced elf, or an outcast faerie, it seemed. Yet Rhys could still not see Glen Elendra proper—the cloud of faeries appeared to rise from the bracken and tangled growth that surrounded the sanctum of the Fae.

Endry had to go through a few simple rules, or so he told them, hovering officiously in the air before the last bend in the path would reveal their destination. "First, don't eat anything. *Any*thing. What looks like a piece of fruit might be a trio of faeries waiting to be born. And if it's not, it's probably poisonous to big folk like you."

"I do not exactly 'eat' in the sense you mean," the sapling said graciously.

"I'm more worried about the elf," Endry said. "Second— don't talk to any Fae but me. They're tricky, and inside Glen Elendra their magic is much more powerful. A trio of faeries could have the two of you drooling into your shoes."

"I don't exactly wear shoes," said the sapling. "Or drool, I should think."

"Your brains can come drooling out of your head, can't they? They can do that, too." Endry cleared his throat and resumed his formal mode of speaking. "Third, if you hear anyone talking *in* your head and it's not the sapling, it means the Great Mother is manipulating you."

"Anything else?" Rhys asked impatiently.

"Yes," said a deeper, slightly more distant voice that definitely did not belong to Endry. Gryffid stepped into the moonlight from around the bend in the path, holding a drawn sword in one hand and batting at the faerie with the other. "Should you encounter the true elves of the Wilt-Leaf defending the greatest and most beautiful corner of the world, surrender immediately and prepare for the death you so richly deserve." The vigilant knocked Endry into the branches of the tree overhanging the path, and Rhys heard a faint yelp before he saw the tiny creature slid down the side of the trunk and lie still.

"So much for the backup plan," Rhys muttered. Elf after magnificent elf emerged from the dark, shadowy undergrowth. Some held drawn bows, the arrows pointed at Rhys and the sapling; others clutching swords like Gryffid's. He felt a wooden hand on his shoulder. *We did not think the glen would be unprotected, Half-Brother,* the sapling told him with a thought. *Remember who you are. You are more than this.*

I won't kill them all, Rhys thought back. *That isn't the answer.*

Rhys, don't—

"I will not surrender," Rhys said, stepping forward and drawing his own battered blade. "I am a safewright of the Wilt-Leaf elves, and what I plan to do is for the good of the Wilt-Leaf Hold. Your quarrel is not with this noble tree-folk or the faerie you so casually abused. Tell your troops to withdraw and face me, Gryffid. I'm the one you want to kill, and not because you're defending Glen Elendra. Your hate's getting the better of you."

Gryffid laughed, a dry sound with little humor in it. "Yes, of course. Though I outnumber you, for some reason I should give up that advantage and give you a chance to murder me."

"Honor demands it," Rhys said.

"My duty demands more."

Rhys fairly shouted, "Do you recognize this sapling? What she is? That's a yew tree. Surely even you are aware—"

"I know of your dabbling in treefolk mysticism, and I remember your 'mentor,'" said the vigilant. "We are protected against such treachery. The Wilt-Leaf elves have entered into a glorious alliance with she who is the most exalted of all things: Oona, Queen of the Fae. It is she who extinguished the Destroyer, and she who will protect the spires of Cayr Ulios until order is restored."

"You're a fool, Gryffid," Rhys said sadly. "I, for one, am ready to seize control of my own destiny. I say no more Oonas, no more Maralens or Sources or Destroyers." He took a step toward Gryffid, who did not retreat. Gryffid pointed to the sapling and then to Endry, and the yew extended a five-foot arm to scoop the unconscious faerie up in her boughs.

Gryffid opened his mouth to speak, but the words appeared to die on his lips. Instead his eyes grew wide and bright. Keeping his blade trained on his former friend, Rhys opened his stance and looked back over his shoulder at the softly glowing form of Ashling, standing in the middle of the path. She was alone, but after a moment, several shuffling, shambling, smoldering shapes emerged from the edges of the tree line. "Cinders," Gryffid finally managed.

"Hello, Gryffid," Ashling said. "Rhys, it's good to see you. I'm—I have a lot to tell you, but for now just that we're here to help."

The sapling turned to the proud vigilant and his hunting pack of prouder elves. "Now may we pass?"

"Never," Gryffid said, but there was a waver in his voice. The sapling extended a hand with a dry rustle, and Endry buzzed from the needles.

The faerie spun in midair amid a shower of sparks and glittering dust. After a few seconds, he said, "Message sent. They're on their way, and they're bringing Kiel."

"Kiel?" Gryffid asked. "Who is—" He clamped his mouth shut. "No matter, traitor," he continued, "You will not enter here."

"I think we will," Endry said. Already Rhys could feel the rumbling in the spongy ground beneath his feet. Something heavy—very heavy and none too distant—was rising, and with a series of increasingly loud crashes, once again walking.

"Your phalanx of noble defenders is about to be outnumbered," Rhys said. "A lot of them are going to die if you don't step aside. Listen to me, Gryffid. Whatever you think of me, I've never done anything without considering the good of the

Wilt-Leaf. I don't want to kill my own kin, even if you want me dead a thousand times over, not when you could be keeping Cayr Ulios safe *right this instant*." Gryffid's expression didn't change. "Gryffid. You don't even know what's happening up there, do you? Oona sent you here to protect this place."

"Yes," Gryffid said grudgingly. "She is caring for Cayr Ulios in our stead. The elves have been sent to protect the many secret safeholds scattered throughout the land. And other sites which Oona told us were important." The vigilant's sword dropped an inch, but he still stood his ground.

"She's gotten into your minds," Rhys said. "You left the first safehold in the hands of a creature like that? Are you mad?"

"We are safe," Gryffid said. "We must keep Oona safe in return. And we will. I'm not suffering from any illusions, traitor. The Great Mother is not mentally controlling me, and I realize the compromises our people have made. The compromises have preserved us through the Destroyer's rampages. She preserved the Wilt-Leaf, and so we will preserve the glen."

"There is a war going on at Cayr Ulios," Rhys said. "The Fae are fighting each other in the first safehold, and Oona is fighting her—well, her rival, for all intents and purposes. If you let us pass, we can stop that. We can save the city and most of the Wilt-Leaf. But if you fight us, more elves will die and we might lose our chance to strike at Oona's seat of power." The outcast safewright pointed at the receding cloud of faeries heading toward Cayr Ulios. "Use your own eyes, Gryff, look where they're headed. She's planning to use the safehold as a battlefield, and retire here after Cayr Ulios is a ruin. That's where your duty lies."

With a crash and several snapped tree branches, Kiel emerged from the trees. "Kiel, stop!" the sapling called, and the giant froze in his tracks.

"Well, which is it?" the giant rumbled. "Come quick, smash all the elves. Stop, don't step on all the elves."

"We'll let you know in a moment," the sapling replied.

The path to Glen Elendra was remarkably quiet except for the buzzing of faerie wings and the wheezy breathing of the impatient giant. "Well?" Rhys asked. "Which is it?"

Gryffid nodded once, raised his hand and signaled. The other elves relaxed or sheathed their weapons, though they did not yet withdraw. The vigilant put two fingers to his mouth and whistled, summoning a half-dozen tall riding cervins, their white hides gleaming in the moonlight. Gryffid ordered a lieutenant to take his mount, then five others he chose seemingly at random, though Rhys was certain he had good reason for choosing each one. Gryffid was a better commander than Rhys had ever been or ever would be—the outcast was certain of it. And the better commander was backing down, precisely because he was the better commander.

As if reading his mind—please, Rhys thought, don't let *Gryffid* start reading my mind now—the vigilant said, "Duren, head straight to Cayr Ulios, and stop for nothing. We will follow on foot, but until my arrival you are to act according to your best judgment of the conditions there. If what the traitor says is true, do—" He coughed, and Rhys realized with a guilty shock that Gryffid was almost overcome with emotion at what he was doing. "Do what you can. If you feel you cannot survive or there is nothing left to save, rendezvous with us at the Barrenclay Crossings. Otherwise, we will meet in the throne room and make our reports to the king and queen. Understood?"

"Yes, sir," said the lieutenant. With a yell and a kick, he spurred the small cavalry unit into action, causing a moment of panic for Rhys when he saw Kiel considering pulling his foot up to allow them passage. He didn't trust the giant's balance on one foot for any extended period of time, and managed to kick Kiel's big toe.

"Just stay put, Kiel."

"At least you decided something," the giant said.

Gryffid said, "Traitor. I am leaving to investigate claims of a disaster in Cayr Ulios."

"You're welcome. Go home, save them if you can. I'll save them if *I* can."

Gryffid grimaced and spat on the ground.

"Or," the sapling said. "He might do that. Perhaps it is best we simply go our several ways?"

"Perhaps," Gryffid said. He nodded to his troops, who one by one turned to follow him in a somber march back up the path that would take them to Cayr Ulios. As each of them passed Ashling and the small pack of seething cinders, a glare was exchanged, a word here and there, but mercifully no actual blows.

"That," said Endry, "did not go as I expected. Shall we?"

"All of us?" Nora called from atop the giant's shoulder.

"One moment," Rhys said, eyeing the flamekin and her cinder wolf pack. "Ashling? That is your name, yes?"

"And assuming that is the case," Endry interrupted, "Ashling of Tanufel, which we *know* is your name (and Rhys should really try keeping up), I would like to ask on behalf of all of us here who don't like being on fire (no offense to those of you who do): Are you planning on, well, destroying anything? Are you feeling at all, in any way, destructive?"

The cinders laughed ominously, though Ashling merely smiled. Only these eight of the many more cinders who had followed the Destroyer now followed Ashling. They seemed drawn to her even though her powers were clearly diminished. She was ablaze, but that was about all.

"It's over, Endry," Ashling said. "That part of it, anyway.

Someone else has that power now, remember? I'm just Ashling."

"But you're—you're burning," the faerie said. "But not all that hot. And you're not bony and crumbly and kind of brainless. No offense to your friends."

"Yes, I'm burning. I—Endry, I remember. I'm still what I was, but I don't know how or why."

"Well don't ask me," Endry said. "I didn't do it. Now, are we all going into Glen Elendra or what?"

CHAPTER 20

Surrounded by a surprisingly large horde of rebellious Fae, the creature who called herself Maralen wondered if this so-called confrontation would end before it began. If it did end, Maralen was not even sure who the victor would be. Her Fae, numbering in the thousands now, were divided into hundreds of units all flying in organic formations that, viewed from her lofty perch, made Maralen feel every bit like a queen.

Somewhere, down in that fog, was Oona. The real Oona, Great Mother of the Fae. Oona had her turn, but like any living thing her time was coming to an end. She'd left Glen Elendra behind and was meeting her here for a confrontation. It seemed almost too convenient, didn't it?

She thought once more how she probably should have kept Brigid around, if only to observe what she was starting to think of as her "elf mind"—the limited, banal little creature she had been. Her new self, the grander, more awesome Maralen said that Brigid had served her purpose.

You just wanted the power, said the new Maralen.

I did it for them, replied the old.

We did it. And we will defeat Oona.

Everything changes, both Maralens thought, and then changes back.

As one, several thousand Fae said, "Out with the old, in with the new." Maralen could have sworn she heard Iliona distinctly among them.

Her troops were ready. She was ready. But Oona remained hidden in fog, and so were tens of thousands of her Fae defenders. Maralen had been so focused on Oona herself she'd almost forgotten that so many hostile faeries in Cayr Ulios could be disastrous, but if they were lying in wait somewhere else it would be far worse.

No, she could sense them. As three very different forms of power dueled within her, Maralen struggled to think strategically. Naked force might indeed be the problem, not the solution. She needed it to fight Oona, to put an end to the old monster, but how was she to employ it? Oona had been kind enough to choose the elf capital as their battleground instead of making a stand at Glen Elendra. Why?

She half expected Oona's voice in her head to explain it all, but there was nothing but her own troubled, increasingly fractured mind. She forced herself to put aside the question of Oona to focus on Oona's Fae.

Maralen allowed her consciousness to expand outward, touching the minds of her many new children. Adopted children, at that. It was truly remarkable, this feeling; more than any elemental power or magical tricks. The many cliques, outcasts, groundlings, and rogues Iliona had helped her gather were all her children, and they believed in her, even loved her. It was her first real glimpse of what it might be like to be Oona herself.

She honed in on Iliona, who was barking orders to a triple-clique of nine individual faeries, five male and four female. Iliona was describing the different ways the traitorous wretch Sygg would cook their limbs should he catch them unawares, so any sign of merrow should be reported to her immediately.

With the tiniest mental nudge, Maralen told her: *Iliona. I would like to ask your advice. Come to me, please.*

Moments later, the Vendilion faerie was at her side, a half-dozen rebel volunteers in train. "Reporting for duty!" Iliona exclaimed with an elaborate salute. "We're ready for the fight, sir!"

"At ease," Maralen said. "Iliona, I'd like to speak with you privately."

"We're all linked up with your mind magic, Mistress," Iliona replied. "Kind of hard to do anything privately."

"Very well," she said. "I'll be blunt. What is Oona up to? Why is she hiding down there? Where are the other Fae?"

Iliona looked more than a little stunned at the import of all three questions, but she recovered with surprising alacrity. "She's—well, she's in the mist," Iliona said. "She wants you to come after her, I think."

"So she wants a fight," Maralen murmured. "She knows *I* want a fight. Why does she?"

"We've got her scared!" Iliona said. "She knows her time is drawing nigh, and she doesn't want Glen Elendra to get ruined."

"That's what I thought," said Maralen. "Now I'm not so sure."

"As for where the other Fae are, they're down there too. I can hear them."

"In your mind?" Maralen asked.

"In my ears," Iliona said, cupping a hand to the side of her tiny head for emphasis.

"You can tell the difference between all of you and the loyalists?"

"Of course!" Iliona said. "I guess it's a faerie thing. But they're down there all right. You know, if you go in you're going to be walking into a trap."

"I know," Maralen said. "That's why I called you here. I'd like you to walk into that trap instead."

"Ah. So you mean to let her wear herself out killing us to death and then sneak up on her after she's tired? Smart move."

"My reasons are slightly more strategic," Maralen said. "And slightly less wasteful. The elemental fire wants—it wants not to kill, exactly, but to burn with abandon, to consume the most precious fuel it's ever touched. Living things. And the Crescent, the power of the Source, is like the river itself. Going around obstacles, finding the tiniest weak point, and exploiting it." She clutched the Crescent at her breast and shivered as the raging fires within her momentarily threatened to take hold of her thoughts and turn them bloody. Fire and water, opposed but working together through her.

"If you say so," Iliona said.

"I want you to break up into small groups and venture into the mist."

"All right!" one of Iliona's comrades said, drawing a tiny sword, and the others murmured agreement.

"You're only scouting," Maralen said, raising a hand. "Let me handle any killing." She continued, knowing that Iliona was right and her words would instantly be heard throughout the growing rebel swarm. "I haven't offered you all your freedom just so you can throw your lives away. Bring me back the lay of the land down there, and if you find yourself outnumbered, return to me."

"Aw," Iliona said. "You're sure we can't kill anyone?"

"If you have to defend yourselves, do," Maralen said. "But no matter what, when you find Oona, you have to let me know immediately. Iliona, I want you to organize this effort. Understood?"

"Yes, sir!" Iliona said with a grin, and Maralen suspected

she had every intention of finding a way to act in self-defense as soon as possible. She wondered if the elemental fires she carried had infected her follwers with some of that destructive bloodlust. It was only because of Maralen's unique nature and origin that she was able to keep it under control; she could easily understand how Ashling had become consumed by it.

And then, as Iliona's flight groups broke off and descended into the fog enshrouding Cayr Ulios, Maralen heard Oona's voice once again. *What are you doing, rag doll? I thought you wanted a confrontation. I am here, waiting. Will you not come to me?*

Had Oona been silently listening in the entire time? If so, it was no matter. Maralen did not intend to rely on surprise and subterfuge.

Oh, you wound me, Oona continued. *Trying to shame me into emerging from my hiding place.*

Well? Maralen said. *What purpose is served by destroying Cayr Ulios? Come up here, Great Mother of the Fae. Face the one who will replace you.*

There was no response, and for a moment Maralen thought she might have imagined the entire thing. Her mind felt as if it was in so many places at once. She was sharing the observations of her rebel Fae, wrestling with the fiery elemental imprisoned in her own body, maintaining the Crescent's connection to the Source, imagining she heard Oona's reply to her challenges. She was becoming overwhelmed, or perhaps her mind had already snapped.

No, your mind is still intact. Though it is as faulty as ever. Look.

The last word rang in the elf woman's head but was also spoken in Maralen's own voice. Maralen had not known how Oona would choose to present herself to her. No one, not even

Maralen who had been created by and of the Great Mother herself, knew what the true Oona looked like. Now it seemed she never would, for the form Oona had taken for the fight over Cayr Ulios was none other than the form of Maralen the Mornsong elf.

"It seemed only fair," Oona's latest puppet body said with a wicked grin. "As the kithkin might say: I want to give you a sporting chance."

"You think I'm trembling at your secret, hidden power?" Maralen demanded. "You think by coming to me as—as *me,* I'm going to be so terrified at the thought of what you're holding back that I won't fight you with everything I've got?"

"That thought had occurred to me," Oona replied, and she popped her neck in a way that made Maralen feel all the more like she was looking in a mirror—it was a habit of the original Maralen. Even the Perfect Peradala had noticed it and asked her to stop. "Now there's a name I haven't thought of in a while," Oona taunted. "Peradala. So, you still think you're an elf? I must say, this is what I get for working on an accelerated schedule."

"What are you talking about?" Maralen said.

"Perhaps I will explain later," Oona replied. "But please, believe me when I say I don't blame you. I probably should have taken Peradala herself, but you seemed so much more versatile a tool."

"I'm versatile," Maralen said. "And so are my friends." She had almost forgotten she was surrounded by hundreds of potent, albeit tiny, defenders. Oona, on the other hand, appeared to have left all of her servants down in Cayr Ulios. Maralen reached out to the rebels and groundlings—and heard nothing but an echo.

"Now, now," Oona said. "This is between us. You and I. And an elemental, the river, and an army of Fae, apparently."

"You sound scared," Maralen said. "Wouldn't just be stalling for time, would you?"

"I do enjoy you," the Great Mother said in a way a gourmand might describe his feeling toward his favorite dish. "You were an error, but you certainly are an ambitious error. Forgive me for relishing a bit more time with you—we've had precious little."

"That's it?" said Maralen. "You just wanted to talk?"

"Well, that and I wanted to give your little scouts time to get into the safehold. You won't be hearing from them again. Your little rebellion is going to be crushed. But first, go ahead. Hit me."

Maralen watched her own eyes flash on another's face, and she felt the fires within her fighting to be released.

"All right," she said, and then she unleashed a firestorm on the Mother of All Fae.

* * * * *

Gryffid and his pack had left Cayr Ulios a city of glittering spires and silver fountains, but returned to find their home enveloped in a terrible mist. It was as if the mist had replaced all of the elves, for he met no one on the road into the largest and greatest of the safeholds. He met no one at the watch gate, which was still closed. Having to open it—and getting no response—was somehow worse than finding the guards dead at their posts. The mist obscured everything, making common and expected shapes loom like specters, preventing the vigilant from seeing much more than an arm's length or two. He was proud of his remaining hunters and vinebred warriors—the vinebred navigated by other senses now. Smell, touch, but especially sound—even muffled by the dense fog, they could guide the others with their eyes closed.

Gryffid kept telling himself he wanted Rhys to face justice, but more than that he wanted the disgraced safewright dead. Therein lay the problem—Gryffid was a capable commander, and he could recognize the dangers of letting a quest for personal vengeance overcome the mission.

And so he'd led his survivors here, organizing them into a hunting pack along the way, not because he'd forgiven Rhys but because the traitor, if traitor he was, spoke the truth. Gryffid's place was here, defending his home. But as he made his way through the fog-enshrouded structures of the greatest of safeholds, he could feel the complications setting in.

He'd expected to find elves defending the place, for one thing. Far overhead, a sound like a raging thunderstorm and lights that made their way through the mist showed a battle of some kind was going on, but neither he nor his scouts had been able to discern the combatants. If Rhys was right and Oona was involved, the only place Gryffid thought he might find answers would be with the king and queen. "Please," he muttered, "let them, at least, be here."

The safewright barked a few orders to his lieutenants, and the survivors fell into formation. Before moving on, he asked for reports.

"East quarter seems deserted, sir," reported a young elf named Filnar. "Fog's thick as I've ever seen it, and we didn't do a building-by-building search, but if there were people in there they weren't answering. Streets are empty. But you can hear, overhead—"

"Yes, I can," Gryffid said. "Thank you. What about your team, Lysere?"

His second lieutenant had also been thrust in to the job thanks to a "battlefield promotion"—the death of all her superiors save Gryffid—but Lysere struck the vigilant as the wiser and more experienced of the two. Like Filnar, she was one of the remaining non-vinebred hunters in the pack, but she didn't know whether that meant Gryffid favored them with this job. It might well have been an effort to burn off his less useful warriors. But she kept her doubts to herself—vinebred or not, she was an elf.

"Sir, I think the people might be there—some of them, anyway," Lysere reported. "I'm not basing that on anything visual. You can't see there better than you can anywhere else. But again, the fog just goes up to the edge of the city and stops. It's damned odd, sir." She sniffed. "I don't think it's natural."

"The fog also extended to the edge on the east half of the city, sir," Filnar jumped in.

"Thank you," Gryffid said. "That confirms your suspicion, Lysere. What else?"

"These vines." She kicked at the ground, and brought up a length of dry, fibrous, cable of vine with a surface that looked more like dry, wrinkled flesh than wooden plant growth. "They're everywhere." Gryffid took the proffered vine, inwardly cursing himself for not noticing them before. Too busy congratulating himself for navigating through the fog. He examined it closely for only a moment. He was certain he knew where the vine led.

"Oona is here. And apparently doing well for herself."

"Possibly, sir," Lysere told him. "But where is everybody? Why were we sent to that glen?"

"You sound suspicious. I approve."

"Thank you, sir," the lieutenant said.

Determined not to be left out, Filnar piped in, "This is all very, very strange."

Gryffid stifled a sigh. The lieutenant had only been such for a few hours, and he was doing the best he could. He was capable enough—he just didn't know how to act in direct contact with his superiors. The youth hadn't any practice.

"That it is, Filnar," said Gryffid. "We've scouted enough. With this fog, an ambush could be waiting around every corner. Let's get to the palace. If the king and queen are gone, too, we've got to make some hard decisions, and I'm no more eager to do that than Filnar is to make a speech to the court." There was murmured laughter from the group, and Gryffid saw Filnar puff up a little bit with pride at being included. "Now form up, everyone. Verify your position with your ears, and move with me. Filnar, Lysere, you two make sure you can see me at all times, the rank behind the lieutenants keep an eye on them. Second rank, keep your eyes on the third, and so on. After-guards, keep a hand on the person in front of you, but your eyes to the rear." He took his position, pointlessly scanning the fog all around him for some sign of living elves other than those he had with him. Or anything alive other than Oona, who was clearly here and, he guessed, creating the mist. There was nothing, though there could have been an army of boggarts ten feet away and he'd never have known as long as they kept their mouths shut.

Gryffid's ears told him they were still a half-mile from the palace when the ambush struck. The vigilant heard Filnar scream just a few feet away, and then heard the heavy thud of a body dropping to the ground. Lysere barked, "Hunters, counterattack! They're in the air!"

Another female, a new recruit named Terela stationed as one of the rear guards, managed to shout "It's a swarm!" before the sound turned into a scream that ended abruptly and with the sickening sound of torn flesh and bone. Gryffid knew the scream had been hers because it was still etched on her face, which rolled into view at his feet moments later, still attached to her head. The body, however, was lost in the fog. A buzzing was in the air, suddenly terrifyingly loud. He heard Fae—they had to be Fae—tearing through the fog, causing it to curl and roil like an angry thing, pulsating with refracted energy from the titanic battle above.

"Belay that order!" He bellowed and drew his sword. "To me, elves of the Wilt-Leaf! We can't fight them in this fog—take cover in the palace!"

* * * * *

Iliona's wing dived into the mist in perfect formation. The Vendilion Free Air General guided her fierce fighting faeries into a small canyon formed by a wide street and several tall spires built contiguously along its length.

"Iliona, the fog—it's not breaking. We can't see anything!"

"Settle down, Loira," Iliona snapped. "We don't need to see anything. Just wait for her to find our targets."

"This doesn't feel right," said another faerie.

"That's what they all say," said Iliona. "Really, if I hear another one of you say this doesn't feel right again, I'll—contact!"

"You'll contact who?" Loira asked.

"Pay attention!" Iliona cried. "Check your—er—mind. We have targets in the mist!"

The experience of flying by sound alone was, Iliona had to admit to herself, really quite extraordinary, and Iliona knew something about extraordinary these days. Almost immediately her battle clique was surrounded.

"Damn it!" Iliona swore. Maralen had ordered them to retreat in a situation like this, and a quick check showed an opening directly overhead not covered by the angry, snot-nosed thoughts of a loyalist swarm. Beyond those thoughts, nothing.

Maralen was gone. Whether she was dead or had simply abandoned her new children Iliona couldn't say, but she could not sense their New Mother in the skies above.

Echoing her thoughts, a familiar voice came to her from the mist, a voice which took shape moments later on silvery wings—a shape so like Iliona's own, just a little smaller. "She's left you. It's safe now, sister. You and the others are free to return home. You will not be punished, for Oona loves you."

"Veesa?" Iliona said. "Who are they?" She pointed to four large male faeries almost as big as her Vendilion sister. They bore spears that ended in tiny glowing lights held in menacing grips.

"My brothers," Veesa replied. "Our brothers. Heralds of Oona, like me. Return to us. All is forgiven."

Hogwash, Iliona thought, and was delighted to hear similar sentiments from the rest of her rebel squadron. Could Veesa hear them as well? The blissful smile on her sister's face betrayed nothing, so Iliona decided to throw caution to the wind. *I think they're bluffing,* she told the rest of the rebels. Again, general agreement, and an overriding question for Iliona: What do we do?

We fight. We fight our way to the New Mother, she told them, and drew her silver sword, no bigger than a kithkin sewing needle but four times as sharp.

We're with you, the others told her.

"Well?" Veesa said. "You're my sister, Iliona, but this offer will not last forever. Forgiveness is a gift offered by she who gave life to us all, and like that life, it ends sooner than you think."

"I think you're trying to keep us down here because Oona can't control us anymore," Iliona said. "I think you have to ask us to come back because Oona can't *make* us come back."

"Ridiculous. You're trying to find a trap in simple mercy. But if it helps, I'm begging you." Veesa's face, now close enough to read clearly, was truly sad. "Now are you going to give me that sword or are you going to do something foolish?"

"Probably both," Iliona said, and she drove her blade into Veesa's heart.

* * * * *

"More faeries should be here, right?" Kiel asked as he loped along, giving voice to the thought on all of their minds. Endry, Rhys, the sapling, and the groundlings were again on his shoulders, while Ashling and the cinders rode along in the giant's oversized right hand, which Kiel insisted didn't cause him any pain—on the contrary, he'd said it tickled. Rhys simply hoped the giant's bushy arm hair didn't catch fire.

"That's a good question," the sapling said. "I would have thought she would leave some defenders here." There was no need to ask which "she" the sapling meant—here in the heart of Glen Elendra, Oona's lingering presence seemed to watch them from every giant toadstool and bramble bush. "If not Fae, then I would expect animals or plants to be within the Great Mother's sphere of influence, if not the very land itself."

"Let's be grateful for small favors," Rhys said. "I'm more concerned that we really have a destination. I mean, look at this place. It's so much bigger inside than out—how can we destroy it?"

"We cannot destroy Glen Elendra, nor should we. We must strike at Oona's literal seat of power. The place where she dwells. Which she has left for the first time in millennia to do battle with—well, with herself. And that is to our advantage."

"You mean," Ashling said, "she left part of herself behind?

That makes sense. The more of her there is, the harder she is to kill."

"Hello," the sapling said. "You sound more like yourself again, pilgrim."

"And you have remarkable patience with someone who tried to kill you on more than one occasion," the flamekin said.

"I am not certain this is a good idea," Rhys said. "I don't think we should trust her."

Ashling didn't reply. The sapling, after a moment of awkward silence, said, "We could not leave her behind. She is part of our little family, after all." The yew laughed with a creaking sound, and Ashling turned to Rhys.

"I don't want you to forgive me," Ashling said. "I don't deserve it. I went too far, and I can't undo any of it. But I do ask you to believe me: If this Great Aurora, what happened to me, to the douns, to the monastery, all of it—if it is ultimately Oona's fault, I will do whatever I must to stop her. I can take my cinders and go after her alone, or I can help you. What will it be, Safewright?"

Rhys, taken aback, said nothing for a moment. The flamekin continued to look him in the eye, and something about the look was familiar in a way he couldn't explain. He nodded. "The sapling is right," he said. "We're in this together, and we're the only ones who can do it."

"Hooray!" Endry cried, and the groundlings echoed with cheers and predictions of another great groundling victory, though Rhys noticed uncomfortably that Endry's troops now numbered less than a dozen of the more than two hundred he'd assembled at the defense of Kinscaer.

"By the way," the faerie asked the sapling when the cheers died down. "What happens when she's gone?"

"I do not know," the sapling said. "Colfenor didn't know, either. He only knew that what had come to be, a world of either endless summer or permanent night with nothing in between, was wrong. He felt it in his roots, knew it in his heart, and spent his life learning how it had come to pass and how to end it."

"But don't we run the risk of ending—ending everything?" Endry asked. "I mean, what's the world going to be like? Just sort of gray? Are we talking about a never-ending Aurora?"

Kiel laughed, startling his passengers. "Sorry," he rumbled. "Reminded me of an old joke about goats. I think we're here, Boss."

Rhys followed Kiel's open hand as the giant drew to a halt—the cinders and Ashling now stood atop the other, looking in the same direction—and saw the giant was right. The elf had never seen anything so beautiful in all his life. Oona's home was a masterpiece of living sculpture, organic stone shapes flowing into vines, twisting and dancing into bursts of flowers and curving green spines like giant blades of grass. And it glittered with light, impossible light of every color exploding from within and illuminating the glen with a kaleidoscope of power.

"The Heart of Glen Elendra," the sapling said in a hushed voice. "How careless and cold she has become, how arrogant, to leave it unattended. Come, Half-Brother. We must now do what Colfenor asks of us, and turn this object of heartbreaking and irreplaceable beauty into kindling."

Rhys, the sapling, and Ashling walked together toward the heart. Kiel remained at a safe distance—yew poison could fell even a giant without much trouble—while Endry and the groundlings watched over Kiel, and Ashling's cinders guarded the trail behind them all. The light inside Oona's home swirled and flashed at odd times and in ever-changing ways. The elf saw shapes and faces in the misty brightness—old Colfenor, the archer who'd taught him how to hold a bow, his long-dead mother. He thought he might become lost in that light, and then he thought it might not be such a bad thing, being with those you remembered from better times, even if it also meant an end to everything else that—

"Are you truly ready, Rhys?" the sapling asked. "This could prove taxing. Even without her presence, Oona's magic is very strong here. Do you have any doubts?"

"I—no," Rhys said.

"Are you certain?" said the sapling. "You look and feel anxious."

"Of course I'm certain," Rhys said more sharply than he meant to. "This is the only way. I'm not afraid of what will happen any more than I'm afraid of the past." The past. The faces in the light. There was Shae, a childhood friend who had become a dawnhand—something Rhys might have done had he not turned from Colfenor's instruction for duty to his people. Boggarts had slaughtered her along with a half-dozen safewrights when they'd come upon the elves attempting to rebuild a safehold devastated by fire.

"Rhys," the sapling said. "Remember where we are, and remember the ways of the creature we face. Whatever you are seeing in that light is false. Do not give her power by refusing to look, but do not stare and become lost."

Shae's face stretched apart and became nothing more than a swirl of bright, vaporous light once again. "Thank you, sapling," he said.

"The same goes for the rest of you," the sapling said. "Now, Ashling. Your part here is less certain. Colfenor intended to include you in his plan, but my own errors in judgment instead caused you and many others great suffering."

"My desire for revenge caused suffering," Ashling said. "I'm not looking for revenge anymore."

"So, you will help?" Rhys asked.

"Tell me what to do."

"We're going to fill this big glowing plant here with deadly poison," Rhys said. "And then I want you to burn it."

"Sounds simple enough," the flamekin said. "But remember, I'm just me. I only have the fires I was born with."

"The flames are to ensure nothing grows again," the sapling said. "It will be dead before you are needed."

Quite a bold and optimistic prediction, Oona said. *Remarkably inaccurate, however.* Before Rhys could respond or even comprehend what was happening, a fibrous tendril as big around as Kiel's arm and the color of dried blood lashed out of the Heart of Glen Elendra and cut the sapling in two.

CHAPTER 21

Maralen funneled a flaming cyclone of molten rock at her grinning doppelganger. Oona laughed as the deluge washed over her floating form, untouched and unharmed.

Maralen turned the clouds overhead into waves of super-heated steam and slammed them into the Great Mother. She blasted Oona with bolts of solid fire. She screamed as she called down thunderclouds. The Crescent turned to ice against her skin, and twin tongues of lightning converged on Oona's body, lashing it like whips.

"Impressive," Oona said when the smoke cleared. "Now it's my turn." She hurled a fist at Maralen, who was a good twenty yards away. Oona's arm stretched and grew as the fist took on the shape of a gnarled club. By the time it reached the elf woman it was moving at tremendous speed and batted aside the walls of fire and ice Maralen threw up in its path.

When she came to her senses, she was still flying backward through the air. It took her a few precious moments to regain control and head back toward the elven safehold. "Wish I knew that trick," she muttered.

As she barreled through the night sky with moonlight in her eyes, Maralen saw that in the few minutes she'd been out of the picture the mists had begun to withdraw from Cayr Ulios. Oona, still in a body that mirrored Maralen's own, stood atop a column of fog that roiled and curled as she absorbed it into her porcelain white skin.

Maralen heard the pounding of hooves in her head and fought the urge to unleash another wall of flame upon the Queen of the Fae.

"Back so soon?" Oona said serenely. "I imagined you'd enjoy a moment to catch your breath."

"That's all the time you get," Maralen said, and threw a punch of her own, curiosity be damned. Jets of flame erupted from her fingers, cutting into Oona's flesh and bone. Flayed, charred skin fell away in flakes and cauterized flesh cracked and popped like cooking meat. The mists were thin now—Oona appeared to be at the center of a rapidly shrinking storm cloud.

Maralen couldn't believe the queen's body was still in one piece. She could feel her own hands beginning to scream in agony as she poured more and more elemental magic through her fingertips, then her arms, then it felt as if her face were going to burn away. Finally, she had to stop and use the Crescent to cool herself before she burst into flame.

Oona should have been a charred husk. She should have plummeted out of the sky and dropped onto what Maralen now saw were the mostly empty streets of Cayr Ulios. She spotted swarms of faeries buzzing to and fro, but no elves. Instead, Maralen's twin laughed as her cracked, blackened wounds began to close. Hair bloomed forth on her bare, charred scalp, skin returned pale and fresh, and finally even her clothes returned to almost pristine condition.

"Do you feel you are doing well?" Oona asked, floating toward Maralen with a look of maternal affection. "Your Fae think so, because they have begun to kill their brothers and sisters. And they are doing well, for it was time for a culling. They need to do this every few centuries. Helps keep them in fighting trim. Look." Oona pointed a now perfectly healed hand down at the city, which was lit with torches where there had been none before. "My children light up the jewel for all to see. Isn't it pretty?"

Everywhere Maralen looked, she saw tiny black clouds of faeries, colliding, coming together again, in a dance comprising thousands upon thousands of individuals. Much more disturbing, the streets were covered with tiny black dots—dead faeries. And moving among them all, other clouds that avoided the fighting and moved from building to building. Wherever they passed, a torch was lit.

"I'm going to miss the elves," Oona said. "For a while. Then, perhaps, I'll make new ones. Not like you, of course."

Maralen refused to be drawn in by Oona's conversational tone. She certainly wasn't fully recovered from the last prolonged fire blast, so instead she dropped a small lake on the Great Mother's head—not all at once, but in a column of water that took almost half a minute to stop falling. When it did, Oona stood soaking wet but none the worse for wear in the exact same place.

"Didn't you wonder why an elf handmaiden would be so power hungry?" the drenched doppelganger asked. "Didn't you question what you were doing? But then, you were no mere vessel. You were special. Everything was special this time around."

"This time?" Maralen asked despite herself.

"Yes, it was too soon, far too soon," Oona said. "But you're getting ahead of ourselves."

"Where are the elves?" Maralen demanded. "What did you do to them?"

"They'll live on through me," Oona replied.

"The mist," Maralen said with dawning horror. "All the elves."

"Oh, not *all* the elves," Oona said. "That would be a waste. And when the time comes there will be more elves in Cayr Ulios, but for now let that empty safehold serve as a monument to this day, to the faeries who died—and to you, my doomed, imperfect twin, who was only doing what she was meant to do. I am sorry I had to lie to you, but you had to be dealt with well away from me."

"Away from you?" Maralen said, still shaken by the death of all those elves, consumed by a voracious and capricious god-thing. "But you're right here."

"No," the doppelganger replied. "Though I did go out of my way to let you think so. This body is a vessel—like you once were, but without your headstrong independence. I assure you my primary self is far from here . . . probably killing your former friends like my swarm cuts down your rebellious insects. This vessel was created with the sole purpose of dealing with you."

"Why create me in the first place if I'd have to be 'dealt with'?" Maralen demanded. "Don't tell me this was all planned from the start."

"Oh, you've been full of surprises, and so have your friends," Oona said. "I never expected the Destroyer to fail and leave the sapling alive. You did your best, my dear, but even I cannot anticipate everything. Your free will was beyond my control, so I had to ensure you were positioned to act as I'd hoped you would—as I would have in your place."

Maralen knew she should unleash all the power she still had at her command in a last, desperate attempt to make Oona stop. She wanted to, so much that it was nearly overwhelming. But Maralen the elf, Maralen the handmaiden, had to know. "You've said that more than once. Your 'twin.' I don't understand."

"Of course you don't," Oona said. "How could you? You have the knowledge of a million lifetimes within you, the experience of thousand worlds, each ever so slightly different from the last. All because of my influence, and always growing more prefect with each iteration—well, every other iteration, to be honest. Though there is perfection in darkness as well as light, I suppose."

"The Aurora," said Maralen. "The Aurora—it was because of you?"

"I suppose you could say that. It is not my creation so much as my formation of the natural world. Night into day, day into night. I've just stretched the days—"

"And the night as well," Maralen said. "But even if I accept that you've been around long enough to have such influence on the world—what does that have to do with me?"

"You are the result of something unexpected," the doppel-ganger replied. "Around a hundred years before the next Aurora was due, I felt a great disaster far beyond the confines of our world. I know not whence it came or why, only that it was going to bring the change soon, too soon." Oona's eyes turned downward in a surprisingly humble expression, and then grew fierce and fiery when she looked back up. "The change had never affected me before. I didn't allow it. But this disastrously early Aurora was going to throw off the balance, and change even me. If I lost any part of myself, my memories, it would mean disaster for this world."

"So you say," Maralen interrupted. "Sounds to me like it would mean some freedom from your control."

"I *am* this world, my dear," Oona said darkly. "And so rather than risk such a thing—"

"You created another you," Maralen said. "Someone to bear the brunt for you."

"Correct," Oona replied. "You were the vessel I created to ensure that I remained uncorrupted by the change. Imagine my face when I realized you were an unnecessary precaution. Now I am as I always have been, whole and complete, but I am stronger than ever. Now, as I wished, you have come to destroy me. You will fail, and I will be alone again at the pinnacle of this world's hierarchy. Even with the early arrival of the Great Aurora, I think I was able to make the best of things. Don't you agree?"

Maralen's mind was reeling, but she knew it was true. She could feel it in her bones. Every part of her wanted to lash out and destroy Oona—every part except the elf she'd once been. And that, she realized, was the only real weapon that mattered right now. "All right," the elf said, "You want me to kill you? I'll kill *you*. Not this thing you've put up in front of me like a decoy. You shouldn't have used an elf as your template, Oona. You shouldn't have used Maralen. You underestimated her strength, and it lives on in me."

Her eyes fluttered for a moment as she summoned a surge of power from the Crescent and the elemental at the same time, and the crash of thunder and hooves was like a stirring anthem.

Maralen shouted, "And you shouldn't talk so much." With that, she launched herself like an arrow toward Glen Elendra and didn't turn back to see if the doppelganger followed.

* * * * *

Gryffid's pack reached the palace without further casualties, though it was slower going than he would have wished. The hunters were spooked, even the vinebred, and every buzzing sound made even the bravest of them—Gryffid included—flinch and look around in the fog. When the great doors of the royal palace loomed out of the fog only a few feet to the left of where his ears told him they should be, he almost emitted a shout of victory, but instead he called the others around and motioned them to approach silently.

With the pack behind him, Gryffid followed several dozen

of the thick vines and ropy fibers leading up the steps and under the doors. With effort and help from a pair of vinebred he hauled the door on the right open several feet, and gasped at what he saw.

The inner vestibule of the palace was filled with elves, each suspended in the air by one of the ropy vines that now laced all of Cayr Ulios. The vines were strong, holding even armored hunters with ease by the coils around their necks. He could see they were breathing, albeit slowly, so the vines weren't choking them. But the elves weren't conscious, either. Indeed, they appeared to be having fitful dreams, jerking and twitching every few seconds, their eyes closed.

"Sir, what—" Lysere began.

"Quiet," Gryffid said, but the damage was done. Slowly, the occupants of the vestibule turned on their coil-stalks to face them. The vigilant wished they would say something, but they all simply watched him, their eyes fluttering in time with their twitching spasms.

"That's the vizier!" exclaimed one of the vinebred. "Isn't it, sir?"

"Looks like him," Gryffid said. "Come on, there's nothing we can do here, and they're not threatening us. We'll do what we can for them later. If those vines lead where I think they lead, the vizier is only the start."

The throne room wasn't far from the double doors. Kithkin and other visitors to Cayr Ulios sometimes found that odd, saying one would expect a king and a queen to hold themselves above their subjects, especially an *elf* king and queen (kithkin, especially, would arch an eyebrow when reiterating that they were *elves*). In this case, Gryffid wasn't sure whether it was a curse or a blessing. He wouldn't know until they pulled open the inner doors to the throne room itself, but the thick cables of vine weren't promising.

Light erupted from the throne room when the vinebred wrenched the doors open—torchlight, the light of a blazing fireplace set on the east wall of the chamber, and a glorious light of a thousand colors that spilled from the king and queen. The coils held them above a hundred other swaying, twitching elves. Unlike all the others, the vines holding the elf royals kept growing upward like beanstalks, and Gryffid couldn't shake the feeling that something was consuming the light, drawing it upward.

"Are they—are they alive, sir?" Lysere asked.

What could he say? They looked alive. But what if he tried to cut them free and alerted Oona?

He turned to the nearest twitching courtier and followed the coil to the floor. Gryffid picked a spot a few inches to the left of the man's foot, which was brushing the ground. He drew his sword and chopped at the vine like a kithkin farmer cutting down a stalk of corn.

The effect was twofold, immediate, and not exactly what Gryffid would have preferred. The elf dropped like a sack of flour and the vine suspending him in the air flopped on top of the corpse, which ceased twitching and fell still.

Gryffid didn't have a chance to check the body thanks to the other immediate effect: Every elf in the throne room save the King and Queen, almost a hundred lifewards, vigilants, dawnhands and safewrights all, turned and began to stagger toward them.

"Sir, what do we do?" Lysere asked. "Please, sir!"

"The king and queen aren't moving," Gryffid murmured, his mind racing in the few seconds they had before the vine-slaves were on top of them. "Only them. The others are sacrificial, but she *needs* the royals."

Lysere let out a yell and raised her sword.

"Wait!" Gryffid shouted, and grabbed her by the wrist.

"Leave them be; they can't hurt us. It's them we've got to worry about."

"Are you mad?" Lysere said. "That's the king and queen of the Wilt-Leaf Hold, sir! I won't do it!"

"They're either slaves or they're already dead," Gryffid growled. "Look at him," he said, pointing at the body he'd cut free from the vine. "I don't know if he's real or not, but he isn't moving. There's no saving them."

"But what is this?" Lysere demanded. "These vines, the lights—what are they doing?"

"I think Oona's feeding on them. Feeding on their magic. They must be all that's left. The whole city—they've all been consumed, somehow, except the people in here." He gave a shove to a shambling vine-slave and watched it fall over into a couple of others, only to emerge from the tangle a few moments later.

"I came here to save Cayr Ulios," Gryffid said, turning to them. "We all did. We're too late, because we were betrayed, but we can still have some small measure of revenge." He raised his sword, still thick with the viscous sap of the vine, and shouted, "We are dead men, one and all, but we can decide what our death means. Cut them down!"

Lysere and the other survivors of the battle of the Cayr Ulios palace claimed an explosion happened when Gryffid's sword struck home. In truth, it was less an explosion and more an interruption—and once the staggering amount of magical current was interrupted, it had nowhere to go but into Vigilant Gryffid of the Wilt-Leaf elves.

Whatever the cause, moments later there was nothing left but ashes of Gryffid or the exalted monarchs of the Wilt-Leaf Hold.

* * * * *

Rhys saw the tentacle vine strike. He heard the thunderous crack of shattering wood, felt a long, jagged splinter tear into his arm, and then warm blood running down his side, but no sound escaped his throat. In an instant, everything his mentor had ever been and everything the sapling might have become fractured into a thousand pieces, and the elf felt as if his soul had done the same. Rhys dropped to his knees, mouth agape, and stared at the toppled boughs lying next to the torn and splintered stumps of the sapling's sundered trunk.

"Murderer!" Endry cried. To Rhys he sounded distant, like a voice heard through a thick glass window. "Get her!" The elf heard the buzzing of the faerie's wings overhead, and the squawks of the surviving groundling magpies. Heard the screams as they died, struck by bolts of brightly colored energy that lanced from the roiling vines at the center of the glen. And he heard his mentor's voice again. Faint—a whisper.

Tears streaming from his eyes, he forced himself to look at the upper half of his fallen friend, "Rhys," the sapling croaked. His heart racing, the elf lifted himself to his feet and stumbled to her side.

"Are you—"

"Time is short," the sapling said softly. "Maralen has learned the truth, and is coming. She can help you."

"Maralen?" Rhys said. "But she's—"

"She can help you!" the sapling coughed. "Now, quickly. Take what I can give you. Take my blood, and use it. This world must be allowed to find its own destiny without the interference of petty gods and old logs." With that, the yew's eyes went glassy and dark, and her branches shuddered and then were still.

Rhys turned his glare upon Oona's visage, and knew what he had to do. He thrust his hands into the sapling's ruined body, closed his eyes, and drained the corpse of every last bit of poisonous power he could find.

* * * * *

Ashling heard the cinders hiss angrily when the sapling died, but then they did everything angrily. The one-time pilgrim felt angry as well, but it paled in comparison to the rage she had felt as the Destroyer. She could never make up for the things she had done, though she intended to spend the rest of whatever life she had left atoning for her crimes.

She hated the cinders, hated that they thought she was their Extinguisher, and hated that they followed her still, but she would make them useful. Those who'd been her friends before the Aurora and, improbably, had stopped her rampages afterward, had determined Oona must be stopped. Ashling was hard put to disagree. So when the sapling was torn apart, the flamekin pilgrim acted on instinct born of guilt and shame, calling on power hidden deep beneath the stones and soil. Since she'd lost the power of the Destroyer, she hadn't really tried to reach so deep, but in her shock she acted without thinking and found it was easier than she'd ever thought possible.

Ashling picked up a hunk of dirt and set it ablaze, hurling it with all her might at the Heart. Another tentacle lashed out and pulverized the missile before it could reach her, but the spectacular first salvo rallied the half-mindless cinders to attack. They shrugged off blasts of energy from the vine-enshrouded monster, and a few even withstood the whipping coils once or twice. The flamekin took advantage of their sacrifice by sending another blast of fire into the writhing heart, fire that struck in the dead center of the thing, but Oona merely soaked it up like a sponge.

Then Ashling heard the familiar pounding of hooves in the distance growing louder by the second. She turned her eyes to the moonlit sky, seeking some sign of the elemental horse, fearing it but needing to see it again. And there they were—blazing orange wings at the fore of a scarlet jet of flame.

Maralen came at Oona from above, screaming out of the night like a shooting star, and slammed into the Heart of Glen Elendra with a sound of mountain collapsing. Anyone standing was knocked over as the ground shook with the impact—everyone but Ashling.

Ashling was flying, flush with power. Maralen was nowhere to be seen, but the elemental had found its way free of the ersatz elf and returned to a far more comfortable environment.

Control, Ashling told herself. This isn't like the last time. I'm ready for you. I can control you, I won't be controlled by you. By any of you. Elemental or Fae, sage or king.

Control. Memories of pain and hatred wanted to explode. She wanted to feel the burning fury that filled the sky, to consume the very land itself, incinerate them all. Control. Control the power. It's got to go somewhere, so send it somewhere. This is really Oona, not a proxy. Not a vessel. Burn *this* Oona, and maybe it would sate her lust for revenge against those who had corrupted the Path.

Rhys. Ashling. Listen.

Maralen? Ashling thought.

* * * * *

Rhys. Ashling. Listen.

Maralen? Rhys asked the voice inside his head, and heard Ashling doing the same—as if the three of them were in a room together.

I've got her distracted. You've got to strike now. Both of you.

"I'll kill you," Ashling seethed. "Once I release the flames, I won't be able to stop them."

"And the poison—"

You're really worried about me? Maralen asked. *I'm touched, but you shouldn't be. It's nothing less than I deserve. She's down and vulnerable now. Hit her with all you've got.*

* * * * *

Endry saw it all with his own two eyes, but he hoped Nora had too. Wherever she was. All of the groundlings were dead, and Endry had survived only because he'd been at a slightly higher elevation than the rest of them when Oona launched her counterattack against their pathetic assault. Brave, he had to admit, but pathetic. He'd lost a wing, the left one—he held what remained of it in one hand—and from his accidental perch atop a charred and broken old oak tree, Endry watched the Great Mother die.

Rhys and Ashling struck almost simultaneously, and Endry would have been hard pressed to say which one hit Oona first. The poisonous yew magic, like black and green smoke mixed with an oily yellow light, enveloped the royal presence in a filthy cloud. At the same time a light so bright he almost couldn't look at it slammed into the queen from the opposite side. It went on forever, Rhys and Ashling pouring their killing magic into Oona's heart.

Endry. My child.

"No," Endry cried weakly. "I won't."

They're hurting your mother, you little fool. I am suffering. Will you not end your mother's suffering?

Endry examined his broken wing, and watched as more and more deadly force struck the Great Mother.

"You're not my mother," Endry said. "I'm the last of the groundlings now. I'm an outcast."

Endry, remember. You swore you would never betray me.

I made you forget, I was wrong, dear one, I was wrong. Come back to me.

Endry felt as if he'd been doused in icy water as his memory of the contact with Oona returned. "You never let me go," he said quietly, rising horror in his voice. "You wanted me here so you could make me betray my friends if you had no other choice.

Endry, my favorite. My sweetest child, the most handsome and daring—

"And if you didn't need me now?" Endry asked. "What then? Would you just let me die too? I'm nothing to you. Nobody's anything to you except yourself." Like a physical hunger, he felt the pull of Oona's urgent call. He wanted to fly to her and swear fealty and love and devotion and loyalty forever and ever. "But that's not true," Endry told himself. "I don't want that. I want the ones you've killed. The ones who died for stupid power and stupid greed and stupid revenge and no reason at all." He hovered, his entire body shaking as he fought the call.

You would defy me? You would defy your Mother Oona? You pathetic insect. You parasite. Your fleeting life is nothing, your individuality an illusion. A hallucination. You're damaged. Broken. You're going to die.

"Everything dies," Endry said. "Everyone dies. Except maybe you. Let's find out together."

Endry, they're—ENDRY! The last syllable of his name extended into a scream more bloodcurdling than any sound Endry had every heard before or would ever hear again. It caused him physical pain throughout every nerve in his tiny body, and when it was over, he realized he fallen off his perch and was lying next to his broken wing, staring upside-down at the slowly dying Heart of Glen Elendra.

And when the light faded from within and Oona spoke no more to her children, Endry heard another voice. So like the

Great Mother, but utterly unlike her as well. The voice wasn't in his head—it came from within her corpse.

"Endry," Maralen said. "Find someone to help me out of this thing."

CHAPTER 22

"No need to be gentle, Kiel," Rhys said.

"It's sharp," the giant rumbled. "And pointy."

"It's the corpse of the most powerful being this world has ever seen," Ashling said. "And I should know. I used to be one of those."

"Is it dead too, do you think?" Rhys asked. "The elemental?" Rhys had found it hard to believe the entire story, how Ashling had been joined with the elemental during the Aurora, but slowly it seemed less and less far-fetched to him. Perhaps as Oona's influence faded, his memories were returning—or perhaps with all that had happened since he'd been cast out of his home, nothing could really surprise him anymore.

"I don't know," Ashling replied. "All I know is that it left. I can't hear it anymore, or feel it. It could be dead. Maybe that's what it took in the end—for the elemental to sacrifice itself." She crossed her arms and dropped her eyes. "I won't say I miss it. It made me into a monster. But it did feel good to join with it one last time."

"I know how you feel," Rhys said. "The sapling was too young to blossom, and I don't know of any other yews in the world." His eyes, too, were focusing hard on the ground.

They pair were spared further grim reverie by the sound of tearing vines and snapping coils, like giant lute strings breaking under a frenzied strum. Rhys ducked to avoid one dead vine that cracked out like a whip, momentarily convincing him Oona wasn't dead after all. He whirled on the dead heart and saw the giant Kiel standing proudly with two halves of Oona's corpse held aloft like they were greens he intended to boil in a soup. Where the heart had been, only Maralen remained. She was crouched, hugging her knees, but as the sinking moon struck her face her eyes fluttered open and she slowly rose to her feet.

"Maralen?" Rhys asked. "What did you do?"

"I went home," said the elf woman—though Rhys doubted that described her very well at all anymore. "The Crescent got me in, and the two of you forced her to turn her defenses outward. That's when I brought out this." She reached into her blackened, blood-soaked tunic and produced a small white flower missing all but one of its petals.

"Dawnglove," Rhys said. "But something's wrong with it. It's pale and—"

"It's not dawnglove," Ashling said.

"No, it isn't," Maralen said. "It's called moonglove. Even more deadly than your yew poison, I'd wager. It's something I—something Maralen of the Mornsong had with her when Oona killed her to create me. I've been carrying it this entire time, but never realized it until Oona forced me to see I wasn't myself—who I thought I was."

"And are you now?" Rhys asked. "Yourself? If the real Maralen was killed—"

Maralen tucked away the last petal of moonglove and stretched out her hands before her, as if to confirm they were real. "I suppose I am," she said. "I'm not that elf in the flesh, but I'm her. I was also her twin—Oona's. The reflection the Aurora made when she wasn't ready for it. Now that she's gone, I get to live."

Ashling stood abruptly, a blaze erupting around her hand. "Rhys, get away from her."

"I'd think you of all people would be a little quicker to understand," Maralen said. "Destroyer. You were also going to die until I saved you. You would have burned out, just as I would have washed away in the rays of Oona's renewed glory."

The flamekin's hand died down, but she didn't move any closer. "Fair enough. So you're the elf, but you're Oona, too."

"Oona is dead," Maralen said. "I am Maralen. But what was left of Oona's power is within me." She smiled and spread her arms wide, and all around them Glen Elendra awoke as if from a catatonic state. Blossoms burst open, spilling forth with tiny newborn faeries, and soon the air was filled with the buzzing of tiny wings and the almost inaudible voices of the Maralen's new generation.

"Will you stay here?" Rhys asked.

"Certainly not," said the new Queen of the Fae. "Though this will always be our home." She reached back into her tunic and again removed the moonglove flower. She placed it in Rhys's hand. "Keep that. If I ever show signs of making day and night last for centuries at a time, you can feed it to me."

"Day and night?" Ashling asked. "What do you mean?"

Maralen smiled and tapped her forehead. "You'll learn. Think of it as having an Aurora every twelve hours or so. I wonder what it's going to do to people's memories. Maybe you'll finally remember the day we met, Rhys."

"Perhaps," the elf said uncertainly. "But that doesn't really answer the question. What's 'day'?"

Maralen pointed toward the horizon, which was growing brighter by the moment. "That," she said, "is day. It begins with the dawn, and ends with dusk. Between dusk and dawn, well, things might look a bit more familiar to you for a while."

Eventide

The blackened night gave way to a deep, rich blue that became lighter and lighter, taking on tinges of gold and orange, until a glorious, enormous orb peeked over the band of the horizon. Dawn had come to a world that was neither Lorwyn nor Shadowmoor, but something new.

* * * * *

It had taken Endry almost two hours to find the magpie, and another hour to coax it over to him. When the infernal bird finally allowed him aboard, it refused to do anything but sit and squawk at him, stepping back and forth from foot to foot on the ground.

"Come on, bird," he complained. "I'm injured. You're not, I can see that. Fine wings you have there, fine wings. Just—you know, up! Fly! Get a good running start if you have to!"

After a bit more cajoling —a *good* bit more—the bird finally took to the sky, and again Endry faced another obstacle—how to get where he was going and not get lost on the way. He'd always been someone who navigated by instinct. All of the Fae navigated by instinct, of course, but Endry especially. Even if what a faerie called "instinct" really meant "Oona's will." So he didn't spot Cayr Ulios until the sun came up (which didn't surprise Endry in the least) and he had to make three passes before he could get the magpie to head into the safehold proper.

The entire place was abandoned except for the dead. What had begun as a battle between Maralen's rebels and Oona's loyalists had degenerated into a bloodbath, and the tiny corpses littered every street amid dried, dying vines. Odd to see so many dead faeries in an empty elven city, especially with no elves, but he'd heard enough of Maralen's explanations while taming his new mount to accept Oona had done it, and to leave it at that. Dead elves meant little. Dead Fae were another matter.

He found them quickly. As he'd suspected, the sisters had been at the center of the battlefield, and if he didn't miss his guess, they'd probably started it. They had definitely killed each other. Iliona's hand still clutched the sword upon which Veesa had been impaled. Veesa, on the other hand, had chosen an upward thrust, driving a short, jagged little blade that looked like it had been a piece of glass into Iliona's abdomen.

Endry closed their eyes with his palms and pulled their bodies away from the pile. He felt very tired and alone. He patted the magpie's beak, handed it a piece of corn, and shooed it away. Then he lay down beside his sisters and went to sleep. He dreamed for a while, content to leave the harvesting of dreams to others. Younger folk who had both their wings. He dreamed of his sisters, and of Nora, and in this dream they were all flying and laughing together.

Satisfied that this would make a splendid last dream to have, Endry decided not to wake up. His chest rose, then fell. Endry sighed, and then breathed no more.

* * * * *

That night, the sun went down and night returned. People remembered the night, and that night followed the day. Though there were many with doubts, sure enough, the night lasted only a short time, and once again the dawn returned, for the day followed the night.

The cycle was the same, only the interlude was different. Shorter, more immediate, though it didn't feel that way to Oona. No words, as such, existed for the ways in which Oona felt the world, for in all the ways that were important, she was the world. And as she always did, Oona adapted.

*Call me Shadowmoor or Lorwyn. Call me Oona, for I am
both of them and more. Call me this world of vengeful darkness and staggering light.*

In the charred heart of Glen Elendra, a small bud slithered
from the encrusted soil, moving with a determined plant's slow
but inexorable speed.

*I am eternal. I am within the land, the rock, the rushing
currents of air and water. My roots run deep and call to each
other from afar.*

Over seven days, the bud split into three parts and ripened
in the rays of the swift-moving sun. Within the glittering pods,
tiny individual minds were brushed with a mother's caress.

*You will make me whole again. You will answer the calls,
reunite us, make us whole and strong. For we are the Fae,
and we are this world.*

And on the dawn of the eighth day they burst open to release
three new faeries; two female, one male, the first of a new generation. Their glistening wings glittered like diamonds in the
first seeking rays of the morning and they chattered to each
other with expectant glee.

Welcome, their mother said. *Whatever shall we call you?*

* * * * *

Brigid Baeli woke in the manner to which she had become
accustomed: face down in the mud and far from any recogniz-
able landmarks. She ached all over and felt as if she'd gone
thirteen rounds with a birch and a giant and lost to both. She
found a wingbow lodged in the small of her back. She pulled
it free, snapped it into shape—a tear in the third membrane,
but serviceable. It would fly.

The kithkin pushed herself onto her rump and blinked at
the bright morning glare. The ground smelled like fresh rain,

though Brigid herself was surprisingly dry. After patting herself down to make sure nothing was broken—nothing was, although she was covered with superficial cuts and bruises—her hand instinctively wandered to her tunic for the Crescent. It wasn't there.

Panic set in, but only for a moment. The Crescent wasn't there, but she *knew* the Crescent wasn't there. Which meant she knew what the Crescent did, which meant she had her memories after all. On a whim that was half curiosity and half instinct, she reached out to nudge a wisp of steam rising from the dewy grass near her feet, and a thousand tiny drops of water danced like minute faerie lights in the golden sunlight.

"Wait a minute," Brigid said. She stared at the sky with renewed interest and no more confusion than was warranted. "When did the sun come out?"

THE KNIGHTS
Of MYTH DRANNOR

A brand new trilogy by master storyteller

ED GREENWOOD

Join the creator of the FORGOTTEN REALMS® world as he explores
the early adventures of his original and most celebrated
characters from the moment they earn the name "Swords of
Eveningstar" to the day they prove themselves worthy of it.

BOOK I
SWORDS Of EVENINGSTAR

Florin Falconhand has always dreamed of adventure. When he saves the life of
the king of Cormyr, his dream comes true and he earns an adventuring charter for
himself and his friends. Unfortunately for Florin, he has also earned the enmity of
several nobles and the attention of some of Cormyr's most dangerous denizens.

Now available in paperback!

BOOK II
SWORDS Of DRAGONFIRE

Victory never comes without sacrifice. Florin Falconhand and the Swords of
Eveningstar have lost friends in their adventures, but in true heroic fashion, they
press on. Unfortunately, there are those who would see the Swords of Eveningstar
pay for lives lost and damage wrecked, regardless of where the true blame lies.

Available in paperback in April 2008!

BOOK III
THE SWORD NEVER SLEEPS

Fame has found the Swords of Eveningstar, but with fame comes danger. Nefarious
forces have dark designs on these adventurers who seem to overturn the most clever
of plots. And if the Swords will not be made into their tools, they will be destroyed.

August 2008

never been to the FORGOTTEN REALMS® world?

SEMBIA:
GATEWAY TO THE REALMS

Opens the door to our most popular world with stories full of
intrigue, adventure, and fascinating characters. Sembia is a land
of wealth and power, where rival families buy and sell everything
imaginable—even life itself. In that unforgiving realm, the
Uskevren family may hold the rarest commodity of all: honor.

But even the most honorable family is not without its secrets, and
everyone from the maid to the matriarch has something to hide.

TRACY HICKMAN

PRESENTS

THE ANVIL OF TIME

With the power of the Anvil of Time, the Journeyman can travel
the river of time as simply as walking upstream, visiting the
ancient past of Krynn with ease.

VOLUME ONE
THE SELLSWORD
Cam Banks

Vanderjack, a mercenary with a price on his head, agrees out of
desperation to retrieve a priceless treasure for a displaced noble. The
treasure is deep within enemy territory, and he must survive an army of
old foes, a chorus of unhappy ghosts, and the questionable assistance of
a mad gnome to find it.

April 2008

VOLUME TWO
THE SURVIVORS
Dan Willis

A goodhearted dwarf is warned of an apocalyptic flood by the god
Reorx, and he and his motley followers must decide whether the
warning is real—and then survive the disaster that sweeps
through their part of Krynn.

November 2008

EDWARD BOLME

The Couatl's Crucible

The scars of the Last War run deep and damage many: A prelate
willing to murder. A monk without an order. A priestess with
dangerous enemies. When a plot to bring down the Silver Flame
draws them all together, they must decide what's more
important—saving Eberron . . . or saving themselves.

Book I
Traitor to the Sovereign Host
September 2008

And don't miss Edward Bolme's other EBERRON books

Bound by Iron
When the law won't help, a hardened soldier and a slippery
inquisitive will turn to alternate methods to solve a veteran's murder.

The Orb of Xoriat
In the final days of the Last War, the Orb of Xoriat was used only
once. Using it again could rip open a portal to the Plane of Madness.
And it's been stolen.

 EBERRON, WIZARDS OF THE COAST, and their respective logos are trademarks of
Wizards of the Coast, Inc. in the U.S.A. and other countries. ©2008 Wizards.